Under the Dark Moon

Susanne Bellamy

Ransom Women: 1

Copyright © Susanne Bellamy 2022
The moral right of the author to be identified as the author of this work has been asserted.
ISBN 978-0-6454850-0-4

Meg Dorset escapes Darwin after the city is bombed by the Japanese. Travelling south in a truck filled with injured soldiers, she meets the charmer, Seamus Flanagan. In the confines of the army camp at Adelaide River, it doesn't take long for them to fall in love and become engaged. When Seamus is shipped out to join the war in the north, Meg is transferred to the RAAF hospital in Townsville.

On arrival, Meg is dismayed to find she is pregnant, but holds the news to herself to avoid the risk of discharge. Working as head nurse to Dr Geoffrey Ransom, Meg pushes away her growing feelings for this kind and dedicated doctor. She is engaged and carrying her fiancé's child, so she immerses herself into her work.

As her pregnancy develops Meg is torn. How can she continue with the career she is passionate about, and keep her pregnancy a secret?

Ransom Women

Under the Dark Moon

Under the Same Stars

Under the Banyan Tree

Under Clouds of War

Under the Southern Sun

Chapter 1

Darwin, 19 February 1942

Meg Dorset hit the floor with a thud. A terrible roaring filled her ears and her army-issue cot lay on its side across her lower legs. Heat beat at her face. Not the usual summer heat of Darwin; this heat was dry and fierce and—*loud.* Like the droning of a thousand giant mosquitoes circling her.

Disorientated, she pushed herself to her knees and kicked free from the bedsheet and tangle of mosquito netting. The door to the tiny rear room in the nurses' accommodation—the room she shared with Vera Grantham—hung askew on its hinges.

Explosions filled the air, banging one after another, and the floor trembled beneath her palms. Or was she trembling? A woman's scream rose from the floor below and Meg clambered to her feet. She grabbed her tin helmet and slung her first aid kit over her shoulder. Matron had emphasised that they must keep their kit and helmet within reach at all times.

'Although war has not directly touched our shores, it is not far away. Be prepared at all times, Sisters.'

It looked like Matron had been right about the kit and wrong about the war. Aircraft rumbled high overhead. More explosions shook the hotel and dust rained down. Was the roof coming down?

Shoving her feet into her boots, Meg didn't stop to tie the laces. She had to get out of the building.

Heated air scorched her skin as she staggered through the doorway into the smoky hallway. At the far end of the hall where a wall had once been, the port was visible, and Meg gasped.

Flames engulfed a naval ship.

Black smoke columned and thickened like a pyre around the smokestack, consuming the ship. Grey smoke filled the gaping hole in the hotel, hiding the death throes of the ship. Coughing, Meg scrunched her watering eyes and covered her mouth and nose with one arm. The other hand flailed for the handrail.

Her hand found the wood, smooth and warm. Blindly feeling for each step, Meg lunged forward and down the stairs. Down and down she staggered, trying not to breathe until she fell through the doors onto the covered veranda. She bent over, hands on her knees and sucked in a deep breath of smoky air. Her body was wracked by coughing and she fell onto a nearby chair. When the fit passed, she sat up, her chest heavy and heaving with the effort of breathing and looked around. *Christ save us, it's Dante's Inferno.*

Soldiers, some bare-chested, formed a bucket line that branched like a snake's forked tongue where two of them attempted to douse flames rising from the façade of a nearby building.

She bent down and tied her bootlaces, knowing there must be wounded men all over the place. People who needed her help. Where should she go? Thank God the last non-essential civilians had flown out yesterday. As a nursing sister, Meg was one of fewer than a hundred women allowed to remain in Darwin.

She pushed her hair back with shaking hands and turned in a slow half-circle. Thick black smoke poured from a stricken ship. Suddenly a blinding explosion spewed in a gold and black mushroom next to the smokestack.

Dodging debris and soldiers manning the untidy bucket line, she ran towards the carnage, even as common sense screamed at her to run the other way.

Meg reached the bank overlooking a stretch of beach at the waterfront and swallowed, sucking in air and trying to quell the panic rising from her gut and threatening to burst from her throat in a piercing, useless scream.

A skinny private with pimples motioned her over and took her arm and helped her over the steep side.

'Thanks. Any casualties here?'

'Over there, Sister.' He directed her to his right and she hurried across the sand towards a small group of soldiers.

Minor cuts and a possible broken arm by the way one young soldier cradled his elbow against his chest. She headed to him first and kneeled beside him. 'How did it happen?' she asked as she examined his arm.

'Oh my God, look.' Her roommate, Vera whom she'd last seen when her shift changed over this morning, appeared at her side and pointed. 'They've hit the hospital ship.'

Meg's fingers dug into the rolled bandage she had just taken out of her kit. 'It's clearly marked as a hospital ship. What sort of enemy bombs wounded men and doctors and nurses?' Her gut clenched and she stood watching, anger and disbelief churning through her.

A soldier with a bandage around his head glanced at her, his expression harsh and dark. 'That means nothing to the little yellow bastards. I heard they rounded up some nurses and shot them in the islands.'

They shot nurses?

Despite the heat, her skin turned clammy. When she signed up no one had ever mentioned she'd face an enemy that shot nurses. Civilians had no idea such horrific acts happened in war. Surely, Dad would have refused to let her go if he'd had any idea she'd be on the front line? He'd been unhappy about her joining up, but he hadn't stopped her.

The front line. Where they shoot nurses.

Bile rose in her throat, burning. Frantically, she swallowed it down. She had a job to do, and do it she would. Turning back to the private she bandaged his arm then improvised a sling with another bandage.

As she was tying a knot beside his neck, a ragged cheer rose around her. 'The *Peary* is firing on the bastards. Go, *Peary*!'

A single gun on the small American ship continued to fire at the dive-bombers even as other ships around were taking hits. As they watched, the *Peary* took a hit, but she kept bravely firing until the end.

'It's no use. The Japs are too high for our piddling little guns to reach them. The shells are exploding way below the planes.' The soldier with the head wound slumped to the ground, his head bowed.

'Sister? Up here. You're needed.' A man's voice broke through the nightmarish scene and recalled Meg to her duty.

'Coming.' Thankful she'd fallen asleep in her uniform after a twenty-hour shift, Meg stumbled back up the bank and across the rubble-strewn street and dropped to her knees beside a young soldier. He writhed in pain, moaning words that were all unintelligible, except for 'Mum'.

'I'm here to help you. Try to stay still and let me see what you've done.'

One hand gripped her wrist so hard she thought her bone might break. 'Mum—hurts.'

'He copped a bit of guttering when it fell. His shoulder's a mess, Sister.' The soldier who had called for her help rose with not another word. Picking up three empty buckets, he raced off to refill them.

'Can you let go of my arm so I can help you?' Meg looked into the young man's eyes and forced her clenched teeth to part into a smile—her professional, reassuring smile, the one she pinned in place every day at work at the top end of Australia. 'I'll look after you, Private—' She glanced at the dog tag lying on the private's chest. 'Jackson. Look at me. I'm going to check your wound and get you to the hospital, okay?'

He let go of her wrist and gently, she eased him into a sitting position and shuffled around in the dirt until she could see his wound more clearly. The hot jagged metal had cut and burned through his shirt and skin, exposing a sliver of white bone beneath the red mess that had been his shoulder. Her guts heaved, but resolutely, she swallowed and focused only on him. 'I need to cut away your shirt. Do you have a knife, private?'

'Yeah.' His reply was a forced grunt, an exhalation of pain. He pointed with his uninjured arm towards his calf. 'Dad give it me.'

Meg reached for the calf sheath and withdrew a short but sharp knife and set to work removing the remnant of shirtsleeve.

Slicing it, she made a pad of it then dressed the wound with a bandage from her kit. That would hold him until she could get him to the hospital and clean the wound properly. Then she tucked his arm inside the remains of his shirt. No matter how careful she was, each movement elicited a moan. 'Stay with me, private. We'll get you some morphine very soon.'

Looking around for someone to help her, Meg began to grasp the extent of the situation. Everyone was battling fires or searching through rubble.

Where the Post Office had once been, smoke rose from a pile of rubble. Wires dangled from telegraph poles. One leaned crazily against the shell of the remains. The front wall was gone, and most of the building lay in untidy piles, but a solitary desk lay on its side surrounded by two walls. As she watched, they gave way and crashed, sending up a cloud of dust. With communication lines down, no one would know what was happening in Darwin. No one would be coming to help them. Panic welled in her gut but giving in to the churning emotion was a luxury she couldn't afford. Not with a wounded soldier depending on her.

'Looks like it's just you and me.' She squatted beside the young private and slung his good arm across her shoulders. 'Come on, soldier. We need to move out of here and get you to the hospital.'

She exerted gentle pressure to get him on his feet, and he groaned, but she urged him into a shuffling walk, one arm around his waist and the other bracing his injured arm across his chest. Heat surrounded them, flames consumed the ships behind them, and smoke choked them no matter which way they turned. Ash floated in the air like black rain and a sharp pain burned her arm. She shook the ash off, biting back a less than ladylike exclamation. Not that Private Jackson would notice.

His head hung low, but he kept moving beside her. 'Sister? If I don't make it—'

'You'll make it, private.'

'Will you see Dad gets my knife—please?'

'I will, but don't you go wasting my effort to fix you up.'

He grunted, a sound she took as assent as they staggered along the road, skirting debris and running soldiers. Everywhere was noise and chaos and horror. Sweat ran down her face, but Meg couldn't risk relaxing her hold on Private Jackson to wipe it off. Black particles settled into the sweat on Jackson's face. Hers probably looked as black.

'Get down.' As she turned, a soldier ran towards her, and the command rang loud and urgent again. 'Get. Down.'

She glanced up. Lines of bombs were falling out near the edge of town. Lines of bombs from neat formations of planes.

Her breath caught in her throat, but she obeyed the order without question.

Dropping to her knees she dragged the private down with her. The lad passed out and Meg lifted her head. A thunderous roar deafened her as wave after wave of planes flew over the town. Bombs whistled as they fell then cracked and crumped as they exploded.

Dark mosquito shapes. A ragged line of bombs raining on the street ahead of them.

She flung herself over the wounded soldier, shielding him with her body.

Dirt rained on them, and she pressed her face into his good shoulder, one hand instinctively covering her helmet even while she tried to protect his wound.

The patter and thud of chunks of dirt subsided and she raised her head.

The soldier who had told her to get down kneeled in front of her, his hand extended to help her up. 'Sister, you've got to get out of here now.'

Meg looked up. The voice belonged to an Aussie sergeant who reached for her elbow and dragged her to her feet. Blood ran down his cheek from a wound above his right eye.

'I can't leave him. He's badly burnt.'

'Bring your patient this way.'

'He's out cold.'

'Damn it.' The sergeant knelt beside the private then hefted him onto his shoulders. 'They're loading trucks and evacuating the wounded.'

'But I am essential. I'm a nurse and—'

'Move, Sister. They'll need you. Around the next corner.'

Her ears ringing, Meg moved in response to the commanding tone. 'I should get him to the hospital . . .'

'Hospital's on fire. Do what you can for him once you're out of here.' The sergeant's words bounced raggedly as he jogged towards the corner.

A battered truck with wooden slats along the sides and no roof, was parked near the rear gates of the hospital. Benches filled with wounded servicemen lined both sides.

Examining the crammed vehicle, Meg shook her head. 'There's no room on this one.'

'You'll fit. We can squeeze you both in.'

Meg looked up at the sound of a familiar voice. Sister Patricia Carey, who had been on the shift that relieved Meg's three hours earlier, gestured for her to climb aboard. 'Hurry up, Meg.' Pat squeezed past the legs of a couple of patients and held out a hand.

Meg grabbed Pat's hand and scrambled up onto the flat bed, dangling her legs over the tailgate. It was precarious, but there wasn't another inch of space to shuffle into.

The sergeant put the injured private beside her then shouted to the driver. 'That's it. Go.'

Meg eased Private Jackson's good shoulder and head onto her lap as the truck bounced into a pothole—or was it a bomb hole? He groaned as the truck bumped and ground along the road south. Covering his wound as well as she could, Meg looked back at the city.

Dust spewed up behind the truck, almost obliterating the dirt road. Smoke filled the sky and several thick black columns rose from the harbour. How many ships had been hit? How many sunk? Her heart ached at the thought of the men on those ships. Had any sailors escaped?

Pat slid down against Meg's back. 'Okay there? What happened to you?'

'I'm fine, aside from being tipped out of my bed. The hotel was hit, but I made it downstairs to the street. Someone called me to help this chap. What's happened, do you know?'

'Tom said the Japs might try to invade us at the Top End. Looks like he was right.'

'Tom, your brother?' The truck lurched around a bend past the road to the racecourse. Dirt spooled out as they headed south, leaving the town behind. The heavy choking smoke thinned.

'Yes. He's on the *HMAS Kookaburra*. I heard there was a wave of planes hit the harbour and the big guns first. ... Once those were out of action, they started bombing the town. My guess is the airport was probably hit, or will be.'

'The Post Office has gone, and it looked like the telegraph wires are down. No one will know what's happening up here.' Meg went quiet. Her head ached, her eyes were gritty, and hunger pangs hit hard. Exhausted after twenty hours on the ward, she'd fallen asleep without eating. But likely she wouldn't be able to keep any food down. Not after the shock of waking to a world on fire. Her stomach disagreed.

A wooden signpost pointed the way to Mt Isa and Alice Springs, and Brisbane, impossibly far away. The truck slowed with a squeal of brakes and a soldier jumped out from the cab. He knocked the sign names from the post with the butt of his rifle, collected them in his arms and returned to the cab. With a wheezing groan, the truck rolled slowly onwards.

'Any idea where we're going?' They bounced in and out of a depression in the road.

Pat knocked Meg's shoulder and grimaced. 'Right now? Frankly, I don't care so long as it's as far away from here as we can get.'

'Thank goodness most of the civilian population were sent away when the government decided to station our armed forces up here.'

Pat said nothing for several moments, but she leaned across Meg's shoulder and gently checked Private Jackson's wound. 'That's one of the things I like about you, Meg. Even in the direst circumstances, you find something to be grateful for.' A soldier out of Meg's sight called, 'Sister, can you check my mate?' She squeezed Meg's shoulder before rising and clambering between soldiers seated on the floor between the narrow benches.

Rocking and bouncing on the back of the truck, Meg felt oddly detached from events. Praying this was just a nightmare brought on by too little sleep, her eyelids lowered, and her head bent. The angle made her neck ache, but she was too tired to lift her head . . .

A hand gripped her shoulder and shook her. 'Whoa there, Sister, don't nod off or you'll fall out and wake up in the middle of the track.'

Blinking and wishing the cheery voice with a hint of an Irish accent hadn't dragged her from the arms of Morpheus, Meg turned to see who had saved her from tumbling into the road.

A cheeky grin slashed white across a corporal's dirt-streaked face.

She raised her gaze to a pair of blue eyes, bright beneath a bandage and intense as the summer sky.

'Thanks for the save.'

'Can't let the prettiest nurse this side of the Black Stump get lost, can I.'

From somewhere behind, Pat raised her voice. 'Corporal Flanagan, I'm not sure whether to tell you off for being cheeky to Sister Dorset, or take umbrage that you ignored me, who's put up with your shenanigans through all the hours of night and day.'

Flanagan's grin grew wider. Ah, but you're the prettiest *head* nurse, Sister.'

'And you're a rascal I should have discharged this morning.'

'Maybe you'll be glad to have an able-bodied man around.'

Flanagan's sling and bandaged head belied his comment, but

his cheery, cheeky flirting made the terrible morning bearable. And when he reached awkwardly into his breast pocket and drew out a small open packet of chocolate and offered it to Meg, she was glad he was aboard their transport.

'I shouldn't take your rations but thank you.'

'Sister, I'll be offended if you turn down my gift. Besides, I got a wonderful night's sleep thanks to you.' He winked, making sure she took no offence.

Her stomach growled and her mouth watered at the scent of chocolate currently wafting beneath her nose. Flanagan held it close and gave her a small nod. Reluctantly, but unable to keep from refusing his offer, she took the packet and broke off a single piece, offered a quiet 'Thanks' and popped it into her mouth. Closing her eyes, she let the chocolate melt on her tongue.

A swiftly indrawn breath nearby forced her eyes to open.

'What is it? Danger?' She scanned the skies over Darwin and the surrounding bush before looking for an explanation from the corporal.

Flanagan's gaze was fixed on her. His Adam's apple bobbed up and down before he gave her a lop-sided smile. 'I haven't seen anyone enjoy chocolate more, Sister.'

'It's the most delicious food I've ever eaten.' She held out his precious bar of chocolate. 'Thanks.'

'Keep it.'

'But—'

'I'm watching my weight.' He winked, and, in spite of the carnage they'd left behind, Meg's day brightened.

Chapter 2

Late evening 19 February 1942. On the track south.

Soft snores and an occasional groan as a wounded man rolled over in his sleep filled the soft night air as Meg finished her stocktake of their meagre medical supplies. *Just another night on the wards.*

She closed the lid of the battered footlocker co-opted to serve as their medical store. In the wavering light of an army-issue torch held under her arm, she made a note on the clipboard Pat had conjured from heaven knew where, and then got to her feet. Her head swam and she was just able to half turn and sit on the lid of the box before she fell. Head bowed, she breathed through the wave of dizziness.

It's exhaustion. Maybe a touch of shock too. All those bombs . . . She pulled her mind away from memories of bombs dropping— *so many bombs – stop thinking!* She set the clipboard beside her and switched off the torch. Her hands dropped to the cool metal beneath her.

Hard. Cool. Solid.

Real. She clung to the edges, the only solid thing in a topsy-turvy world.

'Are you okay, Sister?' Corporal Flanagan's voice came out of the darkness. *A hint of Irish*, she thought. 'Sister?'

A hand landed awkwardly on her shoulder, light, but offering comfort. Soft shuffling. The roll of a pebble dislodged in the dirt. The brush of material against her knees. He must be standing right in front of her. With a huge effort, she lifted her head. A gleam of teeth in the faint light of a waxing crescent moon confirmed the corporal was on his knees in front of her.

'You remind me of the Cheshire Cat before he disappears.'

'You're blathering, *macushla*. Have you eaten?'

'I'm fine, Corporal, just tired, and yes, I had a most delicious piece of chocolate, thanks to you.'

'*A piece*? As in one piece I watched you eat this morning? Christ—pardon my French. Is that all you've eaten? No wonder you look as though a stiff breeze would knock you over. Where's your bar of chocolate?'

'Here and there.' Her eyes closed.

'Don't tell me you gave it to these blokes. Instead of looking after yourself, you fed it to them. You did, didn't you?' Was that a tinge of anger in his voice?

'Guilty as charged, Corporal. They needed it more than I did.' Her head touched a solid shoulder and rough fabric and Meg let out a soft sigh. Her eyes closed. She was too tired to argue with him. Her nose touched warm skin redolent with male sweat and she nestled closer. 'This is nice, comfy . . .'

A hand stroked her head and she slipped into slumber.

Meg woke slowly, unwilling to give up her pillow and face the day. Would she have another twenty-hour shift or—

Lifting her head, her nose scraped across stubbled skin. Stubbled *male* skin. *Oh, heavens, what happened, where am I?*

'Morning, *macushla*. Did you know you snore?'

Meg sat up abruptly. She dragged her eyes open and found herself looking into the amused blue eyes of Corporal Flanagan. Her hand went to her hair before she looked around.

The truck was parked beneath a tree where the driver had pulled in last night, and small groups of men lay stretched out on the ground. Some clutched blankets but more had nothing but the hard ground beneath their heads. Pat was kneeling beside the burns patient Meg had brought to the truck yesterday.

Her gaze returned to the corporal. 'Did I fall asleep on you?'

'You did, and a more pleasant night I can't recall.' He grinned, a boyish grin that squashed any idea of improper behaviour.

'Pleasant? You said I snored. I'm sure I don't, but if I did—'

'Wee little snores, softer than a Galway breeze that tickled my neck.'

'I'm sorry.' She'd never slept with a man, in either sense of the phrase, but surely no one would see anything wrong in last night. There *was* nothing wrong, aside from her not remembering a thing, but she moved a respectable distance from him.

'Don't be, Sister. You were dead on your feet last night. I was happy to be your pillow, but don't take that the wrong way.'

The corporal wasn't embarrassed, and Meg would follow his lead. 'Thank you, then. You were an excellent pillow.'

Pat rose from the side of Private Jackson, the movement drawing Meg's attention. The head sister's expression was sad.

Meg looked at the soldier, barely more than a boy. His face was covered by Pat's nurse's cap. 'Oh no.' Her stomach, so empty it rumbled with need, clenched. She should be used to losing a patient. It happened from time to time no matter how much nursing she gave, but each loss touched her to her core.

Beside her, the corporal got to his feet awkwardly and followed her as she joined Pat.

'When did he die?'

'Not long ago. There was nothing more we could do for him out here, Meg.'

Flanagan bowed his head and his lips moved in a prayer for the private's soul.

Meg bowed her head and offered her prayers too. When she lifted her head, Corporal Flanagan was watching her. 'No tears, *macushla*. You did all you could for him.'

She nodded slowly. 'I know, but John Donne was right. Each man's death diminishes us because none of us is an island.' She inhaled a long, steadying breath and turned to Pat. 'What do you want me to do first, Sister?'

Flanagan answered before Pat had a chance to. 'Breakfast first, don't you reckon, Sister?' The corporal was a brave man, taking the head nurse's lead.

'Are you going to call up your magic leprechaun to cook something for us, Corporal?' Pat's tone was dry at the best of times, but she looked exhausted too.

'It's not a touch of magic you need, Sister. There *is* food in the bush, but we'll have to gather it.'

'Then go and organise any semi-able-bodied men and do so.' Pat suppressed a yawn.

With a touch of embarrassment, Meg realised Pat must have stayed awake through the night, keeping watch over the wounded men. 'I'm sorry, Sister. I should have stayed awake to assist you.'

'Nonsense, Meg. I know how long your last shift was. You would have been lucky to catch an hour's sleep between it and the start of the bombing. Corporal Ransom, our driver assisted me. Now, let's see if there's *anything* in this truck fit to eat.'

Corporal Flanagan had rounded up a couple of men and they followed him into the bush. Sister headed for the cabin and Meg climbed onto the bed of the truck. A barrel tied onto the slats behind the window of the cabin was the only likely place. The lid was a tight fit and she looked for something to lever it up.

'Need some help, Sister?' The truck driver squinted up through the side slats. 'I've got a decent knife if you're looking to open that.'

'Thanks. Do you know what's inside?'

'No idea. It was already lashed on board when we commandeered the truck. We didn't bother to ask or stop to get rid of it.'

Meg stood aside while the driver, Corporal Ransom, with the polished tone of a city fella, climbed up beside her. He took a lethal-looking hunting knife from a scabbard on his hip, inserted the tip between the lid and the barrel and hit the pommel. Several more hits like that and one side of the lid rose.

Between them, they tugged the lid free. Meg peered inside. Her stomach felt as though it was knocking against her backbone, but she wasn't sure what she hoped for most.

An earthy smell rose. The soldier thrust his hand inside and pulled out a tuberous plant still covered in dirt. He turned it this way and that and held it out to her. 'Any idea what this is, Sister?'

'Sweet potato. We're in luck. One of the nurses who lives in the Territory was telling me her father grows these.'

Pat called from the rear of the truck. 'Have you got something there?'

Meg held up the tuber. 'Madeline Tucker told me her family grow these.'

Pat looked dubious. 'We have no cooking pots.'

'We don't need them. If we dig a fire pit, we can toss them in, and they'll cook in their skins.'

The driver folded his arms and looked sceptical. 'We don't have time to dig a pit or wait for food to cook.'

Corporal Flanagan and his pair of ambulant foragers returned carrying bush food in the shirt of a now bare-chested private. 'It's not much, Sister, but it will keep everyone going for now.'

'Well done.' Pat smiled at the foragers then turned back to their driver. 'We need to eat, Corporal Ransom.'

The driver frowned before heading to the truck. Sounds of static reached them, and the corporal's voice as he contacted a military post.

Meg tuned him out as she relieved the wounded men of their small bundle and began to distribute the bush food, amongst which was some sort of pinkish berry. The men looked at the slim pickings, some with resignation, others, with curiosity. One man asked, 'What is it, Sister?'

'I have no idea, Sergeant, but it's what's available for now. I'm sure we'll get a decent feed when we reach Wherever we're going.'

'Everyone, back on the truck. I've just had a radio message from Adelaide River. We are to proceed there with all speed.'

Meg glanced at the body of Corporal Jackson. 'What about the dead soldier, Corporal? We need to bury him and—'

'We can't wait, Sister. Right, you lot, get on the—'

'We can't leave him under the tree.' Meg stood her ground, but looked around for Pat. 'Sister, tell him. It isn't right.'

The corporal overtalked her. 'Everyone, on board now.'

The wounded who could stand, did. But no one made a move towards the truck. Meg looked at their faces. Pain and fatigue had etched lines on many, but to a man they were resolved to do the right thing.

'Ain't leaving till the private has been buried and we've said a few words over him.' A sergeant with a bandage over one eye leaned heavily on a branch he had picked up for a crutch. He looked in no fit state to dig, but he turned away from the driver and hobbled slowly over to where the dead boy lay. He looked around then pointed to a spot a few yards off the track. 'The ground there looks a bit softer. We'll dig there. Flanagan?'

Corporal Flanagan saluted with his good arm. 'Yes, sir?'

'Organise some men to gather rocks to put over the grave.'

'Yes, sir.'

Meg fought the lump in her throat. 'Thank you, Sergeant.'

'It's the last thing we can do for the lad. Sister, did you see a shovel in the truck?'

'I'll look now.' Meg turned to find Pat watching her. Her friend nodded.

'Well done, Meg. I saw a short-handled shovel in the cab, under the seat. It won't be much use for a deep hole, but if they lay stones over him, he should be safe from any animals.' She climbed into the cabin. A moment later, her backside stuck up in the air as she worked the shovel free from under the seat then clambered back down and carried it to the sergeant.

He looked around the group of soldiers, as though assessing who among them was fit enough to wield the tool.

The driver, the only man in the group who wasn't injured, approached. 'I'll dig his grave.' His cheeks were pink, but his gaze met and held the sergeant's as he held out his hand for the shovel.

'I'll find something to make a cross with.' Meg slipped into the bush on the other side of the track. Two sticks and some vine, if she could find any, would serve as a simple cross for the private.

Sunlight fell on salmon-coloured bark and drew her to a tree she didn't know the name of. It looked like some sort of eucalyptus.

White-grey bark hung in long strips and beneath it, glorious salmon-pink wood almost glowed in the early morning light. Large triangular leaves offered shade, and twigs of varying thickness and length lay around the base of a tree. She selected two of the thickest, straightest twigs then looked around for a flexible plant to tie them together.

Stepping between bushes, she slipped, her feet went out from under her, and she landed hard. 'Oof. Ow.'

Leaves crunched, a hand took her elbow and a familiar voice spoke beside her. 'Are you okay, Sister?'

She looked up into the concerned eyes of Corporal Flanagan. 'I'm fine, thank you, Corporal.' But tears sprang to her eyes. She dashed them away with the back of her hand and sucked in a calming breath.

'A fall will do that to you. It shakes everything loose inside and when that happens, it's best to let the excess moisture out.'

'It's not the fall, Corporal. It's just—Private Jackson was so young.'

'He was. Old men send young men off to fight wars. Cemeteries are full of the graves of the young.'

'But he'll be buried here so far from home and his loved ones won't know where he is. They won't be able to visit or bring flowers to his grave or—' Meg tipped her head back to stop more tears falling. Blinking hard, she concentrated on the shifting patterns of leaves above their heads. 'Sorry. I'm not usually so emotional. Nurses can't afford to be.'

'But you *are* human, and you looked after the lad as well as you could. He had a soft lap to lay his head and a tender hand to soothe him at the end. No man can ask for more.'

'His family around him at the end of a long and happy life would be better, don't you think?'

'Yes, but under the circumstances, you gave him the comfort of one who cared about him. What you did back there, standing up to the driver like that, was brave.'

'Good heavens, I'm not brave, Corporal.'

'Brave and fierce. You know, Sister, in your own way, you're a warrior too.'

Pinning him with her disbelieving gaze, Meg shook her head. 'Aren't you leading a rock hunting party?'

'Sure I am, but when I heard you slip, I needed to see you were all right.' He pushed her elbow gently and, turning her around, checked her backside. 'A bit of dust and leaves. Do you want my help cleaning it off?'

Heat of a different sort raced through her at the thought of Corporal Flanagan's hand skimming her backside. 'Definitely not, thank you.'

He laughed. 'If you're sure. We can't go on meeting like this without knowing each other's names. Corporal and Sister are just plain wrong, especially after you slept on my shoulder. Michael Seamus Flanagan, at your service.'

'Corporal Flanagan.'

'My family call me Seamus though, 'cos my da is Michael too.'

'Margaret Olivia Dorset. Meg, to my friends.' Hesitantly, she extended her hand and Seamus—she wasn't sure about using his first name though—solemnly shook hers.

'So, can I help you with anything?'

His offer brought back the task ahead. She held up the two sticks. 'I was looking for some vine to tie these together.'

Seamus frowned then took her free hand and led her a little further on. 'I saw some clumping grass. The fronds are long, and I reckon they'll be easy to weave around the arms of your cross.' They headed in the direction of the truck and the solemn work happening under the tree next to Private Jackson's body.

A few injured soldiers were lugging stones between them and stacking them beside the driver digging in the shallow grave.

'Here, Meg.'

The long grass rose high in the centre and fell in an elegant arc like the fuchsias beside the back door at home. How she wished she were there now, sitting with Mum and having a cuppa. Meg tamped down the memory. She'd shed enough tears today and what good had they done anyone? Sniffing and pressing her lips together, she set the sticks on the ground and grabbed a couple of the longest blades of grass. The plant resisted her efforts and she stood up.

'Do you have a knife?'

Seamus pulled a penknife from his pocket and handed it to her.

'Thanks.' She cut two pieces, carefully wiped the blade on her dusty skirt, and closed it before handing it back to him. They returned to the truck and Meg sat on the step of the cabin where there was shade from the early morning sun. Her fingers were nimble. She'd crocheted often enough with Mum, even if she'd never woven grass. A few minutes later, she held the rough cross up to check the connection just as Seamus passed her. He clutched a bowling ball-sized stone to his stomach.

'It's a bit wonky. What do you think?'

'Looks fine. Back in two shakes of a lamb's tail.' He grunted with the effort of lowering the stone onto the pile and brushed off his shirt. Something or someone out of Meg's sight caught his eye. He raised a hand in a 'back in a moment' gesture.

Meg fiddled with the grass ties, but nothing she did made a difference. Her cross remained wonky.

'Here.' Seamus thrust a small bouquet of wildflowers towards her. 'If you want to, you could tie these onto the cross.'

Pressing her lips together, Meg nodded. 'That's a lovely idea, thank you.' With Seamus's hand to hold the flowers in place, she made a decent job of attaching them. When she was done, the crude cross was still simple but more fitting to farewell a young man.

They laid the private's body in the shallow grave, his face covered by Pat's nurse's veil, and filled the hole as best they could. The sound of rocks thudding as they were piled over him sounded sad and final amid the bright calls of birds. When the last rock was in place and Meg's simple cross was wedged at the head of his grave, the sergeant stood behind it and bowed his head.

'We've no minister with us, but I reckon God will hear our

prayers.' All heads bowed before the sergeant continued. 'Our Father in Heaven, take up the soul of George Jackson to be with you in eternal life. May he live in your House in peace forever. We pray for him, and his family, and for a swift victory in this terrible war. Amen.'

Meg whispered 'Amen' and raised her head. Seamus murmured words she couldn't make out then crossed himself before meeting her eyes. Of course, he was Irish, and a Catholic.

A muscle flickered in his cheek, and he sighed. 'This bloody war.' He looked at her. 'Sorry, Meg, but it's enough to make a saint swear.'

She nodded. 'It is. Come on. We'd better not miss our ride.'

They were the last to climb aboard, and as the truck chugged and shuddered along the track, her gaze remained on Private Jackson's last resting place until dust and distance hid it from sight. Only then did she close her eyes and tip her face to the sun. Despite their prayers, she recognised the attack on Darwin was only the beginning of the next stage of this bloody, bloody war.

A hand, rough and male and very warm, closed over hers and Seamus spoke softly, his warm breath brushing her ear. 'Don't dwell on it, Meg. Find something good in each day and focus on that.'

Seamus's hand. That felt strong and solid and comforting. Today, Seamus was her something good. She nodded, and held tight to that thought, and his comforting presence by her side.

Chapter 3

Adelaide River

After a night spent sleeping in the back of the truck, even with Seamus's shoulder for a pillow, the basic accommodation offered at Adelaide River felt luxurious. Sister Mary O'Dea welcomed Meg and Pat before Pat slipped away to meet the matron. Off-duty when the truck rolled into the River, Mary offered Meg both conversation and a spare uniform. 'This place started out as a rest camp and farm area, but since Pearl Harbour we've been sent more staff. The radio's been running hot all morning and the army's gearing up. I reckon the River will become more important now Darwin's been bombed.'

'Do you feel safe here?' Meg gratefully took the proffered uniform. It was ridiculous asking, but that *'they shot nurses'* comment on the beach in Darwin resurfaced the moment she tried to relax. 'If the Japs land in Darwin, it's only a hop and a skip to Adelaide River.'

'I can't imagine them being interested in an Outback hospital. It's not like we've got an airbase right on our doorstep, is it? Besides, we're nurses. We should be safe enough.'

Meg chose not to reply. Why frighten Mary and the others with an unsubstantiated story? A short shower and a borrowed uniform while Meg washed hers made it possible to return to ward duty with her usual smile in place.

Pat was standing beside the matron as Meg entered. She excused herself and met Meg near the door. 'Sister Dorset, Matron was just passing on orders from the Army. I'm to continue with the most severe cases to the nearest railway. You'll stay here with the ambulatory and nearly recovered patients. The army will arrange transport for them in a few days. I've suggested Corporal Flanagan as a temporary orderly to assist with the extra patients. His arm is healing, and he's shown himself competent at solving problems.'

A little flutter stirred in Meg's belly. It would be nice to have Seamus around for a bit longer. 'Yes, Sister. Am I to be transferred here, or will I be returning to Darwin?'

'I don't know. Right now, I can't imagine what it's like up there.' She leaned in and drew Meg close to the entrance. 'I did hear there was another bombing raid after we left. The airport was hit hard and badly damaged. There might not be anything left to return to.'

'There must have been so many casualties to care for.' Following orders had been drilled into Meg in training and she'd climbed into the truck when told to by a sergeant. But the news there had been more raids left her feeling as guilty as if she'd deserted her post.

'And we were short-staffed before the bombing.'

Meg looked north along the track they'd taken, her chest, tight with anxiety. 'Do you think the Japs will invade?'

Pat shrugged and pulled a slip of paper from her pocket. 'It's possible. Nothing in war is certain. Look, if you ever find yourself in Brisbane, here's my address. If I'm not there, Mum would still love to chat with you and at the very least, you'll get fed a decent meal.'

'Thanks. Are you leaving soon?'

'Oi, Sister Carey! We're ready to go.'

Pat glanced over her shoulder and took a deep breath. 'Now, by the looks of it.'

Meg clutched Pat's hand then pulled her into a quick, fierce hug. 'I'll miss you. Stay safe.'

'I will. I'm glad Corporal Flanagan is staying with you. For all he's a charmer, I trust him. If ever he tells you to run, do it.' With a final squeeze of Meg's hand, Pat strode to the truck. Corporal Ransom helped her to climb into the back with her charges. As the truck pulled out, she raised a hand in farewell before a turn in the track swallowed the truck whole.

'So many goodbyes, aren't there.' Seamus set down the bucket he'd been carrying and pulled his handkerchief from his pocket. 'Here.'

Meg looked, wondering why he offered it before she registered her damp cheeks. Shaking her head at the hanky, she wiped her hands over her cheeks and sniffed. 'Sorry. I don't know why I'm such a watering pot today.'

'Don't you, *macushla*? First a funeral and now farewelling a friend, on top of a tough couple of days with little sleep? Why, I feel like sitting down and sobbing meself.' He pulled a comical expression that drew a snort and a smile from her.

'Then it's a good thing I didn't accept your hanky, isn't it?' She sniffed once more, smoothed her hands over her skirt and huffed out decisively. 'Right then, we need to crack on with our jobs. I'd better see what Matron has planned for me.'

'That's the ticket. You'll be all right, Meg—Sister.' His glance slid past Meg's shoulder and he tipped his chin the tiniest bit.

She turned as Seamus bent and picked up his bucket. Matron stood in the doorway, an expression of disapproval furrowing her brow.

'Matron, I was just—'

'I have drawn up a list of duties which you will commence immediately, Sister Dorset. Corporal Flanagan has been assigned to the ward as an orderly. Corporal—' She pinned him with a look that assured Meg she wasn't a woman to mess with. 'Keep that label in mind every time you step into *my* ward.'

'To be sure, Matron. I'll be the orderliest orderly you've seen.' A subtle wink in Meg's direction and he headed off, whistling '*It's a Long Way to Tipperary*'.

Avoiding Matron's eye, Meg slipped back into the ward. She made her way to Matron's desk, little more than card table size, but neat for all its lack of space, and stood, shoulders back and hands folded in front of her.

Matron took her seat and picked up a pencil, running the unsharpened end down lines of small print. Leaving a nurse waiting to make the point who was in charge had been a favourite trick of Meg's superior at the teaching hospital in Sydney. But Meg was no fool. Stepping in to explain herself would guarantee an extra shift, or bedpan duty for as long as she was here. Meg waited.

At last, Matron looked up. 'Even in a war zone—*especially* in a war zone—it's important to keep your distance and follow the rules, Sister.'

'I understand, Matron. That was drummed into us by Matron Phillips during training. *"Compassion, caring, but no cuddling"* was her advice.'

Soft whistling in the ward caught Meg's attention—*Tipperary*.

Matron glanced past Meg and pressed her lips together. 'Excellent advice. Make sure you follow it, Dorset.'

'Yes, Matron. Which patients would you like me to check first?'

'Start with Simpson in the far corner.' The pencil pointed towards a patient with two arms in plaster. Her tone and expression softened. 'And Sister, I know you lost a patient this morning, but don't let it discourage you. There will be many more losses—and wins—before this is over. Every soldier you nurse back to health is a victory. Remember that.'

Touched by her superior's words, Meg lifted her chin and found her smile. As far as chastisements went, she'd got off lightly. 'Thank you, Matron. I won't forget that.'

Chapter 4
Adelaide River

'For a bush hospital, this place isn't bad, hey, Meg?' Seamus sat on a nearby rock, his dinner cradled awkwardly in his injured arm. After several weeks in plaster, it was pale and skinnier than his other wrist, and he would have to work to build up muscle strength. 'Good tucker.' He scooped another spoonful into his mouth.

'Pretty good, especially since the cook has to feed more mouths than he had supplies for. He's rationed the meat, but with all the vegetables they grow here—'

'And the tropical fruits. Don't forget them.'

'Army food isn't so bad here, but I look forward to when bush turkey isn't the only meat served.'

Seamus had shot a bush turkey to add to the pot, his second in two days. One-handed and therefore slower to complete tasks, his humorous quips on the ward lifted the spirits of patients and staff alike, and his hunting skill had eased the cook's worries about making supplies last. 'Mind you, I've never eaten bush turkey before. Are they always so—chewy?'

'Plenty of them in the bush around our farm.' A cheeky grin lit his face. 'Tough old bird, but boil the guts out of it and you get—'

'Still a tough old bird.' Meg laughed. 'And a good jaw workout while you eat.'

'Ah, Meg, you know how to cut a man's delusions of being a great white hunter down to size.'

'I didn't mean—'

'No offence taken, *macushla*. I'm teasing, is all.'

'You've been wonderful, the way you help everyone.'

'Wonderful, is it now? You'll give me a big head.' He scraped the last of the meal onto his spoon and set his bowl down with a sigh of satisfaction. 'Tough, but tasty.'

'If you're finished, I'll wash your plate, and you can tell me what that word means while we have a cuppa.'

'What word would that be?'

'The "mac" word you call me.'

'*Macushla*?' His gaze darkened, deepened, pinning her on her rocky seat. The way he said it—with that lilt of a remembered Irish accent— was . . . She thought about it for a moment before she answered. Possessive, almost, but in a good way.

'That word, yes.' Her voice came out soft, and filled with hunger for something—precisely what, she didn't know.

He stood abruptly. 'I'll get us both a mug of tea and meet you yonder.' He nodded towards the growing darkness at the edge of camp then turned away and strode to the mess tent.

In a haze of unfamiliar emotions, Meg washed and dried their plates and set them on the neat pile ready for the morning meal. Innocent of a man's touch though she was, Seamus stirred feelings in her. Feelings that made sense of the romantic poetry she'd read late at night in bed in the nurses' quarters in Sydney.

She bit her thumb and peered into the gathering darkness where Seamus waited with her tea. *It's just tea, for goodness' sake. Just a cup of tea.*

But she knew she lied.

Seamus's gaze had promised knowledge and an answer to the fluttering in her stomach whenever he was near. If she walked down the track to the edge of camp, she would break Matron's rule of no cuddling. She knew there would be cuddling. She knew there would be no turning back.

The sky was filling with stars and a tropical moon, big and white and full, had risen, bathing the landscape in a wash of magical light.

Drawing a deep breath, Meg stepped onto the track, following it to Seamus.

He was perched on a fallen log, his legs stretched in front of him and crossed at the ankles. Meg stepped through his long moon-shadow and sat beside him, crossing her ankles and tucking her feet to the side. Silently, he handed her a mug, the brew strong and black, but redolent of home and comfort.

Like the man by her side. In a handful of days, Seamus had become her comfort. Being with him was like returning home.

'You're my North Star, Meg.' His voice was low, thoughtful, romantic—like the lush tropical night enveloping them. Lover-like. She'd seen *Gone with the Wind*, almost swooned at Rhett Butler's voice, but Seamus's voice thrilled her more. Thrilled and comforted and excited her.

'You promised to tell me what that word means.'

'Aye, I did. What do you think it is?'

Had he leaned closer? Had she? 'Something—nice, I think. Little one?'

'Darling. It means my darling Meg. Do you mind?'

'Mind, no.' Her heart zinged at the sweet Irish word, and what it seemed to say about Seamus, and how he felt about her. How it made her feel. 'It feels special.'

'You are special, Meg. A man could fall in love with you over a bar of chocolate.'

Her breath caught, stuttered, then rushed out in a quick exhale. *Love? Was Seamus saying he loved her?* She sipped her tea and looked up at the stars, too numerous to count. 'People don't fall in love at first sight.'

'Most don't. Perhaps some do, the lucky ones. The moment you looked up at me on the truck with your big blue eyes wide with surprise, I knew it could happen.'

Meg dug her short fingernails into her palms and turned to look at him. Starlight and moonlight gathered in his eyes. She had to be dreaming. No man could make such a beautiful declaration in real life. It was poetry and romance. It was perfect.

And it was happening to her.

Seamus lifted her mug from her hand and set it beside his on the ground then he took her hand. 'I want to kiss you, Meg.'

'Yes,' she whispered then more loudly, 'Yes, please.' If this moment was a dream, she would be brave. 'I'd like to kiss you too.'

He held her face, his hands gentle, for all they were callused, and leaned closer. And then soft lips pressed against hers. She had little idea how to kiss well. A few fumbling, sloppy meetings of lips in the back of the movie theatre hardly counted, and yet Seamus's lips on hers felt natural. Wonderful. She parted her lips to tell him so, but he caught her lower lip and then his tongue traced her mouth. She gasped and drew back.

'Sorry, Meg. I'll try not to do it if you don't like it.'

She touched her lips lightly, her fingers tracing the path his tongue had taken. 'I—haven't had many kisses, and if I think about that last bit, it's strange. Kind of nice, but strange.'

'I can live with *kind of nice.* And you kiss perfectly well. I like your kisses. A lot.'

Seamus's response made her feel on top of the world. He gave her the confidence to ask, 'Can I try what you did? With your tongue?'

'Sure, and just so you know, I'll like whatever sort of kisses you decide to give me. Do whatever feels nice. Okay?' His smile tugged at one corner of his mouth as she set her hands on his face, the same as he'd held hers.

Emboldened by his smile, she kept her eyes open and kissed him. Lips to lips first, then, when his parted, tentatively she traced his with her tongue. He tasted of tea and bush turkey stew, but beyond that, overtaking the sense of wonder at her first magical kiss, was an overwhelming sense of coming home.

I love you. I love you. I love you.

Her thoughts whirled around that single unalterable fact, but she held onto the discovery and stayed silent. There would be time later to consider what her feelings meant. For now, she simply *felt*, and lost herself in kissing Seamus.

***

Two nights and many kisses later, as they left the dinner queue with their trays and headed out of the mess tent, Seamus balanced his tray on one hand and guided her with his free hand past their regular dinner spot.

'Aren't we sitting here tonight?'

'I've a surprise for you.' His hand on her waist felt natural and right. Hungering for his touch occupied her mind when he wasn't near.

And then yesterday, wonder of wonders, the doctor had allowed Seamus to remove his sling. Now he had two arms to hold her, two hands to touch her. And touch her he did, every opportunity he could find.

It wasn't that his embrace had been *less* wonderful before his sling came off, before he was able to fully enfold her in his arms. It was just that two arms were *more*. Two arms invited her to meld with him until she was certain they were simply two parts of one whole, meant to be together to make the world right.

Seamus took her into his arms the moment they were out of sight, and she was the same. If Seamus came into the ward, she had a sudden urgent need to check medical supplies or roll bandages. Seamus would slip in behind the curtain and, like filings to a magnet, she stepped into his arms.

If Matron was likely to return, they made no sound, but the look Seamus gave her needed no words. Like his expression now as she raised an eyebrow and glanced over her shoulder. Matron had been tolerant—and surprisingly silent on the subject of one of her nurses sitting outside the mess tent with a soldier—but Meg doubted she would be as accepting if she saw Meg and Seamus disappearing with their dinner.

'Matron's in a meeting with the captain. Don't worry about her. Just close your eyes and hang onto me.' She balanced her tray on one hand and, trusting him completely, enjoyed a burst of pleasure at the change in routine.

The dirt track beneath her feet felt as if he was leading her to their special place beyond the edge of camp. Even though the moon hadn't risen and closing her eyes barely changed her ability to see, or not to see in this case, walking blind made her feel she was stepping into her own adventure, and she smiled. *An adventure with Seamus.*

'You realise I do know where I am still? The scent of those pink flowers is unmistakeable.'

'Dead giveaway, hey? But you don't know what else you're going to find, and that's the surprise, *macushla.*' He stopped her at the edge of the track and released her arm.

The slight ridge where dirt gave way to long scraggly grass was just there—she put one foot forward and tapped the ground. A grass stem brushed her bare leg, tickling her skin. Cocking her head, she heard a familiar scraping sound. Was Seamus lighting a match? He knew she didn't like smoking and had refrained whenever they were together. 'What are you doing?'

'Nearly ready. Keep your eyes closed and give me your meal.'

She held the tray out, felt him take it and waited. Anticipation bubbled within her, heady as the Champagne she'd drunk once on New Year's Eve, back before their world went mad. Whatever Seamus had planned, he made her feel like she was looking forward to that Champagne New Year's Eve again. Like the world wasn't on fire and a future awaited.

A future with Seamus?

He set a hand on her shoulder and took her free hand in his. 'Open your eyes, Meg.' His warm breath tickled her ear before she did as he said.

Before her, neatly set out on a hospital blanket, a lamp cast a cosy glow over their dinner trays and a bunch of wildflowers. He'd folded two clean handkerchiefs for serviettes, and a bottle of beer and a bottle of soft drink sat to one side, flanked by two tin mugs.

Meg was delighted. And touched by his thoughtfulness. 'What made you think of doing this?' She dropped onto her knees on a corner of the blanket and picked up the flowers. He'd included some of the perfumed pink flowers in the bunch. Bringing it to her nose, she inhaled their heady scent.

Seamus sat opposite her and grinned. 'I can't take my girl out to dinner at a fancy restaurant, so I made our own private dining room. Do you like it?'

'I love it. I think it's the nicest thing anyone has ever done for me. However did you find beer and soft drink out here?'

'Ah—' He tapped the side of his nose. 'I can't reveal my sources, but let's just say the cook was grateful for the bush tucker I've brought him. He has a private store of beer. As for the soft drink, the Aussies have an army canteen service making it. They told me tamarind is the most popular flavour.' He picked up the beer bottle and knocked off the top then held it towards her, showing the label like a waiter offering the finest wine. 'Would Madam like to taste the beer?'

Meg hesitated. She'd never drunk beer, but tonight felt like the beginning of something. Since there was no Champagne to be had . . . 'Yes, please.'

He half-filled both their mugs and she lifted hers, sipping the brew. Her first taste of beer made her screw up her nose. It was bitter, but she wasn't about to say so to Seamus. 'I'm sure it will compliment our meal perfectly.'

'And here was me thinking you'd find it bitter and that I'd have to drink the lot by myself.'

She picked up her mug, gave him a sweet smile then took a mouthful. Her nose wrinkled again but she made herself swallow. Exhaling an audible sigh of feigned delight, she met his amused gaze. 'Absolutely delicious.'

Raising the bottle, he made to top up her mug.

Quickly, she put her hand over the top. 'I'll just work my way through this, thank you. Share and share alike and all that. Is the soft drink to go with dessert?'

Seamus grinned. 'Maybe. Next time I'll make sure to bring you Champagne and the finest foods, but for now, all I can give you is beer and cook's stew.'

Reaching out, she touched his hand. 'This is so much more than beer and stew. It's magic and moonlight, and flowers and—you. You've made a little patch of joy amidst this horrid war. Thank you, Seamus.'

He caught her hand and kissed it, then turned it over and pressed a lingering kiss in her palm.

A queer little flibbertigibbet danced in her stomach.

Breathless at his touch, she eased her hand from his hold. 'We should eat our meal before it gets cold.'

'That we should. Sadly, it doesn't improve with age.'

When she'd eaten as much as she could—in Seamus's case, he cleaned his plate, although she had no idea how he managed it—she raised her mug. 'To moonlit picnics among the gum trees.'

'And to many more dinners with you, Meg.'

They finished the beer and then Meg began tidying the remains of their meal. She stacked the trays and moved the beer and soft drink bottles and lamp to one corner of the blanket. Smoothing out a wrinkle, she turned and sat in the middle, patting a spot beside her. 'I want to look at the stars and make a wish.'

Seamus sat beside her and put an arm over her shoulders. 'What are you going to wish for?'

'Aside from an immediate end to this war?' She tipped her head to the sky. 'For this moment to never end. Look at those stars. They're so big and bright. Nothing like what I see from my home in the middle of Sydney.'

'You've got stars in your eyes, *macushla*.' Seamus kissed her cheek then trailed his lips over her skin to her neck, and the little spot just below her ear he'd discovered last night. The magic of the night and Seamus's lovely surprise heightened her senses. She was relaxed and on edge at the same time, wanting him to never stop what he was doing.

Wanting him to do more.

More than kiss her face and neck. More than give her goosebumps, although they were wonderful too.

She lay back on the blanket and looked up at him. Stroking his cheek, feeling that stubble that always grew back by the end of the day, no matter how close a shave he made in the morning, she knew she wanted all of him.

Her hand slipped around his nape and drew him down until she could kiss his lips and her free hand could reach around his waist and draw him closer. With a hand that trembled only a little, she tugged his shirt from his trousers and trailed her fingers across his back. Smooth. Warm. Bare.

He stretched out beside her and, reaching down, pulled her dress up and bared her thigh. The lightest of touches sent need spiking through her belly. It seemed to concentrate on that private place between her thighs and at last, she knew what desire was. That soaring need poets wrote of, and singers crooned about.

'Seamus, I want you.'

He rose up on one elbow, pulling back from her unwillingly, she thought, and looked at her in the light of the newly risen moon. His breathing seemed heavy, as though he'd been running, and something hard in his pocket poked at her leg. 'What are you asking for, Meg?'

'You. All of you. I—think I love you. I want what people in love share with each other.'

'Mother of God, how can I refuse anything you ask for. But Meg, are you sure you want this? Do you know what you're asking for? Because, hard as it will be—*hard* as I am right now—I'll wait if you're not sure.'

'I don't know what you mean about *being hard*,' although he did sound as though he was in some pain, 'but I *am* sure that I want you, in every way a woman wants the man she loves. Show me, *macushla*?'

Seamus closed his eyes and tipped his face to the sky. 'I can't deny you, Meg, because I want you so much it hurts.' He exhaled, a long, slow breath, and sat up. Reefing his shirt over his head, he dropped it beside him then rolled onto his elbow and stroked her face. 'I'll make this good for you, Meg, I promise.'

Slowly, he unbuttoned her shirt and eased it off her shoulders, followed by her skirt. Beneath them, she had worn a borrowed slip and army-issue knickers, both of which he slid off her body with reverent, slow fingers.

'You're beautiful. Your skin is like silk and your—' Words dried up as he cupped her breast.

She pressed into his hand, sure she shouldn't be enjoying his touch so much. A good girl would be embarrassed about exposing her body to a man who wasn't her husband. A good girl wouldn't have asked a man to make love to her, or even gone off with a man to a private spot in the first place.

But she wasn't a good girl. She was a woman about to lie with the man she loved.

Knowingly.

Rushing—headlong into sin.

Seamus lowered his head and gently sucked her breast.

She closed her eyes and concentrated on the feeling. The way desire ran through her body from his mouth to the very core of her.

Hadn't her mother advised her sister the night before her wedding to *lie back and think of England*? Meg couldn't imagine thinking of anything but Seamus's touch and *oh!*—the scrape of his stubbled chin on her skin, her soft belly, her thighs. Her hips rose, pressing against his mouth.

Sublime.

Divine.

Seamus's breath huffed over her most private place and she felt no embarrassment. Just a deep need to know all and share it with him. 'That feels so good, but I'm sure there's more than just this touching and kissing.'

'There is, my love. So much more. I want to take my time exploring every inch of your body, but I don't think I can wait much longer to make you mine. Are you ready?'

'I feel ready. I feel restless and ~~wonderful~~wonderful, and I want to be yours.'

His hand slipped between her thighs. 'You're so wet.'

'Is that good?'

'Perfect.'

She wished she knew more about *the marital act*. Even though they weren't married, that *act* was what they were about to do. Of course, as a nurse, she knew in theory what happened. But already, she was certain the experience would be something special. *Because I love Seamus?*

'This may hurt a bit the first time.' He positioned himself

over her and that hard thing she'd thought was something in his pocket nudged between her legs and dipped into her. *His penis.* She knew the vocabulary from her studies, but she'd never imagined it would feel so hard and so silky at the same time.

'Okay so far?'

She nodded and raised her hips. 'Yes.'

'This may sting.' He kissed her lips then rose onto his elbows and surged into her.

She gasped, blinked back unexpected tears at the pain, and bit her lip.

Seamus froze. 'Are you hurt? I'm so sorry, Meg, I—'

She shook her head. Gradually, the sting was fading, replaced by a new sensation. 'It did, but now it's—' Moving her hips gently, a strange full pleasure replaced the pain. 'Oh, it's changing. It's—'

Seamus moved within her, slowly at first until her gasps of pleasure broke through his fear of hurting her. Faster and faster he pumped, in and out, and then it was as though stars and worlds collided and she broke into a million pieces and soared into the starry night.

Chapter 5
Adelaide River

The easterly wind carried a cloud of dust towards Meg as an army truck pulled up in front of the mess hall, brakes squealing in protest. At least it had arrived from the south, so that meant no new patients. A good thing, given how full the wards were. Shading her eyes against the grit and slowly settling dust, and keen to see what supplies had arrived, Meg waited for the unloading to begin. The tailgate dropped and bags of cement and metal rods came into view.

Doubtful her replacement issue of uniform items would have accompanied a load of building materials, she sighed and slipped into the mess tent. 'Any chance of a late lunch, Cookie? Even a sandwich?'

Burly arms and a crooked nose gave Cookie the look of an aging pugilist rather than a cook, but he was a kind man. Not much taller than Meg, he had to lift his chin to peer into the pot he was stirring. Apparently satisfied, he banged the ladle on the rim and set the utensil down. 'No problem, Sister. You sit yourself down and I'll bring you a tray.'

'You're a legend, Cookie. Thank you. I'll be happy with a Spam sandwich this late in the day.' Her stomach gurgled, betraying her desperate need for food. There was precious little time for rest or relaxation, or sometimes even grabbing a meal since the 119 Australian General Hospital had moved south following the bombing of Darwin. Precious little time with Seamus, and never enough to satisfy, but they cobbled together enough snatched moments to keep them both going. At least they were both stationed in the same place.

For now. She sat at the end of the long table nearest the front of the mess and watched the first few bags of cement being tossed down.

Cookie handed over a tray with a generous serving of hash and veggies then set a cup of tea in front of her. 'Get that into you, Sister.' He leaned on the table and watched the unloading. 'That cement will be to make blast walls for the new telephone exchange.'

'We're getting a telephone exchange here? That seems excessive when Darwin's just up the road.'

Rolls of camouflage netting were tossed from the back of the truck on top of the bags of cement and Cookie nodded at them. 'Blast walls and camo netting. They're setting up a bigger military post here. The River is going to become a key part of our northern defences.'

'Are they abandoning Darwin then?'

Cookie met her eyes. Sympathy had filled his each time she mentioned Darwin, and she wondered if her fear still showed. Nightmares about the bombing haunted most of her nights, but Mary, with whom she shared a tent, simply shook her awake and chatted until Meg settled.

'We won't abandon the port, but it suffered so much damage, it will take time to make it fully operational again. Even when it is, think about how exposed it is. We need heavy artillery up there for the next time the Japs attack.'

'The next—' Her heart thudded hard. The shakes that came with the memory of falling bombs were almost as bad as her nightmares, but worse, they were visible. Anyone and everyone could see and know she was a coward. Clenching her hands, she pressed her nails into her palms and swallowed the lump of fear. A nurse had to be stronger than this. A nurse had to make her patients feel safe. Meg sucked in a painful breath. 'So you think they will? Attack, that is?' The hash she'd managed to eat sat heavy in her stomach and she dropped her fork onto the food heaped on her tray.

'For sure. Darwin's a strategic port.'

A chill rose in Meg, like a slow leaching away of heat and life. Of course the Japanese would return. Of course they would drop more bombs on Darwin. And every other town and city they could reach from their aircraft carriers. The only way she could do her job was to push the knowledge deep into her mind where it couldn't sit on her shoulder like a vulture.

'But the Japs won't catch our RAAF like sitting ducks again.

Those blokes can grade a short bush runway faster than the Japs can bomb one, and I heard tell there's likely to be a few hidden in the bush. Not A-class ones, but still. Reckon we'll be safe enough here, Sister.'

Safe enough? Meg nodded and summoned a smile. She wasn't sure anywhere was *safe* in this war, but Cookie's optimism helped bury the vulture. For now. 'In that case, I'll relax and enjoy this delicious meal then write a bright and happy letter to my parents.'

'Good idea, and—Sister?'

'What is it, Cookie?'

'Any time you need cheering up, just pop into my kitchen. I've a broad shoulder and a fund of jokes, and if all else fails, there's my secret stash of chocolate.' He grinned and patted her shoulder.

'Thanks, Cookie. That means a lot.'

##

Meg wrung out her washing, shook out her shirt then pegged it on the line Seamus had strung for her and Mary between their tent and a twelve-foot sapling. The late summer heat would dry her shirt and undergarments quickly, which was just as well. Two sets of clothes—one in the wash and one on her back—weren't enough. Not when she lost a gallon of sweat in the normal course of a day. Sweat, dust, and flies – *the summer trifecta*, Dad called it.

She took a wooden peg from her pocket and hung her knickers as a pair of hands slid around her waist. In that first moment, Meg gasped before Seamus nuzzled her ear. 'It's just me. How's my girl today?'

Setting her hands over his, she leaned against Seamus's chest and closed her eyes. 'Better now you're here. Gosh, I'm tired.'

'Long shift?'

She bit her lip and nodded. 'And another nightmare. Honestly, I don't know how Mary puts up with me.'

'She must be a saint. You know I'd willingly replace her if I could. In my arms—' His lips trailed kisses up her neck and she tipped her head to make it easier for him. 'You wouldn't have nightmares, *macushla.*'

If only Seamus could be by my side.

She lifted a hand and touched his cheek then slipped it around his neck, holding him like she'd never let him go. She didn't want to let him go. Not ever. 'Mmm, you make all my aches and fears disappear when you do that.'

'What—this?' He turned her around in his arms and claimed her lips. She had no chance to tell him to be careful or that someone might see them. She barely had time to draw breath before Seamus's kiss made her forget where they were. Warm lips. Soft lips. Seamus's lips. Even the war disappeared as she lost herself in him.

Am I in love?

When she was with him, she was certain of her feelings. Seamus was adventure and excitement, but he was also home. Safety. With him by her side she felt whole again.

Her arms encircled his neck as she pressed against him, loving him.

Love? The word felt right, and as he lifted his head and looked into her eyes, she tested it in her mind. *I love you.*

Seamus took a quick breath and set his forehead against hers. 'Ah, Meg, when you look at me like that, I see all that's good and beautiful in this world, and all I want is to be with you. To love you.'

'You have the silver tongue of a poet.'

'If it's true, 'tis you who brings out the poet in me. I look at you and think of Galway's green fields and summer rain soft as a butterfly wing on my cheek. One day, *macushla*, I'll take you there and show you where I was born.' He raised his head and his blue eyes—*blue as the summer sea*, she thought—pinned her.

'Would you come with me, Meg?'

Her breath caught. His question was so much more than mere words. It was a promise. Hope. A future.

Would she leave her home and follow Seamus across the sea to Ireland?

'Yes.'

##

'Sister Dorset?' Seamus stopped beside her at the foot of Simpson's bed and spoke more softly. 'Meg, can you get away for a few minutes?'

Meg finished writing up Simpson's medical notes and gave her patient a smile before turning to Seamus. 'I'll be relieved in twenty minutes. Will that do?'

He glanced through the doorway and Meg's gaze followed his. An army truck was offloading supplies into the mess tent and a small pile of kitbags sat off to one side. Gripping his arm, she asked, 'Have your orders come through?'

He nodded, and a muscle in his cheek jumped. He took her hand and tugged her towards the supply 'cupboard', the curtained off section offering a little privacy.

Meg pulled the curtain across then gripped his hands. 'Where are you going?' She had to be strong. She would not cry. A handful wonderful nights making love with Seamus under the stars were not enough, but she wouldn't send him off with tears and a blotchy face to remember her by.

'Townsville for a start, then who knows. We've got to stop the Japs before they reach our shores.'

'Active duty? But you're not ready for that.'

'My arm's coming good, and I reckon the army needs all the able-bodied men it can get.' He released one hand and tucked a loose strand of hair behind her ears, his fingers trailing away down her cheek. 'You've got to admit, *macushla*—I'm definitely *able-bodied*.'

She caught his hand before it left her face and pressed her cheek into his palm. 'In army jargon, your equipment's all in excellent working order.' Her smile trembled, and she blinked away tears that threatened to fall, despite her best intentions. 'I'll miss you, Seamus.'

'And I, you. Meg, I know our time has been short, but—will you wait for me? Wait till I come home.'

'You know I'm your girl.'

'That you are, *macushla*. But I want more than that. I want to marry you and make a life together. Say you'll marry me, Meg?'

Meg frowned. With all her heart she wanted to say yes, but she'd heard her mother's stories about wartime weddings from the Great War. 'They say wartime romances happen quickly because we don't know which day will be our last. Is that why you're asking me, Seamus?'

He slid both arms around her waist and pulled her close. 'Of course we don't know when our last day will be, but that's true of life in or out of wartime. But I want to marry you because I love you, Meg. The only question is, do you love me enough to wait?'

She nodded slowly, slid her arms around his neck then pressed her lips to his. Seamus's kisses made her forget the sounds of the ward, forget the war raging to the north. He made her forget everything except how wonderful she felt in his arms. The kind of wonderful she wanted to hold onto for the rest of her life. The kind of wonderful she had discovered on their blanket beneath the stars.

When he finally raised his head and rested his forehead against hers, his words were soft. 'So that's a yes then?'

A soft smile lifted the corners of her mouth. 'Yes.'

'She said yes.' The loud voice belonged to Private Sanders in the bed closest to them.

Clapping erupted on the other side of the curtain, and when Seamus pulled it back, most of the patients were watching them.

Heat rose in Meg's cheeks and her hands rose to cover them. She was happy. Deliriously happy. It lasted for thirty seconds, until Matron stepped into the ward, Meg and Seamus in her sights.

'Have we won the war, and someone forgot to tell me?' Her voice had a frosty edge at odds with the building heat outside and her gaze swept over each side of the ward, finally returning to Seamus standing tall by Meg's side and holding her hand.

'Corporal Flanagan, please unhand Sister Dorset.'

Seamus turned to Meg and raised her hand to his lips before releasing his hold. 'Only a direct order could make me let you go.' He walked towards Matron. 'Will you spare my *fiancée* for a few minutes so we can say our goodbyes, pretty please, Matron?'

'Fiancée, is it? Since when?'

'About a minute ago, Matron,' Simpson called out from his bed.

'Right romantic it was, Matron,' added Johnny Matthews in the bed next to Simpson.

Matron held up both hands and the good-natured joshing subsided. 'Since you've apparently accepted this soldier's proposal—*against* all advice to the contrary, Sister—you may have five minutes to send him on his way.'

'Thank you, Matron.' Meg grabbed Seamus's hand on the way out of the ward and ran with him along the side of the hospital until they were out of sight of the soldiers unloading the truck. The unloading was almost finished, and Meg knew they had little time to say goodbye.

Her chest felt tight. She wasn't ready to say goodbye, but that was the way of this beastly war. Too many goodbyes and no time to prepare for them.

At the rear of the hospital Seamus pulled her into his arms and kissed her, kisses that told her how much he loved her. Hers were more than a little desperate at the thought of not seeing him for weeks—months. She pulled back and held his face in her hands. 'Don't you dare let anything happen to you. Come back to me in one piece.'

'You have my promise.' He let her go, reached behind his neck and removed the chain she'd noticed under his dog tags. He held it out for her to see. 'I don't have a ring to give you, Meg, but I want you to wear my St Christopher medal. I know you aren't Catholic, but, even though he's the patron saint of travellers, I believe he'll keep you safe while I'm away. Will you wear it?'

'What about you? You're the one going off to fight. I want you to stay safe. Why don't you—'

Seamus reached around her neck and did up the clasp then kissed her, a soft kiss full of promise. 'With my St Christopher medal, I take you as my bride-to-be.'

From the track, a truck horn blared, insistent, not to be refused.

'I've got to go. Remember, I love you, Meg. I always will.' He jogged backwards, blew her a kiss then turned the corner of the building and was gone.

Meg picked up the medal, warm from his skin. She pressed it to her lips. *I'm engaged!* Excitement coursed through her, mixed with a sharp sense of loss. His proposal was crazy and ridiculously quick and wonderful all at the same time.

How long would it be before he returned, and they could be married? How long before she became both wife and mother? Hugging herself, she let tears of both joy and sadness run down her cheeks and clung to the memory of Seamus's kisses. Memory was all she had until he returned.

***

The signal from the Armed Forces radio show cut in and out before it settled. Frank Sinatra was crooning *This Love of Mine*, a big hit from the previous year. Meg looked around the group of off duty staff, both Aussies and a few Americans from down the road, and ambulatory patients. They were gathered in the mess tent to listen to the radio and drink tea. The Americans served alcohol at their social gatherings, so Mary had told her, but Meg had traded places to avoid such get togethers until tonight. Tonight, Mary had practically marched her into the mess tent and pushed her onto a chair.

'Repeat after me: I *will* enjoy myself.'

'I will try, Mary. I promise.' With Seamus gone, Meg doubted her ability to enjoy the evening, but for her friend's sake, she smiled. 'Thanks for swapping shifts.'

'Heaven knows, you've done the same for others. Dance, have fun, be young.' Mary gave her a brief one-armed hug and hurried back to the ward.

Meg looked around to see who else had the night off. In the corner, Dr Hampton turned his back on the assembly and held his mug out. Cookie glanced towards Matron, who had agreed to one dance with Captain Keller. As the captain turned her away from them, Cookie— the source of Seamus' beer that wonderful night they'd made love for the first time—tipped something into Doc's mug and grinned before slipping the bottle into his pocket.

Meg rested her chin on her hand and set her elbow on her knee and sighed, wishing Seamus were here to dance with her. If she closed her eyes, she could see him and imagine him standing in front of her and saying—

'Sister, may I have this dance?'

Her eyes sprang open and she sat up straight. Private Matthews, newly out of his hospital bed, stood in front of her, one hand extended and waiting for her answer.

Meg jumped to her feet. There were too few nurses, or too many men to make a refusal possible, no matter how much she wanted only to be in Seamus' arms. 'I'd be delighted, thank you, Matthews.'

'I'll try not to step on your toes, Sister.' *These Are the Things I Love* began to play and Matthews grinned. 'Jimmy Dorsey and his Orchestra with Bob Eberly—this is a top song, Sister. I'm going to learn to play it on my saxophone after I get home.' He took her in his arms, not too close, and, as they began a slow circuit around the makeshift dance floor, he began humming, singing occasional snatches with the singer. '*The gleam of love light in your lovely eyes'*. He looked into hers. 'Reckon that's you, Sister, with love light in your eyes. Have you heard from your fiancé, if I'm not being forward in asking?'

She summoned a smile and shook her head, feeling the loss of Seamus like a physical weight on her heart. 'Not yet, but it's only been a couple of weeks.'

'He'll write when he can. All the blokes know you're his girl and how sweet on you he is.'

'A real whirlwind romance.' Her gaze slipped over Matthews's shoulder into the darkness beyond the tent. Out there was *their* special place, where they'd made a little slice of heaven all their own. Where Seamus had looked at her with love in his eyes. Where she'd told him she loved him too.

'*The look you give in answer to my pleas . . .*' The singer built to the song's finale but the voice she heard belonged to

Seamus: '*Your sweet voice whispering darling, I love you, These are the things I love.*'

As the song ended and Matthews escorted her back to her seat, thanking her for the dance, her thoughts winged to her beloved.

Stay safe, Seamus, wherever you are. I love you.

Chapter 6

Meg's stomach contracted, bile rushed up her throat and she threw up again. She pushed back a loose tendril of hair and rocked back on her heels.

Heavens, do I have food poisoning?

When she felt there couldn't be anything left in her stomach, she spat out the awful taste. Her eyes were streaming, and her head was heavy, but other than that, it was just this horrid retching.

Feeling shaky, she stood, shovelled dirt into the hole and stepped through the flap of the open-roofed latrine. Crossing to the washing station, she scrubbed her hands and hoped Matron didn't need her early on the ward. At least not until her stomach had settled.

'Sister Dorset!' Jimmy, the captain's clerk, waved at her. He raced over and presented her with a letter. 'It's from Corporal Flanagan, Sister. I thought you'd want it straight away. I haven't even given Matron her mail yet.'

Touched at how wonderful the men were about her and Seamus, she patted his arm and smiled. 'Thanks, Private Langdon.'

With a wink and a smile in return, Jimmy raced back to his post and continued sorting the mail.

Sucking in a deep breath, Meg headed into the mess tent. No one else seemed to be unwell and breakfast was almost over. Maybe she had just been unlucky, but the thought of food sent her stomach into backflips. As Cook approached and lifted the lid on the leavings of scrambled eggs, Meg's stomach gave another of those uncomfortable flips. She stepped away from the food, waved her hands as though she could magic up a barrier, and shook her head. 'Just tea, thanks, Cookie.'

'You'll waste away, Sister.' He nodded at the letter she clutched in her lap as he set a mug of tea in front of her. 'News from your soldier, hey?'

'Yes. It's been a while. Matron hasn't sent for me yet and

I've half an hour until my shift starts.'

'I'll leave you to enjoy your letter.' He shuffled back to his pots and pans.

Meg set Seamus's letter on the table and ran a hand over the writing. An unfamiliar hand, since she'd never seen anything he had written while they were together, and yet she thought she would have known it was from him even without his details in the top corner. She examined them, running a finger over his name. No location, just his company.

A sip of tea slipped down easily, and her stomach behaved. She opened his letter. Chunks of writing had been blacked out, censored by some clerk who had read Seamus's words before they reached her. She frowned, knowing it was necessary, but resenting it all the same. She took another sip of tea and told herself off. They were in the middle of a war and such details were not important. What *was* important was that Seamus had written and she had his letter in her hand. Greedy to hear his voice in his words, she read:

Meg, macushla,

I love you and miss you madly. Got to say the most important things first in case I have to finish writing this quickly. I'll be [section blacked out].

No idea how long it will be until I can hold you in my arms again.

Our captain says [section blacked out]. Not the greatest news, but as we expected.

Expected? She decided that meant he was being sent overseas. Seamus had said as much before he left. Perhaps Townsville was a major launch point for the Allied efforts. Where would he be sent?

Little news had reached them here at Adelaide River, but she knew from the trucks rattling through to and from Darwin that the northern city had taken a severe battering and the Japanese were pressing forward through islands to the north. Injured servicemen on their way south and drivers heading north had all offered similar information. Some trucks rested at the River overnight, and those times were the busiest. Meg didn't mind though. Being busy kept her mind off wondering about Seamus as she tended young men's wounds.

She held the double-sided page up and continued reading.

Do you fancy a big white wedding or shall we 'tie the knot' with only a pair of witnesses? I fancy the latter choice, and the sooner, the better. I can't wait to make you my wife.

Dad and Mum would prefer the big white wedding, but how 'white' could it be with the restrictions that were in place. Sydney was so far away, and heaven knew when they would get leave, let along enough to travel south and get married.

If we can even travel that far for personal reasons.

Meg stared through the open door of the mess without really seeing anything. Her top priority was to marry Seamus, and if two witnesses and a minister was all the law required, she'd marry him tomorrow.

'Sister Dorset?' Meg looked up as Jimmy skidded to a halt in front of her. 'Matron wants you at the hospital right away.'

'Thanks, Jimmy. On my way!' She gulped down a large mouthful of tea, slipped Seamus's letter into its envelope, and stood. A wave of dizziness engulfed her. Her hand shot out and she leaned on the table, eyes closed for several moments.

'Sister, are you okay?'

Sucking a draft of air through her mouth, Meg opened her eyes to see Cookie standing beside Jimmy. Cookie shook his head, but he looked concerned. 'She didn't eat any breakfast and then expects to go work on the ward all day.'

'You can't survive on love alone, Sister.' Jimmy frowned and, she wasn't sure if she imagined it, his gaze flicked down her body. But Jimmy wasn't like that, ogling the nurses. It must have been the dizziness making her see things.

'I'm fine but thank you both. I promise I'll come back and get some food if I can after I find out why Matron wants me.' Fixing a smile in place and touched anew by how caring the men were, she put back her shoulders and headed off to the hospital.

But the memory of Jimmy's gaze flickering down her body—to her waist, she felt sure—sent unease niggling through her mind as she catalogued her illness this morning. Was she—could she possibly be—pregnant?

The idea jumped fully formed into her mind. She stopped abruptly; hands pressed against her stomach. She and Seamus hadn't used any form of protection when they'd made love. They hadn't even talked about the possibility of a baby resulting from their love. *A baby!*

She couldn't. Being engaged to be married wouldn't satisfy the neighbours back home. No sex before the '*I do's*' had been exchanged, no matter that young men were heading off to fight—and some to die—for King and Country. How long would it be before Seamus got leave? Would he return in time for them to be married before their baby was born?

She pulled herself up short. *I don't even know if I am pregnant.*

But throwing up before breakfast wasn't like her. She swallowed her fears, drew a deep breath, and covered the last few yards into the hospital ward.

'Sister Dorset, I've received word that you're to be transferred to a hospital in Townsville.'

Meg's heart leapt. Seamus was in Townsville. When she got there, she could find out for sure if she carried his child, and perhaps they could be wed before he went overseas. 'When do I leave?'

'On the next truck heading south. I'll be sorry to lose you, Meg, especially the way the River is expanding. You're a good nurse, but Townsville might get heavy casualties soon and they'll need nurses with combat wound experience. I've put your name forward for immediate advanced training in theatre. From what your patients out of Darwin said, and what I've seen of you here, you don't lose your head in tough situations.'

'Thank you, Matron. I appreciate your faith in me, and the

opportunity to increase my skills.'

'Have you eaten? You look peaky.'

Meg shook her head. She was unwilling to mention her throwing up to Matron. 'I got a letter from my fiancé this morning and was too excited reading it to eat.'

'Go and eat now. I'll see you in twenty minutes, and Sister—'

'Yes, Matron?'

'Food first, every day. If you collapse, how will you nurse your patients?'

'Understood, Matron. It won't happen again.'

Hopeful that she was wrong or would find a way to overcome her morning sickness if she *was* pregnant, Meg hightailed it back to the mess tent. Jimmy and Cookie were in a huddle beside the army-sized teapot, but, when Jimmy spotted her, he said something to Cookie before carrying a mug of steaming tea to her.

'Please don't take this the wrong way, and my apologies if I've got the wrong end of the stick, Sister, but I heard you throwing up, and then when Cookie said you weren't eating breakfast—well— it's not like you. My sister used to drink ginger tea when her stomach was upset. Said it worked a treat for her, and I thought you might like to try some.'

'That's very kind of you, Jimmy. Thank you.' She lifted the mug and sniffed the pale brew. Pieces of chopped ginger floated in the water, but her stomach didn't flip at the aroma. It smelled enticing. 'Did your sister suffer often with an upset tummy?'

Jimmy's cheeks turned beetroot-red, and he dropped his gaze. 'Only when she was in the family way, Sister.' He looked up and met her gaze. 'I don't mean to suggest you are too—in the family way, I mean—but I thought, if it helped Doris then, it might help your upset stomach now.'

Meg froze. How could Jimmy know? *Did* Jimmy know what she had only begun to suspect?

'I'm sure my upset stomach will be fine soon, but thanks, Jimmy.'

'My pleasure, Sister.' His smile was quick and then he was gone.

Meg blew over the top of the brew, sending a stream of steam into the day then sipped. Delicious. However it worked, the important thing was that she felt better as she drank, and when Cookie brought over a couple of slices of toast with a thin scraping of Vegemite, she felt confident of getting through the day.

'You're not to leave until you've finished what's on your plate, Sister.' He folded his arms across his chest, and she knew he wasn't going to budge unless she began eating.

'Thanks, Cookie.' With Cookie hovering like a mother hen, she bit into the toast, chewed and swallowed. 'I feel better already. And I promise I won't skip a meal tomorrow.' She took another bite and gave an exaggerated 'Yummy!'

Cookie unfolded his brawny arms and nodded. 'Better. And so you know, I've got plenty of fresh ginger to make you more tea—' He looked a little uncomfortable. 'If you need it. Jimmy found a clump of ginger not far from camp.'

'Good to know.' Had Jimmy guessed her condition and shared it with Cookie? Unable to meet Cookie's eye, Meg kept her head down and focused on eating every bite of toast. She finished her ginger tea and felt more settled in herself, but only marginally less embarrassed. Good girls didn't make love with men before they married them. Good girls didn't fall pregnant out of wedlock. Had her love for Seamus turned her into—*a bad girl*?

By the time she'd washed her mug and plate, she was no nearer finding an answer and had to hustle to make it into the ward for the start of her shift.

Meg sat in front of Jimmy Langdon's radio and looked up at him. He was young, just turned nineteen, he'd told her, but practical and organised. For once, the army had got the right person in the job, she thought.

'You're sure you won't get into trouble for this?'

'No, Sister, it's all good, but keep it short, okay.' He glanced over his shoulder before he nodded to her. 'Go ahead. I'll be just outside keeping watch.'

'Thank you.'

Jimmy took up a position near the entrance, struck a match and lit a cigarette. He should have been at university studying the classics, not fighting in this dreadful, dreadful war. He should have been dating girls and going to dances and having fun, like all the other young men.

She pressed her lips together and turned her full attention to his radio set and suddenly, there was Seamus's voice coming down the line.

'Meg, my sweet. How are you?'

'Fine. Well.'

We might be having a baby and I've been throwing up and it's awful, but . . .

Her courage failed her as she stared at the dark machine. It was wrong to tell him she might be pregnant like this – over the radio. He deserved to hear it from her lips, and she wanted her lips close enough to his when she told him. Close enough to kiss her; his arms close enough to enfold her. 'How are you?'

'Delighted to hear your voice, my darling. Are you sure everything's okay? This call is risky.'

She cleared her throat. 'I just had to let you know - I'm being transferred to Townsville. My orders just came through.'

'Meg, *macushla*, grand news. Do you want me to see if I can chase up a priest so we can . . .?'

'Not a priest. I'm not Catholic, remember?' But it thrilled her that he was so keen to marry her. *Her*, not the maybe-mother of his baby. Why, she might even have her wedding night this week!

'Hmm, what about an army chaplain? All-denominations catered for. Shall I ask around, Meg?'

Jimmy began whistling *Tipperary*. Someone was approaching.

'Yes. Do it. I've got to go. I love you, Seamus.'

'I love you, Meg. See you soon.'

Meg stood abruptly and shoved Jimmy's seat back under the radio table then took up her agreed position behind the seat, a couple of pieces of paper in her hand.

Jimmy stuck his head inside and spoke clearly. 'I'm sorry, Sister, but I'll have to deal with your request a bit later. The captain needs me.'

Meg took a deep breath and stepped outside. 'No problem, Private. I'll come back after my shift.' She saluted Captain Keller. 'Sir.'

'Sorry to interrupt your business, Sister.'

'It can wait, sir. I'm needed on the ward.'

She turned on her heel and headed towards the hospital, her steps matching the joyful refrain running through her mind.

This week. I'll be marrying Seamus this week.

Chapter 7
Townsville

Truck, train, car . . . *I only need to take a boat and a plane, and I'll have used every form of transport known to man.*

Travel-weary, Meg leaned against the telegraph pole outside the RAAF supply-store and waited for a ride to her new posting. A duffle bag containing her new set of uniforms lay at her feet. The clerk had grudgingly handed over a replacement kit when she told him hers had been lost in the Darwin bombing. The paperwork had been painful, but it hadn't been worth getting into a long explanation with him. Most of what she'd lost had been uniform items, but she regretted the loss of her family photos. And given her poor recall for mundane details, the loss of her little address book limited her ability to write to friends.

But she'd memorised the information about Seamus's company. In her first free moment, she was going to contact him. Had he teed up an army chaplain already? At least she'd have a new uniform to walk down the aisle in, but a small part of her regretted not being able to dress up for him. He'd never seen her dressed to the nines and she was just vain enough to want to wow him on her wedding day.

A jeep pulled up beside her and a corporal leaned across the passenger seat. 'Lt Dorset?' Meg nodded and the driver patted the seat. 'Hop in.' He came around her side of the jeep and tossed her duffle bag onto the back seat while she climbed in. 'I'm to take you to the MRS, Central Sick Quarters.'

Her tired brain couldn't remember what she'd heard about this unit. 'Central? Does it serve all defence forces?' Meg prayed it included the army. Surely it would be easier to find Seamus if she were based in a hospital that included the army.

'It serves the squadrons out at Garbutt Airfield. Central Sick Quarters is a RAAF acquisition. It's an old home that's been acquired. We've taken out walls to make two wards and now we're turning the rear rooms into an operating theatre.'

Matron had promised Meg she would be furthering her skills as a theatre nurse. It looked like she was coming in on the ground floor, but the news she was to be stationed in a RAAF hospital wasn't so promising. Not when she still had to find Seamus. Grateful he hadn't yet been deployed, her mind turned over her driver's comments, and thrilled to the information about the operating theatre. In Darwin, before the bombing had changed everything, she'd already decided that being a theatre nurse was where she felt most at home, and she had requested as much time there as her matron was prepared to give her.

'Do you know where my barracks will be?'

'On site at *Currajong*. There are huts for the nurses around the croquet green. *Croquet*, hey! The owners must have been posh.' Her driver said no more until they turned a corner and he pointed ahead. A soldier was guiding a reversing truck down a driveway while another stood in the middle of the street, holding back a single civilian car until the truck cleared the road. 'That's you, where the truck just turned in.'

He pulled up near the front corner of the property and Meg clambered out of the jeep. Turning back to grab her duffle bag she asked, 'Where and to whom do I report?'

The corporal was halfway to the front steps when he flicked an abrupt finger along the driveway. 'Down the side that way. Temporary office in the first hut you come to. Can't miss it. I've got to get back to work.' With no more small talk, he strode up the front steps and through the door.

Meg looked at the building set well back from the road. The front garden must have been sizable judging by the cleared ground. Sounds of hammering came through the open front door of what, despite the army's worst efforts, had clearly once been a beautiful home.

Palm trees filled one corner of the property but churned up earth surrounded them, and Meg wondered if their days were numbered as she approached the fence line. Two prefabricated tents with wooden flooring had been erected and wooden pegs indicated where others would be added.

The house was a grand structure, gracious and beautifully proportioned, with a wide veranda running down each side. Soldiers were in the process of adding flyscreening and materials for multiple beds were stacked nearby. This was a major facility and Meg more fully appreciated Matron's recommending her for the transfer. The size and scope of what was happening here would be good experience and once the war was over, she hoped it would help her to find work in a surgical hospital.

Following the churned-up driveway, the sounds of hammering and sawing grew louder, and she glimpsed her driver on a ladder climbing onto the roof. Rounding the corner, she understood why he hadn't bothered to escort her further. Overgrown grass, lush, but contained within a croquet-shaped area was surrounded by huts. She'd found the nurses' accommodation, but nowhere stood out as an office where she could report her arrival.

Slowing her pace, she strolled towards the nearest hut. At the open door she peeked inside. A WAAAF officer sat at a file-covered desk, a set of shelves lining the wall behind. The woman looked up suddenly. 'Can I help you?'

Meg stepped into the room, lowered her duffle bag, and stood at attention. 'Lt Dorset reporting for duty, ma'am.'

'Dorset? You were in Darwin during the bombing, weren't you?'

'Yes, ma'am.'

'And after that?'

'On an evac truck to Adelaide River where I've been since Darwin.'

The woman sorted through a pile of files, pulled one out and opened it. Meg could just make out 'Dorset, Margaret Olivia-Lt. Nurse' on the tab. 'You're coming in as a theatre nurse. Good. The matron at Adelaide River recommended you as being cool and calm in difficult circumstances.' Closing the file, she stood and came around the desk to join Meg. 'I'll show you to your quarters. Fifteen minutes to freshen up and then I'll introduce you to Dr Ransom. You'll be on his team and answerable to him in the first instance.'

Meg nodded. Why did that name sound familiar? Tired from the constant travelling to get to Townsville, her sludgy brain took a while to remember where she'd heard it before—Corporal Ransom had been their driver as they escaped from Darwin. As she followed the WAAAF officer to a hut two doors down from the office, she wondered if the corporal was related to the doctor she was to work under.

'You're the first to move in here, Dorset. Ablutions are in that building.' Meg followed the pointing finger. Not that she needed to be told. Signs clearly labelled the block, and the nearby mess hut. Beyond these buildings and at a distance stood a separate building, as yet unnamed.

'What's that far building for?'

'The morgue. Come back to my office when you've tidied up. I'm Lt Breeks.' Turning on her heel, the lieutenant strode back the way they'd come.

Meg stepped into the basic hut and looked around. Two double-bunk beds were set at right angles along two walls. Four upright metal lockers and four hooks lined the third wall, and she stood in the doorway in the fourth wall, surveying what was to be her home for the foreseeable future.

Unless I'm pregnant or married.

If Seamus had arranged their wedding, she would have to remain quiet about the fact. Married women were not acceptable as nurses, and pregnant nurses—they were unheard of. Shelving the pregnancy question until there was something she could do about finding out, she chose a bottom bunk and set out a fresh uniform, grabbed her toiletry bag and headed to the ablutions block for a quick shower. The water was warm and plentiful, and washed away dust and her fatigue so that, when she presented herself to Lt Breeks fifteen minutes later, she felt ready to cope with anything.

Lt Breeks handed her a manual. 'Dr Ransom has arrived. I'll introduce you first, then you are to familiarise yourself with the contents of that before tomorrow. You'll be helping the doctor to set up the operating theatre as soon as it's finished.'

'Yes, ma'am.' Once again, she followed the lieutenant, this time to a hut on the other side of the croquet lawn.

The lieutenant tapped on the open door and waited until an authoritative male voice bade them enter. Snapping a smart salute, she stood aside, and Meg got her first glimpse of the doctor. She scrutinised his face but couldn't tell if he might be related to the corporal from her Darwin trip.

A one-sided tilt of his lips suggested he was holding back a smile. 'Do I have something on my face, Sister?'

Her eyes widened and she stood straighter. 'No, sir, sorry, sir. It's just—the corporal who drove us down from Darwin was named Ransom too. It's a somewhat unusual name and I wondered . . .' Her cheeks heated and she kept her gaze on the loop on his shoulder. *Stop blathering like an idiot and show him you're a professional.* 'Sorry, sir.'

'As it happens, I do have a younger brother who is a corporal. It could have been him. Now, Lt Dorset, isn't it?'

Meg nodded.

'We need experienced theatre nurses. More than are available. You have been recommended for this position. I've been told our operating theatre will be complete and ready to go operational soon, as in by tomorrow. I like my operating theatre to run in a certain way so I will train you to assist me since it seems most of our nursing staff won't be arriving for a few days.'

'Excuse me, Doctor, but am I the only nurse to have arrived so far?'

'You are the first, Sister, and so you will have the task of helping me set up once we are able to access the theatre. Before we begin receiving patients, I will test you in procedures until you can do them in your sleep, and believe me, Sister, there will be times when you will feel as though you're doing just that.'

'Sir, I'm looking forward to improving and learning new skills.'

'Good. I see Lt Breeks has given you the manual on setting up an operating theatre. Tomorrow, I'll test you on the instruments and handling procedures. I trust you will quickly learn to anticipate my needs and meet them.'

'Yes, sir.'

'Dismissed.'

Meg turned to go, but before she reached the door, Dr Ransom stopped her. 'On a personal note, how was my brother when you saw him?'

Memories of Pte Jackson's death on the track were crystal clear in her mind, but she chose the most suitable to share. 'Your brother was well and helpful. He dug a grave for a young soldier we couldn't save in the evacuation from Darwin on the drive down to Adelaide River. I knew him for little more than a day.'

'Trust Terry to be in Darwin when it was bombed. But we're safe here—all those aircraft at the air base to defend us, right, Sister? I'll see you at 0800 tomorrow.'

'Yes, sir.' Meg left clutching the manual. First, she'd make a cuppa and then she planned to find a shady patch of grass and become familiar with how to set up an operating theatre. And after that she would find someone who could tell her where Seamus was.

The wide central hall of the house channelled a breeze towards Meg as she held the handset of the wall-mounted phone. Soon, an operator picked up, and Meg asked for, 'Army HQ please.' She'd read the manual on setting up an operating theatre from cover to cover and would read it again, but now she was going to find Seamus. Just hearing his voice would be enough for the moment, but she wanted his arms around her soon. And she needed to tell him that she might be carrying their child. She needed—

Had someone picked up the phone on the other end? Drawing a breath ready to answer, she pressed the telephone to her ear and waited . . . and waited. She could hear men's voices at the other end of the line and wondered if the soldier who had answered her call had forgotten her. At last, he returned. 'Are you there, Sister?'

'I'm here. Did you find Corporal Flanagan, my fiancé?'

'I traced him. Sorry, Sister, but he shipped out two days ago.'

Her heart nose-dived, if one could say that of such a central organ. Nose-dived and sank without trace as reality hit. Seamus wasn't here. Seamus probably wasn't even in the same country as her now. She couldn't speak to him; couldn't tell him about their perhaps-baby; couldn't marry him right away. All she could do was accept that, like so many others, this war was keeping them apart. Her breath juddered as she drew it in. She pushed out a soft 'Thank you.' At least, she thought she said the words before she hung up the phone.

Two days. She'd missed him by two days. It might as well be a year. It wouldn't have mattered if there had been room on a passing truck a day earlier. She'd still have missed him. A lone tear slid down her cheek. She leaned her head against the wall beside the phone and wiped it away.

'What's the matter, Sister? Bad news?' Of course Dr Ransom had chosen that moment to walk down the hallway. Of course he had seen Meg crying, but right now, she didn't care. Well—maybe she cared a little.

Quickly she wiped both cheeks and took a deep breath before turning to him. 'Sort of, though not the worst. I was hoping to see my fiancé, but he shipped out. Two days ago.'

'I'm sorry. That's lousy timing. Let's start your first lesson. That should help take your mind off it for a bit. We'll set up the autoclave.'

In some ways, Dr Ransom was not so much unsympathetic as practical. She would do well to emulate his attitude. Everyone had disappointments. Everyone had to face absences of loved ones in a war. No matter how much her heart hurt, she was no different.

Standing tall, she dug her short nails into her palms and nodded. 'I'm ready, doctor.' She followed him into the operating theatre and stopped by his side. He lifted the lid of the metal box. Inside, the metal drainer was similar to the one she had used in Darwin. 'When will the other nurses arrive?'

He shrugged and set the lid down beside the autoclave. 'A day or two or three. I have no idea, but what I do know is that all of you will require training in preparation for when the worst happens and we're inundated with casualties. You're here so I'll train you. If you live up to your matron's recommendation, you might become my head nurse. When the other sisters arrive, we will both teach them what you have learned. Okay, so—you've used an autoclave before?'

Meg nodded. 'Autoclaving is the most effective method of sterilising equipment, which we do after each procedure.'

He picked up a handful of medical instruments and set them in a single layer on the metal drainer then replaced the lid. 'Always like that; never in an untidy pile, which, believe me, I have seen happen. Once the lid is in place and secure, turn the power on and note the time. We can't expect that all of our nurses will be fully trained and competent. I want to reduce the chance of errors, so I want the autoclaving times for various instruments and beakers posted on the wall above.'

He moved on to a tray of surgical instruments. 'Set these out according to the diagram in the manual. There is logic and reason for the order. When we operate, I expect immediate delivery of whatever I ask for. Let's see your technique. Hold out your hand, palm up and flat.'

Meg did as she was told and Dr Ransom firmly placed a scalpel in her hand. 'Like that, Sister. That's what I expect from you. Your delivery of the instrument should be firm without smacking into my hand. The handle should be placed so that when I close my hand, the instrument is facing the right way ready to be used. In emergency cases, speed is as important as precision. Now, hand me that scalpel.'

Nervous at first, Meg took three attempts to set it in Dr Ransom's hand firmly enough to suit him. 'I'm sorry, doctor.'

'Don't be. You picked up my preference quickly. Sister Dorset, I'm confident that, with practice, you will become a good theatre nurse. Now, I'll explain the procedure I expect for bringing a patient in and preparing him, and after that, I think we'll have a break for lunch.'

##

'Knock, knock.'

Meg looked up from the filing notes in her hand. A young corporal stood in the doorway and pulled off his cap when she noticed him.

'Ah, Lieutenant, I have a package for a Sister Margaret Dorset, to be delivered to her hand only. Can you tell me where I might find—'

Meg pushed her chair back and held out her hand. 'I'm Lt Dorset, Corporal.'

'Then this is for you—' He paused, and colour seeped across his cheeks. He pulled off his cap and gripped it between both hands. Clearing his throat, he met her gaze. 'With much love, and a thousand apologies. I was told to say that.' His cheeks flamed red as he handed over the package, and he shuffled his feet. 'Corporal Flanagan made me swear on my granny's grave that I'd be sure to tell you that. Especially the love bit.'

Heart thudding at this wonderful and unexpected gift from Seamus, Meg smiled. 'Then I'll be sure to let him know how perfectly fine your delivery of his message was when I next write to him. Thank you, Corporal.'

The bright red in the lad's face eased, and his cheeks puffed with round good health as he smiled. 'My pleasure, Lieutenant. I'm sorry I couldn't get it to you any earlier.' He saluted and disappeared down the hallway.

Meg sat slowly, thoughtful as her fingers teased out the shape inside Seamus's package. A book.

She set the package on the desk and slipped off the string holding the brown paper wrapping in place. Folding the paper back, she saw it was a slim volume of poetry. Not new. Well-thumbed. Loved by its owner.

She lifted the front board and first page and held them open. There, in the top left corner, was written in a neat, schoolboy script:

'M. Seamus Flanagan, 1932'.

Below, in a similar but adult version of the same hand, Seamus had written:

For my Meg
With all my love, always,
Seamus xx

She traced the letters of his name, read the inscription softly, and then fanned the pages of the book. Had he written a letter? A note? Perhaps he had marked his favourite poem for her? As she reached the back board of the volume, a single sheet of paper fell onto the desk. Ripped from a notebook, both sides were covered in pencilled words, scrawled, perhaps written hurriedly. She picked the paper up and tipped it towards the window. There was no attribution or year, and no other message to her, but Seamus had felt this important enough to include with his gift. She read:

SONG: WHEREVER WE MAY BE
Wherever we may be
There is mindlessness and mind,
There is self, there is unself,
Within and without;
There is plus, there is minus;
There is empty, there is full;
There is God, the busy question
In denial of doubt.

There is mindlessness and mind,
There is deathlessness, and death,
There is waking, there is sleeping,
There is false, there is true,
There is going, there is coming,
But upon the stroke of midnight
Wherever we may be,

There am I, there are you.

She sat, staring through the glass as afternoon sunlight filtered through the branches of a tree outside her window. Seamus was telling her they each existed because the other did. At least, she thought that was what he meant. Irish poets could be esoteric, her father had told her, and Seamus was both Irish, and a poet of sorts. But his gift was precious; something of his, treasured since he was fourteen, carried with him in his duffle bag, and now gifted to her.

Meg pressed the paper to her breast and closed her eyes. 'I love you, Seamus. Wherever you are, I am with you, my love.'

Chapter 8
Townsville

By the end of her second day at *Currajong*, there was still no sign of the new nurses from Brisbane, but word was that the hospital's first patients would be arriving in two days. Meg wondered if Dr Ransom would require her to assist in an operation without a full support team.

She set the instruments into the autoclave and turned it on, barely glancing at the chart of times she had stuck on the wall above the machine. Already she was familiar with the requirements of the new machine. Movement in her peripheral vision caught her attention and she registered Dr Ransom's presence.

'Sister, our entire medical staff has been invited to a dance over at the Americans' recreation hall. Since our medical staff currently consists of you and me, will you accompany me?'

'Just two of us?' A dance required more energy and smiling than Meg felt capable of. While she hadn't thrown up since that morning at Adelaide River, neither had her monthlies come. By the end of each day, she was tired, wanting nothing more than her bed, and the hope of dreaming about Seamus. 'I'm—not really in the mood for it, Doctor.'

'That's a pity because the request to join with our American allies and make them feel welcome came from HQ.'

'So, it's an order?' Her thoughts winged to the half-written letter sitting in her locker. Her preference was to crawl into bed with a hot cup of cocoa and finish writing to Seamus.

'Call it an unofficial expectation. I can go alone, but I don't think the Yanks will want to dance with me.' He grinned and folded his arms over his chest. 'What do you say, Sister? Want to help me with hands across the sea or, in this case, feet on the dance floor? All in the name of friendship.'

Summoning a smile, Meg nodded. 'Of course, Doctor. What time are we expected?'

He glanced at his watch. 'How about I pick you up at your hut in an hour? That should be enough time to get dolled up and eat.'

Meg's expectations for the evening tanked. 'Dolled up? I left Darwin with nothing but the clothes on my back and for all I know, what I had there went up in smoke. The only clothes I have are uniforms and the Q sergeant wasn't happy about issuing me with another set. I don't have any civvies.'

'Uniform is fine, and probably worthwhile as a reminder that you are a serving member of our defence force.' A frown appeared and he hesitated before adding, 'I've heard stories of some unbecoming behaviour from soldiers in Brisbane. If anyone shows you disrespect, or if you're worried by unwanted attentions, tell me.'

Touched by his concern and reassured by his comment about wearing her uniform, Meg smiled. 'Thank you, Doctor. I'd better get cleaned up ready to *schmooze*. I think that's the word I heard.'

Doc, as she privately thought of him, laughed, a carefree shout of laughter that crinkled the corners of his brown eyes and bracketed his nose with two deep laugh lines. It was so at odds with his regular manner that she did a double take. 'You, *schmoozing*? This, I have got to see, Sister. See you in an hour.'

By the time she had eaten, showered and put on a clean uniform, Meg felt better and surprised to discover a little part of her was looking forward to dancing again. How long had it been since she had danced without a care in the world? Long before her dance with the recuperating Private Matthews at the River. Tonight, it didn't matter that she wore a uniform and had scraped out the last of a piece of lipstick donated by one of the nurses at the River. Victory Red wasn't her colour, but it was what was available in these dark days, so she painted her lips red and smiled at her reflection in the small mirror beside the lockers.

A knock sounded at her door. She called out, 'Coming', rolled her lips and glanced in the mirror then dropped the tiny lipstick into her handbag and opened the door.

Doctor Ransom in full dress uniform with his hair slicked back took her by surprise. In the theatre, he worked in short sleeves, no tie, and sometimes ran his fingers through his hair so it stood up in disarray. She had no idea why she hadn't realised what a good-looking man he was. Not that she was tempted by his looks or his position. Seamus was her man, but a woman would have to be dead or blind not to notice the doctor. He offered his arm and she took it, stepping out past the croquet lawn and down the rutted driveway.

Dr Ransom kept a firm grip on her as they picked their way over the rough ground. 'I've requested the driveway be smoothed and gravel put down to eliminate the dust as soon as possible. Anything we can do to create a dust-free environment is better for our patients, especially as the plan is keep those who are dangerously ill in the veranda ward facing the driveway.'

Meg began labelling the wards in her mind with information gleaned over the past couple of days. 'The ruts will make their ride very uncomfortable. I imagine the owners of *Currajong* kept their driveway in excellent condition. It's a shame our trucks made such a mess of it when the renovations were carried out.'

'It's probably worse than it should be. There was heavy rain during the period they were building and the trucks caused a lot of damage. But the work had to be completed in a short time frame. Look at our hospital—we've built and set up wards and an operating theatre in record time.'

Record time suggested the army knew they would need these facilities sooner, not later. Did that mean Seamus was in danger?

Of course he's in danger. He's gone off to fight in a war.

A shiver ran down Meg's back, chilling her heart.

'Are you cold, Sister?' Dr Ransom's voice was considerate as they stood on the footpath waiting for their ride. 'I thought the night was quite warm, but do you need a coat?'

'No, Doctor. Just thinking about the speed with which our unit was built—and I'm sure there are plenty of others like ours. It suggests the army expects a lot of casualties to come through Townsville. It's hard thinking of the young men who will be wounded—or die.' She sent up a quick prayer for Seamus.

'True, but the important thing to remember is that the closer we are to the fighting, the sooner we can tend the wounded, and the more likely we are to save them. That's a good thing, don't you think?' He took out a cigarette and bent his head to a lighter. In the brief flare that lit his face before he snapped the lighter shut, Meg saw—he believed in the good they could do more than in the evil of war.

Another of his attitudes she would do well to adopt if she wasn't to go crazy with worry about Seamus. 'But if time is of the essence, why aren't we closer to the front line?'

'Townsville is the most northerly city. It's not likely the Japanese will risk flying so far south to bomb facilities. It's an ideal base for our army, navy, and air force. That also makes it the safest and closest location for hospitals.' Dr Ransom turned to her. Lacking street lighting or a sliver of moonlight, she could only sense the tension in the faint outline of his body. 'Would you volunteer for service in a field hospital?'

Would it be like the bombing of Darwin? Meg peeked through the gap in the curtain of her memories and shuddered. Bombs falling nearby had been hell on earth. The idea of bombs falling while working on a patient scared her witless. Only a fool willingly put herself in harm's way but, even as she thought of the danger and the rumours about how the Japs had mistreated—*shot?* —nurses in some of the islands, she asked, 'Why not me? Why should I stay safe at home when our men are overseas fighting for our freedom? I'm young and fit, and I have vital skills that could help them. Maybe I should volunteer to care for our injured men on the front lines?'

Headlights swung around the corner into Fulham Road, lighting a tight path as a vehicle rapidly approached. Blinded after the lack of light on the street, Meg shaded her eyes and blinked until she could see the ground. A jeep pulled up and Dr Ransom handed her into the back seat of the vehicle. She hadn't got an answer to her question, but she wasn't sure she wanted one. If only Seamus were here to talk about the idea with her. As much as her comment was based on a genuine belief that women who had the necessary skills should be assigned to theatres of war, she feared that, with the possibility of her pregnancy, she was mouthing nothing more than bravado.

Pondering how honest she had been filled the journey. The jeep pulled up near the American servicemen's recreation hall from which light spilled through wide double doors. No one seemed concerned that, when the doors opened, bright yellow light streamed through, flouting blackout orders. Loud jazz music filled the air and, when Meg reached the doorway, the blare of music and the jumping dancers vibrated up through her soles. Music and an almost forgotten anticipation washed over her, seeped through her pores and insinuated itself into her feet. All at once, she was glad she had been given no choice about coming.

At the coat-check desk, Dr Ransom leaned towards her, a necessary closeness if he wanted to be heard over the mix of music and loud voices. 'Can I fetch you a glass of punch, Sister, or would you like to hit the dance floor first?'

Meg collected the ticket for her bag and tucked it in her pocket. Her foot was tapping as a jitterbug finished and a new song began, one she recognised as a new Frank Sinatra song from the Armed Forces radio show back in Adelaide River. 'I'd love to dance since you're asking, thank you.'

He led her towards the dance floor. The song was a ballad and the dance was slow—perfect if Seamus were here. But he was far away, and tonight—well, it would be good for her morale if she let it. Smiling at her partner, Meg focused on the music, and the joy of dancing once more.

Dr Ransom danced well, considerate of her in the crush of dancers. A few slow turns into the dance, he smiled at her. 'Thank goodness.'

Wondering what had caught his attention she looked around then met his eyes. 'Who or what are you thankful for, Doctor?'

'You look as though you're enjoying yourself, Sister. Finally. I admit I was a bit concerned that you only accompanied me because you felt it was your duty. I may have fudged the truth a little to get you to come tonight.'

'What do you mean?'

'HQ didn't really say we *had* to come, but you've worked hard assisting with the setting up of the theatre and I thought you deserved a night out. This invitation came from an American doctor I recently met. It seemed just the ticket. Forgive me?'

Struck by this social side of Dr Ransom and increasingly comfortable in his company, Meg saw no problem. 'There's nothing to forgive. It's very kind of you to offer this treat, Doctor.'

'Geoffrey, please, or Geoff if you prefer. While we're here, at least.'

The song ended and the bandmaster informed them the orchestra would be taking a ten-minute break. 'But don't go far, folks. We'll be back with another new one from the 1942 hit parade.'

'Doctor—'

'Geoffrey.' He looked past her, waved then took her elbow. 'Come and meet Dr Newton. He's a surgeon with the American hospital at— 'Don, hello.' Geoffrey extended a hand to the man who had stopped beside her.

'Don, this is Lt Margaret Dorset who is my new theatre nurse. Margaret, Dr Newton.'

She smiled. 'Pleased to meet you, Doctor.'

He took her hand, but instead of shaking it, held it between both of his.

'Margaret. And do they call you Meg for short?' His smile was wide and white and even, like the film stars in her favourite movies. Like Clark Gable in *Gone with the Wind*. But his accent was more like John Wayne's drawl in the last cowboy movie she'd seen. The name of the movie escaped her.

'Margaret?' Geoffrey's use of her name brought her back to earth.

'Most people call me Margaret.' *Meg* belonged to Seamus, and to her family. 'I prefer Margaret.'

Dr Newton offered his arm and smiled. 'May I escort you to the refreshments, Margaret? If that's okay by you, Geoff?'

Geoffrey looked to her for her agreement. When she nodded, he stepped aside. 'I'll see you later, Sister.'

As they approached a long trestle table laden with food, and bowls into which a cook was tipping what looked like miniature hamburgers, Meg's tastebuds woke up and yahooed. The Americans had more variety of food than she'd seen in months. 'I'd heard you weren't on rations, but this is amazing. There's even oranges!'

'Help yourself. Take a couple back home if you like. Would you prefer a glass of punch, or something with more of a mule kick to it?'

'Punch please.'

'Are you sure you wouldn't like a bourbon. I can add Coke if you don't want it neat.' Behind the bar, a bartender rested his knuckles on the wood, waiting for the doctor's drink order.

'Just punch, thanks.'

While the American doctor ordered a bourbon for himself and a punch for *the little lady*, Meg selected one of the small hamburgers and an orange and—just because she could—added a slice of some kind of sticky, nutty tart.

When Dr Newton returned with their drinks, he nodded towards the rear of the dance floor. Once there, a wall and the edge of the stage created a small space around them. Meg set her plate on the edge of the stage and gratefully sipped her punch. 'It's hot in here with so many bodies, isn't it? Hotter than where I come from at this time of year.'

'Sure is. We could go outside, but the way Geoff looked at you, I don't think I should risk raising his hackles.'

Meg frowned. 'What do you mean?'

Don frowned right back at her, but there was a glint in his eyes. 'Are you telling me there's nothing between you two?'

'We met a few days ago. Dr Ransom is my superior officer. That's all.'

'So you're not taken. Well, that's good news. Would you like to go out—'

'Dr Newton, there is nothing between me and Dr Ransom,

but I *am* engaged. To a soldier who's just been sent overseas.'

The glint in his eyes diminished, but not entirely. 'My apologies, Margaret. I don't poach another man's lady, but I thought . . . Never mind. I hope you'll forget I asked you outside.'

'Forgotten, Doctor.' She smiled as further assurance no offence had been taken. 'So, were you a surgeon before you joined up?'

'Sort of. I'm newly come to the soldiering side of it. I started out as an obstetric gynaecologist.' His gaze pinned hers over his glass before he drank. 'Go ahead and say it. Everyone else does.'

'There are no women soldiers so—'

'So why include an obstetrician, right? Yeah, well, where I come from, and no one seems to know why this is, I ended up having to perform more surgeries on patients with problems other than the usual procedures in gynaecological surgery. I figured if I was doing those surgeries, I wanted to expand my surgical training. I mean, when you're the *only* surgeon in a broad area of a county, it pays to know as much as possible. When the Japs hit Pearl Harbour, I was most of the way through my training. The army convinced me to join up, and here I am.'

Strange as it was that she'd met an obstetrician in a town on the edge of a war, Dr Newton might be the answer to her need. 'Do you think it would be possible for me to consult you—in your capacity as an obstetrician?'

Dr Newton's eyes narrowed. 'For a medical condition?'

Shaking her head, Meg shored up her courage. *In for a penny, in for a pound.* She'd raised the topic. Dr Newton might well decline, but she had to know for certain so she could plan her departure if necessary. 'I might be pregnant, but I'm not sure. I don't feel that I can ask Dr Ransom, not when we have to work together.'

'To your fiancé?'

'Yes. I was hoping to tell him when I arrived in Townsville so we could be married straightaway, but he was sent overseas before I arrived. Her voice dropped and her gaze fell to her glass. 'This wretched war.'

'Margaret, I'd be happy to help. I'll need time to find a rabbit, or maybe a toad. I hear they're pretty common around sugarcane farms. When I have, I'll set up a time to see you.'

Meg extended a hand. 'Thank you, Doctor. I am so appreciative, but please don't tell Dr Ransom. If the test is negative, I don't want him to know it happened, and if it's positive, I want to be the one to tell him. He's put so much time into giving me further training as a theatre nurse.'

'You have my word.'

The band returned to the stage and Dr Newton held out a hand. 'I believe this is my dance. Shall we?'

##

It was after eleven when the jeep dropped them back to *Currajong*. Geoffrey—*Dr Ransom, now we're back here*, she reminded herself—took her arm for the walk down the driveway. A sliver of moon cast just enough light for them to pick their way over the rutted ground. At the door to her hut, they stopped, and Dr Ransom put his hands in his pockets. 'Did you enjoy yourself tonight, Sister?'

'I did, thank you, Doctor. It was just the tonic I needed.'

'Excellent. See you at eight sharp in theatre.'

'Yes, Doctor. And with luck, the rest of your nurses might arrive tomorrow.' How she hoped they did, especially now they had a firm arrival time for their first intake of patients. She'd feel guilty if she had to leave before she had trained up her replacement for Dr Ransom.

'One can hope, but our first patients *will definitely* be arriving so we know we'll be busy.' He waited until she found her key and opened the door. 'Well, good night, Sister.'

'Good night, Doctor.' As he strolled towards his cabin, his lighter flared and the smell of a cigarette wafted across before she closed her door and switched on the light.

The single bulb barely gave the room a dim gloom after the bright lights of the Americans' recreation hall. Her unfinished letter to Seamus lay beside her bed. Hours earlier, it had seemed like the most important thing in her evening. Then she had met Don Newton.

She really should finish writing now but, energised as she had been by the dancing, a wave of fatigue crashed over her. With just enough rational thought to know it would be sensible to wait until she had her test results from Dr Newton, she washed her face and stripped off her uniform before falling into bed.

Chapter 9
Townsville – Currajong

The new nurse followed Meg into her hut and looked around. 'All this space for just the two of us? Nice.'

Meg pointed to her lower bunk. 'Until the next intake of nurses arrive anyway. That's mine. Take your pick of the others.'

Sister Geraldine Platt dropped her suitcase at the end of the bunk at right angles to Meg's and flopped back onto the bed. 'Every bone in my body aches. Overnight train trips sitting up are the pits, but that was two nights of torture. Ugh.' She dropped her arm across her eyes like a melodrama queen and sighed. 'Please tell me we aren't expected to report for duty until tomorrow.'

Meg perched on the edge of her bunk, concerned that her cabin mate, one of only five nurses to arrive at *Currajong* early this morning, wouldn't measure up to Dr Ransom's expectations. 'You have until morning tea to settle in, but then we need all hands on deck. Our first patients will be arriving after lunch, and there's not much time to show you everything. I was worried it would only be me on duty to get them settled in, so I'm thrilled five of you turned up today.'

'I peeked into the theatre on our walk-through of the house. It looks fully set up so why were you worried?'

'Dr Ransom and I set it up. They were still building it when I arrived.'

Geraldine lifted her arm and rolled onto her side, resting her head on her arm. 'Do you mean you were the only nurse here all that time? Goodness, how did you manage?'

Meg shrugged. 'You just do. And the doctor is a really good teacher. This is my first posting as head theatre nurse, and I feel as though I have a reasonable grasp of my duties thanks to him. What about you, Geraldine, what's your background?'

'Call me Gerry. *Geraldine* sounds like my great-aunt and she's a relic.' Gerry rolled her eyes then grinned. For someone who claimed not to have slept sitting up on the train, she was vivacious and funny and for some reason, Meg's qualms about her new cabin mate eased.

'My great-aunt's name is Augusta and *she* lives up to her name. Talk about taking the role of matriarch of the family seriously.' Despite her occasionally judgemental comments, Meg felt affection for Aunt Augie.

'Families can be *so* interesting. Anyway, you asked about my nursing experience. I worked in Brisbane at two different hospitals. General ward duties, a stint in theatre, and some time in maternity. It was the theatre work that sealed this posting for me.'

'I doubt there'll be much call for maternity nursing up here.' Meg hoped she wouldn't end up proving the exception.

Gerry swung her legs over the edge of the bed, hauled her suitcase up beside her and opened it. 'I don't know about that. I saw some *hunky* Yankee soldiers as we drove in from the station. I bet they've got a few hearts on strings already.'

Those Meg had met were clean-cut, with flashy, white-toothed smiles and bucketloads of confidence. 'Perhaps. I met a few last night at a dance they hosted. They seemed pleasant. And Dr Ransom is friendly with one of their surgeons.'

'Oh goody—inter-forces recreation! When's their next dance?' Gerry lifted a red dress out of her case and shook it, inserted a hanger and looked around the cabin. 'Okay if I hang it here?' She hooked it over one of the wall pegs.

'That's fine. Gosh, that's pretty. And that beading work is exquisite.' She moved closer to study the silver and red beaded bird sitting below one shoulder. 'Where did you find it? I've seen nothing like it in the shops since—before the war I should think.'

Gerry's eyes were bright as she ran a fingertip over the bird. 'I made it. It's how I relax. For all I complain about my great-aunt, she's an incredible dressmaker. She's also one of the biggest hoarders I know. You should see the dressmaking supplies she has in her back room, all from before the war, I hasten to add. Mum taught me to sew, but Geraldine taught me to *couture up* an outfit—her words.'

As Meg rubbed the material between her fingers, a quick thrust of envy stabbed her. She had nothing but a uniform to welcome Seamus when he finally came home. 'You'll be the belle of the ball in this, although last night, all the women—and there were few enough of us—wore uniform.'

'Tch, we'll convince whoever thought that was a good idea that it's not.'

Meg shrugged, glanced at her watch and crossed to the door. 'All I have are uniforms. Any personal gear I had probably got blown to kingdom come in Darwin. I'll see you at ten hundred sharp for morning tea and a revision session on theatre procedures before I introduce everyone to Dr Ransom.'

Quietly, she closed the door behind her before Gerry could commiserate. If she was quick—and lucky—she could ring Dr Newton and find out how long it might be before he could do her pregnancy test. Until that was either confirmed or knocked on the head, pretty dresses and frippery were the last thing she should be feeling envious about. Thank goodness she'd left her morning sickness behind at Adelaide River.

##

Meg stood in front of her small team of nurses, marvelling that the simple fact of arriving a few days ahead of them and being personally trained by Dr Ransom had put her in charge. For all that she was young to be taking on such a responsible position, he'd reassured her and in his keen eyes, she'd seen his certainty she was ready.

'All the nurses coming up have volunteered, but of those coming to us, none have what I consider to be sufficient training in an operating theatre. You will do a fine job, Margaret. I wouldn't have asked you if I wasn't certain you'd be a capable head nurse.' His words had filled her with confidence, but now, with five pairs of eyes on her, she doubted herself. She met each sister's eyes: Gerry's were encouraging; Sister Thomas and the two nurses flanking her were attentive; and Sister Smith—there was something mean in her narrow-eyed glare. Meg sensed trouble ahead.

Sister Eva Smith had a chip on her shoulder the size of Sydney Harbour. 'We're the brave ones. I reckon what happened in Darwin frightened a lot of nurses. They want to stay safe down in Brisbane and as far south as they can get in case the Japanese invade.' Sister Smith's round, ruddy-cheeks and thin lips turned down in scorn. 'Cowards, they are.'

'We shouldn't judge others when we know nothing of their circumstances.' Sister Catherine Thomas had been quiet, but now she turned to Eva. 'Not every woman is in a position to volunteer for duty close to a war zone. Lots of them have taken on the work our men were doing before they joined up, and others are raising their families. All of it is vital to winning this war.'

'Hmph. Maybe not all of them.' Unwilling to press her argument after Catherine's calm response, Eva pulled a face and looked at Meg. 'You're young like us. Why are you in charge?'

Grateful that Gerry and not Eva had chosen to share her cabin, Meg pitied Catherine. Her quiet response was almost saintly against Eva's brashness. 'Dr Ransom has been training me since I arrived here a few days ago. As surgeon-in-charge, he made the decision.'

Eva sat forward on her chair, her eyes hard. 'Have you been in a war zone? Any one of us could as easily do the job. Why should it be yours more than mine?'

Seated at the end of the row, Gerry leaned an arm against the bench and pinned Eva with a look that could freeze a man at ten paces. 'Sister Dorset was in Darwin when it was bombed. If you want to trade places with her, get that experience first.'

Eva's face blanched but she shut up. Meg saw she would have to toughen her management style to manage the nurse. They weren't all equal. She had to show Eva who was in charge through her skills and the knowledge she had so recently acquired. Channelling her tone and attitude from her matrons in Sydney, Darwin, and Adelaide River, she called their attention to the small blackboard in the cabin allocated for training. 'Let's make a start.

Sponge count—the first step is to set out sponges on a sterile towel and count them. Before the patient is sewed back up, you must recount the sponges to ensure none are accidentally left in the patient.'

By the time she had covered theatre theory, and safety points in the use of the autoclave, Dr Ransom appeared to greet his team. 'Sisters, I am so glad to see you. We have patients arriving after lunch and two wards of beds to make up before then.' He turned to Meg. 'Sister Dorset, would you oversee that then bring your staff to theatre. I have a number of procedural items to run through with everyone.'

'Of course, Doctor.' She led the way out of the hut, Gerry beside her as they walked across the croquet lawn.

Gerry glanced over her shoulder then leaned close. 'Well done in there. You showed Eva you're in charge.'

'I tried to emulate the matrons I've worked under. I admired each for different skills they demonstrated, but I've got a lot to learn. Eva seems—difficult.'

'She was a real pain on the train, whinging about everything from the lack of a sleeper to the bloke in front of her who snored on and off. I think she kicked the back of his seat a couple of times. Honestly, I could cheerfully have shoved her through the door at one of the river crossings, but Catherine seems to manage her pretty well. When we were told we would be two to a cabin for the time being, I jumped in and offered to pair with the new nurse, sight unseen.' Gerry nudged Meg with a discreet elbow. 'I got lucky and Catherine seems fine about drawing the short straw.'

Meg smiled like the conspirator she knew herself to be. 'I thought much the same thing back there.' She opened the door into the supply room, so much more spacious and secure than the curtained-off area at the River. Setting one hand on a pile of pillowcases, she pointed to the sheets, folded into pairs for expediency. 'Drop one set on each bed then we'll pair up to make the beds.'

Predictably, Eva was the one to question her. 'Why do we

have to work in pairs? Why can't we—'

Meg raised one hand and pinned Eva with what she hoped was a fair imitation of a matron. 'I read a time and motion study in one of the manuals that explained why that method is quicker, but aside from that, this will be the last time I allow you to question my directions, Sister Smith. You will do it that way because I have directed you to do so. Is that understood?'

Eva's mouth fell open and Meg wondered if the nurse was used to getting away with disrespect, or if she was one of those people who forever defied authority.

'Is that clear, Sister?'

'Yes, Sister.' Eva's eyes fixed on a pile of sheets, but as she lifted them off the shelf, a mulish expression pulled her mouth down.

Round two to Sister-in-charge, Meg thought before leading the way into the long central hallway. 'Sisters Thomas and Platt, you take the veranda ward beside the driveway. Sisters Gilroy and Maxwell, the inside ward on the left. Sister Smith will work with me on the inner right side.' By choice, Meg would have preferred to work with any of the other nurses but working side by side with the reluctant nurse would establish their working relationship and remind Eva that they were a team.

Catherine and Gerry finished one bed ahead of both Meg and Eva, and the other pair. Gerry leaned against the doorjamb. 'Looks like we won. Anything else you'd like us to do while you finish up, Sister Dorset?'

Meg glanced up as she folded a neat hospital corner. 'Head on into the theatre and let Dr Ransom know we'll be there in a minute please.' She and Eva added a light blanket, tucked it in then folded the edge of the top sheet over and tucked in the sides. Centring the pillow, Meg looked at Eva. 'Good work, Sister.'

Eva sniffed, a small sound but indicative that she wasn't yet ready to work under Meg. Perhaps she never would be, but Meg would make it her mission to create a smoothly functioning team both in and out of the operating theatre. Their task was to nurse wounded soldiers, not grudges, and Meg was determined to do her job to the best of her ability. If that meant dragging a reluctant Eva into behaving like a decent human being, so be it.

Chapter 10
Townsville

Meg sat quietly as Dr Newton took his seat behind the desk, opened an envelope and pulled out a folded piece of paper. His face gave away nothing, no hint of the answer she craved. But then, she wasn't sure if she wanted her results to prove she *was* carrying Seamus's child. Her work as sister-in-charge at *Currajong* was fulfilling in ways she hadn't expected. Responsibility for her small staff of nurses, now grown to eight, and for the soldier patients who had begun arriving several weeks earlier challenged her—as did Eva, who had settled only a little—but still, Meg's satisfaction with what they were achieving was high.

Don Newton set the paper on the desk and sat forward, his hands loosely clasped. 'What result are you hoping for, Margaret?'

How she wished she could get a read of the result from his expression, but Dr Newton had perfected the professional give-nothing-away look. She admired it, except for now when she teetered on the edge of a great unknown. 'To be honest, I'm not sure. I don't want to have to leave my work, but if I'm to have Seamus's child, I can't be unhappy about that either.' Her gut tightened and her hands, hidden beneath the desk, curled into fists on her lap, but his expression remained neutral. 'Well, what's the news?'

'The rabbit died. You're with child, Margaret. About eight weeks I would guess. If you can remember dates when you last had relations with your fiancé that would give me a better idea, but you'll have your baby around Christmas.'

She sat silently, waiting to feel something. Was she happy or sad? In her heart she'd known the truth, suspected it as the time for her monthly passed again without needing to take out her issue of sanitary products. But to hear her pregnancy confirmed felt—strange. 'Thank you, Dr Newton.' Even her voice sounded unfamiliar in her ears as she stood.

I'm carrying Seamus's baby.

'Are you okay with this news? Can I do anything to help?'

Meg looked around. What was she meant to be doing? Abruptly, she sat back on her chair and gripped the edges. 'Do you have to report this to anyone?'

'No, Margaret. You consulted me on a private matter. Besides, you're part of a different army to me. It's up to you when you decide to let your lot know. First babies often don't show for quite a while. You're fit and healthy—there's no reason you can't keep working for now.' He walked around and perched on the desk in front of her. 'I would advise you not to drink alcohol and, in spite of all the advertising to the contrary, my personal belief is that smoking is not in the best interests of your baby. Everything you ingest and imbibe will affect him or her. If you like, I'd be happy to remain your consultant for as long as you choose to continue working.'

At last Meg looked up into eyes full of sympathy. Now he'd delivered the news, he looked more like the man she'd danced with. A man willing to keep confidential the secret she carried. 'Thank you. I must write to Seamus now I know for certain. Dr Newton, I can't tell you how much I appreciate your willingness to care for me.' She touched her tongue to the corner of her mouth and drew in an audible breath. 'Our doctor back home in Sydney wouldn't be so accepting of my condition since Seamus and I are not yet married. In fact, I think he might have tossed me out of his consulting room.'

She wished that were a joke, but her family and their circle of friends were pillars of the church, staunch believers in the sanctity of marriage. Unmarried mothers barely existed in their world, except as charity cases. Hidden away, they were fallen women with no hope for salvation and their children, poor little ones, were taken away to be adopted by married couples who had not been blessed with their own family.

She pressed her knuckles against her mouth. Her free hand covered her stomach, still flat although, now she knew she was pregnant, the hint of a baby bump was obvious to Meg. Until Seamus returned and they were married, she couldn't say anything about her baby.

I'll have to fudge our wedding date if my family is to accept my baby.

'Margaret, making a baby takes two people, and if they have made a promise to each other to wed, I can understand pre-empting the wedding night, especially in wartime. When we don't know when—or if—we'll see each other again, the instinct to create new life can be powerful.'

'Most people of my acquaintance don't see it that way.'

'Being judgemental helps no one, especially when—' Dr Newton's gaze slid away. When he looked at her again, his neutral expression surprised her. 'Now, do you have any questions for me at this stage?'

Meg shook her head. 'I need time to get used to the idea I'm going to be a mother.'

'In that case, I'll see you in a month, if not on the dance floor next week.' He offered his hand.

Meg took it, rose, and stepped towards the privacy screen but stopped short. 'Is it safe for me to continue working?'

'It should be, but no heavy lifting. Let the other nurses do that. Should be easy enough since you're in charge.' He winked, a friendly, conspiratorial wink that reassured her of his support before he left her in complete privacy to change.

##

Meg's driver set her down on the footpath in front of *Currajong*. As she walked along the now smooth driveway, one of the new nurses exited the tent closest to Fulham Road. The venereal disease tent ward on what had once been grassy front lawn was busier than she had expected, and she frowned at the activity. After her consultation with Dr Newton and his compassion for her situation, she viewed it differently.

Don't be judgemental. It's wartime and people need love wherever they can find it. She had certainly embraced Seamus.

Her mind spun with her news and the decisions she would have to make alone. If only she had a close friend she could talk to.

Gerry might one day become that—their connection and like-mindedness was a bulwark against Eva's antipathy—but Meg didn't know her well enough to be certain yet, despite how well they dealt together. Keeping her secret locked away was safer, at least for now.

Cigarette smoke alerted her to the presence of another person before she rounded the corner of the hut where she'd met Lt Breek on her first day at *Currajong*. Eva was sitting in front of the hut, a cigarette held between two fingers.

Eva tipped her face up and blew out a stream of smoke before she caught sight of Meg. 'I'm on my break, *Sister*.'

Meg just nodded and walked past Eva and into her cabin. She changed out of her RAAF uniform into her nursing uniform and tidied her hair before locking her door behind her. For several reasons, locking her door had become the sensible routine since the arrival of Sister Smith, and now, with delicate news to impart, she couldn't risk the woman snooping through her things and discovering the letter she had started to Seamus.

'Anything to report, Sister Smith?'

'Nothing out of the ordinary while you were—out, Sister.' Eva pushed to her feet, her rotund shape making the move ungainly. She took a final drag of her cigarette before dropping it and toeing it out. Her glare at Meg bordered on insolent, but, after a pause of several seconds during which she seemed to be waiting for Meg to chew her out over the dropped butt, she picked it up and pushed it into the metal bin that sat outside the hut.

'I'm pleased to hear that.' Keeping her tone deliberately mild, Meg added, 'In that case, I'm going to have a quick cuppa before I go back on duty.'

Dr Ransom appeared from his hut and raised his hand in a brief welcome wave. 'Sister Dorset, might I have a word before you go back to the ward?'

Eva strolled towards the hospital, not so fast that Meg might think she was keen to get back to work, but fast enough that Dr Ransom didn't tell her to hurry up.

Dr Ransom watched Eva depart until she was well out of

hearing range then met Meg's curious gaze. 'I'm sensing some hostility from Sister Smith. Is everything okay with her?'

'She's doing her work, but I wouldn't rate her skills, personal or professional, very high, unless she's talking to a good-looking patient above the rank of corporal.'

'Hmm, I'm not happy with her performance in the operating theatre. See if you can make her pull her boots up or, shortage or not, I'll be requesting her transfer out.'

'Certainly, Doctor.'

'Thank you, Sister.' He headed towards the hospital leaving Meg to make her much-needed cup of tea.

For a moment, Meg imagined leaving Eva to flail and fail. How much nicer the ward would be without Eva's sniping and monopolising certain patients at the expense of the lower ranks. But with barely enough nurses to care for their patients until the next round of transfers increased their staff, Meg had to find a way to reach Eva and draw out her better nature.

If she has one.

And she had to ensure a smooth transition for whomever followed her as Dr Ransom's head nurse, because she doubted she could continue in the role once he—and therefore HQ—knew she was with child. Her hand slipped over her stomach before she realised the action would be a dead giveaway. How long did she have before she could no longer disguise her condition? July? Maybe August or, if she were very lucky, September?

Sipping her tea and gazing across the croquet lawn through blurring steam, her mind wandered back to the few precious times Seamus had made love to her. Mid- to late March, and on one of those occasions their love had created new life. So now, nearing the end of autumn, she must be about six or eight weeks along, as Dr Newton had guessed.

By the time she finished her tea and was returning to the hospital, a flurry of activity around the operating theatre hastened her steps.

Catherine turned out of the supply room in front of her.

'Sorry, Sister Dorset.'

'What's happened?'

'An appendectomy, urgent. The ambulance is on its way.'

'I'll scrub up. Have you begun the sponge count?'

'Eva's doing that now.'

Meg slipped into a surgical gown and pulled on a cap as she was brought up to speed. Why hadn't Dr Ransom mentioned the case when they'd spoken? 'When did the call come in?'

'Five minutes ago. Apparently, the drill sergeant keeled over on the parade ground. Shall I do up your ties?'

Meg turned and Catherine, calm, unflappable Catherine, did up her gown then picked up her bundle of small cloths and continued on her way to theatre. She would make a very good head nurse once Meg left.

Better than Gerry?

Meg scrubbed and then, as her fellow nurses went about their tasks while she checked the instrument tray was complete and in the correct order, she kept track of their progress. Early on, just after the first five nurses arrived, Dr Ransom had requested she keep notes on the progress of each nurse. She had, with dates and new skills listed, but more than that would be necessary in the next three months, four at most. Tonight, she would stay back in her cubbyhole of an office and add to them; things like ability to take on increased responsibility, deal with pressure, organisational skills. At least then, her suggestion as to her replacement to Dr Ransom would be based on facts and not personal loyalty.

Catherine or Gerry? Or is one of the newcomers still to show her mettle?

Maybe she should also make a note of their personality aptitude for the position, although . . . She hadn't seen herself as ready to be a head nurse before she arrived. Some things you simply learned as you went along because you had to.

Like motherhood.

Would she learn to be a good mother to Seamus's baby?

Dr Ransom poked his head around the door of the scrub

room. His surgical gown flapped loose and he held his hands up and away from his body as water dripped down them. 'Sister Dorset, is the theatre prepped?'

She handed him a sterile cloth. 'Yes, Doctor. We're ready.'

'Good. Sounds like we have a severe case of appendicitis. I hope they get him here before the appendix ruptures.'

They'd only just got the appendix out in time and the atmosphere in the theatre had been tense as Dr Ransom carefully lifted it into a specimen tray. 'Another hour and the sergeant might not have made it.' He'd directed her to administer penicillin and keep a check on the patient's reaction. 'I've been called to HQ for a meeting. Dam—dashed inconvenient.'

'Yes, Doctor.'

'I'm glad you came here, Margaret. You're an excellent head nurse.' She wasn't certain what the look he'd given her was about, but his compliment made her feel less tired as she stripped off her surgical gown and tossed it into the laundry hamper then pulled off the cap.

Eva appeared at the door with a clipboard. She was on duty until midnight and Meg needed to eat. Now! It was past three o'clock. She'd had no breakfast and was almost shaking with the need to eat.

'Sister Smith, I'm going to get a late lunch. I need you to do hourly checks on Sgt Draper. Look out for a rash forming, or nausea, diarrhea, vomiting . . .'

'Allergic reactions. I get it, Sister.'

'It's vital you check regularly, Sister. There can be reactions to penicillin ranging from mild to severe. After saving his life with an appendectomy, we don't want to lose him to anaphylactoid shock.'

Eva pressed her lips together and wrote on her clipboard. 'Yes, Sister.'

After Meg finished giving Eva instructions to cover the period while she ate, she hesitated then added, 'I trust you, Sister. I know you'll do your best by all your patients.'

Eva blinked, drew in an audible breath and nodded. 'Thank you, Sister Dorset.' As she turned to head into the ward, Meg thought she caught the edge of a smile.

Maybe that was what Eva had been missing—what Meg hadn't given enough of as she felt her way in her new role as head nurse.

Trust and acknowledgement. Everyone needed to be seen, and perhaps Eva hadn't received much of either.

Feeling lighter in spirit, Meg made her way to the mess hut, hoping to scrounge up a sandwich. And another cup of tea if she were lucky, given how her stomach reacted to the smell of coffee. Her supply of ginger from the River had long since been used up, but Dr Newton had connections and he'd procured some for her since she couldn't very well ask Dr Ransom without raising suspicion as to why she wanted it.

Food—and another night of dancing. She was looking forward to both.

And soon, her baby would be another exciting event to focus on—once she adjusted to the idea of impending motherhood. So what if she had to fudge the year of her wedding? In the midst of a war, her baby was a promise of new life.

Chapter 11

'Meg, what did Dr Ransom say about wearing civvies to the dance with the Americans? Please tell me you asked him?' Gerry held her red dress against her waist, dancing from foot to foot and making the skirt swish. The dress was a triumph of a skilled dressmaker's art, and although the silhouette was slim, thanks to restrictions on material, the fluted edge flicked up as she moved.

Meg turned from the mirror, a precious new tube of lipstick in her hand thanks to her mother's care package. Not that Mum approved of bright red lipstick—or any make up for that matter—but *Victory Red* was patriotic, if only by name. Enough to assuage Mum's scruples. 'I did ask him, but the answer is still no.' She turned back and carefully added colour to her bottom lip.

'Blast. Why not, did he say?' Gerry seemed disappointed but resigned as she set the hanger back on a hook.

Meg rolled her lips together and leaned close to the mirror. 'For the same reason he gave me when we attended the first dance.' Satisfied with the look of her lips, she met Gerry's disappointed gaze. 'If we are in uniform, it reminds everyone we are serving members of the Australian defence forces and deserving of their respect for our service.'

'But we're deserving of respect as attractive women too, so why not brighten everyone's night and let us doll up? I'd love to see more than beige, navy, and drab greens for once.' Gerry sighed and ran her hand over the beading on her red dress. 'Sorry, little bird. Not this time.'

'I'm sorry, Gerry. I know you were hoping to take your dress out for a spin. You know, when Doc first said that, I thought it was because I had nothing but a uniform to wear and he was trying to make me feel better. Now, I think he believes it. Doc is nothing if not honest.'

'It's fine, Maggie darling. I kind of like how protective Doc is of all of us. I sometimes think he likes you. Turn around.'

'What? Wherever did you get that idea?' She turned at the insistent push of a hand and faced the mirror.

Gerry adjusted a hairpin in Meg's hair then set both hands on Meg's shoulders and spoke over her shoulder to their reflections. 'If you weren't engaged, I think he'd be asking you out on a date. He watches you when you aren't looking, you know.'

Meg spun around, needing to see more than Gerry's reflection. Her friend wasn't joking. She sank onto the bunk, clutching her lipstick. 'You're wrong, Gerry. You have to be. We *work* together. *And* I'm engaged.'

'Don't get me wrong. I'm pretty sure he's too honourable to act on his feelings, but he does like you. Just saying . . .' Gerry's voice trailed off and she gripped Meg's shoulder. 'Hey, I shouldn't have spoken out of turn. You know me, Gerry Bigmouth. Forget I said anything . . . Please?'

Meg's heart thudded as though she'd run the whole way from the beach to the hospital, a feat she would never achieve. Had she really been blind to signs Gerry had seen? Was it possible that Geoff's interest in her—an interest she'd noticed, but put down to his pleasure in her developing professional skills—was something more personal? The shock of Gerry's revelation prickled across her skin like a spring allergy. 'I—I've got reports to finish writing. I won't go tonight.'

'Margaret Olivia Dorset! Is this the same nurse who faced the bombing of Darwin then tended a truckload of wounded men on a track in the Territory? Don't turn coward, Maggie.'

Meg shook her head. 'I need time to think about what you said.'

'What's there to think about? Are you going to act on it now you know? I seriously doubt it.' Gerry took both her hands and pulled her to her feet.

'Even if you were right—and I'm not saying you are—we've

got a job to do. *And again*, I'm engaged. Of course I'm not going to act on it.'

'Then why not come to the dance tonight? Have some fun, relax, flirt a little. It's harmless. Surely you can have one dance with Doc and not make a goose of yourself?' Genuinely upset, Gerry pleaded both with words and with her eyes. 'Come on, Maggie. Please?'

Dr Ransom would also expect to claim a dance, and he'd invited her *outside* before he learned of her engagement. What was going on? Were there too few women amongst so many men geed up for war? Or was it the doctor-nurse thing she'd heard about when she was training in Sydney, common because they spent hours working together? Suddenly the whole evening just felt too hard.

If she stayed, she could write up personnel reports in peace. And there was another benefit, one she wouldn't share with Gerry. Maybe she could do something unexpected and nice for Eva that would help the nurse settle down. Unbuttoning her jacket, she turned her back on Gerry. 'Eva can go. I'm staying.'

'No, you can't. You deserve an evening out. I won't let you, Maggie.'

'Sue me.'

'What?' Gerry tipped her head and frowned.

Deflated yet sure staying home was the safe move, Meg shrugged. 'It's an American expression I heard. Sort of means, what can you do about it?'

Folding her arms across her chest, Gerry tapped her toes and pinned Meg with the look of a woman on a mission. 'I wonder if Doc Ransom will allow his head nurse to work late while the rest of us go out and have fun?'

'You wouldn't dare tell him.'

'Why should you cover Eva's shift? It's her bad luck it just happened to fall on the night the Yanks decided to have another dance. Besides, what about the other nurses on night duty? How are you going to make it fair to them? And why can't Cate and I have a night away from Eva?'

Meg recognised the last-ditch attempt to guilt her into going. Gerry hadn't warmed to Eva, and Cate put up with her at work and off duty, although if Doc's information was correct, more nurses would arrive on the next train and dilute the "Eva-effect", as Meg privately called it. 'I've already been to one, so if I swap with her this time, I can stay and write my reports in peace *and* keep an eye on our appendicitis case.'

'Maggie—'

'My mind is made up.' She began changing uniforms and shooed Gerry out the door. 'Go tell them to wait a few minutes while Eva gets changed. My bet is she'll be there in record time.'

'You're mad. Or a saint. I can't decide which.' Gerry blew her a kiss. 'Wish me luck.'

'Luck. Now go.' She finished changing and went straight to the ward, hoping to avoid encounters and explanations with Doc.

Not Doc—Dr Ransom. Think formal, act normal.

When Meg stepped into the ward, Eva's mouth turned down in a look Meg's mother would have warned her against. *'Don't pull that face or it will stay like that when the wind changes.'*

'Sister Smith, I'm here to relieve you. Go and get changed for the dance. The others will wait five minutes for you.'

Eva's eyes grew wide. Her mouth opened and no words came out, but she sprang to her feet.

'You'd better get going.' Hoping she'd made the right choice, Meg jerked her head towards the door. 'Be quick, Sister.'

'Really? You mean . . . Yes, Sister—thanks.' One hand holding her cap in place, Eva took off leaving Meg in her dust.

'Thanks, Sister Dorset.' The voice came from Sgt Draper who had been placed in the bed closest to the nurse's station. He sounded tired, and his voice was weak, not like she imagined a drill sergeant's to be. Probably the after-effects of the anaesthetic.

'Would you like a few sips of water?'

He shook his head.

Meg walked over and straightened the bedsheet across his chest. 'I'm not sure why you're thanking me, Sergeant.'

'Now I've got the prettiest nurse here looking after me.'

'Sergeant, are you flirting with the nurse in charge of your wellbeing?' Meg looked at his chart then her watch. His next vitals check was due in a few minutes.

'You can't blame a man for speaking the truth when he's coming out of anaesthetics.'

Attaching the cuff, she checked his blood pressure. It was a little low and when she checked his pulse, it was elevated. The sergeant was suffering from shock.

His free hand scratched his chest through the sheet and light blanket. 'You're wearing lipstick on the ward too. Is that to cheer me up?'

'Does it cheer you up, Sergeant?' Telling herself his flirty comments meant nothing, Meg set his arm down gently and picked up his chart to record his pulse. Patients often imagined themselves smitten with their nurses. Nodding at the hand scratching his chest with increasing urgency she asked, 'Are you feeling itchy anywhere else, Sergeant?'

He glanced down at his chest and frowned. 'Now you mention it, yes.'

'Do you mind if I have a look?'

Awkwardly, he pushed the blanket down. Light as it was, its weight over his surgical dressing drew a grimace.

Meg folded it down to his hips, easing that discomfort, unbuttoned his pyjama shirt and moved so the night light from the desk fell onto his chest. Angry red welts rose in two patches. 'Where else feels itchy?'

'My right leg, my scalp, and my gut hurts, more than just where the doc took out my appendix. It's been getting worse since I came around.'

Meg checked both his leg and scalp then gently palpated his stomach. His indrawn breath hissed as he bit back a groan and she was certain.

'I'll be back in a moment.' She walked smartly to the front door, hoping against hope Doc and the nurses hadn't left yet, but Eva must have changed super-fast. There was no sign of the group. Slowly she returned to her patient.

'I believe you're having a reaction to the penicillin. A small number of patients have an allergic reaction to the drug. Looks like you're one of them.' Her voice remained calm and she smiled as she spoke. 'I'm going to phone the doctor and ask if he'll allow me to administer something called anti-histamine. It will ease the pain and the itching should go away soon after. Don't go away.'

'Not if you promise to come back soon, Sister.' His smile was a gritted-teeth, not-going-to-show-how-bad-I'm-feeling, quick pull back of his lips.

Meg touched his shoulder in acknowledgement then picked up the extension on the nurse's desk and asked to be put through to the American recreation hall.

The phone rang so long she feared no one could hear it above the music, but just as she began to despair and considered taking action without the doctor's permission, it was picked up. The background noise was *loud* as the soldier on the other end asked what she wanted.

'Dr Ransom—Ransom—Australian doctor. I need to speak with him now. It's urgent.'

After several loud repetitions, the listener understood and, moments later, the music stopped. Meg heard a call for Dr Ransom over the stage microphone. Shortly after, a door banged and the doctor himself picked up the phone. With the music muted she explained the sergeant's reaction. 'Do you need to see for yourself, or are you happy for me to give him the anti-histamine now, Doctor?'

Some would consider she'd overstepped her boundary as a nurse, but, watching the sergeant's increasingly frantic scratching, and a worrying, high-pitched wheezing, his condition was rapidly getting worse.

'Go ahead and give him one standard dose for now and monitor him closely. I'll find a ride and get there as soon as I can. Oh, and Margaret, have a bucket ready. He may throw up before the anti-histamine begins to work.' There was a click as he ended the call.

Meg fetched a large specimen tray and set it within reach. 'I'm going to prepare the injection, Sergeant. The tray is just in case you need to—'

'Chuck up?'

'Yes.'

This time he barely managed a nod and as Meg prepared a small tray with the anti-histamine, she heard sounds of retching. Glad that she had sent Eva off to the dance and taken her place, she grabbed a small cloth to cover the tray. Sgt Draper's face was pale as she moved the tray of vomit out of the way and gave him the injection. Rubbing the spot where the needle had gone in, she spoke in a brisk tone, knowing the sound of her voice telling him he would be okay was as much a part of settling him as the injection.

'There you are, Sergeant Draper. You'll feel much better very soon. The doctor is on his way back from the dance and he'll check you over. Not many people get a reaction like you did.'

'Lucky me.' His eyes had been closed, but now he opened them.

'Well, I'm not sure I'd call an allergic reaction *lucky*, although I guess it is good luck that we have an antidote close by.'

His Adam's apple bobbed up and down and she wondered if she needed to get a fresh tray for him, but he swallowed. The sergeant was made of stern stuff. He dragged in a slow breath then exhaled, the latter sound less forced, as though the drug was beginning to have an effect on him. 'Yeah, that's lucky too. But I meant I'm lucky to have an angel looking after me. You've a kind way with patients, Sister. Not like—'

'Ssh, enough now. I need you to close your eyes and rest. The doctor will be here soon.' But she wondered what Eva had done—or not done—to elicit such a negative tone.

'Did you give up going to the dance to look after me, Sister?' Sergeant Draper's eyelids closed as inexorably as the playing of Taps darkened a barracks.

'How could a dance compare with the pleasure of your company, Sergeant?'

A less than gentle snore was her only response. Meg's head tipped back and she glanced through the window. The night sky was black beyond the glass, which reflected a soft spill of light from her desk and the indistinct form of her patient. Wanting to believe that Sister Smith would have tended their patient as well as she had, she couldn't help but believe that her decision to swap places meant some higher being was looking out for the sergeant.

After all she'd seen, questioning the existence of a God who allowed such terrible wars and painful, savage deaths to occur had seemed her only course. But tonight, perhaps He had found a way to bring her back to Him.

Casting a glance at her special patient and seeing him fast asleep, she slipped onto the veranda and checked the two patients there. Sound asleep and snores from both beds. She looked through the flyscreens at the sky. Out here, the night seemed luminous up high, while the horizon was a velvety black. She leaned on the railing, searching for the twin pointer stars. Lying in Seamus's arms in their secret glade at the River, he'd begun pointing out various constellations, but her favourite was the Southern Cross. And tonight, after stopping what had been shaping up to be a serious allergic reaction, it seemed fitting that she sent a silent thanks to *her* constellation.

Narrow beams of headlights cut through the darkness followed by the sound of a vehicle pulling up in front of *Currajong*. Doc must be back from the dance and she had good news for him. But as she stepped back inside the ward Gerry's comment—the one that had made Meg take Eva's place instead of attending the dance—drifted back. Now, instead of being amongst a happy, noisy throng, she was about to be alone with him in a darkened ward. At least there were patients, even if sleeping.

And I've got tickets on myself if I believe what Gerry said.

Steeling herself to be *normal*, whatever the heck that was these days, she sat at her desk next to Sergeant Draper's bed and opened the personnel files she'd planned to work on.

Soft footfalls approached along the hallway and Dr Ransom appeared. 'Good evening, Sister. How's your patient doing?'

Meg stood and faced him, all professional competence with no hint of uncertainty in her manner. 'Sergeant Draper responded well to the anti-histamine injection. He fell asleep soon after.'

'Keep up the IV fluids.' Doc ran a hand through his hair. He looked tired but determined and Meg appreciated his dedication more than ever. Catching Meg's gaze, he smiled ruefully. 'Heaven knows this war is shocking, but one good thing is the advances in medicine and surgical techniques in response to what we're encountering day by day. Even non-war related problems like the sergeant's appendicitis.'

'I'm sorry you had to leave the dance, but at the time I felt—'

He held up a hand. 'Never apologise for putting a patient's needs first, Margaret. But I didn't manage to get a drink at the dance, so how about a cup of tea?'

'Certainly. I'll put the kettle on.'

'Margaret—' He touched her arm and shook his head. '*I'll* put the kettle on. I was the one who suggested it after all. But tell me, do you know where the biscuits are hidden? I think a small treat is in order, don't you?'

His smile made him look younger, less care-worn perhaps. She wanted to keep it there, despite the reasons she'd earlier convinced herself of for keeping her distance from Geoffrey.

'Third cupboard on the left, on the top shelf.' Her smile came naturally. That was the thing about Geoffrey; he made her feel good in spite of her resolution to maintain professional distance.

'Don't go away.'

Meg watched until the dark hallway swallowed him then turned back and checked the sergeant's pulse and blood pressure again, reassuring herself the injection was doing its job. Glancing at the files waiting on her desk, she turned away. Five minutes to relax and watch the stars wouldn't hurt. Five minutes – time to remind herself she was in love with Seamus, the father of her child.

Chapter 12
Late July

Meg tapped on the door of the nurses' hut before entering, clipboard in hand. Five faces turned towards her as she sniffed the air appreciatively. 'Please tell me you made a pot of hot cocoa and there's some left!'

Catherine picked up a mug and poured in the last of the contents of the pot. 'Sorry, only the dregs I'm afraid. If you'd been here two minutes earlier—'

Meg tucked her clipboard under her arm and wrapped both hands around the mug. 'Dregs or not, this is welcome. Considering how warm the days are, I'm never quite prepared for the cool nights here.' She buried her nose in the mug then sipped and sighed with pleasure. 'It's good.'

Gerry nudged the nurse next to her. 'Squish up a bit, Pam. Maggie, take a load off your feet.'

Meg perched on the edge of the bunk and looked around. Three of the occupants of number two hut, which included Catherine, plus Gerry and Mary Donovan from Meg's hut were relaxing together. 'Where's Eva? Isn't she off-duty too?'

Catherine and Gerry shared a look, but it was Eva's cabin mate who answered. 'You know Bill Grossman, the supply sergeant she met at one of the dances? He picked her up when she came off duty and whisked her away. I heard him remark how lovely moonlight on the water is as they strolled down the driveway.'

Gerry drained her mug and set it at her feet. 'Working in Supply means he's got easy access to the car pool. My guess is he's taking her down to The Strand and I don't think he wants to show her the view, if you get my drift.'

Pam laughed. 'A car, a beach, and moonlight on the water. Sounds like a seduction to me.'

A sigh from Gerry filtered through the laughter of the other nurses. 'How come Eva's the lucky one to hit on one of the few blokes with access to a vehicle? And on a Saturday night.'

Mary's expression turned wistful. 'I can hardly remember what Saturday nights were like before the war.'

'Are you envious of Eva, Gerry?' For all that Gerry was attractive, she hadn't taken a shine to any of the men she'd met. American or Australian, not one had caught her interest beyond socialising at the occasional dances, and yet she loved fine clothes and good times, dressing up and flirting.

Gerry shrugged and leaned back on her elbows. 'Not envious of her. Just tired of being confined here. Five or six miles is a bit far to walk to a beach when we're off duty.'

'True.' Meg finished her cocoa and stood with a sigh. It had been a long day on the ward for all of them. Two patients had been brought in with malaria and a jeep had gone into a ditch near Garbutt air base. Then, while the other nurses went off duty and relaxed, Meg had stayed back and written up the roster.

She glanced at the page on her clipboard. Doc had asked her to join him at a gathering of medical supervisors and head nurses, but despite the fact it was technically still work, she felt guilty about taking an evening off.

'I'll post the roster for the next seven days on the board. Any urgent changes, find someone you can switch with before you okay it with me. Thanks for the pick-me-up cocoa. Good night, ladies.'

##

Meg sat up abruptly. Something out of the ordinary had woken her, beyond an occasional snore that interrupted the gentle breathing of her cabin mates. Slipping her feet into her boots and pulling on her dressing gown, she slipped out of the hut and looked around. The moon was almost full and silvery light lent an ethereal grace to the workday ugliness of surrounding huts.

It was probably a possum.

And since she was awake, she might as well visit the nurses' loo. A recent need to *go* more often reminded her she didn't have much time to choose a nominee for her position. Telling Doc would be hard, but if she could at least recommend a replacement backed up by her notes on nursing personnel, she'd feel a bit better about deserting him—them. No one was indispensable, but the anticipation of having Seamus's baby wasn't enough to make her feel their timing wasn't terrible. Not now the war in the Pacific had grown fiercer, and the battleground in Papua New Guinea was on their doorstep.

As she returned to her hut, a hunched figure at the edge of the croquet lawn resolved into Eva. In uniform. Sobbing. Meg approached cautiously and quietly, but Eva didn't look up, not even when Meg put a hand on her shoulder.

'Has something happened, Eva?'

The nurse struggled to take more than a short breath, and the moonlight was enough to reveal the wreck of her make up. 'They're—coming!' She choked on the word and flung herself into Meg's arms.

Several minutes of cajoling and soothing passed before Eva settled enough to make sense and when she did, her words chilled Meg to the bone.

'Bill and I were parked above one of the beaches when we saw them. Three or four planes—I don't know for sure, but they dropped lots of bombs. Bill reckoned they all landed in the sea, but after the first one hit, I hid my eyes. Oh, God, they're coming here, aren't they? They're going to invade us.' Eva began rocking back and forth, moaning softly.

Holding Eva and patting her back, Meg's mind raced. Had Eva even witnessed a real bombing? There hadn't been any alarm raised, although the alarm that had sounded before the bombing in Darwin had been almost useless. Two minutes' warning about an attack of that size was ridiculous. But if the Japanese had dropped bombs, why hadn't the hospital been put on alert?

'Come on, Eva. Let's get you inside and—'

'Sisters, good evening. Or is it morning?' Dr Ransom appeared from the direction of the hospital, his stethoscope draped around his neck. Coming from a late call to a patient, Meg reasoned, but she was glad to see him. 'Is everything okay?'

'Good morning, Doctor. Sister Smith is a bit shaken up. She said she saw some Japanese planes dropping bombs.'

Eva's shoulders tensed beneath Meg's hands. She sat straight and sniffed loudly. 'I did see them. I'm not making it up. They all fell into the water.'

Dr Ransom offered a hand to help first Meg, then Eva up from the ground. 'Perhaps a hot cup of tea might help?'

'I'll see what I can rustle up. Come with me, Eva.'

'I'd rather go to bed.'

Maybe she was embarrassed about breaking down in Meg's arms. Against her better judgement, she allowed the tremor in Eva's voice to convince her. 'If you're sure?'

'I'm sure.' Eva pushed hair off her face and walked a less than straight line to her hut.

'Do you suspect her of drinking, Margaret?'

Meg shook her head and rubbed her upper arms. The night was cool and she hadn't felt warm even before she left the hut. 'I didn't smell alcohol on her, but she arrived back from her evening much later than permitted, and she was genuinely distraught. But if there was a bombing raid, why didn't we hear any alarms?'

Dr Ransom rubbed a thumb over his lower lip and frowned. 'That is odd. I'll call Garbutt air base and see what I can find out. Come into my office while I make the call.'

They passed a line of sleeping patients on the way to Doc's office in the front corner of the veranda. He pushed open the door and closed it behind Meg before turning on a desk lamp. A neat pile of case notes was stacked in one corner, but the ink blotter showed signs of recent writing. He opened the lowest filing drawer, took out a bottle of bourbon and two glasses. 'Care to join me, Margaret? It will warm you up.'

Mindful of Don Newton's comments about not imbibing spirits, she shook her head. 'I don't drink, but thank you.'

He poured a small glass for himself and tossed it back before replacing the bottle and glasses in the drawer. 'I'm not a fan of bourbon, but Don gave it to me after I helped him with advice on an unusual surgery. I'd prefer a good malt whisky, but beggars can't be choosers. Now, that call.' He picked up the receiver and waited for the operator. At this time of night, the connection was quickly made, but whomever Doc wanted to speak to was slow coming to the phone.

By the time he ended the call, Meg decided that all doctors must be taught how to suppress their emotions, because she had no idea from his expression whether the answers he'd been given were good or bad. 'Well? Was there a raid?'

'Yes. Reports vary between two and four planes, but Japanese flying boats dropped six bombs, all of which landed in the sea. Probably going after the harbour installations, which were lit up like a da—like a fairyland. In the end, the Americans either smashed or shot out the harbour lights. It seems no one knew whose job it was to switch them off.'

'Why didn't we hear a siren?'

'The ones in town worked, but the electrical system servicing our area sirens failed. None sounded near here or out at Garbutt. There was no aerial response, and the colonel I spoke with is of a mind that the Japs were—pardon the pun—testing the waters to see what our response might be.'

'I hope there is one next time—a response, I mean.' Praying she wouldn't go through another bombing like Darwin, Meg let out a sigh. 'Should I tell my nurses or are we to keep quiet about tonight?'

'Best to give them the facts in case Sister Smith's retelling exaggerates the size of the raid. And be sure to tell them the air force will be on watch from now on. We've got what pilots call a bomber's moon. The Japs might try again, but we'll be ready for them. This won't be like Darwin. You'll be safe here, Margaret. Would you like to have that cup of tea we talked about?'

Her head lifted at his tone. Not quite intimate, but personal and caring enough to remind her she was alone with him in a sleeping ward. Enough to remind her how appealing a man who cared could be. Enough to remind her of Gerry's comment that Doc liked her. His care and concern for her could slip under her guard and make her forget her engaged status if she wasn't careful.

Seamus trusts me to wait for him, and I will. Me and our baby.

Folding her arms across her chest, she accepted that she liked Doc. It was impossible not to appreciate his fine qualities. But she would *not* like him in *that* way. 'I pray we'll all be safe. Thank you for sharing the information with me, Doctor. I'll give the tea a miss and say good night. With luck I might catch a few more hours of sleep.'

'Probably a good idea. Good night, Margaret. Sleep well.' Was she imagining disappointment that she was leaving? A midnight conversation with her superior was one thing, but they'd teetered on the edge of something more—of being simply a man and a woman together in the wee hours of morning.

Witching hours, when people made wrong turns.

She slipped out of the room through the smallest opening of his door so as not to disturb the patients nearest to his office then gently closed the door behind her. With swift steps, she left the ward and hurried down the path back to her hut. It was all very well talking about sleeping through the rest of the night. In truth, she was certain sleep would elude her.

As she let herself back into her hut, her mind whirled. Japanese bombers attacking Townsville, and Dr Ransom offering tea and comfort in the dead of night. Neither event was conducive to sleep, but she snuggled beneath her blankets, closed her eyes and prayed. 'Please keep Seamus safe, keep our pilots alert, and please dear Lord, remind me every day how lucky I am to have found the love of my life. Keep me steadfast and true. Amen.'

##

By the time Meg joined the other nurses at breakfast, Eva was preening over what had become her starring role in the attack.

'. . . and then we raced back to Bill's HQ to report what we'd seen. It was ever so frightening, but it was lucky we were there to see and report it.'

'Weren't you scared silly?' Mary asked.

'Of course, but we were eyewitnesses. We had to tell what we saw.'

Meg stayed quiet about Eva's confession—that she'd buried her face in the sergeant's shoulder and not looked up after the first bomb fell. But Doc had been right about Eva's tendency to exaggerate.

Meg tapped on her mug with a spoon and waited till all eyes turned her way. 'I've been asked to give you the official information pertaining to the encounter Sister Smith told you about.' Meg recounted the details passed on via Doc from Garbutt Airfield and ended with a request for calm. 'The air force will be on high alert over the next few nights due to what they call a bomber's moon, which makes it easier for pilots to pick out their targets. If you hear an alarm, remember the drill. Tin hat, shelter as per orders. There will be a practice drill later today. Take time to check your equipment prior to it happening.'

Murmurs of 'Yes, Sister,' drifted up to where she sat at the head of the table before the group fell back into conversation punctuated by the occasional exclamation of concern. Eva threw her a dirty look for stealing her limelight and turned away. Last night, Meg had put her curtness down to shock, but now—

As she stood and lifted her breakfast tray, Meg spoke over the buzz of chatter. 'Sister Smith, report to my office in ten minutes.' The other nurses fell quiet. Those either side of Eva suddenly found their breakfast of intense interest when Eva's mulish expression returned. Her assent was given through gritted teeth. Disciplining a nurse was still a challenge for Meg, but Eva's attitude was making it easier to formulate what she had to say.

By the time Eva knocked on Meg's office door—two minutes late, Meg noted—she had contrived to change her expression into something vaguely pleasant. 'You wanted to see me, Sister Dorset?'

'Come in, Sister, and close the door.' Picking the time after the night shift ended and while the nurses on the morning shift were occupied with the morning routine had been deliberate. 'Last night, you were out well past the time your leave pass allowed.'

'We had to report what we'd seen, Sister. There was a *bombing* raid!' The last words were delivered with a *Remember!* implied by her tone. A certain amount of smugness was almost always guaranteed when speaking to Eva, but her attitude this morning took smug to a whole new level.

Leaving a pause during which she simply looked at Eva gave Meg time to bite back a sarcastic remark. Taking a deep breath, she adjusted her tone to mimic her Sydney matron's following the one time Meg had raced in five minutes late coming in from seeing a movie. 'That would be understandable, and acceptable if the raid had occurred earlier in the evening, but the official reports place it around midnight. You were required to be back by eleven. Your excuse for being late only serves to highlight that you had already disregarded your leave entitlement.'

Eva's expression lost its smugness as she realised her error. 'We—we'd broken down and Bill had to fix the engine. It wasn't my fault.'

'Are you telling me your date magically fixed this—breakdown—as soon as the raid ended?'

'He's very good with his hands—' Dull colour raced up Eva's neck and over her cheeks. 'I mean—'

Meg raised one hand. If Eva kept talking, she'd dig herself all the way to China. 'Spare me the details, Sister Smith. I have no choice but to place you on report and refuse requests for a leave pass until further notice.'

'But that means I'll miss the next dance. That's not fair!'

'Those are the rules. This is not up for discussion. Dismissed, Sister.' Meg opened Eva's file, bent her head and picked up her pen.

Eva made no move to leave.

Pausing before she wrote a single word, Meg glanced up. Eva's cheeks were mottled red, and her fists clenched at her sides. Meg raised her eyebrows in a manner that should intimidate even Eva, although naked hatred glared through her eyes before she wrenched the door open and fled. The door banged and bounced off the filing cabinet.

Sucking in a breath and exhaling a soft *whew*, Meg set her pen down and gripped her hands together. Eva's infraction was bad enough, but as far as Meg was concerned, that response had sealed her fate. Doc had been right to—

Doc appeared in the doorway, hands in the pockets of his white coat and jerked his head in the direction taken by Eva. 'I see the interview with Sister Smith went over like a lead balloon.'

Speak of the devil!

Meg rose and nodded. 'Unfortunately, when presented with the fact that she'd already blown her leave pass by not returning on time, she offered a lie. Claimed they had broken down at the beach before the raid.'

'Easy to establish—or discredit. I'll call the Supply Sergeant's superior officer and find out what his story is, but if, as I suspect, he owns up to the truth, then I'll be requesting Smith's transfer out. If she can't follow rules or keep a civil tongue in her head, she's not suited to the work we do here. Well handled by the way, Sister.'

'You heard us?'

'By chance only. I was coming to talk to you about the training meeting on Tuesday evening when I saw Smith at your door, so I waited. I didn't think you'd be with her for long.'

Meg nodded. Doc's approval of how she'd handled the situation felt good and, difficult as she found the discipline side of her position, Meg knew she'd done the right thing. 'You mentioned something about the meeting?'

'Ah yes. There's some *top brass* visiting, as Don would say, so they've changed the training to Wednesday the twenty-ninth to accommodate them and added dinner afterwards. We'll leave here at 1700 hours. The training session will start at 1730 hours.'

Mentally adjusting her night off on the current roster, Meg nodded. 'Nice of them to feed us.'

Be quiet, Meg. That sounds too friendly. Formal is normal.

She cleared her throat and rested her hands on Eva's

personnel file. 'Will that be all, Doctor?'

Sirens wailed, cutting through the night and dragging Meg out of a dream that disappeared the moment she opened her eyes.

'Come on, Maggie.' Gerry switched on the light and the four nurses grabbed their tin hats and raced out towards the nearest slit trench.

Meg managed to get both arms into her dressing gown before sliding over the lip of the trench in a shower of dirt. One foot clipped a body.

'Oi, watch it!' The male owner of the voice grabbed her, easing her down into the relative safety of the trench. 'There you go, luv.'

'Sorry.' Recognising the voice as belonging to Corporal Davis, one of the orderlies known for his spiky sense of humour, Meg felt relief. Davis was sensible, for all he enjoyed a laugh and a joke, and he swiftly organised those sheltering with him.

'Another body incoming. Scrunch up a bit, luv.'

Meg hunkered down and shielded her head as someone joined them, sending small chunks of dirt over her helmet. Davis wasn't concerned who was in his trench, only that they were safe. Which reminded Meg . . . Calling names softly, she checked that each of the nurses from her cabin and Catherine's next door were in the trench then peered into the slice of sky above. 'Davis, do you know what's happening?'

'Maybe another raid? I heard a single plane go over. Sounded like it circled over the sea and headed north, then there were several *crumps*. Could have been bombs falling. Hard to tell, Sister.'

Crouching in the trench, packed in with unseen others, Meg shivered. It stayed quiet. If this was a raid, were there more explosions to come? Maybe on top of them? The huge red cross on the hospital ship in Darwin Harbour hadn't stopped a bomb hitting them. Bombs—or maybe the pilots who dropped them—were no respecters of symbols. Bombs dropped, detonated, destroyed.

Each breath Meg drew sounded loud and shaky in her ears.

Too loud? Could the others hear her fear? What about setting a good example? She forced herself to inhale slowly, hold the breath while she counted to five then exhale slowly. *Not so bad,* she thought, and repeated the pattern.

By the time the all-clear siren was sounded, Meg's nerves were still tightly strung, but she had control of her breathing. No bombs had fallen on them and they were safe. As Davis and another orderly switched on their torches and helped them out of the trench, she became aware of someone softly sobbing and looked around.

Eva.

'I think we all need hot drinks. Come on, everyone.' Taking Eva by the arm, Meg rounded up her nurses and headed for the mess tent. She called over her shoulder, 'Davis, spread the word, will you. Tea and bikkies for whoever turns up.'

'Yes, Sister.' His torch bobbed away across the green and Meg issued directions for two of the nurses to set water to boil and find the cook's supply of biscuits. If ever they needed a sweet treat, it was tonight. She glanced at her watch as she settled Eva at a back table. After two in the morning. Whether or not bombs had been dropped, the enemy had disrupted routine and set them all on edge.

'Sister Smith? Eva?' The nurse was a mess—again. Even without her disregard for the rules it was becoming clear to Meg. Eva would not cope if they came under a concerted enemy attack. 'Eva, listen to me. You're fine. There aren't any bombs falling. You're safe, do you hear?'

Catherine approached, an eyebrow raised, asking if she could join them. Meg nodded.

'We're safe, Eva. Nothing more will happen tonight.' Catherine slipped an arm around her shoulders and at last, Eva gave a small nod.

Watching her, Meg was certain Catherine would make an excellent replacement for her. The thought was bittersweet. Just as she had begun to feel comfortable in her role as head nurse on Doc's team, she was running out of time.

Two big pots of tea and trays of mugs were set on the table

and plates of biscuits were handed around. Meg took one and nibbled it, aiming to make it last as long as possible. Scanning those gathered, she sensed all aside from Eva were coping, at least outwardly.

'Sister Dorset?' Davis leaned close and spoke softly. 'Doc Ransom said to let everyone know it was a single airboat that dropped eight bombs. They landed north of town near Many Peaks Range.'

'Thanks, Davis. I'll tell them. Did he say if the RAAF engaged the bomber?'

Davis shook his head. 'That's all he told me. Okay if I grab a cuppa now, Sister?'

'Go ahead.' Standing at the end of the table, Meg called for attention and passed on the details before encouraging everyone to drink up, stay positive, and get some sleep. 'I know it's hard after the *excitement* of tonight—'

'It's morning, Sister,' someone called from the other side of the mess.

Meg nodded and continued. 'After *this morning's* excitement, but I expect you all to be as rested as possible in the morning. *Later* this morning.' Grateful for the touch of humour, she caught the eye of the nurse who had corrected her and smiled. Cradling her mug in both hands, Meg waited until most of the others had left then encouraged the stragglers to find their beds.

As for her, she knew sleep would come late. She understood the nerve-shattering fear of looking up and seeing bombs raining down around her. What they'd experienced here was little more than a warning of what would come if their defence forces failed to push the Japs back in those island countries to the north. How much worse must it be for Seamus and the others, under constant enemy bombardment?

As she walked back to her hut, she paused and looked for the Southern Cross. The same stars shone in the sky as they had at the River but, without Seamus, they were cold and comfortless. She hurried the last few yards to her hut and closed out the night and the war.

Chapter 13

The lecture on a new surgical technique ended with a round of polite applause. Meg closed her notebook and stood, hand on lower back, and stretched. Beside her, Doctors Ransom and Newton became involved in a discussion of the technique.

Meg looked around at the assembled medical personnel, inspired by what they were collectively achieving. Honoured at being one of the youngest sisters-in-charge, she was also excited. They were on the cutting edge of surgical advances and medical treatments, and she had a small, but important, role to play. Tomorrow, she would instruct her nurses on the changes from tonight's lecture. But her delight at being part of this had been tempered by the commander's introduction, that more medical advances occurred during wars than in peace time. New weapons, often more devastating to the human body, required new surgical techniques.

'Sister Dorset?' The woman's voice was familiar and Meg turned to discover an old friend.

'Pat!' They exchanged a happy, one-armed hug and looked at each other. 'You look well. Where are you stationed?'

'You wouldn't believe my luck. I was sent to Brisbane after the evac from Darwin, and, as luck would have it, I was in the right place at the right time. Maybe because I'd been in Darwin during the bombing—I don't know—but I was selected for this visit to the north. Where did you end up?'

'*Currajong*, Central Sick Quarters here in Townsville.'

'How is it?'

'I love it. I've learned so much, and the doctor in charge of my team made me his head nurse. I reckon that was luck at work too. I was the first and only nurse for the first few days so he trained me to his requirements and put me in charge. Can you imagine?'

'Well done. Are you staying for the dinner? I hope so. I want to catch up now. We can sit together and chat.'

'I should check if that's okay with Dr Ransom. Hang on a minute.' She stepped up beside Doc and waited until he finished talking to Don Newton then asked if he minded if she sat with a friend.

Doc glanced at Pat and smiled. 'Of course.' He resumed his conversation and Meg hurried back to Pat.

'*That's* your doctor? You lucky duck! He's cute, and his Yankee friend's not bad either.' Envy tinged Pat's voice and she nodded towards a portly, middle-aged man standing near the door. 'Behold, my travelling companion. Want to swap?'

Meg laughed and threaded an arm through Pat's. 'I'll hold onto mine for now, thanks.' They headed into the dining hall and found seats together near the door, away from the bigwigs at the head table.

'So tell me, do you have a thing for your Dr Gorgeous?' Pat flicked her serviette open and set it across her lap as lower-ranked soldiers co-opted to wait on table began serving bowls of soup.

'Of course not.'

'Why not?'

'Because I'm engaged.'

'What? When?' Pat set a hand on her arm and peered into her eyes. 'It's only been—what, five months since I saw you and there was no fiancé then.'

'Remember Corporal Flanagan? Seamus and I worked at Adelaide River for several weeks. We fell in love and he asked me to marry him.'

'Flanagan? My goodness, Meg. I thought you'd have aimed higher. You could easily catch a doctor. Why settle for a corporal?'

Pat's cavalier attitude stung. Meg hadn't taken her for a social climber, but maybe that's what came of working with the higher ups in the service. She shrugged. 'When you fall in love with someone, that's all there is to it. As soon as he gets back on leave, we'll marry.'

Doc and Don Newton arrived late to the table, still deep in

conversation. They stopped, looked around and, discovering two empty chairs across the table from Meg and Pat, took them.

'Margaret, who's your friend?' Geoff smiled at her.

Conversation flowed and Meg gradually relaxed. Pat's comment wasn't anything new. Most nurses would set their caps at a doctor, and why not? But Meg had fallen in love with Seamus and his poetic soul. She admired Geoff in much the same way as she admired Don Newton. Of course Geoff would be a *good catch*. *If* she wasn't already engaged, and *if* she wasn't in love with her fiancé, she might have fallen for him.

Meg set her cutlery on her plate and turned to her friend. 'Tell me about working in Brisbane, Pat.'

Over post-dinner drinks, Geoff introduced Meg to a small group of surgeons as 'my excellent head nurse, Margaret Dorset, a matron in the making if ever I saw one'. She gave an embarrassed half smile and sipped her soft drink.

A tiny flutter in her womb as she had sat at the dining table gave her a moment of wonder, quickly followed by a heavy sense of guilt. By rights she should have told Doc about her pregnancy and accepted whatever decision he made for the good of the unit, but she had clung to the idea of training up her replacement before she told him. This flutter meant her baby was *real*. If her pregnancy went well, he or she would arrive in four or five months. The baby would be dependent on her for everything since she doubted Seamus would be home. The war wasn't going to end just because she wanted it to, but her responsibility for this little person was just beginning.

Worries circled in her mind, chasing one another around and around. She had no answers. Not yet. Going home to her parents wasn't an option. Unmarried, she would be a stain on their good name. A different city then. How would she cope alone? Where would she live? No, where would *they* live?

It was late as Meg climbed into the jeep beside Doc. The meal had been better than she was used to, and once Pat got over her disappointment in Meg's engagement to Seamus, they had chatted non-stop. Then Doc had been so intent on connecting with as many surgeons from other units as he could that it was nearly midnight. Suppressing a yawn, a wave of fatigue hit Meg.

Doc laughed. 'Clearly you're out of practice enjoying yourself at a party, Margaret.' He started the engine, put the jeep into gear, and headed towards the sentry at the front gate. 'Is everything okay? You were quiet after dinner.'

'Too much work makes Jill a dull girl and all that.' She set an elbow on the door rim and cupped her cheek. 'I apologise in advance if I fall asleep on the way home. I've had enough excitement for one day.'

'Then I'll endeavour to avoid all potholes, so I don't wake you, unless you snore?'

'Thanks, although I can't comment on the snoring.'

It would be so easy to misconstrue his light-hearted question and familiar tone for more than it was. Doc knew she was engaged, but he was an honourable man.

Beneath bright moonlight the road unwound north to Townsville. Trees tipped with silver loaned the night a special magic. Imagining they were on the way home from a party, Meg dozed off.

Air raid sirens wailed.

Meg shot up in her seat, praying they were a nightmare. Ahead, the road lay clear in the bright light of a full moon. Above, a steady droning noise.

'It's a bomber's moon all right. Blackout restrictions won't help now.'

'Should we turn back to Oonoonba?' Meg held her hat and tipped her head back, scanning the sky. 'There! He's right above us.'

'I'm pulling off the road.' Doc wrenched the steering wheel and slid to a stop on the shoulder. 'Get out of the car, Margaret. Now!'

She scrambled out, her legs like jelly, but she ran.

Doc grabbed her hand and drew her into the cover of some spindly trees. 'Get down.' His free hand pushed on her back and the other pulled her down.

Meg sprawled in the grass. Both hands covered her head, but the drone of the plane was clear. Inside her, something fierce and brave was awakened and she rolled onto her side. Under the light of the moon, the bomber pilot would be able to see the coast and the town. If she was going to die in a bombing raid, she preferred to face it.

A bomb dropped out of the belly of the plane and headed for them and suddenly Margaret wasn't certain she wanted to see her end plummeting towards her. The bomb exploded further back along the road they'd travelled from Oonoonba. Was that the ground shuddering from the impact, or her frightened body losing control?

Unable to look away she watched the plane, waiting for more bombs to drop, accepting whatever fate had in store for her.

Light machine guns began firing from somewhere not far away. Doc shook his head. 'The plane's well out of their range, but look, Margaret. Look at the sky.'

More than a dozen searchlights criss-crossed, sweeping, seeking, trapping the enemy plane in their beams. They held it perfectly as it flew towards the town.

Rapid-fire artillery followed along the lines of light and burst in puffy explosions. She'd seen it before, that valiant, useless firing. 'The ack-ack shells aren't reaching it. They're exploding way too low. The same happened in Darwin.'

But it wasn't the same. This was night time. There were no waves of planes flying in formation and raining death and destruction on a vulnerable town. The searchlights had located and held a single bomber.

The ack-ack guns fired again before several RAAF fighter planes joined the aerial dance. Meg kneeled up, willing them to bring down the enemy plane. Red tracer bullets lit up a path towards the bomber. One long burst hit the bomber's tail and a yellow light erupted.

Meg clasped her hands under her chin. 'He's hit! I think the bomber's losing height.'

'Maybe. It's difficult to tell from here. Look, the fighter plane's going back around. He'll have another go at him. Damn, they're moving out of our line of sight.' Doc pushed to his feet and offered his hand to Meg.

She took it but stumbled in the tussocky grass.

Doc's hands shot out and caught her as she fell sideways against him.

Her shoulder knocked into his chest, but the moment his hand touched her stomach, he stilled.

Meg froze. The moonlight revealed his frown. Surprise, disbelief, followed by indecision as he seemed to weigh up whether to ask her outright.

He knows. Confess it now and see what he says.

She moistened her lips and stepped away from him.

'Margaret?'

'Yes, Dr Ransom, I *am* pregnant. I was planning to have worked out who should be my replacement and have her up to speed before I told you. I apologise for the manner in which you found out. It wasn't what I intended.' Proud of how she held it together, Meg knew she'd taken *formal* to a new high, but there was no instruction manual for handling such a situation.

She held her head high, but the look on Doc's face made her wish for a dark moon. Then she wouldn't have to see his disappointment. But then, the bomber wouldn't have menaced them and she wouldn't have been in this awkward spot.

'How many months?' At last, he spoke.

'About four. I missed seeing Seamus by two days or we'd have tried to get married before he shipped out.'

'I see. Does anyone at *Currajong* know? Your—replacement?'

'I've told no one. You were to be the first. You *are* the first.'

'Thank you for that.' His gaze caught and held hers.

'Are you going to send me away now? It's not impacting on my work, and I feel well. Surprisingly well.'

Doc rubbed the back of his neck then shoved both hands in

his pockets. 'I should.' He turned away, walked a few steps and looked over the stretch of open country. She had no idea what he was thinking, although—when had she ever known for sure?

He turned back but didn't approach. 'Do you want to leave the unit now?'

'I don't want to leave until I have to.'

He nodded and fell silent. He hadn't told her to go. Maybe he wouldn't put her on the first train south. Maybe he'd let her stay on for a while.

Praying she'd interpreted that silence correctly, she took a step towards him. 'Besides, you're sending Sister Smith back to Brisbane. We'll be short-staffed until a replacement arrives for her. While I can do my job properly, I want to stay here, and I was thinking—' What would Doc think of her suggestion? New mothers were supposed to be with their babies. They were supposed to *want* to stay with their babies, but Meg couldn't imagine experiencing such a feeling. Not when there was so much work to do here. Not when she was needed in an active role in the war effort.

'If I can find someone to care for my baby, I'd like to come back after the birth.'

Doc's nod was non-committal, but before he replied, another jeep pulled up beside them.

Dr Newton called out, 'Anyone hurt? We were still at the meeting site when that bomb hit and— Geoff, Meg, I didn't see it was you.'

Doc approached the jeep. 'We pulled off and took shelter when that bugger flew straight over and dropped his load. No damage done.'

'The all clear sounded. Sure you're both okay?' Don Newton peered in Margaret's direction.

Moving out of the shadow of the trees, an idle thought about hiding in moon-shadows played in her mind. 'I'm fine although I might have a bruise or two from flinging myself onto the ground. It looks like our chaps hit the Jap's plane.'

'Here's hoping. Well, if you're both okay . . .' Dr Newton

put the jeep in gear and gave them a casual wave. 'I expect we'll read all about it in the *Townsville Bulletin* in a few days. Geoff, don't forget to send me that article on vascular developments. Night.' He pulled away leaving them to dust themselves off and clamber back into their jeep.

With a pang of regret for their interrupted discussion, Meg waited for Doc to resume the conversation, but he drove home in silence, only speaking to wish her a good night before leaving her to her thoughts. She strolled along the driveway, seeing activity in the veranda ward as nurses settled patients into their beds after the raid. Sneaking into her hut so as not to disturb the others if they had gone to bed proved useless. She eased the door open to find three pairs of eyes turn to her.

'You're awake still?'

'Why would you think we'd be asleep after another bombing raid?' Gerry asked. 'Eva treated us to another attack of hysteria. That girl would be useless anywhere near a front line.'

If Meg had given the nurse another thought, she'd have expected nothing less. She shrugged and, seeing they were keen to talk, told them about seeing the enemy plane and taking cover and the bomb.

'Ah, that explains the dirt on your skirt and grass in your hair.'

'What?' Meg jumped up and looked at her reflection, plucking a grass stem from her hair and brushing off her skirt. 'Oh dear. I hoped not to have to fit in doing more laundry for a few days, but this dirt isn't going to come out.'

'So . . . did you only take cover because of the plane, or did Doc—you know?' Seated on the end of her bunk, Gerry nudged Meg and gave her an exaggerated wink.

'Gerry! Honestly, you know—'

'You're an engaged person, I know. You tell us that so often I sometimes wonder if you feel you have to remind yourself. Come on, Maggie, I'm only kidding. But it could have been fun.'

Desperate to divert Gerry from her comments, Meg shook

her head. 'I'm beginning to wonder about these raids that are hardly raids. Either the Japs have lousy aim, or their plan isn't to bomb the heck out of us, but to tire us into making mistakes. I know the pilot dropped one bomb this time. It landed not far from us.' Her near miss elicited shocked exclamations. Jokes about Doc and *a good time* vanished.

'Oh my God, Maggie, are you okay?' Gerry's grip on her arm was hard and fierce, and Meg felt real fear roll off her friend.

'I stared at his plane and prayed he didn't drop another on top of us. It was so close the ground quaked—or it might have been me shaking in my boots.'

Mary made a sound of disgust. 'You were in the thick of it with an actual bomb and meanwhile our Eva carried on like a pork chop—*again*. Do you think she should stay here? What if the bombing gets more accurate and we have to deal with casualties? She'd be squawking and useless.'

Soon they would have to tell Eva that she was being sent south. Meg doubted any of the staff would see her departure as a negative, especially after tonight's repeat performance. 'So far, the bombs have landed either in the sea or in the mountains outside of town. The pilots had to have seen the town lying open and clear under the moonlight, so—'

Pam leaned forward, nodding. 'Your idea makes a weird kind of sense you know. Three out of four nights with disturbed sleep hasn't done me any favours, I can tell you.'

'Did you offer everyone tea again?'

Gerry jumped in. 'Hot cocoa, but most people just wanted to go to bed. Do you want—'

'No thanks. I'm going to crawl into bed and beg Morpheus to clobber me. Night, girls.' Kicking off her shoes, Meg turned off the light then made short work of removing her uniform and dropping it at the end of the bunk. Why bother folding it when she'd have to work hard to remove dirt and grass stains tomorrow?

A rustling of bedclothes and Mary's soft sniffs, always a prelude to her falling asleep, sent Meg hurrying into her bed. Hoping for sleep, she burrowed under her blankets and curled up on her side. Tomorrow, Doc might decide to send her home and Meg, for all the fright of tonight, didn't want to leave. Not yet.

Chapter 14

'Maggie! Have you seen the *Bulletin* today?' Gerry slipped in beside Meg, moved her mug aside and set the newspaper on the table. She stabbed her finger at an article. 'My God, you were lucky not to be any nearer to that bomb. Look!'

'Move your finger.' Meg drew the paper closer and angled it towards the light. As she skimmed the article, her knees ached with remembered pain when she'd slammed into the ground as the bomber overflew them.

Pat rapped on the table. 'Read it aloud please, Margaret. A few days ago, after the first raid, the paper reported that the enemy planes appeared to be some sort of long distance flying boat. Was this the same? Let's hear what they have to say about your encounter.'

'Okay. Let me see—seven bombs landed in Cleveland Bay . . .' She skimmed further. 'Oh, this bit refers to the bomb that hit near Oonoonba.' Leaning an elbow on the table, she read:

The lesson of the Japanese bombing last week was that people must remain in their shelters while enemy aircraft are in the neighbourhood. The only "casualty" to be seen in the Townsville area, after three raids, is a lone coconut tree, which was struck by a flying bomb splinter. Some 14 feet up, the splinter struck the nine-inch diameter trunk a glancing blow, cutting its way through, and the top of the tree promptly toppled over. Near the ground can be seen two marks caused by splinter bits. Twenty yards from the bomb crater two posts in a wire fence, three inches in diameter, were cut off at ground level.

'They lopped a coconut tree? That's it?' Mary shook her head.

'A bomb *splinter* lopped the tree and two fence posts this thick—' Pat held her hands three inches apart and peered through them then circled her fingers around Mary's upper arm.

Meg stared at Pat's demonstration. Bomb splinters had sliced through fence posts as thick as an arm. Cut them off at ground level. Near her. If she and Doc had pulled off only a little further down the road . . .

Bile rose in her throat.

'A bomb splinter could lop off a man's arm—' If she and Doc had been closer to the bomb, she might not be here now, or she might be minus a limb or . . . 'Excuse me.'

She barely made it to the lavatory before she threw up. When the heaving subsided, she sank onto her heels and rested her head in one hand. What was she thinking, remaining up here where flying boats dropped bombs like that? Where a *splinter* from a bomb could fell a tree as easily as a knife cut through butter.

What sort of mother put her baby in such danger?

'Maggie?' Gerry tapped on the door and a moment later, it creaked open and she popped her head around. 'Are you okay?' She took one look at Meg's face and pushed the door wide, dropping onto the floor and grabbing Meg in a tight hug. 'I'm so sorry. I wasn't thinking about how that news story would make you feel. I'm an idiot, a horrible person, I'm—'

'Not your fault, Gerry.' Meg sucked in a breath that shuddered through her. 'It was Pat's demonstration of the size of the fence posts that made it hit home. We were so lucky to have left the meeting when we did. A few minutes later and we might have been hit like—' Swallowing down a fresh surge of bile, she breathed through her mouth. 'Like the palm tree. But we weren't and I should be focused on that, not how close it could have been.'

She pushed herself up, and, with trembling fingers, wiped moisture from her eyes. 'I need to rinse my mouth and splash water over my face.'

'Of course. Will you come back to the mess? Can I get you a cuppa?'

'I'm fine, honestly. But after that piece of—news—I do want to talk to Doc about how we're protecting patients who can't be moved from raids.'

'And Eva? She's really not coping.'

Meg just nodded. It was too much effort to explain what had already been decided. Besides, she owed it to Eva to tell her first. 'I'll see you on the ward.'

She tapped on the door of Doc's office, wondering if she should have delayed speaking to him until she had planned her approach.

'Come in.' He sounded distracted and when she stopped in the doorway, an untidy pile of mail sat front and centre on his desk. 'Sister, what can I do for you?'

'Is this a bad time? I can come back later.'

Doc tunnelled his fingers through his hair, looked at the envelopes then at her. 'No, now is fine. There's never a *good* time in this man's army.'

'I have two items to discuss. The first is about Sister Smith. Apparently, she became hysterical during last night's raid and—'

'So I heard. I've just signed her transfer papers, effective immediately. Will you let her know she's to be on the fourteen hundred train to Brisbane?'

'Certainly, Doctor. So, the second item—'

Doc held up a hand and pinned her with a look she interpreted as resigned. 'You want to know what I've decided about your—situation. By rights and all that's sane and safe, I should have signed your papers and arranged for you to accompany Sister Smith to Brisbane. But I haven't, and not because we'll be short-staffed without you but—'

The pause was uncharacteristic for Doc. Self-assured and confident in his decisions, Meg was hard put to remember another time when he had faltered. But the fact he had gave her hope. 'You aren't sending me south with Sister Smith because . . .'

'Because I'm a selfish bast—ahem, a selfish man. I know your *situation*, but even knowing that, I don't want you to go. I like you, Margaret—a lot. You're a damned good nurse too and I'm lucky to have you. I think we might be able to stretch out your time here another month or so. What do you think?'

Was he saying what she thought he was? Understanding that he wanted her to stay because of her nursing skills was one thing, but beyond that, his self-accusation and his *'I like you a lot'* seemed weightier than the simple statements first appeared. They seemed to support Gerry's theory that Doc *liked* her as more than a friend. In which case, wouldn't it be better for her to leave now? That would be the sensible option, the *safe* option. She gripped her hands tightly together.

'I'd be happy to stay for as long as I can do my job properly. As long as you'll have me. Thank you, Doctor.'

Doc released a soft breath. Had he imagined she would leave before she had secured a seamless transition to Catherine?

He cleared his throat. 'Good. Well, better get on with—'

'Doctor, there is the second matter I wanted to raise with you.'

'I thought your position here was it?'

Meg rolled her lips and shook her head. 'No. After reading the *Bulletin's* account of the raid over Oonoonba and the effect of bomb splinters on local fence posts and vegetation—' Goodness, she sounded formal, but how else was she to describe it without the urge to throw up again.

'Ah, the coconut tree, yes?'

'I was thinking about how to shelter patients who cannot be moved during air raids.'

Doc's gaze softened and held hers. 'Of course you were. Margaret, I—'

A quick double tap on the door drew Meg's attention. Eva stood there, her face pale, her eyes still shooting defiance at Meg.

'Sister Smith, what is it?' Doc's expression morphed into his usual neutral mask. The change was swift and subtle, and Meg couldn't explain it. It simply *happened.*

Eva stepped into the room and stood beside Meg. 'I want to go home. I want to get out of this place—please.'

Doc tapped his fingers on the transfer papers. 'Already

arranged, Sister Smith. Sister Dorset was about to let you know the details. You can go and pack while I finish discussing hospital matters with her.' Doc handed over the transfer papers and Eva grinned.

'I'm going today? That's great, that's— Thank you.' Her sullen aggression dropped away making her look younger than she had since her arrival. She all but skipped out of the office.

Meg watched her go. 'One less task on today's list, unless I need to arrange her transport to the train?'

Doc sat and pulled a paper from the top of a pile. 'Already taken care of. But if you have a moment, we haven't talked about your idea for sheltering patients, and—a heads up—I've heard that *Currajong* is to become 3 Medical Receiving Station. I'm waiting on further details, but it might not happen until after your departure.'

'What do I need to do in preparation, Dr Ransom?'

'When I know more, I'll let you know. But tell me about your idea.'

'We need to protect patients who can't be moved to trenches or shelters from bomb splinters . . .'

##

Eva's departure changed the mood at the nurses' table and, over dinner, conversation flowed more freely. Meg noted the change and promised herself that on any future wards she took charge of, she would pay closer attention to how nurses worked together.

Catherine seemed a little more relaxed, and Lesley and Janet, who had shared the hut with her and Eva in the months since their transfers in, conversed softly. They looked at Meg, but it was Lesley who asked, 'Are we getting another nurse to take Eva's place?'

Meg stirred a little sugar into her tea and set the spoon on the table. 'Perhaps. I believe there may be changes coming, but no, I don't have firm information yet. For the time being, you three can spread out and enjoy a little more space.'

'I wonder if Eva felt any regrets at leaving her Supply Sergeant?' Trust Gerry to bring up other people's love lives.

Catherine shook her head. 'I don't think so. She gave him a

sound telling off for ratting her out. Something about him not supporting her story about their jeep breaking down?'

Gerry leaned across the table. 'And how do you know that, Sister I-never-listen-to-other-people's-conversations?'

A frown creased Catherine's usually serene expression. 'I wish I hadn't heard her. I was doing the stock take when she made a call on the extension outside the supply room. Once she started telling him off, I felt I couldn't make my presence known.'

'Too right. She'd have had a go at you for eavesdropping, the silly girl.' Pam tossed off her cup of tea and banged the mug on the table. 'I don't think anyone here will really miss her.'

Catherine's expression looked uncertain. 'That's not really fair. I'm sure she had her good points.'

Gerry tut-tutted and shook her head. 'You're way too nice, Catherine. If Eva had any, she hid them well. And I won't miss her trying to go through my belongings.' Gerry had never warmed to Eva and it seemed to Meg that Eva had been more of a thorn in the side of her nursing mates than she'd known.

'How do you know that?'

Gerry heaved a sigh. 'I caught her red-handed one day. She was pawing my red dress and my locker was wide open. When I challenged her about it, she said you'd sent her to our hut to pick up something and she'd opened the wrong locker. As if she couldn't read our names!'

Janet nodded. 'Same with me. She said she pulled open my locker by mistake for hers.'

Meg's thoughts raced through the letters she'd written to Seamus and his, to her. Had she locked them away after every reading? Could Eva have read their loving words and excitement about the baby?

But no, Eva wouldn't have kept something like that to herself. She'd have found a way to use the information to somehow make life easier for herself. Not for the first time, Meg wondered why Eva had become a nurse. A calling to serve others hadn't been a hallmark of her time at *Currajong*, so what had attracted her to nursing?

Shaking her head, Meg could only be grateful that Gerry had caught Eva before she'd caused any mischief. 'Ladies, if tomorrow proves to be a quiet day, I thought those of us who are off duty might go for a picnic on The Strand. Who's in?'

For a winter day, the weather was warm and inviting, and while Meg didn't plan on swimming, the thought of paddling in the sea lifted her spirits. Doc had readily agreed to authorise the use of a jeep. 'An excellent suggestion to keep morale up, Sister. Such a shame I can't join all of you.' But his eyes stayed on her face a moment too long. She wondered if his answer would have been the same if she'd invited him to join her alone.

Gerry begged to drive. 'I'm an excellent driver, Maggie, and I know the shortest way there, and the best spots for swimming.'

Happy to simply be a passenger and enjoy the moment of freedom from duty and responsibility, Meg agreed. In her absence Catherine was in charge. While there was nothing major scheduled, it would be an opportunity for Doc to watch and assess her in the role.

She removed her hat, leaned back, as much as one could in a jeep, and tipped her face to the sky. The air was balmy and pleasantly cool on her skin. Squished into the back seat, Lesley and Janet, and Ria, a nurse from hut three, sang, their voices growing louder as the jeep approached the southern end of Castle Hill. Driving past a truck of Aussie soldiers, they waved at the men.

'Oi, where are you off to, luv?'

'The beach!' Ria yelled back, and Janet let out a loud 'Wheeeeee!' that lasted all the way around the dogleg corner on Sturt Road. Ahead of them, Castle Hill loomed redly, its bulk too often blocking cooling sea breezes from *Currajong*.

St James Cathedral passed on their right as they crested a hill and suddenly, there it was—a vista of sea and palm trees. Across the water rose the bulk of Magnetic Island. Sunlight tipped small waves in diamond bursts of light, and nearer in, dotted amongst the green, it reflected off tin roofs.

'I wouldn't mind living in one of these houses,' Ria said, turning to keep a beautiful wood and stone building in her sight before Gerry turned onto a road that ran along the beach.

'You seem to know where you're going, Gerry.' Meg appreciated the brief reprieve from making decisions. For a few hours, she could forget the war and just have fun in the sun.

'The supply sergeant told me we should stay at this end of The Strand so we're out of the way. There's a rock pool big enough to sit in, he said, but we shouldn't go further north than Rowes Bay.'

Janet piped in. 'Aren't there gun emplacements up at Pallarenda? I shouldn't think it would be very nice that far up. Bet they've got barbed wire and barriers in place. Let's stay near the rock pool.'

Gerry pulled off the road beneath the shade of a huge Moreton Bay fig tree. She looked at Meg who raised an eyebrow and climbed out. 'What? The water's not far and the shade will keep the car and our food cool.'

Meg raised both hands in surrender. 'Good thinking. You're in charge of the jeep. Choice of parking is yours to make.' Grinning, she lifted her arms high and turned a full circle. 'What a glorious day. Look at the colour of that water, and the red of Castle Hill and the island. It's shimmering under the sun.'

Gerry stopped beside her, a towel slung around her neck. 'Yeah, the colours are intense. If I was an artist, I'd like to capture the day on canvas, but seeing all I've got is this—' From behind her back, Gerry produced a Box Brownie camera. 'I'm going to record our outing for posterity. Sit on that bit of fence all of you and look at me.'

Four nurses perched side by side on the round wooden railing. Janet and Ria put an arm around each other's neck, and Meg rested both hands beside her.

'Smile, ladies.' Gerry peered down into the viewing screen, taking her time. Meg's cheeks ached with holding a smile, but finally Gerry announced, 'Got it! One more.'

'You should be in the next one, Gerry.' Meg pushed off the fence and held out her hand for the camera. 'I know what to do. Go take my place.'

Gerry scurried over to the others and leaned in, her arm sliding around Janet's shoulder before she raised her other arm. 'Smile, everyone!'

As soon as Meg clicked the shutter, Ria jumped to her feet and set off running, down the slope and across to the sand. She stopped long enough to pull off her shoes and drop them next to her bag then headed for the water, Janet and Lesley close behind. Meg handed the camera to Gerry who stowed it safely in her bag. Together they sauntered in the direction of the untidy pile of bags dropped by the others.

'I'm not swimming, but I might paddle for a bit. Feel free to join the others.'

'Are you sure?' Gerry eyed her thoughtfully. 'Why come to the beach if you're not swimming?'

'Wrong time of the month.' The lie slipped out, glib and far too easy. It didn't sit well with Meg, but the truth wasn't for sharing. Not yet.

Gerry set her bag down and glanced in the direction of the other nurses. All three were thigh deep and engaged in splashing each other. She turned back and met Meg's eyes. 'Don't take this the wrong way but I haven't seen you collecting your allotment of disposable pads.'

'What?' Her breath caught, hooked by the lie she had told. The lie she had to hold onto so she could stay in Townsville a little longer. 'What is there to take the wrong way about that?'

'Since I arrived you haven't once brought pads into the hut or stuffed them into your toiletry bag. Are you just really irregular or are you—' Gerry's gaze flicked to Meg's waist. 'Pregnant?'

The lie wouldn't come. Sunlight became blinding. A buzzing in her ears blocked every other sound—her nurses frolicking in the water, trucks rumbling past; the cawing of seagulls overhead. Meg stared at Gerry as everything slipped from her grasp. Around her the day blurred.

Gerry grabbed Meg's wrists as she sank onto the warm sand and squatted in front of her. 'It's okay. Breathe, Maggie. Don't worry, I'm not going to tell anyone if you are.'

Meg shook her head, unable to meet Gerry's searching gaze. She'd been so careful about everything else. Not changing in front of the others, blousing her top over her skirt to disguise the undone button, the slow increase in her waist. Missed periods had seemed one of the few positives among the changes in her body, but now they were to be her undoing. 'I guess I should be grateful Eagle-eyes Eva wasn't sharing our hut.'

'So it's true?'

She nodded. 'I had hoped to see Seamus before he shipped out, but I missed him. I think it happened around the end of March, while we were in Adelaide River.'

'Didn't you want to go home when you found out? Maggie— what on earth are you doing staying in a war zone?'

'I've asked myself that a dozen times since the Oonoonba raid, and I know I'm probably crazy, but Gerry, I love my work. I love the responsibility and learning so many new things. I don't want to lose all that.'

'But you will, no matter how long you wait here before someone finds out. Someone else I mean. At some point, and I reckon you'll be lucky to last another month before that happens, you'll have to tell Doc and then you'll be sent south.'

'I know.' Even now, she held back sharing that Doc already knew. While nobody else knew that he knew, he couldn't get into trouble for her choices, her decisions. For the choice he had knowingly made in allowing her to stay. 'Please don't tell anyone. It's difficult enough that Seamus and I weren't married before he left, but—I want to find someone in Brisbane to look after the baby so I can return and keep nursing.'

Gerry sat with a thump. 'Are you really going to give up your baby to keep nursing?'

'I didn't mean I'm giving my baby away!' The thought of

never knowing her and Seamus's child chilled her to the bone. 'I want a temporary mother for my child, just until Seamus returns and we can be married. When he comes home, we'll marry and be a family and maybe then I can help out at a local hospital. Maybe that will be enough.'

'And if it isn't?' Gerry's voice was soft, but the question had played on Meg's mind before now. 'What if being a wife and mother isn't enough for you?'

'It will have to be. Unless the laws change to allow married women to keep working.'

'What a lousy choice we women have.'

Meg shrugged. 'Home and children, or single and a career. It's a man's world all right. I can't see it changing any time soon, even though the army has just changed the rules so married nurses can keep working.'

'And yet, Maggie, here we are in this man's army, and women back home are doing jobs men used to do while they're away fighting. Maybe that should give us hope that things *can* change because they *have to* change.' Gerry gripped Meg's hand between hers. 'As to your choice about returning to work after your baby is born—I know a nun. We were friends at school; now we're both *sisters*.' She grinned at her quip. 'The thing is, she lives at Magdalen House in Wooloowin. They look after unmarried mums and bubs there. I could write to her and ask if she knows of someone who can help. If you like?'

'Thank you, Gerry. Yes, I'd love for you to write and ask. It will be such a relief to know it's all sorted before I have my baby.'

Squeals of pleasure erupted from the trio in the water, and Ria waved at them. 'Come on in, you two. The water is wonderful.'

'Go on, Gerry. Get in and enjoy your swim. I'll walk up that way.' She pointed towards a rocky section. 'Maybe I'll dip my toes in a rock pool.'

'If you're sure you don't mind?'

'With your kind offer and this balmy day, I can relax now. And to be honest, I'll love a little solitude.'

Gerry smiled then ran across the sand and joined the others.

Meg kicked off her shoes, had a drink from her water bottle then set off towards the rocks. Sand squished up between her toes and the wind tossed loose hair across her eyes. She clambered onto the rocks, shaded her eyes and looked across the water. Magnetic Island seemed to doze in midday heat hot enough even in winter to create a light haze. She knew there were gun emplacements at strategic points, but from here, without a pair of binoculars, they were invisible.

Probably even if I had a pair, I wouldn't see them.

But she could imagine them. Davis had described the emplacements built into the hill up Pallarenda way. Hidden beneath flat concrete roofs, he'd spotted one when he was out bird watching on a rare half day off. He'd described his find in a quiet moment one day on the ward. Meg and one of their patients, another bird-watcher, had been so involved in Davis's poetic descriptions of bird life on the Town Common, they hadn't noticed Doc's approach until he tapped her on the shoulder and requested '*a moment of your time, Sister*'.

A seagull glided down onto the rocks not far from her and sat at the edge of a small pool of water, its beady black eyes searching for food. Here on the sun-soaked rocks, the warmth of midday had drawn a line of sweat along Meg's upper lip. She lifted her hair off her neck and looked around. Sun glinted off water in a bigger rock pool than the seagull had claimed.

Meg climbed carefully down to the big pool, examined the sandy bottom for other life then stepped into the water. If she'd brought a bathing suit, she could have fully submersed herself. As it was, she tucked her skirt up and waded, even scooping water over her arms. A sea breeze cooled her wet skin, enough that she no longer felt envious of the others frolicking in the shallows.

Spying a pretty purple-tinged shell, she plunged her arm into the water and drew it out. Shaking the water off she held it between two fingers and examined it. As the shell dried its colour dimmed, but it gave her an idea. Collecting shells was as good a disguise as any for not swimming and the bonus was, she could show them to her patient in bed four. When he'd learned she was heading off to the beach, Rollings had cheekily asked her to bring him something.

She pocketed the shell and splashed her arms again. Feeling cool and fresh, she set one foot on a small ledge to climb out. Recently she had been feeling off balance so she pushed off the bottom with extra vigour. Next thing she knew, she was completely wet. 'Damn it.' Spluttering and surprised by the exclamation that slipped out, a word she *never* used, Meg stood. Both hands pushed hair out of her eyes. So much for not wearing shorts and keeping her clothes dry. She was the wettest of them all now.

Taking extra care, she climbed out of the rock pool and dripped her way off the rocks onto the sand. *At least now I'll stay cool.*

Since she was already wet, she waded in the shallows, her gaze drifting from searching for shells to looking at the island. Her toe nudged something hard and she looked down. A small group of sea snail shells rolled with the ebb and flow of water. Tiny fish darted about her ankles, bright flashes of colour as they moved out of her shadow. She moved closer to the lacy froth of sea spume marking the place where sea met land. Tiny holes pocked the sand and endless bubbles rose around the edges.

She squatted and watched, still and quiet. Soon, an army of little white crabs with grey camouflage spots, crabs no bigger than the length of her thumb, scurried over the muddy sand.

Engrossed in watching them, she didn't hear Gerry calling her to lunch until her friend stepped in front of her.

'I see you decided to bathe in private after all. One tip: might be a better idea to take some clothes off first.'

Meg rose, a small selection of empty shells in hand. 'I'll try to remember that next time I'm falling into a rock pool.'

Gerry frowned. 'Are you okay? I mean, you didn't hurt yourself?'

'I'm fine. Just not as sure-footed as I used to be. Can't think why.'

'Try to take it easy, Maggie. A fall could harm you and—you know what I mean.'

'Don't mollycoddle me, Gerry. Truly, I'm okay. Now let's eat and enjoy this moment of peace.'

Chapter 15

Meg slipped the voluminous apron over her head and loosely tied the waist ties behind her back. Despite Gerry's whispered reassurances that no one could yet tell she was pregnant, she felt fat and awkward and her feet seemed too big for her shoes. What she was going to do when the temperature climbed and her feet really swelled up, heaven knew.

'It's a lovely day outside, Private. Wouldn't you like to get up and enjoy some sunshine?' She shook the thermometer, slipped it under Wharton's tongue before he could answer then, picking up his wrist, checked his pulse. He had been slow to recover from a traumatic head wound, and his memory was still erratic, but the nineteen-year-old's smile today suggested he was a little better.

She checked the temperature and set the thermometer in its jar to sterilise. 'How are you feeling, Private Wharton? Any pain?'

'Only when you leave my side, Sister.'

'Hmm, sounds like you're flirting with me. You must be feeling better.' She recorded Wharton's temperature and pulse, noting the improvements. Doc would be around soon to do his morning rounds and—

'Sister Dorset, do you have a moment?' She checked her watch. Doc was always on time, which made his early appearance significant.

'I'll be with you in one moment, Doctor.'

She turned back to her patient, conscious of Doc's eyes on her. They both knew her departure was rapidly approaching, but Doc had treated her no differently, except for this increased surveillance. He'd been watching her like a hawk since the night he learned she was pregnant. Or maybe it just seemed that way.

She tidied the sheets, setting them straight, and, with a smile for her patient, she headed towards Doc who jerked his head towards her office. Once inside, Doc closed the door.

'Am I correct that you're now about five months along? How are you feeling, Margaret?'

'And good morning to you, Doctor. I'm well, though a little tired at the end of the day. I don't believe my work has been affected—' God, she'd never forgive herself if her desire to work for as long as she could led to an error that affected a patient. 'Have I done something wrong? Missed something?'

Doc shook his head and Meg sank onto her chair. Relief felt like— Her mind winged to her day at the beach. Cool water over heated skin.

'Your work continues to be exemplary, but I'm sure you know that, Margaret. I'm also certain if you thought otherwise, you'd have been knocking on my office door requesting a leave of absence. No, I wanted to let you know, I've received word that 3 MRS is taking over this site and I was wondering what your plans are?'

Thinking about the likely changes, Meg nodded. 'This would be the time for me to take leave.' The time had arrived, not like a clock counting down to New Year, but sneaking up on her like a hunter until it was too late to dodge. Too late to change course.

'Come to dinner with me tonight, in town. We should mark the occasion with something more than mess food.'

'That's kind of you, Doctor, but—'

'No buts, Margaret. I'll pick you up at eighteen hundred.'

'How about I meet you out front of *Currajong*?'

His eyebrow rose, a faint disappointment quickly masked. 'As you wish.'

For the rest of the day, Meg moved through the motions, aware that she was ticking a list of "*lasts*". Regardless of whether she left tomorrow or the next day, she was counting down. Determined to leave her work complete, she finalised notes on the personnel files, checked the latest supplies lists, and began her letter to Doc requesting leave to attend to 'medical issues'. That didn't feel right, and she left the letter in her own file, to be completed after her discussion with Doc.

Geoffrey. Why can't I think of him by name?

Self-preservation, answered her subconscious. *Geoffrey* was a whole other level of friendship, which, as an engaged woman, she couldn't contemplate. Although— Was it possible to have feelings for two men at the same time?

Rubbing her forehead, she looked at the time. In twenty minutes, she was meeting Doc and if she didn't get a wriggle on, she'd be late. She put away the files she'd worked on and left two to be completed sitting on her desk. Of all the nurses, she still couldn't separate Gerry and Catherine as possible successors. Early on, Gerry had seemed flighty, but her friend had a core of goodness and strength and paid attention to others' needs. Catherine was the more organised of the two, but Meg wasn't certain she saw beneath the professional veneer as well as Gerry. If only they could both do the job.

Setting her chair under the desk, Meg switched off the desk lamp and closed the door.

***

Doc parked the jeep across the road from the quaintly neo-Byzantine Queen's Hotel on The Strand and strode to Meg's side, offering her his arm to alight.

'What a beautiful building, but I hope they don't leave the lights glowing like that after dark.'

'I shouldn't think they do. Since the raids last month, regulations have been tightened.' He led her inside and they were taken to a table with an outlook over The Strand. Meg set her handbag at her feet and glanced through the window. The sun had set as they left *Currajong* and Magnetic Island was melting into the darkness. Soon, the curtains would be drawn and the view, lost.

'I thought it would be easier to talk away from the hospital.' Doc raised a glass of whisky and tapped it against Meg's water glass. 'I hear the roast is good, and the management still seems to have no problem sourcing vegetables, despite the shortages mentioned in news articles.'

Plenty of Allied personnel filled the restaurant, but Meg saw no locals at the tables. 'I wonder if that's because their customers are mostly army? I've noticed more and more private gardens around the hospital have pulled out their flower beds and planted veggies.'

Doc looked around. 'Possibly. I imagine the army claims a lot of the supplies before they ever reach the locals. Townsville has become a defence forces town.'

'It must be tough for those not in the services. Even between the allied groups there are problems over perceived rights.' Meg thought about the ugly scene she and Gerry had witnessed after going to see a movie in town. Walking to a local café for coffee after they came out, the sounds of men shouting had drawn them a little way along the street. In front of a building boasting a shaded red light, half a dozen Aussie and Yankee soldiers were throwing punches, egged on by their mates. Gerry had grabbed her arm and hustled her back to the café. 'Maybe that explains the fights breaking out around the harbour. And the increasing numbers in the VD ward.'

Doc raised his eyebrows but made no comment. 'How's your fiancé?'

Like Gerry, Doc probably thought the harbour was the last place two nurses should be. Thankful to have avoided a lecture, she went with the change of subject. 'He said he was fine in his last letter.' But when had that been? Longer ago than Meg could remember. She sipped her water and frowned. 'It's been a while.'

'Don't worry too much, Margaret. Mail gets held up all the time, but—he knows about your baby, doesn't he? You told him?'

'Yes, and I had a letter from him after that although—' Thinking about the timing of Seamus's last letter, the loving words he'd written had been no different from his early letters, and she didn't think the censors would have blacked out references to her baby. 'I wondered if that letter arrived after he sent his.'

'He didn't mention your baby?'

She shook her head slowly. 'I haven't had another letter since then.' Oh dear God, was that it? Seamus had changed his mind about loving her? Marrying her? Chills ran through her body, freezing her heart, her mind. She didn't even feel nauseous because every part of her had numbed. Had word of her baby frightened him away?

'Margaret—' Doc covered her hand where it lay beside her water glass. 'Your skin is so cold. He'll be okay. Don't worry. Here, drink this.'

She took the glass he held up and drank—and coughed. 'That's whisky.' More coughing, then she grabbed her water and drank. 'I shouldn't be drinking alcohol.'

'Don Newton's advice I presume. It was only a sip. At least now you have some colour back in your cheeks. You thought the worst, didn't you, but you would have heard if anything had happened to him. That's the one sort of mail that always come through.'

Meg stared at Doc. Comprehension was slow in coming, but when it did, fresh waves of denial flowed. Her hand slipped to her belly, protecting her unborn child from the worst. 'I thought perhaps he'd changed his mind, but he could have been wounded. Why didn't I think of that first?'

Knowing Seamus for such a short time, falling in love with him so hard and fast that she'd tossed aside her beliefs and made love before she wore his wedding ring—these things had been slowly eating away at her certainty of his love. Now Doc had given her a different set of concerns. She met Doc's worried eyes.

His gaze was intense. 'Margaret, I—' for only the second time since she'd come to know him, Doc was lost for words. He looked down at the table and, picking up his whisky, drank. Clearing his throat, he reached again for her hand and looked into her eyes.

The strangest feeling of déjà vu came over Meg and then—

'Margaret, should either of those eventualities come to pass, God forbid, I would be honoured if you would become my wife. I have feelings for you, perhaps not love, not yet, but I have the greatest respect for you and would go into our marriage knowing about your baby.'

How did one respond to an offer of marriage when one was already engaged, but to a fiancé from whom one hadn't heard since sharing news of the child they had created?

'Please don't feel you have to answer me. I'm not asking you to marry me tonight, but I want you to know I would like you to, if you find yourself—available.'

Holding his gaze had never felt so difficult, or so necessary. 'Thank you, Geoffrey. You are a good and kind man—'

'I sense a *but* coming.'

She shook her head. 'No *but*. To be honest, I can't think beyond the fact I haven't heard from Seamus in some time. Of course, there are plenty of reasons why that may be so.'

He bowed his head for a moment then nodded. 'A proposal that isn't a proposal isn't what a woman wants to hear. I simply wish you to know I am here, *if* your situation changes. We deal very well together. Should it come to pass that we were to marry and you wished to continue working, I would support your choice.'

'Then *should* my situation change, please know I won't hold you to tonight's offer, but I would be happy to hear it again—if you still feel the same.'

'You can count on it.' Doc's smile rose on one side, wry and aware that he could expect no more than this.

'Two roast beefs, sir. More drinks?'

The appearance of the waitress with their dinner put an end to their strange discussion, but Doc's offer gave Meg much to think about. Her appetite had returned, but she cut her meal into small pieces and took her time, chatting about less consequential matters. Like her imminent departure and the best reasons to give to HQ.

Meg woke to an insistent pain in her lower abdomen. She caught her breath and pressed her lips together, stifling the groan that welled within her. Swinging her feet out of bed and into her shoes, she groped for her torch, grabbed her dressing gown from the foot of her bed and staggered to the door.

'Maggie, are you okay?' Gerry's whisper cut through the fog of pain.

'Hurts.' Meg bent over and clutched her stomach.

Gerry jumped out of bed and set her arms around Meg's shoulders. 'Come outside.' Gerry grabbed her dressing gown and led Meg from the hut, down to the shaded single light in the mess. Sitting Meg on a bench, her friend hunkered down in front of her and gripped her hands. 'Now talk to me. Tell me what you're feeling. Is the pain sharp or niggling?'

'Heavy, like pressure building. Oh God, am I losing my baby?'

Gerry frowned, stood and reached towards Meg's stomach, stopping short as she made eye contact. 'May I?'

Meg nodded and Gerry helped her lie back on the bench then felt her stomach. Stretched out, the pain seemed to settle in one area, easing a little with Gerry's gentle probing.

'Did you eat a big meal tonight?'

'Bigger than normal, yes. It was the first time I've actually felt like eating since early on.'

'And you haven't had any bleeding?' Gerry's fingers settled around her wrist, checking her pulse.

At Meg's shake of her head Gerry sat beside her. 'Gas. Most likely the unfamiliar big meal has put pressure on the surrounding organs, including your stomach. It feels a bit bloated. Big meals can give you constipation and gas, especially during the middle and late stages of your pregnancy. I saw women come in with similar symptoms often enough during my time on the maternity ward. The solution is easy. Instead of three regular meals, try eating smaller and more frequent meals. And drink plenty of water.'

'You're sure my baby's fine?' But the question was moot. Gerry's explanation made sense now Meg had stopped panicking and listened to her body.

'I'm as sure as I can be. I'll get you some water. Wait there.'

Meg released a long shuddery breath and closed her eyes. Hands splayed over her baby bump, she wondered about the other changes in her body. As a nurse she'd thought she knew a lot about most areas of medicine, but her own pregnancy had revealed gaps in her training. What else didn't she know about having a baby? What else should she have known that, if she were home—and married—her mother might have shared with her?

Gerry was back quickly with water. 'I don't want to assume here but you said your training was mostly in theatre and general ward work before that. Anything I can help with, in your pregnancy I mean, just ask.'

Meg sat up and accepted the mug. 'That's part of my problem; I don't know what I don't know. Maybe when I'm in Brisbane I should find some pamphlets on what to do and how to prepare for my baby's birth.' She drank half the contents, surprised at how thirsty she was. 'I've been feeling pretty good since the morning sickness disappeared. This—*gas*—it threw me. I wish I'd done a stint in maternity like you so I knew more.'

'You've done really well so far. But Maggie, it might be time to consider taking leave. Have you seen your ankles lately?'

'Ugh. My ankles have let me know they're not happy with me, but yes, I will be leaving soon. I spoke with Doc tonight about my departure.'

'Good.' Gerry slid her a sideways look. Nonchalant, it wasn't, and given what Gerry thought she knew about Doc, Meg knew what was coming.

'How did Doc take it?'

'He asked if I'd heard from Seamus and I reacted badly. It's been way too long since I had a letter. I hadn't realised just how long. We've been so busy and time slips by faster than the blink of an eye and—'

'I know we're busy. Get back to Doc. How did he take it when you told him you were expecting?'

Meg sucked in a deep breath. 'Please don't be cross. He figured it out the night of the Oonoonba bombing when we deserted the jeep and flung ourselves to the ground. I slipped and he grabbed me and—well, I might not be very big yet but he's a doctor.'

Gerry's eyes widened and she gave a long drawn-out *hmmm* that clearly meant *I told you so*. 'So, Doc said nothing and let you keep working. Here. *With him*.'

'He's been keeping an eye on me since then.'

'Since I first met you, you mean. I swear if you weren't engaged, Doc would have asked you out.'

'He kind of did last night.'

'Oh. My. Goodness.'

'That sounds really odd. You probably think I've encouraged him. I haven't, not at all. But we were talking about me leaving and why Seamus might not have replied to my letter about the baby. I thought Seamus may have realised he didn't love me and didn't want to get married. Doc suggested he may not be able to write if he was wounded.'

'That makes sense. You would have heard if he was KIA.'

'In a selfish way, I hope a wound is the reason why I haven't heard from him.'

'I'll wound him myself if he's changed his mind.' Gerry squeezed her hand. 'You're in love with him though, so why would you think he doesn't want to marry you?'

'Everything happened so quickly between Seamus and me and I guess I need reassurance that we aren't just another side story of the war.'

Gerry nudged Meg. 'If you weren't so gassy and pregnant, I'd shake you for thinking that. Seriously, Maggie, I doubt *you* would make such a mistake about Seamus. You're practical and sensible and—'

'And in love.'

'That too.'

'Don't they say love is blind? What if I—misunderstood Seamus's attentions and let myself get caught up in the whole wartime romance thing. Picnicking under a tropical moon, the pressure of knowing one or both of us could be posted elsewhere in the blink of an eye?' Second-guessing why Seamus hadn't written had done awful things to her self-confidence. 'How well do I really know my fiancé?'

'How well do any of us know each other? You liked what you saw of him enough to accept his proposal.'

The speed of her courtship, if those weeks in Adelaide River could be so called, stunned Meg. 'Everything is different during a war. Emotions are more intense. Time is condensed.'

She frowned. 'Actually, I'm not sure *condensed* is the right word. Time saunters and strolls and then suddenly it gallops like a horse in the Melbourne Cup. It doesn't run smoothly like it used to. Nothing is like it was.'

'No, it isn't, and I don't think it will ever be the same again.'

They sat quiet and companionable while Meg's thoughts chased each other through her mind without settling on an answer.

'Do you doubt Seamus is true?'

Gerry's question could have popped out of Meg's brain. She set one foot on the bench, wrapped her arms around her leg and rested her chin on her knee. 'Of course, I don't want to think that. But—it is possible. There's another thing. What if he picked up on something in my letters?'

'*Something* as in—what?' Gerry's eyes narrowed, perhaps sensing Meg's turmoil.

Resting her cheek on her knee Meg wondered about the power of night. Caught in this dim patch of light enveloped by darkness was like she imagined a Catholic confessional to be, with Gerry as the priest. Or maybe it was less Catholic and her friend was an ancient high priestess. Either way, spilling her guts released some of her fears. 'I like Doc. I respect his work, but maybe I've written too much about him when I only meant to describe what's happened in the hospital. What if Seamus thinks I've fallen for a man who's with me every day?'

'Hmm. What if you're only just realising that in fact you *have* fallen for Doc like I'm sure he's fallen for you? Would that be such a terrible thing?'

'Yes, when I'm carrying another man's child.'

'Doc knows about the baby, and yet he still invited you out. That has to tell you something.'

Meg met Gerry's gaze and drew a deep breath. 'Doc proposed.'

'What—' Gerry was thunderstruck, wordless in a very un-Gerry-like way. Because the news had changed how she saw Meg?

'His proposal was in the sense of *he'd like to marry me, but only if the worst had happened.* Something like that. Well?'

Gerry could have been the poster for *stunned mullet*, she was so quiet.

'Talk to me. Tell me I haven't done anything wrong.'

Shaking her head, Gerry blinked. 'I've always said Doc is a decent man, but that is some proposal. You're engaged to another man and having his baby and Doc was still able to propose and make it seem—special.'

'You don't think I'm to blame?'

'Not at all, sweet Maggie. You've behaved like a paragon. So has Doc, but wow! —that is some attraction he has for you.'

'It should feel all kinds of wrong, but it doesn't. It just feels—*nice.*'

'He loves you. I told you he'd fallen for you.'

'Actually, he said he has feelings for me—maybe not love yet, but he respects me and, what's really important to me, he would be fine with me continuing to work if we were to marry. It came as a shock.'

'What answer did you give him?'

'I thanked him and said I couldn't think beyond waiting to hear from Seamus. He was—accepting of that. Gerry, can I ask you something?'

'About the baby? Ask away.'

'No, about men. I've done nothing to lead Doc on. I've been faithful to Seamus and I still intend to marry him, but— Do you think it's possible to be in love with two men at the same time?'

Gerry leaned back against the table and tipped her head in thought. 'I think it's possible. Who's to say we can only love one person at a time?' She pinned Meg with a look that bored right through to her heart. 'Are you saying you might have feelings for Doc too?'

'Maybe? Or maybe I'm feeling mellow because he's a good

and kind man who, for whatever reason, seems to care about me.'
She set her foot down and stood, tugging the belt of her dressing
gown tighter. 'I'm sorry I woke you before, but thanks for the
midnight medical consultation, and Gerry—thanks for being the best
friend a woman could ask for. I'm going to miss you.'

Gerry slipped her arm through Meg's and together they left
the mess tent. 'I'll miss you too but leaving is the best thing for both
you and your baby. By the way, I've had a letter from my friend, the
nun. Sister Rosemary. She invited you to meet her at Magdalen
House when you get to Brisbane and she'll let you know if she's
found a home for your baby.'

Meg gripped Gerry's hand where it rested on her arm. 'How
can I thank you for all your help?'

'Gerry is a great name for a girl or a boy.' She winked and
patted Meg's hand, making a hand sandwich. 'Seriously, I have a
widowed aunt who would love to fuss over you. She lives on
Brunswick Street near New Farm Park.'

'I'll look her up when I get there.'

Chapter 16

Brisbane

Heading south, rushing towards a new life she wasn't ready for, the train whistle was too cheerful for Meg's mood as she looked through the window. Cane fields and small settlements and occasional glimpses of a distant blue ocean passed by beyond the window frame, but nothing lightened her low spirits.

Although, she reminded herself, Doc *had* managed to arrange 'leave' from duty for her to travel to Brisbane for 'medical treatment'. With any other superior officer—she supposed that included everyone who hadn't proposed to her—she'd have been sent away as soon as her pregnancy had become known. For that, she must be grateful. Given the expectation that a woman would be married before she had a child, most didn't have a choice to keep working once they were married.

Except army nurses.

Was that meant to include nurses in other arms of the services?

Frowning, she took out and unfolded the newspaper cutting Mum had clipped from the *Newcastle Morning Herald and Miners' Advocate* from mid-June:

MARRIED ARMY NURSES
CAN KEEP JOBS
MELBOURNE
Tuesday. - Australian Army nurses who are already married or who marry while in the service may retain their appointments in the A.A.N.S., provided their marriage does not interfere with the

performance of their normal nursing duties.

This was announced to-day by the Minister for the Army (Mr. Forde).

Previously, the appointment of a member of the A.A.N.S. who married or was found to be married was terminated.

Under the new arrangement, army nurses may retain their appointments at the discretion of the Director-General Medical Services.

The report was unclear, but if she could find care for her child, she would return to Townsville. Doc had gone out on a limb for her, so she supposed he really didn't want to lose her. She thought of his proposal again, and about how willing he was to marry her if Seamus didn't return.

Still no letter had arrived, but she consoled herself with the thought that neither had she received a telegram *regretfully informing her* of his death.

'Excuse me, miss, do you have your ticket?' The raspy voice came from a ticket inspector in an old-fashioned cutaway coat.

'Yes.' Meg ferreted through her handbag, certain she'd put the ticket in her purse. 'It's here somewhere.' Unable to find it amongst the coins and a couple of one-pound notes, in a moment of anxious annoyance she upended the contents into her lap. 'Here it is. Sorry.'

'A nice cup of tea helps settle the nerves, miss. Just head down that way to the dining car.' The inspector pointed towards the next carriage, touched the brim of his hat in a polite but very un-army salute and moved onto the next row of passengers.

Muttering softly to herself, Meg tidied her bag and snapped the clasp shut. 'Settles the nerves indeed. What does he think I am?' She was proud of her uniform, and her rank in the RAAFNS had been earned, like any serving soldier. Why did most men—Doc not included—insist on treating women as weak creatures?

When did I become so bolshie?

Her mother would look askance were Meg to express such

views, but Gerry would agree and cheer her on.

Deciding she needed to stretch her legs and get out of her own head, Meg set off for the dining car. If Don Newton hadn't recommended a no alcohol diet, she'd have ordered a Whisky Sour and sat sipping it as the ticket inspector worked his way through the carriage. Maybe she'd have raised it in a mock toast to him and said something sophisticated like, 'Real women prefer whisky'.

The silly image cheered her, as did an egg sandwich, and she decided she'd follow Gerry's recommendation of several smaller meals more often in the day.

Gerry—did I make the right choice?

Doc had accepted her recommendation of Gerry to fill her shoes while she was away, but Catherine had seemed a little disappointed when the announcement was made yesterday. On paper, Meg hadn't been able to select one set of skills above the other. In the end, her instinct—perhaps swayed by their close friendship? —led her to choose Gerry.

'Can I get you anything else, miss?' The attendant removed her plate and nodded at her empty Queensland Railways mug. 'Another cuppa, on the house?'

'Yes please. That'd be lovely. Do you know when we'll get into Brisbane?'

Her mug was filled and the oversized QR teapot set down before she got her answer. 'Well, generally the powers-that-be claim it takes forty-eight hours. Our top speed is thirty-five miles per hour, so that's probably right, but there are often delays at switch points. We have to give way to northbound military trains of course.'

'Of course.' Meg sipped her drink. The tea was well and truly stewed, stronger than she normally liked, but it was hot and wet and all that mattered right now. 'What about Ambulance trains? Are they allowed to pass us?'

The attendant shrugged. 'You'd hope so, but I don't know.'

Another passenger raised an imperious finger for attention and Meg was left alone.

Back in her allocated seat, Meg tried to concentrate on her

new novel, delivered in the most recent care package from her mother. But her thoughts rambled and even Agatha Christie's *Evil Under the Sun* couldn't hold her attention. It dropped into her lap and she turned to the window, watching the long day pass into a gradual fading into night.

***

Meg had almost reached the river end of Brunswick Street when she stopped to check the address on the slip of paper. The second to last house was a beautiful Queenslander set high on stumps with bull-nosed roofing shading wide, deep verandas around which Cupids frolicked in wrought iron railings. If this was her destination, Gerry's aunt must be well to do.

The address matched the street number on the letterbox and Meg looked more closely at the home. How wonderfully cool it would be sitting out on the veranda in the summer heat.

If Gerry's aunt has room for me.

Meg set a hand in the small of her back and stretched. After walking from the railway station her feet were sore and her back ached and she prayed Gerry's aunt, who lived across from New Farm Park at the river end of Brunswick Street, was expecting her. Otherwise, she might curl up in a ball beneath one of the massive Moreton Bay fig trees and never get up.

Cream frangipani overhung the front fence and, on the river side of the garden, magenta bougainvillaea provided a bright splash of colour. Behind the house a huge mango tree shaded much of the back yard, but the front garden beds were filled with vegetables.

Meg opened the gate beneath an archway covered in purple wisteria, cringing when it squeaked both on opening and closing. Crossing her fingers that Gerry's aunt was home, she followed a narrow brick path to the stairs.

Before she set a foot on the lowest tread, a woman's voice called out, 'I'm coming,' and a moment later, a woman appeared around the corner of the building. 'Can I help you?'

'Good afternoon. Are you Mrs Burnett?'

'Yes . . . Are you Geraldine's friend?'

'Margaret Dorset, yes.' At least her arrival wasn't a total surprise for Gerry's aunt thank goodness. 'Did Gerry—Geraldine mention—'

'That you've come to Brisbane to have your baby, yes, my dear, she did. Come in and put your feet up. Would you like a cool drink or a cuppa?' As they climbed the front stairs side by side, Mrs Burnett tugged off her gardening gloves and removed her broad-brimmed straw hat and patted her hair.

'Either or both, thank you.' Meg removed her hat and fanned her face. The weather was pleasant and less humid than in Townsville, but she was sure her cheeks were red and shiny after walking so far.

'Let me just show you to your room and you can freshen up while I put the kettle on.'

Mrs Burnett showed her to a small but pleasant bedroom that opened via a pair of French doors off the end of the veranda. The single bed was dressed in a pastel patchwork quilt with a matching cushion on a cane chair. A small table could serve as both desk and dressing table if Meg was thoughtful about how she divided the space.

She set her case down at the foot of the bed and turned to her new landlady. 'It's lovely. Thank you so much for taking me in.'

'You're welcome, my dear. Geraldine told me you are her particular friend and she was sure we'd get along famously. She's rarely wrong about people.' Pausing at the door, she added, 'Come along to the kitchen when you've unpacked. I baked last night in the hopes you'd arrive today.' The door closed gently behind her.

Meg unbuttoned her jacket and draped it over the bed end then opened the window. She tipped her head back and lifted her hair off her neck. A breeze, soft but steady, cooled her damp skin. Bliss. Through slitted eyes, she took in the view. Between the trees of the neighbouring property, the wide brown water of the Brisbane River swirled past on its way to the port and the ocean. She drew in a deep breath and the smell of mud mixed with the scent of flowers surprised her. Shouldn't the river smell clean and fresh, like the sea?

Making use of the jug and bowl she had a quick wash then changed into the only non-uniform dress she owned. Grateful for Gerry's dressmaking skill and kindness, Meg tied the wrap-front dress to one side, smoothed the skirt and followed her nose to the kitchen.

'There you are, my dear, and what a lovely dress.' Mrs Burnett drew nearer and peered more closely at the ties. 'Such a clever design to take you all the way through to the birth of your baby. Where on earth did you find it?'

'Gerry made it for me before I left. Heaven knows how she found such pretty fabric in Townsville. That girl has talent.'

'She gets it from my side of the family. My aunt Geraldine, after whom she was named, is a superlative dressmaker. I always thought if either had lived in Paris, they would have been designing for one of the *couture* houses.' Gerry's aunt sighed. 'But Geraldine decided she had a calling and there she is now, nursing the sick and wounded. How was she?'

'I'm delighted to tell you Gerry is now acting sister-in-charge of the theatre nurses at our hospital.'

'Of course she is. That girl is destined for great things.' Her aunt smiled. Picking up the teapot, she poured tea into two dainty cups painted with a variety of pastel flowers barely contained within heavy gold rims.

Meg picked up the fine china cup and saucer very carefully. 'These are beautiful. So wonderful after army-issue tin mugs.'

'They're Royal Albert's *Spring Meadow*. The set was a wedding gift from my husband's family.'

'And where is Mr Burnett now?'

'Pushing up daisies, my dear. He passed away before the war. This current war that is. He was injured in France and his lungs never fully recovered.'

'I'm sorry, Mrs Burnett.'

'Don't be, and please call me Vera, dear. We had a good life. A good marriage, even though it was cut short.' She gestured around the kitchen, a broad, sweeping gesture that encompassed the room and possibly the whole building. 'Reg built this house in the Twenties. He said it would be high enough to escape flooding, and cool through our Queensland summers. He was right—on both counts.'

'It invites one to enjoy the outside while being perfectly comfortable inside. Your husband must have been a real craftsman. All that beautiful woodwork.' Impressed by the attention to detail in the fretwork above the doors and the high ceiling, Meg promised herself she would live in a home like Vera's.

'You're right about that. I spend time outside most every day. Working in one's garden is so satisfying, don't you think?'

Meg nodded. 'I'm not much of a gardener myself, but I love being outside.'

'You'll find spring here is lovely, but the midday sun can be enervating. At least I found it so when I was with child.' Vera's gaze dropped to her teacup shuttering her expression. 'I only had the one child, a son called Phillip. He was the bonniest little fellow, but he died when he was not quite two years old. Perfectly healthy one day and gone the next.'

Meg's throat constricted with pity for Vera and fear for her unborn baby. With all that medicine could do to save lives, why did such things still happen? Why did God let such awful things happen to innocents?

Instinctively she reached for Vera's hand: mother to mother; woman to woman in the age-old need to comfort. 'I'm so sorry, Vera.'

Vera smiled, a cross between reassurance and a grimace, and patted Meg's hand. 'You're a sweet girl to care so, but I shouldn't be talking about such memories. Not when you're looking forward to the birth of your own babe. When is he due?'

'By Christmas, my doctor said. Maybe a little before.'

'Perfect. He can be Baby Jesus in the manger for the Nativity play.'

A jolt of possessive anxiety skittered through Meg. Her hands settled over her still small baby bump. The idea of allowing her as yet unseen baby to be placed in a crib surrounded by excitable, child-sized shepherds was unthinkable. For the first time since her pregnancy had been confirmed, she found herself keen to meet this little stranger. *Her* stranger, the child of her and Seamus's love. The welling of unfamiliar maternal feelings threatened to overturn her. Fumbling in her pocket for a handkerchief she said, 'Let's wait and see when he or she decides to arrive. It might not be until the New Year.'

***

Despite the warmth of the mid-September day, as Meg turned the corner into Chalk Street in Wooloowin, a chill went through her at the sight of the Holy Cross Magdalen Asylum. An oppressive air clung to the stern brick building with small, shuttered windows and a high fence. It had few redeeming features other than its function, but it was where Gerry's friend, Sister Rosemary lived and worked. The nun belonged to the Order of the Sisters of Mercy who, according to a discreet sign beside the door, ran the home for unmarried mothers, disabled girls and infants. From the outside, a less welcoming sight Meg couldn't imagine.

Unless it was a planeload of Japanese bombs descending on her.

A smaller sign below pointed the way to the laundry operated by the inmates and brought to mind Gran's story about spending time in a London workhouse after her husband left them to fend for themselves. Weren't they decades past such institutions? Meg shivered.

Stop being silly. You're not going to end up here.

Putting her shoulders back, Meg stepped up to the front door and lifted the heavy knocker, letting it fall in two quick raps before stepping back to wait. Time passed slowly, reluctantly it seemed; but her anxiety about the dark institution fed on memories of Gran's pinched mouth as she recounted her bitter experience.

Finally, a latch clicked, and the door opened, revealing a sister with a young-old face framed by her white wimple and dark habit. Her gaze flicked over Meg, pausing at her thickening waist before lifting to look her in the eye. 'How may I help you?'

'Good morning. I wish to speak with Sister Rosemary. I have a message for her from an old friend with whom I was working.'

The door opened wide enough to allow her to enter and closed behind with a soft thud. 'Wait here.'

A narrow bench hard enough to be a discard from a church was the only seat in the cool foyer. Faded linoleum covered the floor and a strong smell of carbolic soap and cabbage wafted in the air. Meg perched; her handbag clenched between gloved hands on her lap. Why she was nervous within these religious walls she couldn't say. Perhaps it was the foreignness of it compared with the Church of England rectory back home. Raising her eyes she met the all-seeing gaze of a benign Jesus, His plaster hand raised in blessing. At least it wasn't one of those stabbed-through-the-heart statues casting agonised eyes over the world in the Catholic Church down the road from home. *That* one had seemed out of place at the wedding of her neighbour's daughter. Why remind worshippers of such pain and suffering instead of offering them light and life? And hope.

Footsteps approached, tapping along the corridor to her left. Meg stared at the doorway, hoping Gerry's friend had been found; hoping she had found a home for Meg's baby, although in the past couple of days in the peace of Vera's home, Meg had begun to wonder about leaving her baby when she returned to work. The pamphlet she had picked up spoke about the unique bond formed between mother and baby in the early months. If she returned to Townsville and the hospital, would she destroy that precious bond with her child?

The nun who approached was young, with cheerful blue eyes and a gentle smile as she held out a hand and shook Meg's. 'You must be Margaret. Gerry wrote glowingly of you. How is she?'

'Sister Rosemary, good morning. Gerry is well and doing my job now I'm down here in Brisbane.'

'We are both sisters to different callings now, but we were best friends in school.' The nun drew Meg back to the hard bench and sat, still holding her hand. 'I believe I have found a suitable home for your baby when you are ready to return to work, but I wasn't sure if you preferred a wet nurse or would be happy for your child to be bottle-fed? It's becoming popular with mothers now, so I've heard, and supposed to be better for the baby.'

Meg had barely begun to think of all the decisions she would have to make regarding the care of her child, let alone changing social and health practices. 'I'm not sure yet. I'm still waiting to hear from Seamus.'

'Your husband?'

The word dropped like a stone into the well of quiet expectation.

Could she tell such a bald-faced lie and claim she and Seamus were wed? With Jesus looking down on her, could she lie to a nun who was willing to help her?

Above the door through which Sister Rosemary had entered a clock ticked loudly; ticking away seconds; ticking away her chance to hold her secret. Ticking away her time to agree and move on and live with the lie.

The minute hand moved onto the half-hour with a loud tick and Meg met the nun's eyes. 'He will be as soon as he gets home on leave.'

'Ah.' Sister Rosemary rolled her lips as though she might hold Meg's secret.

'I missed him by two days or we'd already be married. I'm sure he'll get leave before our baby is born.'

Lifting her chin, the nun patted Meg's hand before standing and folding her arms inside the wide sleeves of her habit. 'There are many such *consequences* in this war. Our home is kept fully occupied with such children and mothers still waiting, with hopes pinned on a man's return. I regret your baby's placement cannot go ahead as planned.'

'But why not? If this woman is willing to take my baby—' Dread curled in Meg's stomach like a ball of lead, weighing down her baby. The message was clear; unassailable and unbending in its judgement.

Unmarried mother, unwelcome baby.

Her chest hurt where the hard knowledge lodged in her heart, and she prepared to plead her case even as the nun shook her head. 'The foster mother *was* willing because she believed the parents to be married. As a devout Catholic, she cannot accept a child such as yours into her God-fearing home. I'm sorry. We can take your child in and offer him or her for adoption?'

Sucking in a breath that was not enough to feed her heavy heart or fill the void opening inside her, Meg rose and faced the nun. 'My child will not grow up unknowing of his parents, or of the love we share. Thank you for your time, Sister. I'll see myself out.'

Later, Meg wasn't sure how she made it out of the asylum, or how she made her way back to New Farm Park. Her feet simply took her to the bus stop and back along the path she had walked this morning. The path she had blithely taken, trusting in the goodness of Gerry's friend.

She passed the stone commemorating the park's opening by the
Queensland Governor Hamilton Goold-Adams, which had been delayed until July 1919 because of World War I. So many things were delayed because of war.

Including my wedding.

Why were words spoken in a church any more binding than promises made beneath the moonlight? A promise was a promise, whether spoken before God in a church or in one's heart. If Meg didn't believe that, then Seamus wasn't going to return to her. To *them.*

But she did, as much as Gerry had believed her friend the nun would help Meg find a home for her child. How had Gerry got it so wrong with her old friend, or had she forgotten how rigid Catholic teaching was?

She must have been raised a Catholic to have been best friends at school with the nun, and yet Meg's lack of a wedding ring didn't deter Gerry from being her friend too. How could two people raised in the same faith react so differently to the same circumstances?

Setting a hand protectively over her child, Meg wandered down to the riverbank and sank onto the grass. Breezes blew intermittently, ruffling the surface of the water into wavelets. A branch floated by, its leaves clinging tenaciously to its tip. She tipped her face to the sky and prayed for Divine inspiration. *Whatever happens*, she promised her baby, *I'll do the right thing by you. I love you.*

It was late in the afternoon; so late that golden light tipped the trees in the park as Meg wandered home from the river. Vera was pulling weeds from the bed next to the gate when Meg pushed the front gate open. As the hinge squeaked, Vera stood with more speed than grace and put a hand on her chest. 'Thank goodness. I was hopeful you were meeting a family when you didn't arrive home for lunch. Did it go well?' Meg met her gaze and Vera's voice trailed away. 'Oh no . . .'

Meg stood on the brick path; her hat held loosely in front of her stomach and shook her head. 'Not very well. In fact, it's safe to say it went terribly.'

'Oh, my dear, I'm sorry to hear that. Come onto the veranda. I'll make a nice pot of tea and you can tell me about it.' Vera settled Meg on the swing seat Reg had hung for his wife years earlier before hurrying away to the kitchen.

Meg closed her eyes. The sounds of the city were muted here, and it was easy to lose herself in the domesticity and simple pleasure of being looked after by Vera. Gentle sounds – of fine china cups and silver teaspoons chinking onto saucers – floated down the hallway and melded with the sounds from the river – chugging boats and the slap of waves against the bank – and gleeful calls of children in the park.

'Here we are.' Meg opened her eyes and Vera set down a wooden tray on a round table, beautifully carved in patterns like the fretwork above the doors. 'Nothing like a strong cuppa to forget the worst of days.' Vera poured two cups, handed one to Meg then sat beside her. Pushing lightly, she set the swing seat gently rocking and sat quietly, easy company after the *disappointment* of today. They rocked back and forth, slow and steady, calming, soothing, and Meg's thoughts wandered from river to park and park to river like water flowing to the sea.

Eventually, Vera set her feet down and stopped the motion of the swing. 'Another cup?'

'Yes please.' Meg handed her cup and saucer to Vera for topping up.

'It was never going to happen, Vera, not while Seamus and I are unwed. Our love, this war – nothing changes the fact that in the eyes of the church we've committed a terrible sin by making a baby before we took our marriage vows.'

'So, Gerry's friend couldn't or wouldn't find someone to help you?'

'Oh, there *was* a woman lined up. Sister Rosemary spoke on behalf of the God-fearing woman when she declined to allow a bastard child to taint her household. But she did offer to have my baby adopted through their asylum.' Subdued undertones of anger buzzed beneath her words in spite of the hours spent in contemplation on the riverbank.

Vera's move, turning to face Meg, set the swing wobbling. 'The very idea of— The gall of that woman! Did you tell her Seamus will be marrying you when he comes home on leave?'

'It made no difference. She didn't believe me—no, that's not quite right. She believed I was just one more deluded and deserted fallen woman who had no right to bring a child into the world and expect more than her *offer* of adoption by some worthy *married* couple. As if a single woman is any less capable of caring for her own child than, say, a widow.'

Vera patted Meg's shoulder. 'I've never liked the look of that place, but it's the last resort for some women and it does put a roof over heads that would otherwise have none. Still—' Pushing gently, she set the swing seat gently rocking again and they sat companionably sipping tea and watching the sky darken into hot pink, purple, and finally midnight blue dotted with stars.

'Margaret—' Vera's voice from the darkness beside her had a new note, one Meg hadn't heard before.

'Do you have an idea?'

'I do, though what you might think of it I can't say. How would it be if I were to care for your child?' She sounded hesitant and hopeful at the same time.

Bless Gerry for sending me to Vera and bless Vera for everything.

'I'd say you are a wonderful woman to even think of it.' Meg set down her cup and saucer and, reaching for Vera's hands, held them between hers. 'Yes, and thank you. A thousand times, thank you.' Happy tears spilled over and ran down her cheeks.

Lambent light showed Vera's smile, as wide as the Cheshire Cat's, before she pulled Meg into a fierce embrace. 'Thank you for trusting me. I'll care for your little one as I would for my own.'

Chapter 17

The heat grew as September rolled into October and then November, although Meg wasn't entirely certain it wasn't her rapidly growing belly attracting the sun's rays whenever she poked her nose into the garden or took a leisurely stroll around the park or down to the river to watch the boats go by.

On a day of high humidity and thunderheads promising an afternoon storm, three letters arrived together from Seamus. Meg opened all three to find the right order then settled on the swing seat to read them as Vera came in from the garden. She waved the first one at Vera. 'Finally, news from the front.'

'You look happy. I'll leave you to read in peace while I get clean. Would you like a cool drink when I come out?'

'That would be lovely, thank you.' Meg turned her attention back to Seamus's letter, the one she had been waiting for since she wrote with the news of her pregnancy.

My darling Meg,

What wonderful news! We're having a baby, although I had hoped we would be enjoying some months of wedded bliss before the arrival of a little one. I still hope to get leave and return to you in time to walk you down the aisle before we two become three, but I don't think the captain can do without me. I am sorry.

I've been promoted – I'm Sergeant Flanagan now, with a little extra in pay. That will come in handy since we're to have our first child by Christmas. I wish I could be with you, but the army seems to value my presence more than my absence. A nuisance when all I want is to be with you, but there it is. Also, you should know I've listed you as my next of kin. The captain said I could, even though we haven't quite managed to say our vows. But he knows when I say I'll do a thing, it happens. Not sure if he expects an invitation to our wedding!

The fighting here is (blacked out lines) . . .

I fall asleep each night thinking of you, and before I open my eyes each morning, I imagine I'll wake to see your sweet smile beside me. I cannot wait to make you mine.

All my love to you and our little one.

Seamus

Meg ran her fingers over the writing. Seamus had a way with words; these were so poetic she could almost hear his lilting Irish voice speaking to her beneath the moon at Adelaide River.

'By that look on your face I'm guessing your man has written something special.' Vera set the wooden tray down. Two glasses of cold water beaded and puddled on the tray beside a plate of Vera's latest batch of biscuits. A small but precious blob of jam had set like a jewel in the centre of each.

'I've been so worried not hearing from him, but this one—' She waggled the letter she'd just read— 'this reminds me why I fell in love with him. He's happy about the baby, and said he'll try to get leave so we can marry before he or she is born.'

'That's wonderful, Margaret. But he'd better get a wriggle on or you'll pop before he sees you in all your beautiful glow.'

'Glow? I feel fat and frumpy, not beautiful. Any *glow* is from the heat.' Just saying that made her aware of how hot she felt and she fanned her face with Seamus's letter.

'No, you *are* beautiful. Impending motherhood suits you, especially now you've heard from your man. You've a look in your eyes like you hold Heaven within.'

'Vera, you know how to make me feel good, even when I'm melting into a puddle of sweat.'

'Did you see the parcel on the table in the hallway? From Gerry.'

'No, I came out through my bedroom doors onto the veranda. I'll go and get it now.'

Vera touched her arm. 'I'll get it. Stay where you're comfortable.' Moments later she returned with a brown paper-wrapped parcel tied with so much string Meg laughed.

'By the amount of string she used, she must have sent me the Crown Jewels!'

Vera offered a pair of scissors and sat beside Meg. The arrival of a parcel was an occasion to be savoured, especially in these lean times. 'Can you cut it carefully so I can re-use the string please?'

Examining the knots, Meg found one tiny end of string poking out. She cut it as close to the knot as she could, and the ties fell into her lap. Reaching forward to lay the scissors on the table set the swing seat moving and Meg grabbed the parcel before it fell from her lap.

What lap, she thought. 'I'm all belly when I sit these days.' Not wanting to lose the contents she moved the parcel to the space between them, opened the flaps of brown paper and sighed with delight. She brushed a hand over the finely smocked top, enjoying the feel of the raised stitches. 'Gerry's made a layette for the baby. Look at the baby bunnies in the smocking. They're gorgeous!'

'That girl should open a shop when this war is over.'

'If she wasn't such a great nurse, I'd agree. She's one of those special people who's good at everything she does.' Meg took each tiny item from the parcel, marvelled at the delicate stitching and thrilled to imagine her baby dressed for a walk in the park. She would push the pram and— 'Oh my, I need to find a pram. Vera, where in Brisbane should I go to find one? I've been lying about like a seal on a beach when I should have been out looking for all sorts of things for my baby.'

'I still have Phillip's pram in the nursery. And all of his little outfits are packed in the trunk in there. We'll have a washing day and you can decide what you'd like to use for your baby—if you like.' That brief pause and the hesitance in the final phrase tugged Meg's heartstrings. Vera had taken her lost son—Phillip—for rides in the pram and dressed him in the little outfits she now offered to Meg. Would they retain a hint of his smell? How would Vera bear to see another woman's child using his things?

Vera squeezed her hand as though she were answering Meg.

'It will be good to see another baby enjoying an outing in Phillip's pram. I look forward to taking him to the park.'

A fresh surge of gratitude welled within Meg for the continuing kindness of Gerry and her aunt. She had so much love to give, and Meg began to understand that Vera's offer was as much about her need to fill the void left by her lost son as to help Meg. 'Thank you, Vera. I'd love that.'

***

Vera hung up a pair of rompers on the line in the backyard. 'There, that's the last of the baby clothes washed. I think we deserve a break. Do you feel up to a walk in the park, or would you prefer to stay in the shade on the veranda?'

'How about I shout you an ice-cream if the cart is in the park?'

'Yes please. I'll get my hat and be back in two shakes of a lamb's tail.'

'That long?' Meg grinned. The day was fine and hot and she had all the time in the world to enjoy it. What better way than with a friend, for that was what Vera had become in the weeks Meg had boarded with her.

Soon, they were strolling through the park towards the new Powerhouse where the red and beige ice-cream cart was parked beneath a broad, shady tree. Red wheel trims gave it a happy air and a small blackboard proclaiming the ice creams to be the creamiest and sweetest of all was set at an angle near the rear fender. Pasted on a side window was a faded list of flavours next to the open servery window.

'Which flavour do you fancy?' Meg stood to one side allowing Vera to make her selection. 'Let me guess—chocolate?'

Meg had discovered Vera's sweet tooth the first time they came across the ice-cream cart. Now, she ordered and paid for two cones. Her vanilla ice cream arrived first. Swirling her tongue around the cold confection, Meg almost groaned with pleasure. 'This is the life. How can anything be bad when there's ice cream?'

The vendor leaned through the window and presented Vera's

chocolate cone with a flourish. 'Mind if I use that line, love?'

'Be my guest.' Meg grinned and licked the ice cream mound into a peak. The tip rose high, curled over and slowly sank back into the already softening mass.

They set off in search of an empty seat in the shade and found one looking out over the river. Meg held her cone to one side over the end of the seat in an attempt to avoid drips on her dress or down her front. 'This is so good.'

'Thanks for the treat.' Vera smiled then glanced past Meg's shoulder and frowned.

'What's the matter, Vera?'

'The telegram delivery boy is coming down the street. I haven't seen him down this way since Johnny Oliver's mother got news of—' She left the sentence unfinished and took a big bite of her cone.

'News of his death on the front lines?'

Vera nodded. 'Sorry. The sight of him just now sent a shiver down my spine, but telegrams can contain good news too. I shouldn't expect the worst just because— Oh, no.'

Meg struggled to turn around and when she did, she wished she hadn't. He's going into your gate.' Blindly she reached for Vera's hand. She whispered, more to herself than to Vera, 'Please don't let there have been another bombing of Townsville. Please be safe, Gerry.' *And Doc and everyone she'd known and worked with.*

Vera dropped the remains of her cone and ran, Meg following as fast as she could, one arm cradling her belly. The telegram boy was just closing Vera's front gate when she reached him. From a distance, Meg imagined the conversation and the dread coursing through her friend.

By the time she reached them, the boy had clambered onto his bicycle and headed back down Brunswick Street. Vera was standing as still as stone and staring at the window of the telegram. Meg couldn't bear the thought of the news contained within. She reached Vera and set an arm around her waist. They would need to support each other if they were to bear bad news about Gerry.

'Do you want me to open it for you, Vera?'

Slowly, Vera met her gaze and held out the telegram. Her voice whispered, softer than a summer breeze, sadder than winter snow. 'I'm so sorry, Margaret. It's for you.'

Not Gerry, thank God, not Gerry.

Meg's fingers closed on the envelope while her mind tried to catch up.

If not Gerry then . . .

Vera drew her along the path and up the stairs, sat her down on the swing then sat beside her as Meg read *her* name on the envelope.

Lt Margaret Dorset RAAFNS c/- . . .

The telegram had come for her, the one every woman feared. Swallowing the lump of fear, she slipped a finger under the flap and drew out the yellow paper.

Deeply regret to inform you of death of your fiancé Sgt Michael Seamus Flanagan occurred 18 November.

The Minister for War joins with Australian Army in expressing profound sympathy.

Her vision blurred and the telegram fluttered to the floor.

***

Days passed, and Meg had no memory of what happened over their course. She lay on her bed staring at the ceiling, or rocked in the veranda seat, or found herself sitting on the bench in the park with no memory of walking there. The only constant was reliving each precious hour she'd spent with Seamus at the River. Try as she may, she wasn't certain of the exact shade of blue in his eyes, or the precise inflection in his voice as he told her he loved her. Loss stalked her dreams, and sadness filled her days. Seamus was slipping from her mind as surely as he'd slipped away from life and nothing—*nothing* could hold him to her.

She stroked her swollen belly. Tucked safe inside her body, her baby was quiet. Did he already sense he would be born fatherless?

Bats swooped on the mango fruit in the backyard, screeching

as the almost-summer heat lay thick and heavy in the early evening. Meg knew it was hot because the mercury had been sitting in the high nineties all afternoon, but she couldn't get warm. She hitched the blanket up around her shoulders and shivered. The swing creaked, a soft little squeak each time it began its forward journey. Seamus's book of poems slid from her lap onto the seat. She left it where it fell, the book, with its pencilled poem from Seamus tucked between the back pages. His promise that he would *be*, so long as she was.

Well, she was here, and Seamus was—nowhere. He was gone, never to return.

Emptiness swelled inside her, taking over the space where her heart should have beaten with love for him. He'd promised to come back to her. To *them*.

Such sweet promises.

He'd broken them all.

Illogical though she knew it to be, she was angry with Seamus. Her head tipped, resting against the chain holding the swing seat. Logic told her that, by choice, he wouldn't have left them. Still, she couldn't help feeling he'd deserted her when she needed him most.

She was angry. Empty. Alone.

Her gaze fell on the abandoned sewing on the table.

Vera had kept her busy sewing lightweight swaddling cloths from an old bed sheet, soft from many washings. She'd hemmed the edges in tiny slip stitches that sat straight as lines of little soldiers.

'It's good to give your hands something to do, my dear. Think of your little one and try to find comfort that soon he'll bring joy to your world again.'

'Will he, Vera? Will he be enough?'

'He will. Because he has to be. You can choose to mourn Seamus for the rest of your life or you can, after time dulls the worst of your pain, choose to live again. There is a choice, my dear. Not an easy one, I grant you, but a choice nonetheless.' Vera patted her shoulder, her gaze compassionate and determined in equal measure.

'I hope one day in the months or years to come you will choose life.'

Meg tipped her head back and half closed her eyes. Seeing the park through a blurry fringe of wet eyelashes, she swung gently and cradled her baby through her belly that connected yet separated them. She stroked her belly and whispered to the tiny being, 'Together, we will be enough, my darling.'

Her baby kicked, hard enough that her upper hand felt the shape of a tiny foot. Hard enough and in perfect answer to the question she had asked of Vera a lifetime ago.

No. She wasn't alone. Not with Vera looking out for her.

##

Hours later, Meg lay wide awake in bed. While she listened as the wind picked up and waves slapped against the riverbank, brief niggling pains started, reminding her she was alive and distracting her from the fog of grief she'd been wallowing in. Rolling onto her side, she sought a more comfortable position.

False labour, she told herself. *It's too early for my baby to be born.*

The pains grew more insistent, more like—contractions? Struggling to get out of bed, she stood. Water gushed down her legs and she gasped.

'Vera.' Meg lurched forward and planted a hand on the doorframe. She pulled the door open and called before the next contraction hit. 'Vera!'

The hallway light flicked on, and Vera hurried from her bedroom, pulling on her dressing gown.

'What's the matter? I thought—' He gaze caught on Meg's saturated nightclothes. 'Ah, he's decided you need company now, not in a couple of weeks. How much time between contractions?'

Panic fizzed through her veins like electricity. 'I don't know, but he's too early.'

'Maybe by a couple of weeks. Perfectly normal, Meg. Babies decide when they are ready to join us, and yours clearly knows you need to hold him in your arms.' She guided Meg back to her bed and helped her to change out of her wet clothes. The practicality of

Vera's actions and her calm voice eased Meg's worry enough that she did as she was told, half-reclining against the two pillows at her back.

'Now, you stay there while I set a pot of water to boil. I'll call the midwife and ask her advice then I'll be back soon. You know you're not alone. I'm here for you.'

Meg rolled her lips together and nodded. 'Thanks, Vera.' Slowing her breathing, she concentrated on counting the time between contractions.

Her baby was born late the following morning, a sweet-faced bundle of joy. Meg held her daughter close and stroked her downy head and soft cheeks. Big blue eyes looked at Meg as though she was her baby's entire world.

Vera sat carefully on the edge of the bed, leaned over and peered at the baby's face. 'You did well, both of you. She's a bonny baby.'

'And not the boy I thought she was going to be.'

'Have you decided on her name?'

'Jennifer Mary Dorset. Mary is after Seamus's mother.' Lost for hours in the fog of delivering her baby, Meg noticed Vera was no longer wearing her dressing gown, but properly dressed in street clothes. 'Are you going out?'

Vera nodded. 'Only up to the corner store for milk. The midwife recommended you drink plenty of fluids over the next couple of days.'

The midwife stuck her head around the bedroom door and Meg looked at her properly for the first time. She was a kindly, competent woman around Vera's age, and something about her reminded Meg of Gerry.

'All good in here?'

'We're fine. Thanks, Sister.'

'You're welcome, Meg. Now take it easy for the next few days. I'll pop in to see you both next Monday. Vera, a moment of your time please.' The two women left Meg alone with her daughter.

As she held Jennifer's tiny hand in hers, love—fierce and pure for her child—welled within and, at last, she understood what Vera meant about choices. Her little girl had arrived and they were at the beginning of a new life together, one *she* would shape by the decisions she made for both of them. Kissing her daughter's head she whispered, 'We will be more than enough for each other, my darling, and together, we'll take on the world.'

***

Jennifer lay in her crib at Meg's side, her rosebud mouth making little sucking motions. 'You're two weeks old today, my darling.' Meg tucked the light sheet around her daughter and gazed her fill. Her hand lingered on Jennifer's chest, feeling the rhythmic rise and fall of each breath as she slept. This was what love felt like, the now-and-forever kind that bound her to her child. The kind of love that would hold them together like the Earth and Moon, although Meg wasn't sure which role she filled. Wherever Jennifer was, Meg was drawn to her. *Perhaps I'm the Moon?*

Reluctantly, she turned to the desk. With her daughter settled and a cup of tea at hand, she picked up the letter that had arrived from Doc and read over it again.

My dear Margaret,

How do I offer both sympathy and congratulations in the same lines? I am joyful to hear of the birth of your daughter, but at the same time, words cannot convey my sorrow for your loss. My most sincere condolences. I know how much in love you were with your fiancé, and how much you were looking forward to his return before your baby was born. I am sorry things did not turn out the way you dreamed they might.

This is not the time to remind you of our conversation at the Queens Hotel but know that I meant every word. If I get the opportunity to take leave, I should like to visit you and your daughter in Brisbane. Would that be agreeable to you? I promise I will not press you for an answer, since I asked no direct question of you.

For now, I stand your friend. Should you need anything that is in my power to provide, do not hesitate to ask.

Know that you have my thoughts and prayers at this difficult time.

Warm regards,
Geoffrey

Dear, sweet, kind Geoffrey. Perhaps it was time to think of him by that name. For months, she'd kept him at a distance by thinking of him as Doc, but he had reminded her of the relationship offered months ago. An offer that, for all it was implied, had been repeated without any pressure on her to reply. If she accepted it, Jennifer would have a father. All she had to do . . .

Seamus. What do you think of me for considering another man's offer when you're barely cold in the ground?

But Geoffrey wasn't pressuring her. There had been no formal declaration of intent or love. Just *"feelings"*. And a gentle reminder he was her friend. That was as much as she could cope with for now.

Shaking her head, she picked up her pen and wrote:

Dear Geoffrey,

Thank you for your kind letter offering your condolences on the death of Seamus ...

Black words on white paper, phrases she'd written after the death of her grandfather, when Grandma had been so distraught, she'd been unable to hold a pen. Although sad at his loss, Meg had scribed for Gran, but the words hadn't laid her low. Not like now.

Meg stared at those same words. Polite, social words that

buzzed in her brain, but were meaningless. Kind words and condolences wouldn't fill the emptiness of Seamus's absence. They wouldn't give Jennifer the father she would never know.

What would Seamus think?

The worst has happened, but I'm still here, and now I have our child to care for. Lowering her head onto her clasped hands, Meg tried to think, but her mind was a fog of grief and loss and indecision.

She dropped the pen, pushed her chair away from the desk and strolled to the French doors. Pulling them open, she stepped onto the veranda and leaned on the railing, drawing in a deep breath. Air, heavy with sweet floral scents and summer heat lay thick around her.

Cumulo-nimbus clouds had built up in the east. Another afternoon storm was on its way, and she had no idea what to tell Geoffrey.

Practical Geoffrey. Kind and caring and *there*, giving her whatever time she needed.

He knew she wasn't in love with him, but he had feelings for her.

Do I have feelings for him? What do I tell him?

She watched when the storm broke and breathed in the earthy smell of rain on Vera's lush garden. She watched until the sky darkened, and still had no idea what to write. Where was the Southern Cross? She needed to find it and think of Seamus. Small snuffling sounds reached her, a prelude to Jennifer waking and hungry.

Later. When Jennifer had been fed and changed, Meg would bring her out and introduce her to the same stars Seamus had shown her but for now, her daughter needed her.

Geoffrey's letter lay unanswered on the desk.

Chapter 18
Late February, 1943

'Shakespeare wrote that *parting is such sweet sorrow*, and now I know what he meant.' Tears prickled in Meg's eyes as she kissed each tiny bare baby foot. Jennifer's little fingers clung to one of hers and big blue eyes gazed up at her in wide-eyed wonder and joy. Her rosebud mouth had begun to form the sweetest smile, and, at almost three months of age, Jennifer was the prettiest child Meg had ever seen. 'Why am I even thinking of leaving you, my darling?'

Vera was standing at a little distance, giving Meg space to say goodbye but ready to take Jennifer and care for her like her own child. 'I can't imagine how hard this is, but you'd better get a hustle on or you'll miss your train.'

Meg drew in a deep breath and unclasped the St Christopher medal from her neck. Her engagement gift from Seamus belonged to their daughter. She dangled the medallion in front of Jennifer. Little arms pumped and flung forward, uncoordinated and joyful as she knocked the medal and set it swinging.

'This was your daddy's promise we'd have a life together, my darling. He was so pleased to know about you. I only wish you could have known him, but when you're older, I'll tell you stories about him.' She set the chain in Jennifer's hand and picked up her baby.

Kissing her forehead, Meg inhaled her sweet baby's scent, trying to memorise the feel of her daughter in her arms against the long, lonely nights that lay ahead. 'I love you so much, but I have to go north and care for the soldiers who have fought like your daddy. I have to do this for him, and maybe for me, but I'll be back as soon as I can, my darling girl. Be good for your Aunt Vera.' With a final kiss she handed Jennifer to Vera and squeezed her friend's shoulder because she had no more words.

'I'll write often with news of how she's doing. Take care, Margaret, as I will take care of Jennifer, and give my love to that niece of mine. You have the package for her?'

Meg sniffed, nodded, then picked up her suitcase and walked down the brick path to the front gate. Opening it and stepping through, she forced herself to concentrate on putting one foot in front of the other, leaving her daughter in a step-by-step withdrawal that left the biggest part of her heart here by the river in Brisbane.

The day was bright, her uniform was hot, and her sadness weighed heavily and yet, there was something energising about the future. Leaving Jennifer was impossibly hard but going back to work felt right. It felt like the only choice she *could* make. And even if the Brisbane Line that the Government Minister, Mr Ward had claimed existed, her daughter would be safe with Vera.

The train journey to Townsville passed in a blur. Arms aching to hold her daughter, Meg's mind slowly drew her onward to the work that lay ahead. In the time she'd been gone, her unit at *Currajong* had undergone changes—of name, of command, of personnel, including Doc who had been transferred. All leave had been cancelled following Allied progress in the Pacific arena, and he hadn't been able to get down to Brisbane to visit before he'd left to oversee the setting up of new forward stations.

But he had written each week, kind letters inquiring about Jennifer and how they were managing in Brisbane, and snippets of news about the hospital that somehow evaded the censor's black pen. He said no more about his offer, and for that, Meg was grateful.

Meg laced her fingers in her lap. Her ability to focus on tasks had been affected by lack of sleep in the first couple of months after Jennifer's birth. In one sense, she was also grateful. Being tired had dulled her sense of loss, but even as she battled her grief for Seamus and being apart from Jennifer, her motivation to care for other soldiers now Seamus was gone, gave her the will to go on. A couple of good nights' sleep would see her right. God, she hoped they would.

The train pulled into the Townsville station with a hiss of

steam and squealing of brakes. Burning-coal smells combined with the heat rising off the platform as Meg stepped down and turned to lift her suitcase. Missing Jennifer as she did, still this return felt like some sort of coming home.

A corporal, his arms crossed over his chest and legs crossed at the ankles, leaned against a jeep outside the station. As she approached, his gaze flicked over her before he stood straight and offered a less than snappy salute. 'Lt Dorset?'

She returned his salute. 'Yes. Are we going straight to *Currajong*?'

'Yes, Lieutenant. Corporal Williams, at your service.'

'Are you attached to the hospital?' she asked when he'd stowed her suitcase behind her seat.

'No, Lieutenant. I usually drive an ambulance, but today's been quiet, so they sent me to collect you. I drew the lucky straw.'

'What lucky straw?' Meg asked, although she could make an educated guess.

'All the blokes want to pick up the new nurses when they arrive—' His gaze slid sideways, and he grinned.

'Then you lucked out, Corporal. I'm returning to duty. I was the Sister-in-charge at *Currajong*.'

Williams's grin slipped and his hands tightened on the steering wheel. 'Ah, right. Then – welcome back?' He seemed disappointed and took a corner faster than she imagined an ambulance driver should.

Meg grabbed the top of the windscreen and pressed her lips together. Blinking against the bright, late-summer sunlight, Meg watched houses and shops slide past. Nothing had changed since she left, but everything in her life was different. *She* was different. How would she fit back into the familiar world of *Currajong*? Would it be familiar in its new incarnation, without Geoffrey?

The jeep slowed then stopped in front of the hospital, and Meg climbed out. 'Thanks, Williams.' She was stiff and her neck ached from trying to sleep sitting up for two nights. Praying whoever was in charge didn't expect her to start a shift without time to recover, she straightened her shoulders and climbed the front stairs and headed towards the Medical Officer's office. A piece of cardboard tacked to the door read: Lt. Col. Smythe.

She set her suitcase at her feet, twitched her jacket into a perfect line, and knocked.

'Come in.' The voice sounded older than Geoffrey's, and weary.

She opened the door, stepped into the office and saluted. 'Lt Dorset reporting for duty, sir.'

'At ease, Lieutenant.' Despite the hot summer day, the MO wore an army-issue tie, and his sleeves were buttoned at the wrist. When he stood, the crease in his trousers was visible, if a little flattened by the humidity. Geoffrey had dressed more casually when he was operating, but Lt. Col. Smythe appeared to be regular army, with a no-nonsense, maintain discipline, keep up appearance look. Greying temples and a surfeit of wrinkles made Meg revise her early estimate of his age to nearing retirement.

'You were sister-in-charge until your departure. Your file says you've been on medical leave.' Her superior looked up at her from under bushy, grey-caterpillar eyebrows and his gaze narrowed. 'Hmph. Are you fit for duty, Lieutenant?'

'Yes, sir. Fit and ready to begin.'

'Good. Nothing like diving straight back in. Report to Sister Platt for your assignment. Dismissed.'

Meg saluted, turned smartly on her heel and closed the door behind her, grateful Gerry was still in charge.

Meg stepped into the ward. Gerry was seated at the desk beside the bed they used for patients needing constant monitoring. It was currently empty, but the moment Gerry looked up and saw Meg, she stood. 'Follow me, Sister.' Gerry led her through the back door. At her old hut, she dropped off her suitcase then continued down to the mess where Gerry asked for, and was given, two cups of coffee. Only when they were seated in a back corner did she fling her arms around Meg's neck. 'It is so good to have you back here, Meggins, my girl. So good.'

They rocked in each other's arms until Meg eased out of Gerry's hold, sniffing. Pulling a hanky from her pocket, she dabbed her eyes and nose. 'I promised myself I wouldn't cry when I saw you.'

'Tosh. What's a few tears between friends? How's my amazing niece and my incredibly wonderful auntie?'

Meg blew her nose and stuffed the hanky back in her pocket. 'Loving her role as Jennifer's mother-aunt, and Jennifer adores her.' She took a sip of coffee and set the cup down. 'I have a package for you from Vera, and the latest photos of her and Jennifer. Maybe after dinner we can—'

'Perfect. Now tell me, how are you going?'

'I'll be fine.'

'You look good, Meg. Better than you should after that train trip.'

'Sleep deprivation with a new baby made the trip a piece of cake.' She rubbed the back of her neck and stretched. 'Aside from a kink or two from sleeping sitting up.'

Gerry peered into her eyes, a small, vertical wrinkle furrowing between her eyebrows. Vera had mentioned how worried Gerry was about Meg in each letter since the news of Seamus's death. 'Physical ailments aside, you haven't answered me. How are *you* doing?'

Meg sighed. 'It's still early days, but I will get through it. Working will help. Just knowing that what I'm doing might stop another woman, another family, from feeling like I do—that's a big thing for me.' She sipped her coffee and set the cup back on the table. 'Vera told me I have a choice. I can fall apart and live half a life until I die, or I can pick myself up and live a full life, with Jennifer. I choose a full life, and *this* is what I need to do to stop up that hole in my heart. It doesn't mean I'll stop loving Seamus, but I don't think he'd have wanted me to mourn him forever either.'

Gerry set a hand on her shoulder and gently squeezed. 'Vera knows what it's like. She's a strong woman. So are you.'

'I've come to love her like another mother. I hope you don't mind sharing her?'

Gerry grinned. 'The more, the merrier, especially with my best friend. *And* my newest niece.' Gerry finished her coffee then stood. 'I need to get back on the ward. You're on roster tomorrow at zero six hundred, so relax, sleep if you can today, and I'll see you at dinner. You're bunking with me of course.'

'Perfect, and thanks.' They walked together to their hut where Gerry peeled off and headed to the hospital.

Meg opened the door and looked around. Gerry's red dress still hung from a hook, adding a bright note to the otherwise drab colours. Hanging her jacket and skirt on a spare hook, she climbed onto the spare bunk above Gerry's. With no baby bump to make the climb difficult, the top bunk was fine. She took a moment to look at the new perspective of her old home before sleep claimed her.

##

'Hey, Sleeping Beauty! Up and at 'em.'

Meg's eyelids opened sluggishly, and she found herself looking into an unfamiliar face beneath a nurse's cap. Blinking to clear sleep-grit from her eyes, she sat up. 'I'm up. Who are you?'

'Claire Jones. You must be Meg Dorset. Gerry's been talking about you all week since she found out you were coming back. Guess that means you don't need the grand tour, hey?'

Meg scrambled down from her bunk. 'No, but thanks. What's the time?' She slipped her arms into her shirt and stepped into her skirt.

'Dinner. Gerry asked me to stop by on my way to the mess and see if you were awake. Do you want to eat?'

The word was enough to remind Meg she hadn't bothered with lunch. 'You bet. Give me one minute to tidy myself.' Setting her suitcase on Gerry's bunk, she rifled through for her hairbrush. 'Have you been here long, Claire?'

'A couple of months. One day I was at home recovering from a New Year's Eve party and the next, I was on a train heading north with a headache throbbing in time with the wheels. Still, since I arrived, we've had a few dances with the Americans over at their reccy club. The food's great and the music is good.'

'Good to hear they're still happening. There were a few incidents between the Aussies and the Yanks while I was up here last year. I wondered if they'd managed to settle their differences.' She tossed the brush into the open suitcase and decided lipstick wasn't required. 'I'm ready.'

Claire opened the door and they walked together down the path. 'Boys will be boys. There were a couple of dust-ups just after I got here, but since then, nothing. I heard a rumour that both sides locked up the ringleaders. That must have helped.'

The mess was half-full as they stepped inside, with a short line still waiting to collect their meal.

'Meg!' Pam, who had been in the hut with Gerry and Meg last year waved from a table on the far side of the mess. 'Come and join us.'

Meg waved in acknowledgement. 'As soon as I've got my tray.'

Claire raised an eyebrow. 'So, Pammy has been here since you were here last time? That's good. Anyone else you know?'

Meg scanned the staff already seated and nodded. 'There are a handful of familiar faces.'

But not Doc. Funny how she thought of him by that name now she was back at the hospital. Doc had helped her find her feet and made her time at *Currajong* memorable. Without his support, she'd have been back in Brisbane much earlier, and probably wouldn't have been able to return following Jennifer's birth. She felt his absence keenly, and she owed him—big time.

Resolved to write and thank him as soon as she had free time, dinner passed happily as she caught up with staff who were still based at the hospital, and met new ones.

And when she woke the next morning, Meg was surprised that she'd slept through the night. No dreams, and no nightmares. Just a sense of being back where she belonged.

##

'Letters for you, Sister.' Corporal Davis, who was still working on the ward as an orderly, handed over two envelopes.

'Thanks, Davis.' Having been back at *Currajong* for almost two weeks, she'd been expecting to hear from Vera, but the second letter . . . She flipped both over and read the names of the senders: Vera, and Geoffrey. Tucking the letters into her pocket to read in a quiet moment, she handed him a file. 'Prescott is being transferred to Brisbane. Can you make sure his gear is packed and he's ready to go as soon as the doctor's done his rounds?'

'Sure can, Sister. And there's someone waiting to see you in the office.'

'Who is—' But Davis was already off, delivering letters to patients down the ward and swapping friendly chat with them.

Meg frowned. She didn't like surprises, although Davis would have warned her if the visitor had been important. Or difficult.

She checked on Private Miles in the close supervision bed. His breathing had stabilised, becoming regular over the last couple of hours, and his blood pressure was improving. Reassured she could leave him for a couple of minutes, she slipped along the corridor and opened the door to what had once been her, now Gerry's office.

Sitting in the visitor's chair was Geoffrey.

He rose and turned as she stepped into the room and stopped, hand on the door handle.

'Hello, Margaret.'

'Geoffrey—how on earth—'

'Ah, you weren't expecting me. It seems I beat my letter here.'

Meg's hand went to her pocket and pulled out the two envelopes. 'I'm guessing this is it? The mail just arrived. How are you?' She'd missed his calm presence when she arrived back at the hospital, and the smile he reserved for her, the one that lit his face from within. But now he was here, her feelings zipped all over the place. Folding her hands over her stomach, she looked at him. A few

more crinkles fanned from his eyes, but it had only been—what –
five or six months since their last dinner together?

'It's lovely to see you, of course. I just wasn't expecting . . .
Would you like a cup of tea? But no, I can't leave Private Miles for
more than a few minutes.'

'Margaret, don't worry about tea. I knew you'd be busy, but I
wanted to call in and see how you are, and invite you out to dinner,
if you aren't on duty tonight. It looks like you're on day duty so I'm
in luck.'

'Yes, I—' Meg closed her mouth. Seeing him now, for the
first time since the news of Seamus's death, threw her. His offer to
wed her *should the worst happen, God forbid*, hung in the air
between them. She had no idea how she felt about him, having
thought the occasion would never arise. What should she say?

'It's fine. I'm here as your friend. I'm here to attend a
conference, and I have a couple of days off. Catching up with you
seemed like the nicest way of spending some of that time. So—
would you like to have dinner with me?'

No pressure. We're friends. That's safe.

She sucked in a deep breath. *I can do this.*

'I'd enjoy that, thank you. What time?'

'I'll call for you at six. Will that be enough time to get ready
after your shift ends?' His gaze was steady and seemed to her
anxious mind nothing other than friendly.

The tightness in her chest eased, and she smiled. 'Six is good.
I'm owed a night off. Thank you for the invitation.'

##

Gerry signed off on Meg's leave pass with a huge smile on
her face. 'Doc's first leave in ages and he's come to see you. Are
you sure you don't want to borrow my dress?'

'Don't stress me out like that, Gerry. It's just good friends
catching up. Geoff—*Doc* didn't make it down to Brisbane before his
transfer; that's all this is.'

'I know, but hey, don't rush home.'

Meg took the pass from Gerry and frowned. 'You've extended the time to midnight, why?'

'I want you to have a wonderful night, that's why. Don't overthink everything. You haven't asked for any leave since you got here. You deserve tonight. Just enjoy the evening.'

Now, Meg stood on the footpath and adjusted her hat for the umpteenth time as she waited for Geoffrey. Despite Gerry's excitement, Meg's emotions were nowhere near excited. They were all over the shop. She wanted to spend time with Geoffrey. She didn't want to be unfaithful to Seamus. She longed to simply chat with Doc and regain the simple relationship they had shared last year, but she feared veering towards the personal.

'Argh!' As she bit off a frustrated sigh, Vera's sage advice drifted through her mind. *You can choose, Meg . . . Choose . . .*

Was tonight such a choice? Would she have to choose between being happy or stepping away from what Geoffrey offered?

A jeep approached, slowed, stopped, and a moment later, Geoffrey came around to her side of the vehicle. 'Good evening, Margaret. It's wonderful to see you waiting there.' He opened the door and held out his hand.

'Geoffrey.' She took his hand—it was warm, smooth-skinned, and strong. A hand she trusted in the operating theatre to be steady and to save lives. A hand extended to her in friendship—and something more?

Wait and see what the evening brings. Gerry had nagged her and then sat her done and styled her hair before adding a touch of colour to her cheeks. Meg swallowed against her uncertainty and confusion. Gerry's advice was sensible.

'Where are we going?'

'I managed to get a table at the Queen's Hotel. I hope that's okay. There isn't a lot of choice if you want a decent meal these days.' He started the engine, but they sat unmoving as he looked at her.

'The Queen's will be lovely, thank you.'

'I'm glad you accepted my invitation, Margaret. To be

honest, I wasn't sure you would.' Then he engaged first gear and they rolled down the street.

The breeze from their passage cooled Meg's cheeks. If her welcome this morning had been lacking warmth, what did it say about her? And yet, Geoffrey had persevered and invited her anyway.

Having booked at the last minute, their table at the hotel was in the rear of the dining room. Geoffrey held her chair as she sat then took his own seat. 'No view of the sea, I'm afraid, but we can stroll along the beach later if you like and take in some sea air. Or not. It's up to you, Margaret.'

'That sounds like a fine idea.' Reminding herself how considerate Geoffrey had been helped settle the jitters in her stomach, and when the waitress took their drink orders, Meg dared to order an Old-fashioned.

'Should I take notice that's your preference for the future?'

'I'm not sure. I've never had one before.'

'What do you like? Champagne?'

'On occasion. I'm not much of a drinker.'

'So—does your taking a step towards a new drink mean you're open to change in other areas? I'm just curious, mind you.'

Meg folded her hands on the table and met his gaze. 'I'm still finding my way forward for now, Geoffrey.'

He nodded. 'I understand, and frankly, I expected nothing less from you. I know you're grieving, and you're loyal and true to the memory of your fiancé, but I hope that time will help you to find a new path. I'm waiting on one of them, and hoping that, when you're ready, you'll choose to step onto mine.'

His words echoed Vera's sentiments, and that simple fact lifted a weight from Meg's shoulders. 'Thank you for understanding. For now, I just need to work to get through each day. I need to make a difference in this wretched war, to feel I'm doing all I can to defeat it.'

Geoffrey nodded and covered her hand with his. 'You do make a difference, Margaret—every day in the hospital. I admire your work ethic, your compassion, your skill.'

'All the nurses are skilled, and Gerry's doing a wonderful job.'

'So I hear.' He looked down to where his hand sat over hers and was quiet for several moments. When he looked up, his expression was unreadable. 'What would you like for dinner? I believe the choice is steak, or beef pie.'

After a pot of tea following their meal, Meg took Geoffrey's arm, and they crossed the road and strolled along the Strand. With little moonlight to show the way, they stayed on the edge as they followed the road north. Waves shushed as they ran up the unseen sand, and a steady onshore breeze tousled Meg's hair, tugging several tendrils loose from her hairpins. The dark night surrounded them, stars filled the sky, and Geoffrey made no further reference to *them*. For the first time in what felt like forever, Meg relaxed.

'Thank you for a lovely evening, Geoffrey. You're good company, and so easy to talk to.'

'It's my pleasure, Margaret. I'm only sorry I've been unable to see you before now. My intention was to be there for you.'

'You were, through your letters. They helped to show me I had wonderful friends who cared.'

His arm jerked a little and he sucked in an audible breath. 'Sorry, I mis-stepped. The path is rockier than I thought.'

'Maybe we should head back?'

'If you wish, or we could sit under the tree up ahead. I'm sure I saw a bench when I drove along here today.'

'Then let's find it and sit. It's nice to catch up, and you haven't finished telling me about your work.'

'As I said, there's satisfaction in starting a hospital from scratch. I like building a team that works together like clockwork.'

'I imagine that's even more important if you're operating under fire?'

'Fortunately, we haven't been that close to a front line yet, if you don't count our side firing rockets over our heads. But I vet every staff member carefully for their ability to remain cool under pressure. After that nurse who fell apart last year—'

'Eva.' Meg shuddered. 'Not that she could help it, but she'd be a nightmare if you had someone with her problems on staff.'

They found the bench and sat looking out over the ocean. Soothed by the sounds of water, a sense of peace filled Meg. 'I can just make out the outline of the island. Thank goodness it's not a bomber's moon tonight.'

'Have there been any more bombing raids since last July?'

'Not that I know of, and I'm sure Gerry would have mentioned it if there had been.' Or maybe she wouldn't if anything had happened after the news of Seamus's death. Both Gerry and Vera had been so protective of her.

'That was quite a night.'

She liked hearing his voice and feeling the deep tone wrap around her, while remaining invisible to him. She'd had enough over dinner of being careful about what her expression might reveal, although she missed seeing the warmth in his gaze when they'd sat across the table from one another. Glancing in his direction, she caught a faint glint from his signet ring as his hand settled beside hers. 'Yes, it was quite a night all right.'

'In a way, I'm glad we shared that experience.'

'You're glad we were bombed?' Despite the lack of light, she turned and leaned towards him, as though she could part the darkness and reveal his expression. 'That sounds—'

'Crazy, I know. What I mean is—' He stopped.

She could hear every breath. Even feel the light puffs of air as he exhaled. The silence between them was charged, like waiting for a summer storm to break. She waited for him to go on. Now he'd begun she needed him to explain.

'When I thought we might die, I was glad my last moments on earth were with you.'

Geoffrey wasn't a poet, but the strange sentiment was poetic. Meg's stomach did a flip. Darkness was seductive. It drew her confession to the surface, ready to spill from her mouth. 'I'm glad—I wasn't alone.'

It wouldn't take any effort to move her hand; just a small movement and she would touch his finger. A small shift forward and their lips would meet. Why was it so easy to consider such actions when no one could see her? When Geoffrey couldn't see her?

His breath whispered across her cheek. Was she going to act on her thoughts? Was he?

'Margaret, I—'

Nearby, an engine revved and brakes squealed.

Bang!

They sprang from the bench. Locating the source of the crash by a pair of headlights tilted up at an odd angle, they ran towards the accident.

'Margaret, check the passenger side. I'll get the driver out.'

The car was wedged against a telegraph pole. Steam hissed from the ruptured radiator. Running feet and wavering torchlight approached as Meg felt her way along to the passenger door and wrenched it open. A woman fell sideways into her arms and moaned. Meg struggled to hold her deadweight.

'Injured female this side,' she called.

'Here, miss, let me help with her.' A burly soldier lifted the woman out of the car. Her head lolled back over his arm. 'Where do you want her?'

'I need light over here. And someone call an ambulance.' Torchlight was trained on her, blinding her momentarily before she shielded her eyes. 'That way.' She pointed towards a nearby tree. 'Bring your torch please.'

The soldier set the woman down under the tree and Meg asked the other man to shine his light on the injured woman while she examined her. The woman was in civvies and what was left of her red lipstick was smudged. Blood trickled down the woman's cheek and, as Meg lifted a curl from her forehead, she saw the source of it was a deep cut. Making a pad of her clean hanky, she got the soldier to hold it against the wound while she checked for broken limbs. The woman had lost a shoe, and her ankle was sprained, but her head wound was the worst of her injuries.

Geoffrey appeared beside her. 'How is she?'

'Concussion will be the main problem. She'll need a couple of stitches, but she lost consciousness a couple of minutes ago. How's the driver?'

'Chest compression from the steering wheel and in shock. Ah good, here's the ambulance.' Geoffrey oversaw the loading of both victims into the ambulance, and then gave a statement to the police officer who arrived on his bicycle as the ambulance was pulling away.

By the time all the drama and excitement had ended, Meg wondered at the timing. She'd been about to kiss Geoffrey—at least she'd been thinking about it, and she was fairly sure he had too. Maybe it was for the best, their interrupted interlude.

'Are you okay, Margaret?'

'I'm fine, but I need to get back to the hospital. It wouldn't do to come in late on my first leave pass.' She kept her tone light, and she said nothing about Gerry giving her an extended pass till midnight. What she needed for now was distance from Geoffrey, and time to sort through her response to him.

'Indeed. I can't get into Sister Platt's bad books now if I hope to take you out next time I get to Townsville.' He took her arm and they walked carefully down the road to the jeep.

'So, you think there'll be a next time?'

Geoffrey stopped and turned her towards him. 'Would you like there to be?'

'I think so.' Meg prayed she would know her mind by then.

Chapter 19

Townsville, late 1943

'Damn it, keep pressure on that bleeder, Sister. And I need a clamp.' Dr Hannington, the new surgeon, was young and lacked the fluid movements of Geoffrey, and the steady experience of the lieutenant-colonel, who had been transferred to Brisbane on promotion. Meg prayed the new man would settle in soon. His first two days in theatre had been a trial by blood and Gerry had sent Meg in to assist today after Pam had burst into tears yesterday.

'It's here, Doctor.' Meg set the clamp on his hand. Recalling Geoffrey's training session—oh so long ago—she considered suggesting a similar session for Dr Hannington to express his preferences and establish a workflow in theatre.

By the time they finished closing the patient, Meg's gown was blood-spattered more than the procedure warranted, and she was perspiring so much, she imagined puddling onto the floor, like the Wicked Witch in *The Wizard of Oz*.

'Done.' Dr Hannington tugged down his mask and gulped in air. 'It's a wonder any surgery gets done under these conditions. They're positively primitive. And you, Sister Dorset, you need to pull yourself together. You should have had that clamp ready to hand over.'

Meg blinked and lowered her mask. 'But I did have it ready, Doctor. I was holding it out when you asked for—'

'How dare you talk back to me. *I'm* the surgeon. *I'm* in charge. Not you, *Sister* Dorset. I've a good mind to put you on report for insubordination.'

Meg bit back the retort that sprang to mind. Chain of command had never felt onerous before, but clearly the young surgeon had an overinflated ego. Helpful suggestions would only get her into more hot water. Longing for the days when Geoffrey had presided over the operating theatre, she lowered her gaze, but inside, she began sifting through possible solutions.

'See that you are up to speed next time you work in my operating theatre.' Hannington turned on his heel and stormed out.

Meg huffed out a frustrated sigh and signalled the orderlies to collect their patient and convey him to the ward.

Davis gave her a look of commiseration, glanced over his shoulder then smiled at her. 'He's a tosser, Sister. Don't let him get to you.'

Really, she should tell him not to make remarks like that about a superior officer, but Hannington was making enemies faster than the Japanese following Pearl Harbor. She allowed a little smile and nod before answering. 'We've survived enough bombings to know what's important and what doesn't matter, Davis. Now, careful with the corporal, as always.'

'Yes, Sister.'

Meg tossed her bloodied surgical gown and cap into the hamper and washed her hands thoroughly. As she turned off the tap, Gerry came in behind her.

'Meg, glad I caught you. Come outside.' Gerry's voice sounded flat.

'What is it? What's happened? Vera—'

'No, everyone is fine, but I've been transferred. I'm leaving in the morning, and I've named you my successor.' She grinned. 'Seems only fair to return the favour you did me.'

They sat under a tree next to the croquet lawn. The area of lawn still bore the name, despite the fact they played volleyball and shuttlecock there.

She tried to smile for Gerry's sake, but she hated the idea that they would be separated again. Gerry was her touchstone, her solid ground when missing Jennifer overwhelmed her. 'Is it a promotion?'

'No. Just a change of scenery with the chance of returning here later. But you'll be back in charge.'

Meg grimaced. 'Maybe not. I had an *exchange* with Dr Hannington at the end of surgery. Arrogant little—' Meg glanced around. Indiscrete comments would not help. She pushed her irritation with the green surgeon way down deep inside. 'I'm not sure he'll accept me in the position.'

'It isn't his call to make. It's the new MO's decision, and my recommendation will carry weight especially as I rather think Dr Rieck fancies me.' Gerry fluttered her eyelashes then grinned.

'Where are you heading to?'

'I've been assigned to a training hospital in Brisbane. Top brass likes our success rate and wants us to share what we're doing so well. It should really be you delivering these lectures.'

A pang of longing to hold Jennifer in her arms again hit Meg hard, but Gerry was in charge, not her. 'You'll do it well, and you'll get a chance to spend time with Vera.'

'And my niece. But it doesn't seem fair you'll miss out.'

'Hey, I heard her call me "Mum" last time I got down there. That was special.' But she'd missed her daughter's first tooth, first steps, and it looked like she was going to miss Jennifer's first birthday, since it was unlikely both she and Gerry would be in Brisbane at the same time. 'I'll give you her birthday present to take down with you. You can give her a big hug and kiss from her mummy for me.'

Gerry gave her a quick, one-armed hug and nodded, but her eyes were bright with tears. 'This bloody, bloody war.'

Late that day, Dr Rieck called Meg into his office.

'Sister Dorset, take a seat.'

Meg perched on the edge of the wooden chair. Had Dr Hannington complained about her? Was she in for what Davis would call a right bollocking? She gripped her hands in her lap and met his gaze before he opened her file and looked at the top page.

'Your record indicates you were the sister-in-charge here prior to Sister Platt, and you served with distinction and calm good leadership through several air raids. Sister Platt has also recommended you to fill her position. Congratulations.'

Meg's lips parted. That was not what she had expected to

hear. Gathering herself together, she cleared her throat and said, 'Thank you, sir. However, I should tell you there may be an obstacle that you haven't taken into account. Dr Hannington. He was considering reporting me for insubordination in theatre this morning and—'

Dr Rieck shook his head. 'I appreciate your honesty. He's already spoken to me about the incident. I told him a few home truths and reassured him he'll learn more from his experienced nursing staff if he listens to them. He won't be a problem.' Dr Rieck tapped his fingers on the desk before he spoke again. 'Sometimes new surgeons who are feeling their way take out their—uncertainty, shall we call it, on the nearest nurse. Your record is excellent, and two previous MO's, Lieutenant-Colonel Smythe and a Dr Ransom, thought highly of your work. Now, Sister Platt will be handing over to you at zero eight hundred tomorrow. Is there anything else, Sister?'

'Nothing, thank you, Dr Rieck.'

##

Meg sat in the mess tent with a fresh mug of coffee and took Geoffrey's latest letter from the envelope. He was good at conveying information that escaped the censor's black pen, and she gleaned enough from his wry observations of work near the front lines to know how tough things were. But there was a sense of the tide turning, and an exciting new initiative that would link the far-flung forward stations with mainland hospitals.

She read over his news then looked at her reply so far. Happy that she'd answered his questions, she picked up her pen and continued:

I am enjoying being in charge of the operating theatre again (although I miss Gerry greatly), but I feel there is more I can, and should, be doing. Please understand how grateful I am that you supported my desire to return to Townsville. I can never thank you enough for your belief in me, and for the opportunities that has provided. One of these is the medical evacuation unit – MAETU. I have applied to join it when it begins in the early part of next year. There will be challenges galore, I'm certain, but the prospect of flying closer to wounded soldiers and caring for them as we bring them safely home feels like the right thing to do.

Whenever she wrote to Geoffrey, she adopted more formal language. Just why that was, she didn't know, but it seemed impossible to change now. Maybe her formal tone was appropriate given she still didn't know what she would say when he proposed again, as she was certain he would.

'Sister Dorset.'

Meg looked up. The corporal who delivered the mail was pink-cheeked. Sheepishly, he held out another letter. 'I'm sorry, Sister, but this one is yours too. It got caught up in the MO's pile of mail.'

Meg held out her hand. 'That's fine, Corporal. These things happen.'

He saluted her and slipped away as fast as he could.

The letter was from Gerry and contained a brief note saying she'd be back in *Currajong* just after New Year. Setting the note aside, Meg looked at two photos Gerry had included. One was of Jennifer in the park with Vera, and the other was her daughter, dressed as a fluffy lamb. On the back, Gerry had written: *Jennifer, aged 1, Nativity play, New Farm, Dec. 1943.*

She ran a finger over her daughter's cute costume and cheeky smile then pressed the photo to her lips.

I miss you, sweetheart. Mummy will be home soon.

Chapter 20
January 1944

Jennifer's first birthday came and went, and Christmas passed without Meg being able to visit. She set out the photos Vera had sent each month and lined them up, touching the face of her daughter in the most recent one.

A hand settled on her shoulder before Gerry slid onto the bench, leaned over and plucked the photo from Meg's hand. 'Let me look at my niece.' Angling the photo to the light, she looked at Meg, then at her daughter. 'She's beautiful, Meg. She has your face, but her eyes—are they like Seamus's?'

The air force in all their wisdom had transferred Gerry from the unit a few months earlier and transferred her back a week ago. She brimmed with good cheer to be working with Meg again.

'I'm thinking she'll look grand in a dress made from that sprigged muslin I had Aunt Vera send up to me.'

'You do know you spoil her rotten, don't you?'

'That's what aunts are for, even if we're not blood relatives. Have you written to your family about her yet?'

Every time someone mentioned Meg's family, her stomach clenched. She shook her head. Secrets had a way of growing bigger and bigger until the truth was no longer an option. 'The longer I leave it, the harder it gets. I can't imagine turning up on their doorstep, unmarried and holding my daughter's hand.' It was surprisingly easy and deceptively hard to write to her parents, and her letters were brief and formal, odd bits about her daily work that might pass censorship, yet hardly the words of a loving daughter missing her family.

'They could surprise you.'

'And the war could be over tomorrow, but that won't happen either.'

'Pity Doc hasn't had another leave since that flying visit after you returned to duty.' A soft elbow nudged Meg. 'It's been over a year since Seamus died. Why haven't you agreed to marry him?'

Meg returned the photo of Jennifer to the line-up. One year of her daughter's life in photos she'd not been there for. The loss of all those shared moments was like a physical ache in her heart. 'Two reasons: I don't know if I love him, and he hasn't asked me again.' Not that she'd share that with anyone else, but it surprised her in odd moments when she thought of Geoffrey. Had he changed his mind, or was he waiting for the war to end?

'Hmm, didn't you tell me he said he'd be *there* for you if the worst happened and Seamus didn't come home?'

Meg nodded. 'As you said, he hasn't had another leave.'

But he could have written and asked me.

'Besides, I'm not sure I'd cope with a second wartime engagement. I'm not sure I want to be married to anyone. Maybe he senses that.'

'What's changed? I thought you at least liked him a lot, even if you don't love him.' Gerry rested her head on her hand and fixed her gaze on Meg's face.

'There was a time before Jennifer's birth and before Seamus was killed when I wondered if I had feelings for Geoffrey. Maybe I do. I just don't know. You say it's been over a year since Seamus died, but— I feel like I'm still living in the shadows.'

'What do you mean? Like you haven't moved on?'

Meg shook her head slowly. 'Like I can't love another man and still be true to Seamus's memory.' And yet, the arrival of Geoffrey's letters brightened her day, and she found herself wondering sometimes what life with him might be like.

And there was that *almost* kiss on the Strand. Would things have been different if that had happened?

A sigh from Gerry brought Meg back to the present. 'Okay. I won't ask about him again. It's grand working together again. We make a great team. Have you given any thought to what you'll do after the war? Where you might go with Jennifer?'

Pushed into the deepest recesses of her mind, Meg had firmly refused to think about the future. Living one day at a time was as much energy as she could expend when there was so much to do in the present. 'Not Sydney, but otherwise, I don't know. Maybe I'll look for a position in Brisbane.'

Gerry squealed with delight. 'Yes! We can live with Aunt Vera and work together. That would be something special, wouldn't it?'

'Indeed.' Meg would enjoy that, and Jennifer wouldn't have to leave the one person who'd been a constant in her life. Vera was so attached to Jennifer, Meg was certain she'd be in favour of keeping all *her girls* together if asked. 'Just—don't say anything yet.'

In case Geoffrey proposes again. In case I say yes.

'I won't.' Gerry tipped her watch, pinned upside down to her apron, and jumped to her feet. 'I'm back on duty in thirty seconds. Mustn't let down the head nurse by being late.'

Meg laughed. 'I'll see you in two hours when I come on duty,' she told Gerry's back. She turned to the photos of her daughter, marvelling at how much she had grown in the fourteen months since her birth. Her life had passed so quickly, especially when Meg's leaves had been few and far between, and the train trip south, so long.

Brushing a thumb across her daughter's image, Meg thought about Gerry's comment. Did Jennifer have her father's eyes? Already she found it difficult to recall Seamus's face in much detail. Were his eyes blue or bluey-grey? His smile—*that* lingered still in her memory, and the way his eyes had crinkled when he laughed. But for the rest—Seamus was blurring and disintegrating like a morning mist. One day he would be little more than his name and a beautiful memory of the brief hours they had spent together.

Eventually and inevitably, she would lose the detail of the man she had loved and lost and remember only the idea of him.

Yet one more loss, one more person this war had stolen from her. And soon, she would have to tell Gerry they were parting again, if only for a while. Taking out the letter from HQ, she reread their acceptance of her request to transfer to the newly forming 1MAETU.

The idea of working as a nurse in the first Medical Air Evacuation Transport Unit filled her with pleasure and a sense of pushing forward and breaking another boundary around her sex.

That's one of the few good things to come out of this war, she thought. *Breaking boundaries.*

And Jennifer.

Always Jennifer.

Chapter 21
February 1944 - December 1945 – Nadzab airport, PNG

Meg lifted her hair off her neck and fanned her face with her notebook. The tent was sweltering in the late afternoon humidity, and she'd give anything for even a little sea breeze that had sometimes cooled the hospital in Townsville, but she was a long way north from there.

'Eight hundred and seventy-two miles, Sister.' The flight lieutenant who delivered the nurses to Nadzab airbase had told her. 'Almost due north from your last posting.'

The Americans had built this airbase, northwest of Lae, after they, and an Aussie contingent, had liberated it from the Japanese last year. Although the base wasn't far from the Markham River, Nadzab was twenty-seven miles inland from the coast, and she walked around in a near-constant state of sweat-dampened clothes. All of the staff looked wilted most of the time. But then, neatly ironed uniforms were irrelevant here.

Meg looked around the room at her fellow sisters. Since last October, nurses and physiotherapists had been posted to 2/9th AGH at "Seventeen Mile" near Port Moresby. They had treated some of the wounded from the Kokoda campaign. Now, she was one of fifteen Aussie nurses selected to begin bringing home wounded servicemen. By air! They might look wilted, but a burst of pride hit Meg as she thought about the mission they were embarking on.

She flipped back to an early page in her notebook. Their training had included in-flight medicine and care at altitude, tropical hygiene, and emergency survival procedures—which Meg prayed she would never have to implement. Ditching in the ocean had become the stuff of her most recent nightmares. It didn't help that at best, she was only a mediocre swimmer. Maybe she should try to fit in another training session?

A swimmer, she wasn't, but tomorrow, she would be one of the first of the RAAF medi-evac nurses the men were already dubbing "Flying Angels".

With a concerted effort, she focused her attention back on Major Allen, the doctor heading up their new unit, who was summing up after days of lectures and some scary practical training. Thank goodness she wasn't afraid of heights.

'So, ladies, in conclusion. Air evacuations are the quickest and most effective way to transport seriously wounded troops from the front line in New Guinea and the surrounding islands. The faster we can get a wounded man to expert care, the greater his chance of survival. You, Sisters, will be the difference to these men, and to getting them home alive to their families.'

He stood at the front of the group of nurses, all recruited from the RAAFNS, and smiled for the first time. 'Your flight schedules will be posted in the mess hall at seventeen hundred hours, which is—' He flipped over his wrist and looked at his watch. 'Now. Check when you'll be heading out. Those of you on the first evacuation flight, get your beauty sleep. You'll be expected at breakfast at zero three thirty with take-off at first light. I don't need to tell you in these parts that comes early. Congratulations on passing your training, and good luck. Dismissed.'

Meg gathered her clipboard, set her hat on her head, and edged along the row of chairs following in the footsteps of three of her fellow nurses as they headed towards the mess tent.

Cynthia, Meg's bunk buddy, dropped back from the leading group and took her arm. 'I'm a bundle of nerves. There's a lot of pressure if you're the first cab off the rank tomorrow.'

'Or the first plane off the tarmac in this case. And yes, there is pressure, but it will be so exciting to become a flying nurse.' They both giggled at her silly turn of phrase. 'Do you think they'll give us insignia with wings, like the pilots?'

Cynthia shrugged. 'I wouldn't hold my breath waiting. The top brass takes forever to make major changes that seem obvious to us. I mean, why didn't they let us start these evacuations last year, when the first nurses were permitted to work in forward stations in Papua?'

'Probably because they didn't have a secure airbase close enough to the front lines back then.'

'Hey, girls, the roster is up.' Two nurses who'd led the way to the mess tent stepped to one side as Meg and Cynthia entered the tent.

Meg stopped in front of the board and looked at the orders. There in black type was her name against tomorrow's inaugural flight. She couldn't keep the smile off her face.

'So, Sister Dorset is *Flying Angel Number One*. Ready for all that excitement and pressure, Margaret?' Cynthia gave her a one-armed hug. 'I'm so relieved it's you and not me. You're a leader.'

'What do you mean? You volunteered for this posting, like the rest of us. That's leading the way in my book.'

Cynthia shrugged as she often did when deflecting attention from herself. 'Okay, I'll give you that, but I prefer to follow where others forge a path. But hey, you can tell me all about it when you get back because I'm not on until—' Cynthia ran her finger down the list. 'Three days' time. Flying Angel number four—suits me perfectly.'

##

3.30 A.M./Zero three thirty

Meg blinked furiously and rubbed her eyes, still trying to clear the grit of sleep as she headed into breakfast. It was such an odd time to wake and begin the day, neither late nor early for a nurse used to night shifts.

Her flight team—how her heart sang at those words—drifted into the mess where the poor cook had probably been up since two a.m. preparing their breakfast. Corporal Duncan Jarvis, her orderly, slid along the bench and patted the spot beside him. 'Here you go.'

As she sat next to him, he asked, 'Nervous about taking your first flight, Sister?'

'Yes and no. I think I'm more excited than nervous, but I'll give you an update when we're in the air.' But the rush of adrenaline had the tang of an adventure in it.

'Eat well is my advice. You won't get another meal for a

while.'

Meg did as Duncan suggested and was finishing a mug of tea when the call came to board. Meg slung her bag over her shoulder and headed out into the grey light. A sliver of pale light sat between the earth and a heavy layer of low clouds.

The DC-47 sat on the tarmac with its cargo doors open and engines revving. To Meg's untrained eye, its snub nose made it look like a flying fish, or a child's model airplane. The nearer they drew to the olive-drab Dakota the more deafening the twin engines became. There was no Red Cross insignia on the plane, and a shiver ran down Meg's spine. Camouflage colours reminded her – they were heading into dangerous territory.

Speech was impossible so Duncan signalled for her to board first. Thankful she was wearing trousers, she climbed in. And stared.

The cargo area was jam packed for the outward journey. She knew eighteen stretchers could be stacked three by three in the modified interior. Nine patients per side of the plane and eighteen in total. Two attendants, her and Duncan, would care for the men along a narrow central aisle. That was how it had been described and how it had looked the day they toured a Dak, the pilot's name for his plane.

There was no aisle. There were no seats. Only crates held in place by netting.

She looked around the interior then, turning to Duncan, mouthed, 'Where do we sit?'

He found her a spot on a single crate next to a stack of boxes and barrels covered by a cargo net, leaned close and said, 'Hang on to the net if it gets bumpy.'

She gave him a thumbs up signal and pressed her back against the wall. The engines throbbed and the plane vibrated like a living being. The rumbling bass note rose as the DC-47 raced east along the runway and leapt towards the rising sun.

Blinded by light streaming through the open cockpit door, Meg narrowed her eyes and clung to the cargo net until they banked over the sea before turning north and levelling out.

The noise of the engines increased when they climbed over mountains whose heads touched the clouds. Peak upon magnificent peak passed them by, with jungle like a green fossil all around. Meg clutched the edge of the cockpit doorway, awed by the landscape.

When they were a little way out from their destination, Flight-Lieutenant Roper invited Meg and Duncan into the cockpit. 'As this is the first air evacuation flight, Kipling and I thought you'd like to share in the moment, Sister, Corporal. Kipling, do you have the requisite equipment to make a toast?'

Flt-Lt Kipling raised a silver hip flask and produced three tin mugs. Pouring a little into each, he handed them around before raising the flask.

Roper raised his. 'To "Meet You"'s maiden flight. Let's bring our boys home.'

What a clever nickname, Meg thought. 1 MAETU was affectionately known as *Meet You*— appropriate for a unit that was bringing their men home.

'To *Meet You.*' Meg drank. The brandy was smooth—and strong. She coughed once and swallowed hard. It had been a long time since she had imbibed, but this moment was worth celebrating.

Looking through the windows, she saw blue ocean that stretched to the horizon on either side. White puffs of cloud floated beneath them, and ahead lay a greenish-grey smudge of land anchored to the earth by a steep-sided mountain that grew steadily bigger as they approached their destination.

Their first load of patients was lined up at the end of an exposed coral airstrip. As Meg climbed down from the Dak, the heat hit her like a physical assault. She stumbled and grabbed the side of the plane.

Duncan jumped down beside her. 'Sister, why don't you wait in the shade under the wing. These blokes won't take long to unload the cargo then it'll be our turn to bring the patients on board. Okay.'

'Okay, and I'm fine. Just a little surprised they have the wounded waiting out in this heat. I'll start checking off our patient list with the medical staff.'

'They knew when to expect us, Sister. The pilot radioed ahead, and all the men understand the need for a quick turnaround. We have to get back beyond the PNG ranges by midday, before the afternoon storms hide the mountain peaks.'

'Of course. I'll get started right away.'

It isn't just the enemy we have to keep watch for.

She dug deep for her *I'm-totally-relaxed-and-know-what-I'm-doing* smile and approached an orderly standing beside the first patient in line, clipboard at the ready.

Be quick. Be efficient.

Towering mountain peaks waited like predators in the clouds. Waited to grab the unwary out of the skies and bury them in steep valleys below.

By the time they returned to base, Meg felt both exhausted and ecstatic. Major Allen was on the tarmac to meet the plane and oversee the unloading of the patients. He checked each man as he was lifted from the plane and set inside the shade of waiting ambulances. When the last patient was disembarked, the major posed for a photo with him, Meg and Duncan. 'For the local rags back in Oz.'

The patient, a cheery chap despite two broken legs and a bandage around his head, gave a grin and a thumbs-up gesture to the photographer before he was sent on his way to the hospital.

Major Allen led Meg and her orderly to a waiting jeep. 'I think it's appropriate to raise a glass to the success of our first evacuation flight, don't you, Sister, Corporal?'

Meg and Duncan made eye contact and quickly looked away. 'Indeed, Major, that's kind of you.'

'We'll do a full debriefing after you've both eaten, but tell me now, off the record, how did you find it?'

Duncan deferred to Meg.

'Staff on the ground were brilliant, and patients were loaded in a timely manner with all care for their comfort. The turnaround was quick. Oh—' She reached into her pocket and withdrew a folded envelope. 'The doctor in charge asked me to give you this letter. He said something about sending them appropriate supplies so they could celebrate too.'

Major Allen tucked the envelope into his trouser pocket and climbed in behind the wheel of the jeep. 'Indeed. I'll see to the loading of a crate of special medical supplies to go out on tomorrow's flight.'

Chapter 22

The war had ended in early May in Europe, but in the Pacific arena, it dragged on. For three months after VE Day, Meg and her fellow Flying Angels added to the more than eight thousand patients they and 2MAETU evacuated and brought safely home.

But there was light at the end of the long dark tunnel of war and, in mid-August, Japan unconditionally surrendered. Celebrations on base were loud and long, but now rescue became repatriation and Meg continued as she had before, bringing home men, and a number of nursing sisters who had been prisoners-of-war. Skeletal and weakened by several years of deprivation, these were the ones who tore out her heart.

The DC-47 took off from Kuching airfield in Sarawak, Malaysia. Meg tested the exotic names in her mind. Already such names were beginning to lose the war-dread that had hung over so many parts of the globe. Maybe one day, instead of war-weary soldiers, planes would fly into such places with travellers for holidays. How Jennifer would squeal and clap if she could fly somewhere on holiday with Meg.

As the plane levelled out, Meg began checking her patients. One soldier had been watching her steadily since he'd been loaded onto his bunk, so she hunkered down beside his lower berth. 'Hi, Sergeant – Westall,' she said, reading the hospital label pinned to his shirt. 'Everything okay? Can I get you a glass of Champagne while you enjoy your flight home?'

Sgt Michael Westall frowned and his gaze dropped, enough that Meg wondered if he was one of *those* soldiers who flirted with any female they met.

Except he didn't seem charming. Just intense.

'Are you by any chance called Margaret, Sister Dorset?' His voice rasped, but he had taken shrapnel in his neck. Rough as his voice was, it was a good sign he still had any. With care, he'd recover.

She checked the bandage around his neck and met his gaze. 'As it happens, I am. Was that a good guess, or did you ask the orderly?'

'You looked familiar, and your badge says Dorset. A mate of mine showed me a photo of his fiancée. He was engaged to a nurse called Margaret Dorset, but he called her Meg.'

Meg's hand dropped to the sergeant's shoulder and she stared at him. 'You knew Seamus? Were you with him when he died?'

More than three years since she'd seen him, Seamus's name evoked a strange reaction: part awe that someone other than her remembered him, and regret that she hadn't thought about him in a while. A long while. And that thought made her feel guilty for not thinking about him every day.

'Held him in my arms while he was bleeding out his life and asked me to find you—tell you he loved you. You and your baby. What did you have?'

'A girl. Jennifer.'

Seamus thought of me—of us right at the end.

There was comfort and an aching sadness in the knowledge, but not the gut-wrenching pain she'd known almost three years ago. Now, Meg accepted she'd moved on. Moving on meant she'd made the choice Vera had spoken about and chosen to live a full life for her and her daughter.

Meg came back to herself, realising Sgt Westall still looked at her, waiting, she supposed, for more details. 'She'll be three at the end of November. She's living in Brisbane with Aunt Vera.' Despite the lack of any blood connection, she thought of Vera as Jennifer's aunt. In every way that mattered, she was. 'I can't wait to see her again.'

'I'd like to meet Seamus's daughter, if you'd let me? I have a letter he dictated to the nurse for his child when he knew he wouldn't make it home.'

'Sister?' A patient near the tail end called for her.

If Seamus had written to his child, Meg would ensure the

letter was saved until she was old enough to understand. 'I have to check all my patients, but I'll be back later.' As she walked towards the tail, turbulence hit the plane. She grabbed for the nearest stretcher and a pair of brown eyes peered at her from beneath the bandage around his head. 'Sorry, soldier, but I'm falling for you.'

There were chuckles all around and an invitation to "Fall for me too, Sister!" How she loved the game nature and wry sense of humour of these men. They'd been to Hell and now, heading home, they dug deep and practised their dulled charms on her before they met wives and girlfriends.

'Next lot of turbulence, I'll make sure I fall your way, Flight-Lieutenant.'

A cheeky voice called an order: 'Present—arms!'

Meg joined in the laughter as seventeen pairs of arms opened wide to catch her. The eighteenth pair was encased in full upper body plaster, but their owner quipped, 'Solid landing ground here, Sister.'

When they landed, every man thanked her and wished her well. Sgt Westall repeated his hope of meeting Seamus's daughter before his stretcher was slid into the waiting ambulance. 'Can I write to you, Sister Dorset?'

Before Seamus's friend disappeared, and before she changed her mind, Meg scribbled Vera's address on a piece of paper torn from the bottom of the list of patients and gave it to him. 'That's where I'll be in a few months. You can write to me there.'

Sgt Westall gripped the paper, gave her a casual salute and the ambulance doors closed, cutting him off from her view. She headed back to the main office to hand in the paperwork.

Major Allen called Meg into his office. 'Take a seat, Lieutenant.'

Meg sat, curious about the summons. Her packing was almost done, aside from a few items hanging on the washing line, and Townsville awaited, followed by the train trip to Brisbane and

Jennifer. The only thing she could imagine was an army snafu, a regular occurrence in these post-war days. 'Is there a problem with my demobilisation, Major?'

Major Allen shook his head. 'No problem with your papers, but we have a situation I'm hoping you'll be able to help me with. Lt King, your friend, Cynthia, was rostered on the final round of repatriation flights out of Sarawak. She broke her ankle when she fell during turbulence on yesterday's flight, and I'm scrambling to replace her. As you know, most of our *angels* have already left. Would you consider taking her place? It would only be for five days. Seven at most.'

While Meg's every thought today had been for her daughter, how could she refuse? 'No more than seven days, Major. Are you certain about that?'

'I guarantee you a VIP flight to Townsville after this. I'm only sorry I can't offer one all the way to Brisbane. So, you'll do it?'

'Of course.'

Chapter 23

Early December 1945

Townsville lay somnolent under a heat-hazed sky as Meg transited through on her way home. To all intents and purposes, Brisbane was now home, because that's where Jennifer was. Geoffrey had written asking if he could meet Jennifer, and she'd agreed. If only their travel times had matched up, they could have had the conversation she was certain they would be having before she got home. If—*when* Geoffrey asked her to marry him, she knew what her answer would be. Jennifer deserved to have a father, and she couldn't think of a better man to fill the role.

With time to kill before her train south departed, Meg got a ride to *Currajong*, where Gerry had still been stationed when the war ended. She'd stayed on to manage the soldiers being repatriated through Townsville.

Fronting up to the Medical Officer's door, Meg enquired after her friend. Vera hadn't replied to her last message, and Meg hoped Gerry had heard from her aunt, or better still, that she and Gerry might be travelling south together.

'Sister Platt got a call to return to Brisbane a couple of weeks ago. Some family emergency I think it was.' The young doctor had no more information than that and Meg passed an anxious couple of hours trying to find a phone and place a call to Vera's home. The train's imminent departure cut short her efforts to get through to an operator. The conductor blew his whistle, and she scurried along the platform, jumping onto a carriage step as the shuddering brown caterpillar of a train edged out of the station.

Reassuring herself that Vera would have let her know if some illness or accident had befallen Jennifer, Meg tried to recall if Gerry had mentioned other family members in Brisbane. There'd been a long-ago reference to second cousins, but beyond that, Meg drew a blank.

With no choice but to wait until she reached Brisbane, Meg settled into her seat and let the rhythmic swaying of the train and the regular clickety-clack of the wheels soothe her and lull her to sleep. She was heading home at last, and for good.

Home to Jennifer.

Treating herself to a taxi was perfectly reasonable, Meg decided as familiar storefronts slipped past the cab's windows. Besides which, she was impatient to see Jennifer and cuddle her, and a cab beat walking in the humidity of an early summer's day in Brisbane. What role would Jennifer have in this year's Nativity play? What would be a step up for a three-year-old from the baby sheep she had been for the past two Christmases?

Excited as the taxi pulled up in front of Vera's home, she fixed her gaze on the front door. Any moment now it would open, and Jennifer would tumble through on her chubby little legs, sandy curls caught up in a ribbon and with Vera close behind.

Meg paid off her taxi driver then hurried along the brick path and was halfway up the front stairs when the door finally swung open. Her smile grew when Gerry stepped through and stood, her hands clasped in front of her chest. 'Hi, Gerry. I'm home at last!'

As Meg's eyes adjusted to the deeper shade of the hallway, Gerry's stillness hit her first. Then she noticed Gerry's red eyes.

Meg's smile faded. She dropped her bag beside the door and reached for Gerry's hands. 'What is it? What's the matter? Is it Vera?'

Gerry pressed her lips together and nodded. 'She's gone, Maggie. She died of a heart attack.'

Sorrow settled over Meg that she would never again see the woman who had been more family to her than her own. In the back of her mind, she knew that wasn't fair, that she hadn't given them any opportunity to welcome her and Jennifer, but oh, the sadness of it threatened to overwhelm her.

'I'm so sorry, Gerry. Have you had the funeral yet or am I

too late to say goodbye?'

'Two days ago, but Maggie—' Gerry looked as though a puff of wind would bowl her over and now Meg's eyes had adjusted to the dim hallway, she saw dark shadows beneath Gerry's eyes.

'How about I put the kettle on and then—where's Jennifer? Is she having a nap?'

'Maggie, they took her away when the ambulance came for Vera. I wasn't here, and the nuns took Jennifer. They refused to let me have her back. I'm not her mother, they said. I'm not her family.'

'Nuns?' Her experience with Sister Rosemary was etched as clear and worrying as the day the nun had offered to adopt Meg's baby out. A chill ran through Meg at the memory of that building, and the nun's damning judgement on her for falling pregnant out of wedlock.

She turned back to the street but her taxi had gone. 'We'll get another taxi and go there now. My daughter won't stay another minute in that place. Come on, Gerry, grab your hat and bag.'

The drive to the asylum seemed long, but at last the taxi pulled up out the front. Meg hopped out leaving Gerry to pay the fare while she strode to the front door and knocked loudly. Each knock demanded: *Give me back my daughter.*

A novice with a fringe of dark hair visible but clipped to one side answered her knocking and invited her and Gerry to sit while she found someone who could assist them. The same hard bench waited beside the door and the same benign statue of Jesus looked down on them, hands still raised in a blessing.

The nun who arrived was middle-aged and her headdress and manner marked her as a Mother Superior. She looked down her long, aquiline nose, which exaggerated the disdain emanating from her.

'I understand you are enquiring about a child brought to this house two weeks ago?'

'My daughter, Jennifer, yes. I want to collect her now and take her home with me.'

'That is not possible.'

Gerry stepped up and slipped her arm through Meg's. 'I

understand that you felt you couldn't release her to me but Maggie is Jennifer's mother. We want to take her home.'

'Sister Rosemary explained the circumstances to me at the time the child was brought here. It doesn't matter if this woman is the child's mother.'

'*The child* is my daughter. Her name is Jennifer. Jennifer Dorset. Please bring her to me now, or do I need to call the police to help me get my daughter back?'

A look of distaste flickered over the nun's face before she schooled her expression into blandness again. 'Call who you like. It won't change matters. Your *daughter* is no longer here.'

'Then tell us where you've sent her, and we'll go and get her ourselves.'

'She has been placed with a good Christian family, a *married* couple who have not been blessed with children but who will raise her as their own. They were prepared to overlook the unfortunate circumstance of her birth.'

'Are you telling me you've adopted *my* daughter away?' A shroud of darkness descended. Blindly, she reached for Gerry's arm and sucked in a breath as though it were her last.

Breathe, Meg. Fight for her.

'Without my knowledge or permission? Against my wishes?'

'We have placed the child in a good Christian home where she will learn proper values and her right place in the world. Unfit mothers have no right to children when there are proper parents desperate to give them a good home.'

'Tell me where she is, please? Tell me who has my daughter and I'll—'

'You'll what? Rip the child away from two loving parents? I think not.'

'They've barely had time to get to know her. I'm her mother. I have a home for her. I love her. Please?'

'You will not see the child again. The law protects her, and her adoptive family. As it should. Good day.' The nun disappeared down the hallway.

Meg sank to the ground, Gerry's arm around her shoulders. There was a pounding in her ears. She saw nothing, felt nothing but a huge, gaping hole where her daughter should be. 'They've stolen my Jennifer. What can I do, Gerry? How can I get her back?'

Chapter 24

Had two or three days passed? Meg was hazy about everything except the pain in her chest. Each beat of her heart was like a fist squeezing hard, accusing her of not being here when Jennifer needed her. Of not being a mother to her daughter. The single most important job in her life was caring for her child, and she hadn't been here.

How could she not remember how many days it had been since learning her darling girl had been stolen from her?

She pressed her knuckled fist against her temple and shook her head. 'I can't remember what day of the week it was, Sergeant, but it was the day I arrived home from Townsville.'

The police officer wrote in his small, black notebook then asked Gerry, 'Did you accompany Miss Dorset to the orphanage?'

'I went with *Lieutenant* Dorset to pick up her daughter. Jennifer's father was killed in the war, and we—I am her only family in Brisbane.' Dark shadows lay beneath Gerry's eyes, but in the midst of her grief over Vera, she was the stronger of the two of them right now.

'And what relation are you to Miss—*Lieutenant* Dorset?' Distantly, Meg noticed the slight pause before he used her RAAF rank, as though it pained him to do so.

Accustomed to the chain of command, and the respect given to nurses by most members of the forces, the sergeant's disdain stood out, stark and accusatory. Did he think like the nuns—that she didn't deserve her child because she was unmarried, or was it because she'd passed off her maternal responsibility to go off nursing? 'We aren't blood relations, Sergeant, but we have been as close as family—closer, perhaps, throughout the war.'

'I see. And the woman who was caring for your child—'

Gerry chimed in with, 'My aunt, Mrs Vera Burnett.'

'She was no relation either?'

Sensing where the policeman's questions were leading, anger stirred in Meg, nudging aside the fog of her grief. 'No. She looked after my daughter while I was serving. I was working up north in hospitals and with a medical air evacuation team.'

'My aunt cared for Meg's daughter while Meg was doing her job, Sergeant—saving soldiers' lives.'

The sergeant closed his notebook and tucked both it and his pencil into his pocket. 'From what you've told me, this isn't a police matter. The police cannot force nuns to release information about adoptions. You'll need a solicitor. I'm sorry, Miss—Lieutenant Dorset, but there's nothing I can do for you. Good day, ladies. I'll see myself out.'

Stunned at the abrupt dismissal of her case, Meg watched him retreat down the hallway. The screen door banged shut before she closed her mouth. She looked at Gerry who sat as stunned as Meg. The kitchen clock ticked loudly – ticking away the seconds and minutes of her life without her daughter.

'This is completely wrong.' Gerry pushed her chair back and reached for the kettle. Shoving it under the tap, she turned the water on hard. 'Jennifer's been taken without your consent. It's like she's been abducted, and he's doing nothing. What does he think the police are for if not to help?'

'I'd report him if I thought it would do any good.' Meg thumped both hands on the table and shoved her chair back. The scrape of wood on lino raised goosebumps on her arms. 'Damn and blast it. If I were a man, this wouldn't have happened.'

'If you were a man, I wouldn't be here.'

Meg turned at the sound of Geoffrey's voice. He stood in the hallway, cap in hand, an uncertain half-smile disappearing as their gazes met.

'I passed a policeman as I came through the gate and let myself in when no one answered my knock. What's the matter? Can I help?'

Something stirred in Meg at the sight of him standing there, so calm and practical. Calm—that was what she needed right now.

Holding out both hands she stepped towards him. He took them, and his touch anchored her. She pushed the words out. 'The nuns took Jennifer. An ambulance came for Vera. She died and the nuns took my daughter. They've given her away. Geoffrey, they took Jennifer.'

Vera's kitchen had always been the heart of her home. Cups of tea and biscuits at the table, chats while she cooked dinner and Meg fed Jennifer – memories of love and friendship filled this room.

Geoffrey looked at home sitting in a chair at Vera's table as he listened to Meg. She shared her fruitless efforts to find her daughter, and when she finished, he spoke for the first time since she'd begun.

'I think the policeman was right. You'll need legal representation to crack the code of silence around adoptions. I'm fairly sure they're covered by State law. If it would help, I have an old school friend who works as a solicitor for a big firm in the city. He was injured in a car accident some years ago so couldn't serve, but he became a junior partner in his firm. Shall I phone him and make an appointment?' Geoffrey still held her hand, she realised with surprise. The simple connection was comforting.

'Yes please. Can we see him today?'

'I'll see what I can do. It may depend on whether he's in court or not, but I'll ask. Geraldine, may I use your phone?'

'Of course. It's on the hall stand.'

'Thanks.' Geoffrey walked down the hallway and a few moments later, they heard him giving the operator a number in the city.

Gerry took the kettle off the stove and poured boiling water into the teapot. She put the lid back on and sat down, leaving the tea to brew. 'I don't know about you, but seeing Geoffrey makes me feel better. He's always so unflappable.'

Meg agreed. 'But none of this is his responsibility. It's mine, and the situation only happened because I was determined to keep working.'

'Don't you *dare* blame yourself for this. You did your bit

during the war, and Vera loved caring for Jennifer. She often said caring for Jennifer was the best gift anyone could have given her. You gave her another chance to bring up a child she loved while you were saving lives, so don't blame yourself.'

'But I do, Gerry. If I hadn't been so determined to push boundaries, to show I could do it all—have it all—' Meg tipped her head back and blinked furiously. 'Why should I be any different from the thousands of other women who have children and stay home to raise them? If I hadn't gone back to nursing after Jennifer was born, someone else would have filled my place.'

'Sure, there would have been another body doling out pills and handing over surgical instruments, but Meg, you gave so much more than that.'

'No more than you or every other nurse did.'

'Aside from Eva who did less than anyone. Come on, Meg. You're a born leader. Look at the innovations you made as Sister-in-charge. Consider how smoothly *Currajong* ran under your guidance. Think about how you stepped up when the call went out for nurses to fly on air-evac flights.'

'Others did that too.'

'You were first in line – Flying Angel number one. Remember? And that is no small deal. You underrate what you achieved.'

Geoffrey appeared in the doorway and leaned against the jamb, his hands folded across his chest. 'That's true, Margaret.'

'Did you talk to your friend?' She couldn't waste time talking down their crazy view of her, not when Jennifer was out there somewhere, with a family who wasn't hers.

'I did. He'll call in here after he leaves the office tonight, as a favour to me. Will that be okay, Geraldine?'

'Of course. Do you think he'll stay for dinner?'

'I have no idea, sorry.'

Meg sucked in a deep breath. It felt like the first one that had filled her lungs since she'd collapsed in the convent. 'Thank you. Did he say anything more?'

He glanced at Gerry. 'Can we talk somewhere quiet? Sorry, Geraldine.'

Gerry shook her head. 'Go ahead. Take a cuppa out with you. I'm going to bake some biscuits; one of Vera's recipes.' She poured two cups and put them on a tray beside a small milk jug.

Meg took the tray and led the way out to the swing seat. The most important events in her life had centred around Vera's swing, and Geoffrey's tone had sounded serious. Setting the tray down, she handed a cup of black tea to Geoffrey, added milk to the other and sat beside him.

'I gave Roger, my solicitor friend, a brief outline of your situation. He believes he can help—' Geoffrey set his cup on the tray. Turning sideways, he caught Meg's gaze.

'I sense a 'but' coming. Tell me, Geoffrey. What's the catch?'

'He feels a judge will probably be more amenable to finding in your favour—if you're married.'

There was weight and waiting in his gaze, and sadness. She hadn't expected that. 'Are you suggesting—'

'This isn't the way I planned to ask you, Margaret. I've been waiting a long time— For your grief to ease. For the war to end. Perhaps I shouldn't have waited so long, because now, you might feel you have no choice. I never wanted that for you, but—' He went down on one knee and took her hand in his.

Never in her wildest dreams could Meg have imagined these circumstances for Geoffrey's proposal. She'd considered other settings; the Strand after a dinner at the Queen's Hotel in Townsville had been top of her list, or even a drive up to the heights of Castle Hill once the army allowed public access again. Every imagined setting always had Townsville as the backdrop since it was the only place she had known Geoffrey.

She looked at him kneeling before her, holding her hand, and panic fluttered through her. He was good and kind, caring, and he'd make a wonderful father. He knew about Jennifer and was happy to offer his name and his help.

But I don't know if I love him.

Time had run out. There was no more time. No more choice.

The only answer she could give was the one that would bring her daughter home. Sitting perfectly still, she met his gaze.

'Margaret, will you do me the honour of becoming my wife?'

'I will marry you, thank you, Geoffrey.'

##

Roger Altmann limped into the room, his walking stick tapping on the hardwood floor. He took a seat across the dining table from her, opened his briefcase and set a legal notepad in front of him. He was the same age as Geoffrey but looked older, and his fair hair had begun to recede into a widow's peak. A three-piece suit and gold fob chain added to the impression of an older man, she realised. Perhaps that was useful when you worked for a firm with an old established name, where appearance and reputation counted for much.

'Lt Dorset, how may I be of service?'

'I thought Geoffrey had told you?' She glanced at Geoffrey. He gave an encouraging nod and sat back, folding his arms across his chest.

Mr Altmann uncapped his fountain pen and smiled at her. 'The bare bones only. It would be helpful if you could tell me your story in your own words, starting with your daughter's father.'

Meg nodded and folded her hands together on the table. 'Very well, Mr Altmann.'

'Please – call me Roger. I can't be Mr Altmann to you and Roger to Geoffrey here.'

She nodded. 'In that case, please call me Margaret. I met Jennifer's father – that's Corporal Michael Seamus Flanagan – when we were evacuated from Darwin during the first bombing raid. That was the morning of the nineteenth of February 1942. We travelled down to Adelaide River where we were both instructed to stay and work in the hospital. The River became an important—'

'Can you focus on your relationship with Michael.'

'Seamus. His father was the only Michael in their family, he said.'

Roger underlined Seamus's name in his notes. 'Go on.'

'We fell in love and he asked me to marry him. I said yes the day he was transferred out.'

'And your daughter Jennifer – she was conceived when?'

Heat rose in Meg's cheeks at the clinical dissection of her love. It had been special, and private, but the solicitor wanted to know intimate details. In front of Geoffrey!

Meg cleared her throat. 'At the River. She was conceived one night before I told Seamus I'd marry him.'

There, she thought. *Judge me for that.*

But Roger surprised her. 'Understandable, especially in wartime. And did Seamus know you were with child when he was transferred?'

'You don't think I'm terrible for making a child out of wedlock?'

'It isn't for me to pass judgement, but I don't believe a civilised society has the right to condemn people for their choices. When did you realise you were pregnant?'

Her appreciation of Geoffrey's friend grew, and she began to feel a glimmer of hope. 'I suspected it when I threw up unexpectedly one morning. That was before I was transferred, but my pregnancy was only confirmed after I got to Townsville. I chanced to meet a doctor who was an obstetrician—'

She glanced at Geoffrey. If he hadn't known before that Don Newton had provided the diagnosis, he would now. 'Once Dr Newton confirmed it, I wrote to my fiancé. He was thrilled and said we were to be married when he got leave. He was killed in action. By that time, I was here living with Vera Burnett, who offered to care for my baby when I went back north to nurse.'

'So, this is Vera's house and she cared for your daughter for what – three years?'

Regret clogged Meg's throat. If she hadn't accepted that last rotation in place of her friend and had flown home instead, would she have been able to save Vera? If she'd flown home when she was meant to, for certain Jennifer wouldn't have been taken by the nuns and given away like a Christmas present to some other family.

'Yes, three years.'

On and on went Roger, drawing out details of her visit to the convent, the nuns who had offered only adoption of her baby, and the shock of her recent visit.

'I understand the convent offers the only hope for many young women and abandoned children, but in your case, it is clear they got it wrong. However, there are laws that protect children, and both their biological parents and the adoptive parents. The 1921 Amendments to Infant Life Protection Act are an important aspect here, and probably the key point we need to address. The Act requires that parents renounce all claims upon the child—'

'But I didn't renounce anything.'

Roger held up one hand and nodded. 'I know, but the fact of your leaving your child to be raised by a non-relative is likely to be made use of by the other side. The Catholic Church is powerful, and their solicitors may try to construct a view of you as a mother who abandoned her child in order to pursue her own interests.'

Despite the warmth of the night, a chill ran down Meg's spine. She'd said much the same to Gerry. Would her friend be called as a witness?

Geoffrey shook his head. 'That should be easy enough to disprove. You could subpoena Margaret's service record. That speaks for itself of her commitment to her patients and her nursing. There is nothing frivolous or self-indulgent in the work she undertook. She joined as a RAAF nurse in 1941 and served in several hospitals over the next three years then was on the first medical air evacuation in 1944. She's worked tirelessly since then to recover and repatriate our men and women from Pacific arenas of war.'

Roger made notes on the pad. 'We'll tender her service record of course, but as a single mother, we are fighting a long-held social belief that mothers take care of their children, regardless of their skills in essential areas. The 1905 Act might also be an issue. It focuses more on the needs, as opposed to the rights, of the child. Every child *needs* to be looked after, and people willing to look after another's child are assumed to be 'good'.'

Bile rose in Meg's throat. She saw where Roger was going with this. 'So, if the adoptive parents are *good*, the biological parent must be the opposite. They'll cast me as some kind of Jezebel and claim I'm an unfit mother.'

Roger nodded. 'It's all about constructing the right image. I'll come back to that shortly. Following the Acts of 1905 and 1921, we then have the 1935 Adoption of Children Act. Now this one is a bit of a kicker. Children's needs and rights to permanent legal parents are addressed. The key word is *permanent*. Adoptive parents are considered much more responsible and stable than biological parents and so are seen as more deserving of protection. Their identity is kept secret, although not that of the biological mother. Adoptive parents are now given details of the mother's name.'

'But I'm not allowed to know who has taken my child?'

Geoffrey covered her hands. 'Breathe, Margaret. We'll work it out and with Roger's help, bring Jennifer home.'

Roger's gaze lingered on their joined hands. 'I hope this isn't an indelicate question, but do you have any plans to wed in the near future?'

Meg looked up, her gaze swinging from Roger to Geoffrey. The solicitor must have intimated this solution during the phone conversation.

Geoffrey answered for both of them. 'Margaret has done me the honour of agreeing to be my wife. We'll be married as soon as it can be arranged.'

'Excellent news. Congratulations. Your case will be stronger if you appeal to the court as a married couple. A major focus of the 1935 Act is on the creation of new family units, of which the adopted child is an integral part. However, once you are married, your union will be seen as providing that element of stability and care, especially if Geoffrey formally adopts your daughter.'

'Which I will do.' Geoffrey squeezed her hands and Meg allowed herself to hope. Alone, it was clear she would have fought an impossible battle. With Geoffrey by her side, there was a chance.

Gerry tapped on the door and stopped in the doorway. 'I'm sorry to interrupt, but would you like to stay for dinner, Mr Altmann?'

'Thank you, but no. My wife will have dinner ready when I get home.' He shuffled his notes into order and tucked them first into a folder then into his briefcase before he stood. 'Congratulations again on your impending nuptials. I'd be delighted to act as your witness or best man, whichever way you choose to go.'

Geoffrey held out his hand and they shook on it. 'Thanks, old man. Can't tell you how much we appreciate your help.'

Meg offered her hand too. 'My sincere thanks, Roger.'

The solicitor took her hand between his. 'Rest easy, Margaret. I will do everything in my power to restore your daughter to you.'

'I'll see you out.' Geoffrey followed his friend down the hallway.

Gerry stepped into the room. 'You've decided then? You're going to marry Geoffrey?'

'I am.'

'So you love him – that's good.'

'I wish I could tell you that's true, but I have no idea if it is. But marrying Geoffrey is the only way I can see to find Jennifer and bring her home. I know that makes me a terrible person, but I have to get my daughter back.'

Chapter 25

Brisbane, December 1945

Roses freshly cut from Vera's garden in the early morning scented the air. Gerry had fashioned them into the most beautiful wedding bouquet Meg had ever seen. Trimmed with white ribbon and scraps of lace, it seemed far too elaborate against her white sheath dress.

But Geoffrey smiled and his eyes looked warmly on her as she came down the aisle of Vera's, and now Gerry's local church. The late morning was already nudging ninety degrees, and a nativity scene set up opposite the pulpit highlighted that Christmas was almost upon them. Desperate to reclaim Jennifer and share their first Christmas together, Meg struggled to focus on the ceremony. She glanced at Gerry who stood by her side, fashionable in a slim black dress and white bolero jacket. Her new dress was simple, but without her friend's sewing skill, Meg would have become Geoffrey's wife dressed in her RAAF uniform.

Roger had kept his promise to stand as Geoffrey's best man. As witnesses, they were also the only guests. Neither she nor Geoffrey had family in Brisbane, and Meg still hadn't spoken to him about her family, other than to say they lived in Sydney.

'It's too far for them to come at such short notice,' she'd said, and left it at that. Geoffrey's family lived in the northwest of the state on a large cattle station.

'Same here. We can visit them later – after we've found Jennifer.' His quiet certainty had reassured her, and his presence calmed her anxiety as they had filled in form after government form to make that happen.

Meg was grateful for his help, and grateful too that Geoffrey belonged to the Church of England, like her, as the minister read from Saint Paul's Letter to the Corinthians. But each exhortation about what love should be cut like a knife. She'd left the choice of reading and order of service to Geoffrey. Was the reading from Saint Paul deliberate, chosen to remind her what she had agreed to? They hadn't spoken of love at all; not since his first declaration in the hotel before Jennifer was born when he'd admitted he had feelings for her. Since then, neither had offered a word about love. If only she loved her soon-to-be husband. When the lesson ended, they would make their vows. How could she say them and be true to her promise?

Dear Lord, please see into my heart. When I promise to love, honour, and obey, I'm promising to be the best wife I can be to Geoffrey. You know Seamus has my heart, but I pray I will learn to love my husband.

That was the only way she could plight her troth and mean it. She stumbled through her vows, and marvelled at Geoffrey's clear, firm promise, spoken directly to her. Did he mean the words, or had he made a similar promise to God?

'For as much as this man and this woman . . .'

The ceremony slipped past, and suddenly, it was over.

The minister closed his Bible. 'I now pronounce you husband and wife. You may kiss the bride.'

Three sets of eyes turned to watch them.

Meg gripped her bouquet, willing it not to shake as Geoffrey leaned towards her.

After she had accepted his proposal, Geoffrey had kissed her cheek, respectful of her emotional state given the loss of her daughter. She hadn't considered their first proper kiss would be in front of witnesses.

She looked into her husband's eyes. *Husband.* Applied to Geoffrey, the word felt strange, and it gradually dawned on her what lay ahead. She hadn't thought beyond the fact they were getting married to help reclaim Jennifer, but marriage carried obligations. Responsibilities. *Rights.*

Meg closed her eyes and tried to enjoy the moment. Geoffrey held her shoulders and the clean scent of his aftershave blended with the scent of roses as he pressed his lips to hers. He was gentle and brief.

Our first kiss.

One day, she would look back and feel good about the choice she had made; what she had done. One day – if she worked at it, she hoped to love the man who took her arm and led her to the registry to sign her maiden name for the last time. She picked up the pen and wrote "Margaret Olivia Dorset".

When all four of them had signed the register and their marriage certificate, Geoffrey held out his hand. 'Allow me to escort you to our wedding breakfast, Mrs Ransom.'

Gerry had spent the last couple of days cooking while Geoffrey and Meg completed application forms and crafted a petition to the archbishop, requesting his help in securing information about Jennifer's whereabouts. But now, the forms were set to one side as the four of them ate a roast beef lunch with vegetables from their own vegie patch.

When the main course was finished, Gerry lifted a small, round fruit cake from the sideboard. It sat in the centre of a fine bone china cake plate. 'Time to cut the wedding cake.' She handed a beribboned knife to Meg.

Rationing meant the cake lacked the customary icing, and Gerry had probably used a couple of months' worth of ration coupons to make it, but it looked pretty with its floral centrepiece held together by a 'wedding' ring made of twisted tinfoil. Throughout the war Vera had collected and reused pieces of foil, and the sight of the tinfoil ring brought a lump to Meg's throat.

'If only Vera was here to share today with us.'

Geoffrey's hand covered hers. 'I'm sure she's here in spirit.'

Meg nodded, and together they plunged the knife into the cake. Gerry and Roger clapped as the first wedge was cut then Gerry took over the task of cutting slices and setting them on more of Vera's best china.

Roger gestured to Gerry. 'I think now is a good time, don't

you?'

Grinning, Gerry slipped out of the dining room.

'What have you two been up to?' Geoffrey didn't seem perturbed by the secrecy. He was enjoying their day, but Meg began to feel detached from everything. She was keen to get on with what needed to be done to bring Jennifer home. While the ceremony had been necessary, and she'd gone along with Gerry's enthusiasm in deciding on her dress, did they really need to go through this semblance of a wedding breakfast when her daughter was somewhere out there, alone with strangers, while they ate cake.

'Voilà!' Gerry entered the room carrying a tray on which a bottle of Champagne and four crystal glasses sat. 'Time for a toast.'

'My contribution to your wedding day,' said Roger, unwrapping the foil and carefully releasing the cork. The pop was loud, and champagne erupted from the neck.

Gerry quickly raised a glass and caught most of it. She laughed. 'Can't let good plonk go to waste.' She handed a glass to Meg.

Roger huffed and said, 'Plonk? I'll have you know this is an excellent French Champagne from my father's cellar.'

Gerry parried, 'And plonk is Aussie for the French *blanc*, which means white, see! And I did say it was the good stuff.'

'Droll,' Geoffrey smiled before leaning close to Meg. 'Are you okay, Margaret? You look pale. Is the heat getting to you?'

Drawing the ragged tatters of her patience together, Meg shook her head and managed a smile. 'I'm fine.'

Geoffrey accepted a glass from Gerry, and as soon as their guests had their glasses in hand, raised his towards Meg. 'To my bride. May today be the first of a long and happy life together.' He tapped his glass lightly against hers and drank.

Meg sipped hers. Bubbles tickled her lips, reminding her of happier, more carefree days when the New Year seemed exciting and full of promise.

Stop it, Meg.

Distracted she may be, but she could be gracious. She was

grateful for her husband and friend, and all they were doing and had done for her. Raising her glass in another toast, she said, 'Thank you for today, my friends. This wine and cake, the wonderful lunch, my beautiful dress and flowers – they're lovely gestures. To our friends, may you always share good times with us.'

They finished their glasses, and Roger stood. 'Sadly, some of us have to work. I leave you to enjoy what's left of the champagne in peace.'

Gerry rose and joined Roger at the door. 'Roger has offered me a ride into the city. I'm going to see a movie. I won't be home until six o'clock, so you'll have the house to yourselves.'

Meg half rose, but her dress was caught between her chair and Geoffrey's, and she sat awkwardly again. 'Gerry, don't feel you have to leave on our account.'

Suddenly, she didn't want to be alone with Geoffrey. Alone meant it was time to fulfil her wifely duties. She wasn't ready!

'Nonsense.' Gerry picked up her handbag then slipped her arm through Roger's. 'Sharing a house when you're newlyweds will be hard enough as it is. Take this time as an extra gift from me to you.' She blew them a kiss and disappeared down the hallway, Roger's walking stick tapping out their passage until the front door closed.

As Geoffrey stood, her dress came free, allowing her to stand. He picked up the half full bottle and their wine glasses. 'Shall we finish this in our bedroom—'

She didn't mean to frown, or shake her head, or whatever it was she did, but Geoffrey went still. He looked at her for a long, drawn-out moment then said, 'Or perhaps we could sit on the veranda and see if there's a breeze.'

'That sounds lovely.' She contained her sigh of relief . . . Just.

'The veranda it is. After you, my dear.'

How had that happened?

Meg lay in their bed and stared at the pattern in the pressed metal ceiling. She gripped the sheet as though it was all that kept her there while Geoffrey padded down the hallway to the bathroom.

Once the champagne was finished there had been no reason to linger outside and Geoffrey had escorted her to what had been Vera's bedroom, now theirs. Renting it from Gerry had seemed a good idea, especially with the housing shortage, but the realities of sharing a home as a newlywed had become apparent the moment Geoffrey rose above her and slid home, consummating their marriage.

Wire springs loudly proclaimed what they were doing, and Meg hadn't been able to muffle her cries. Her body had a mind of its own, and it didn't matter about doing her duty or her lost love when Geoffrey made love to her.

It wasn't like it had been with Seamus. At the River, beneath starry skies at the edge of an army camp, making love had been delightful and new. Seamus had kissed every inch of skin, and she'd roared out of her body and climbed to the stars. They'd been in the first flush of new love and Meg had been certain she'd never experience its like again.

Her husband was gentle and considerate at first, and Meg was certain that shattering feeling she'd known was lost with Seamus. But as Geoffrey thrust faster, his breathing, less regular, he stoked a slow burning fire that grew and blazed until it swallowed her whole.

She had known they would consummate their marriage but enjoying it surprised her. She wasn't in love with Geoffrey, and yet, she'd liked making love. More than liked. For that time, nothing else had filled her mind. Not even Jennifer.

As her body became her own again, guilt nudged her conscience.

Geoffrey entered their bedroom and closed the door. 'How do you feel?' He was dressed in an open-necked shirt and dark trousers, and his hair was damp and slicked back. He sat on the edge of the bed, lifted her hand and kissed her palm. Folding her fingers over his kiss, he smiled. 'Do you feel like a stroll along the river?'

Meg nodded. 'I'll have a quick wash first.'

Geoffrey reached for her peignoir, the soft peach silk, his wedding gift to her, and held it while she turned her back and slipped her arms through the sleeves. As she belted the sash, he held her shoulders and dropped a kiss on her neck.

Her shoulders hunched, his hands dropped, and he stepped away.

She turned quickly. 'I'm sorry. I didn't mean to— It's just—'

One hand rose to stop her apology. Hurt flickered in his eyes, there and gone so quickly she almost wondered if she'd imagined it. But why wouldn't he feel hurt when his wife of a few hours pulled away from his touch after they'd just been intimate?

But now his *doctor* face, the one he wore when talking with patients, gave nothing away. 'I'll be in the garden when you're ready. Take your time, Margaret. There's no rush.' He left her in peace. A moment later, the screen door squeaked open and softly closed.

There's no rush.

Guilt and grief crashed over her and clashed within her. He was a good man, and she was behaving as if he'd forced her into their marriage. If anything, it was she who was using him. His sense of honour had led him to repeat his offer when no other way of reclaiming her daughter could be found. In accepting him, she had made him a promise of a life together. A good life.

There and then, she vowed she *would* be a good wife to Geoffrey.

But how did she begin to do that while her daughter was lost to her?

Small, gold-tipped waves caught the late afternoon sun and made the brown water almost pretty. Wash from a steamboat travelling towards the river mouth slapped against the bank in rhythmic waves below them. As they passed the power station and approached the park, Meg was still lost in thought. No matter what bad things happened in her life, the world kept turning. Life went on. Of late, she'd let it drag her along on the ride. She needed to take back control of her life and steer a better course. Starting now. Starting with this kind and good man who walked by her side.

So much had changed; now, she was a wife as well as a mother. Determined to do better, she took her new husband's arm as they turned back into New Farm Park. 'Geoffrey?'

'What is it, my dear?'

'Thank you – for everything. I will be a good wife to you. I didn't mean to pull away when you touched me. It's just that I'm— distracted.'

He was quiet for a moment as they stopped in the shade. 'I understand. Wondering where your daughter is must consume your thoughts, but we *will* find her, Margaret.'

She smiled, feeling her cheeks quiver as she fought to hold it in place. 'I believe you, but it's so hard. All the time I was away from her, I thought – 'this is tough, but it's the right thing to do'. Then the war ended, and it was only going to be a few weeks, just a couple of months bringing home prisoners of war and the wounded, and *that* felt like the right thing to do too. I knew Jennifer was safe with Vera, and I knew I'd see her soon, but there were so many families who'd waited years for their loved ones to come home. How could I not help them to be reunited?'

'And when you finally made it home, it was to a double loss.'

He drew her into a gentle embrace. It comforted her and she drew strength from him, and from his touch. It demanded nothing and gave so much.

'I promise I'll move heaven and earth to bring her home to you.'

She breathed in the clean soap smell of him and the lingering scent of his Old Spice aftershave. 'I know.'

'Tomorrow, we'll visit the archbishop's secretary and deliver our petition then call in and see if Roger has had any luck contacting the Catholic diocese. The mother superior's refusal to hand over

Jennifer's adoption details is frustrating, but perhaps the convent is waiting for permission to hand over the information. Government bureaucracy grinds along slowly too.'

Meg nodded. 'Time seems to go so slowly, but it feels so hard waiting to get my daughter back.'

Geoffrey glanced at his watch and tucked her arm in his. 'It's five-thirty. Let's head back. Gerry will be home soon. After that wonderful lunch, the least we should do is have dinner ready for her when she comes in.'

Chapter 26

The following day

'I'm sorry but we've exhausted all avenues at this point.'

Despite the open windows the office was stuffy with the smell of leather and legal tomes. Roger sat on the other side of his wide desk; Meg's file lay open in front of him. She couldn't lift her gaze from the gilt edging of the green tooled-leather insert. If she did, she would explode. But it wasn't Roger's fault. Clenching her hands in her lap, she worked to control her breathing.

Beside her, Geoffrey set an arm on the desk and leaned forward. 'What you're saying is that there's nothing we can do until the government offices reopen in the new year?'

At last, Meg looked up.

Roger spread his hands and met her gaze. 'I'm sorry to have to give you this news, Margaret, but they refused. I even tried offering to pay a premium if they would put your request through before the office closed for the Christmas holiday, but everyone seems determined to start their celebrations early. No exceptions, they said.'

'So we won't be able to celebrate our first Christmas with Jennifer.'

'Not this year, my dear.' Geoffrey reached across and took her hand in his.

Were all these bad things happening because she was a bad person? In the back of Meg's mind, her father's voice laid down judgement. *Those who do not follow God's will shall be punished.* He'd been referring to a young, unwed mother whose child had been stillborn, but Meg could hear the same response being given to her. After all she'd endured, and in spite of her marriage yesterday, in her parents' eyes, Meg would also be a fallen woman. If bad things happened to her, it was her own fault. The knowledge sat like a stone in her stomach.

Roger was shaking his head. 'I'm afraid not, unless you've had any luck reaching the Anglican archbishop?'

Geoffrey drummed his fingers on the desk. 'Not yet. We delivered our petition requesting his assistance in reuniting our family, but he may not have even seen it yet.'

'In that case, and as hard as it is, all I can suggest is that you make what you can of our first peaceful Christmas in years and be waiting on the doorstep of the records office when they reopen.'

Gripping her handbag in one hand, Meg stood. The muscles in her neck and back were tight but she extended her other hand to Roger. She couldn't muster even half a smile as they shook hands. 'Thank you for what you've done for us so far.'

'I only wish my news were better.'

'You've gone above and beyond for us, Roger. We're very grateful for your help. All the best to you and your family.' Geoffrey set a hand on Meg's back and held the door as she exited. They didn't speak until they were out on the footpath.

Queen Street was abuzz with pedestrians and a bell clanged as a tram approached a nearby stop. The street wore a festive air thanks to the council's encouragement of businesses to decorate. Garlands were strung along shop fronts and even the tram—their number, Meg noted—carried a Christmas wreath in its front window.

So much joy all around. Her sense of loss would crush her if she let it. Reminding herself they had done all they could, she held her head high.

'Would you like to head home, Margaret, or shall we call into the tea shop and revise our plans?'

'Tea would be nice.' She slipped her arm through his and they headed down to the Brisbane Arcade. Her only plan had been watching her daughter opening Christmas presents and sharing their first proper Christmas together. Nothing could replace one more year lost, but Vera was gone, Gerry was grieving, and Geoffrey—dear Geoffrey—deserved so much more than gloom and doom from her.

They turned into the arcade, and natural light from overhead clerestory windows flooded the space. Passing several polished timber shopfronts, they stopped in front of the tearoom. Geoffrey peered through the stained-glass window. 'It's still open.' He opened the door and held it for Meg. 'After you.'

A waitress seated them at a corner table where a piece of blue glass gave Meg the sense of hiding behind it while allowing her to look through an adjacent piece of clear glass at the passing foot traffic.

Geoffrey ordered a pot of tea and a plate of sandwiches then turned his full attention on her. 'I regret that we won't have our daughter with us for our first Christmas.'

Our daughter.

Our belonged to Seamus, and maybe even to Vera who had cared for Jennifer like her own child. And yet each time Geoffrey said that she felt a flutter in her stomach. If they could find Jennifer, the three of them would be a family. *When we find her, not if.*

Clinging to that hope, she dragged in a deep breath and exhaled slowly. 'I'm trying not to think about it for the moment. But I agree we need to revise our plans. We could try to find a chicken for Christmas lunch. What did you have in mind?'

'If you're up to it, we could do some Christmas shopping. I know Jennifer won't be here for Christmas Day, but we can save her presents until she's home. What do you think?'

'Delay Christmas?' She nodded slowly. 'I've dreamed of watching her open her presents since she was born, and last Christmas, when she might have had some idea what it was about, I couldn't get leave.'

'You agree then? After our tea and sandwiches, we go shopping?'

'Yes.' And when they had Jennifer's present, Meg was going to look for a gift for Gerry. And Geoffrey. 'You've already given me my present.'

'The peignoir was for our wedding, Margaret. Christmas is different and—'

'I didn't mean that. What you've given me is far beyond

anything else. It's the greatest gift of all right now. You've given me hope.'

##

Geoffrey set the potted plant on the corner of the table in the lounge room and stepped back to admire the effect. 'You were right. That green tablecloth looks festive under the red leaves. Do you want me to bring in the presents and put them around the tree?'

Meg looked at their makeshift Christmas tree and shook her head. Geoffrey had carefully dug up the small poinsettia with its bright-red leaves and together, they had potted it. 'No, I'll make a few decorations for it first.' Geoffrey was out the back chopping wood for the kitchen range and she was in the middle of adorning the tree when Gerry came home from her first shift back at the Herston Women's Hospital.

She put her bag on the nearest chair and stood beside Meg, unbuttoning her nurse's cape. 'What on earth— I thought we weren't celebrating this year?'

'We weren't, but then Geoffrey and I had a talk. Here – your turn. Put this on the tree.' Meg handed her a star made of foil.

Gerry looked at the decoration lying on her palm before attaching it to the topmost branch of the poinsettia. She tipped her head to one side then the other. 'It's lopsided.'

True, it sat a little wonky, but light glinted off it like tiny slivers of hope. 'That suits what this year has been – wonky.' Meg took Gerry's hand and squeezed. 'This Christmas isn't going to be what we had hoped, not for any of us. Vera is gone and there's nothing we can do to change that. Jennifer is missing, but we've done all that's humanly possible to find her. She *will* come home, soon, please God. But the war is over. We're together and we're safe. We have peace at last, and that *is* worth celebrating, don't you think?'

Gerry nodded. Her eyes were bright with unshed tears, but she smiled – a wonky smile that matched their wonky star. 'You're right. We have to look for the good things and celebrate them.'

'Right. So say your prayers because I'm cooking dinner and you know what sort of cook I am.'

Gerry laughed. 'I'll pray it's edible while I have a quick bath.'

Geoffrey joined them around the tree. His hair was damp and his cheeks flushed from his wood-chopping, but he smiled. 'Are we looking at scrambled eggs and burnt toast then?'

'As long as no one distracts me, it might not be burnt.' She'd never be the best cook in the house, but Meg was determined to make a start on her vow to control her life. Starting with something simple – dinner.

'I'll leave you to it.' Gerry left.

Moments later, Meg heard the bathroom door open and the sound of water splashing into the bathtub.

'I need to make a couple of phone calls. Before I decide between the two positions I've been offered, I need more information.'

'You've had two offers? I didn't know.' She had no idea how that had slipped past her, that Geoffrey had been actively pursuing a civilian job since his arrival.

Geoffrey met her gaze. 'You have enough to worry about without me burdening you further. Unless—'

'I'd like to hear about them.'

'In that case, I'll join you in the kitchen after I've made the calls. If I'm lucky, there might be a beer in the cool box.' He smiled and walked out of the room.

Meg looked at their unusual Christmas tree. They could plant it in the garden later, but it would stay alive in the pot for as long as it took to bring Jennifer home. Then they would share Christmas with her.

Meg took a knife out to the vegie patch and cut lettuce and cherry tomatoes for a salad. She was rinsing the lettuce in a colander when Geoffrey returned. 'You're in luck. There's a bottle of beer.' She turned the tap off, grabbed a clean tea towel, and patted excess moisture from the lettuce leaves.

'Thanks.' Geoffrey sounded distracted as he collected a glass and the bottle of beer and sat at the table. He uncapped the beer then sat looking at the bottle.

'Did you find out what you needed to make your decision?'

'I got the information I needed, but now I'm less sure than ever about which to choose.' He poured the beer, keeping the foamy head to less than half an inch, the way he liked it.

'Are they both surgical positions?' Meg ripped the lettuce leaves into smaller pieces and added them to a salad bowl.

'Yes. One is working under Dr Hepworth.'

She turned and looked at him in surprise. 'The surgeon who's doing facial reconstructive work on soldiers?'

'That's the one. He was trained by Henry Pickerill, the New Zealander who trained under Gillies in England after the first world war.'

'That would be such an opportunity for you.'

'The idea excites me. The position offers a chance to do research and to be hands on as new techniques offer hope. Too often, soldiers with terrible facial wounds struggle with the idea of their loved ones seeing them so changed.' Geoffrey had said he was excited, but he didn't sound as enthused as Meg expected, given how much of an opportunity the position offered. 'What's the catch?'

He sighed. 'The position is in Sydney, and he wants me to start at the beginning of January. I asked if there was any possibility of delaying the start, but he said no. They have long waiting lists of injured soldiers. The second week of January was as late as he would allow.'

'Oh dear.' Meg pulled out a chair and sank onto it. If Geoffrey accepted the position, she couldn't go with him. Not yet. It was unlikely they would have Jennifer restored to them by then, if their experience so far was anything to go by. And then there was the location. Her family, who knew nothing of her child, were in Sydney. But how could she hold him back if this was where he saw his life's work? 'And the second position?'

'Is here in Brisbane. Head of Surgery at the University of

Queensland's medical school in Herston.'

'Surely a position where you are in charge would be preferable?'

'It's definitely tempting to consider shaping the development of the new medical school. I'd be overseeing surgeons who are developing new techniques in a range of surgeries, as well as medical students specialising in surgery.'

'But?'

'I'm torn. If it weren't for Jennifer, I'd jump at the chance of working with Hepworth, but I don't see how I can accept his offer while we're looking for her.'

To Meg, the choice was simple. She had to remain in Brisbane, but she understood Geoffrey's dilemma. 'When do you have to decide?'

'The day after Boxing Day for Hepworth's offer, and the second of January for the university position.' He looked into his glass as though the answer was written in its foam. Suddenly he lifted his head and sniffed. 'The toast – it's burning.'

Meg grabbed the toasting fork out of the fire and tossed it into the sink. The black slice of bread hung off the tines and made a mockery of her efforts at control. If she couldn't toast a simple slice of bread without burning it, how on earth could she help her husband with his dilemma?

Enough negative thinking.

She turned to face him and gripped the edge of the sink behind her. 'Accept the position that will fulfil you. If that's Sydney, then we'll find a way to make it work. I'll stay here with Gerry until I've recovered Jennifer, and we'll join you when we can.'

Late that night, unable to sleep, Meg slipped out of bed and tip-toed out to the swing seat. Curling into a ball, she lay her head on a cushion, and looked across the road at the park. A sliver of starry sky appeared and disappeared as the seat gently rocked. Time passed – she had no idea how much – while her thoughts floated in the darkness.

The front door opened, and Geoffrey stepped out. Sleep-tousled and wearing only pyjama trousers in the hot night, he padded bare-footed to the swing. 'Is everything okay? Did the heat keep you awake?'

'Partly that.' She sat up and made room for him beside her. As he sat, he set the seat rocking.

'And the other part?'

'Not being able to see far turned my thoughts inward. Marriage is about sharing, and—maybe—not keeping secrets from one another.'

'Is there a secret that's keeping you awake?'

'A half-truth. I didn't tell you the whole story about my family.'

'I know you have a couple of siblings; they and your parents all live somewhere in Sydney and couldn't make it to our wedding. Other than that—'

'Your dream job is in *Sydney*.' She couldn't stop the odd inflection her fear of what waited at home gave to the city's name.

He took her hand, twining their fingers together. 'I'm sorry but I'm not seeing what your point is. I know the only important thing right now is finding Jennifer, but I thought you'd be delighted about the prospect of returning to the city where your family lives?'

'It's *all* about Jennifer.' Just not in the way Geoffrey meant.

'We'll stay here in Brisbane, and we'll find her. It might take longer than you would like, but I'll be content with the job at Herston. Heaven knows there'll be plenty to occupy me there.'

'Content isn't the same as excited.'

'Margaret, look at me.' When she met his gaze, he continued. 'I'll be happy wherever we are because we'll be together. I should have immediately thanked Dr Hepworth for his offer and told him that the timing wasn't right for me. I'll call him tomorrow and—'

'On Christmas Day? No. Think about what you're throwing away if you reject his offer.'

'I know what I'll be gaining by staying here – my family. But

I sense something more than timing is an issue. I thought you'd jump at the idea of heading home to your family. Was I wrong?'

'It's complicated.'

'Try me.'

For so long she had bottled up her feelings and now, unstoppering them felt like ripping off a bandage stuck to a wound. But she had to try. Geoffrey needed to understand.

'You know the circumstances of Jennifer's conception and birth, yet you married me anyway, and offered to adopt my daughter as your own. Not once did you judge me for the choices I made.'

'Of course I didn't. No one should.' He paused.

He left a silence that waited for her to agree but saying it would be a betrayal of her parents. She said nothing.

'I imagine your family will be keen to meet her?'

There had always been something about sitting side by side in the dark that seduced her into sharing secrets. She'd done it before, in Townsville. It was the not seeing that made it possible. She spoke to the trees and set free the shattering truth. 'They don't know she exists.'

Silence from Geoffrey. She imagined him grappling with the truth while she rocked, cocooned within the darkness.

At last, he spoke. 'I don't understand. She's three years old.' He set the seat swinging. Even in the shadows of the veranda, she could just make out his frown. 'Why haven't you told them about her?'

'I planned to tell them I was expecting as soon as Seamus and I were married. I thought we'd fudge the month of our wedding—make it the date we got engaged, which was close enough to— Well, you get the idea. If we did that, all would be well. But when he died, I couldn't tell them I was about to become an unwed mother. They would have told me I'd reaped what I'd sown.' Bitterness filled her as she imagined her mother's tone of voice and her father's glare, their disappointment in their only daughter.

'Would they, Margaret? I can't imagine the people who brought you into the world would turn their backs on their daughter and granddaughter.'

'Your family must be more forgiving. Mine are models of rectitude. Acknowledging me and my daughter would mean my father couldn't maintain his position as an elder of their church. It's not possible.'

'But we're married now. Surely that—'

'Will count for nothing. They'll never accept my daughter because of her birth. Illegitimate at birth, barely tolerated through life. That's their *Christian* view.'

'If that's true then it's sad. But can you know that for sure? What if you give them a chance?'

'If you accept the position with Dr Hepworth and we end up in Sydney, there is no way I'll risk them hurting Jennifer by refusing to acknowledge her. It's my job to protect her, even if that means she has nothing to do with my family.'

'I'm—confused. Are you telling me you want me to take the job in Sydney, or that you'll hate going back there?'

'I want you to take the job that makes you happy and if that's in Sydney, then I'll live with it. It's a big city. I mean—it's not likely I'll run into my family when I go shopping. They live a fair way south of the city. We could live in the northern suburbs near the beach. Jennifer would like that.' From reluctantly opening up about her parents, now Meg couldn't stop the flow of words. She was gabbling. She never gabbled but—

'Margaret, enough.' Spoken gently, Geoffrey's soft comment was all it took to settle her.

'You're a practical, level-headed woman, but this situation with your family has you tied in knots. Let's leave it until the morning to unravel them, shall we. Now, would you like some hot cocoa to help you sleep?'

'Yes please.'

He patted her hand and rose, setting the seat rocking with more force than usual. 'Stay there and I'll be back soon.'

Meg curled her legs up and waited for her heartbeat to settle. Geoffrey was right. Whenever she thought about seeing her family, she grew agitated, and emotion clouded her response. He didn't know her family, but he had the advantage of thinking about the situation from a different perspective. Was he right that there might be a way back to them?

Chapter 27

January 1946

'It opens at half-past nine.' Meg turned from the notice and pressed herself against the brick wall at the entrance to the Records office. In typical midsummer fashion, the day had burst forth in a wall of heat and still air, and the narrow patch of shade from the door hood gave little relief. 'It seems hotter than Townsville, but I'm sure that can't be right.'

Geoffrey's head was in the shade but the rest of his body was in the sun. He squinted into the bright light. 'The heat bounces off the pavement as well as rising through the soles of our shoes, so the effect is intensified. Did you bring the thermos of water?'

'Yes. Would you like some now?'

Behind her, the sound of a key being turned in the lock caught her attention.

'They're opening. Let's deal with the paperwork first.'

Meg stepped through the door being held open by a middle-aged man who looked less than pleased to see customers already on his doorstep. Once in the main office, they waited while he raised a hinged flap and stepped behind the polished timber counter before approaching his window.

'How may I be of assistance?' He looked to Geoffrey for an answer.

Meg began to explain, and the clerk's eyebrows rose as he turned his attention from Geoffrey to her. 'The form was handed in before Christmas and—'

'There is quite a back log of work to get through. Christmas is our busiest period. Everyone wants their file attended to first. I'll have a look and see if your form has been submitted or if it's waiting lodgement. Name?'

'Dorset—Ransom. Sorry. We were only just married before Christmas.'

The clerk flicked through a pile of forms, the rubber tip on his finger moving precisely and slowly. Somewhere around the middle he stopped and drew one out. 'Application by Geoffrey and Margaret Ransom for the release of adoption records relating to one Jennifer Dorset.'

'That's us. Jennifer is our daughter.' Geoffrey, bless him, was already claiming Jennifer as his own child.

'No, the form hasn't been lodged yet. From its place in the pile, it will likely be two weeks before we get to it.' The clerk looked at Geoffrey.

His focus on her husband was beginning to irk Meg. This was *her* daughter they were talking about. *Her* child who was lost to *her*. She leaned on the counter and pinned him with the same direct look she used on difficult patients. 'How can we expedite that?'

'Every request takes its turn.'

'But this is about my—our daughter.' There was a sharp edge in her voice she regretted the moment it slipped out. It hinted at loss of control. Quickly, she cleared her throat. *Use your nurse voice. Control. Control. Control.* 'She was wrongfully adopted before we were demobilised and returned home.'

The clerk's gaze narrowed on Meg. 'You were in the services?'

Geoffrey leaned against the counter and nodded. 'Doctor and nurse. My wife was in the Darwin and Townville bombings, and she was the first Flying Angel when we started air evacuations of wounded soldiers.'

Now the clerk was staring at her. 'You were an angel? My son was repatriated late last year. We had him home for Christmas Day. He wouldn't talk about what happened to him over there, but he talked about the flight home. Said he had the prettiest nurse caring for him.' His gaze narrowed on her. 'Could have been you.'

Meg ignored the sideways compliment. There was too much at stake. Normally, she was reticent about her work and the men she had brought home, but the connection was too precious not to make use of. Not when it might mean bringing her little girl home sooner.

'He could have been on my flight. I was one of the last *angels* to leave. That's why my daughter was taken by the nuns; because I was bringing our men home on those final flights.'

'It might have been you.' The clerk set their form on the counter and picked up an official looking stamp. 'I'll see that this form goes in today.'

Meg exhaled, and her relief lent a quiver to her 'Thank you.' She couldn't say more.

The clerk nodded and set the form in an empty tray labelled 'Out'.

Geoffrey took Meg's arm, and they left the building. She could have been walking on air for all she noticed the hot footpath. 'I can't believe it was that easy.'

'Sometimes, good things happen, Margaret. Now, I'm going to catch a tram out to the hospital at Herston. Would you like to accompany me?'

'What would I do while you have your orientation?'

'Look around. If you like what you see, you could apply to work there.' He grinned. 'It could be like old times, working together in theatre.'

Meg felt the old tug of attraction. To be working in an operating theatre beside Geoffrey would be wonderful. Their efficient work flow; the sense of achievement of a surgery that had gone well. 'We were good together, weren't we?' She thought about those times, enjoying the memory.

'What do you say? Will you come with me?'

Meg sighed and shook her head. 'At one time, I'd have jumped at the chance, but when Jennifer comes home, I need to be there for her. She needs her mother. I've missed out on so much of her life already. I can't miss any more.'

'What about when she goes to school?'

'Maybe. I don't know. Once she's in my arms, I don't think I'll ever want to let her go.'

A bell ding-dinged, signalling an approaching tram. Geoffrey glanced around. 'That's mine. Do what you feel is best for Jennifer.

Meanwhile, I'll hope that your '*maybe*' becomes a 'yes' when the time is right. I'll be home for dinner, my dear.'

'Burnt toast notwithstanding?'

'I'll eat whatever comes as long as it's with you sitting across the table.' He hesitated then kissed her cheek before sprinting for the tram.

As it pulled away, she put a hand to her cheek. He'd kissed her. Out in public in the middle of the street. Now what was she to make of that?

She made her way to her tram stop, wondering if that kiss had been Geoffrey distracting her, or a sign of affection.

And if it was affection, and Geoffrey's feelings for her were growing . . . That was the most worrying idea of all. Because he deserved so much more than she could ever give him.

A week passed, then two. Geoffrey began work as the new Head of Surgery at Herston and Gerry sometimes caught a ride in with him when her shift matched his workday. And every day, Meg stayed in the house to be near the phone, except when she heard the postman's whistle. Then, she raced out to the letterbox and opened it, hoping today would be the day she'd hear from the Records office.

Waiting was an almost physical pain. Her remedies were cooking and cleaning the house from top to bottom. Every morning, as soon as she had the house to herself and before the heat of the day became unbearable in the kitchen, Meg pulled out a copy of the Women's Weekly magazine and selected a recipe to cook or bake. By dint of sheer repetition, her cooking skills were beginning to improve.

It's hard to get worse than burnt toast, she thought, and smiled as she stirred a pot of rhubarb and apple jam. With three ration books and a little negotiation, she'd convinced Geoffrey and Gerry to give up part of their sugar ration with the promise of delicious jam.

'You've got to pay attention, Meg. It's not like a stew where it doesn't matter if you cook it a bit longer,' Gerry had warned her. 'You can't leave it and go and do something else.'

'I won't leave the kitchen, I promise. You'll love it.' A good mother would be a good cook and feed her child healthy food and Meg was determined to succeed. For Jennifer's sake, and her own pride.

She checked the time then scooped half a teaspoonful onto a cool saucer. Was it thick enough? She peered at the spreading blob then poked at it with the tip of her finger.

The postie's whistle blew at her gate and Meg put the saucer down and ran. She reached the doorway before she remembered – the pot was still simmering on the stove. Forcing her impatience down, she grabbed two potholders and set the pot in the sink then ran out to the letterbox.

Please be today.

##

Gerry was still at work when Geoffrey walked through the front door and removed his hat. Meg flung herself against his chest. 'We've got an interview!' She waved the letter.

His arms wrapped around her and lifted her clear off the floor. He spun her in dizzying circles and when he set her down, he didn't let her go. 'Wonderful news. When?'

'The day after tomorrow. Eleven o'clock at the Records office.'

Geoffrey frowned then nodded. 'I can fit in most of my morning surgery, but I'll have to ask Dr Higgins to take over one case. It will be too challenging for a new surgeon.'

'Will that be a problem?'

He leaned his forehead against hers and his arms tightened around her waist. 'Nothing is more important than our daughter.'

A fillip of excitement tumbled through her. *Gratitude.* That was all it was. She was grateful for his help, and for his easy acceptance of Jennifer into their lives. With a murmured 'Thank you', she kissed his mouth. Not his cheek, which would have been more suited to a thank you kiss, but his mouth. Her lips met his unerringly. Naturally.

Geoffrey stood perfectly still. She thought he held his breath, so still was he.

Perhaps his very stillness encouraged her to prolong the kiss. Meant to be brief, it grew into something more than simple gratitude. She fell into it like a starving woman.

'Do you want to—'

She wasn't sure if she heard the words, or if the tightening of his arms, the hardening of his body against hers communicated his need – echoing hers.

'Yes.'

They made it to their bedroom and the door crashed behind Geoffrey, before Meg gave herself up to the insistent need of her body.

Chapter 28

'You've no need to be nervous, Margaret. We have all the documents they asked for, plus copies of our records of service. I'm sure they'll decide we are appropriate parents for our child.' Geoffrey reached for her hand and held it until the door behind them was opened and a man entered, with a stenographer following quietly behind, her mid-grey jacket and skirt blending into the shadows. She sat at a small desk in front of the window and opened a notebook without making eye contact.

The middle-aged man in a smart three-piece suit, his thinning hair combed over his bald pate, stopped beside them and held out his hand. 'Dr and Mrs Ransom? I'm Philip Soames, head of the department. Given the regrettable error that allowed the unlawful adoption of your daughter, I'll be conducting this interview today.'

Geoffrey stood and shook Mr Soames's hand. 'Pleased to meet you.'

Soames nodded to Meg then sat behind the desk, reached into his jacket pocket and withdrew a pair of round spectacles which he proceeded to polish in slow, deliberate circles. He held them up to the window. Apparently satisfied with their clarity, he set them on his nose then opened the file that had been sitting on the desk when they arrived. He scanned the first page then turned it over and scanned the next.

Meg sat up straighter, but her grip on her handbag tightened with each ticking minute as he read documents he must surely know well. After all, if the head of the department was meeting with them, it must be because Jennifer's adoption had been illegal and he was in damage control.

Soames reached the end of the third page, folded his hands and looked at Meg. 'Mrs Ransom, please clarify for me: at any time, in written form or by any verbal indication, did you agree to allow the convent to take your child for adoption?'

'Never. When Sister Rosemary, the nun who spoke to me the first time I visited said that they would not accept my child for temporary fostering, only for adoption, I made it very clear that I did not intend to give up my child.'

Soames nodded and his gaze shifted to Geoffrey. 'Do you intend to adopt this child as your own?'

'I do. I've known Margaret since early in 1942, and I've known about her child since before she was born.'

The clock at City Hall chimed noon, and still the questions rolled on, the stenographer recording their answers, and Mr Soames slowly ticking items off a list. Finally, he put the cap back on his fountain pen and looked from Geoffrey to Meg.

Meg jumped into the quiet moment with a question of her own. 'Surely a doctor and a nursing sister must be considered the most fitting of parents for any child, especially given the fact I am Jennifer's biological mother?'

'We must be absolutely certain we have everything correct, Mrs Ransom. The Minister hopes that lessons may be learned from your case, so such an event never happens again. But . . .' He nodded at the stenographer who rose and handed him a typed page. He set it on the desk between them. 'If you would be kind enough to sign this statement, which promises you will not go to the newspapers with your story, I believe we can satisfactorily conclude our meeting.'

'Does that mean—'

'We will take the necessary steps to return your daughter to you. You will never know who she was adopted out to. Their privacy will remain protected. You will be advised of the place and time when you will be able to collect her. Once you've signed the document . . .' He proffered his pen.

Collect her? My daughter is not a parcel to be collected.

But she bit the inside of her cheek and kept the thought to herself. Taking the pen, she signed her name then handed it to Geoffrey, who did likewise and handed the paper and pen back to Soames.

'Excellent. Miss Frobisher, would you also sign as a witness and date the document?'

Miss Frobisher stood at the end of the desk and when she was finished, Mr Soames added his signature. 'You'll be hearing from us soon.'

'Mr Soames?' Now she knew Jennifer would be coming home, Meg's confidence grew.

'Yes, Mrs Ransom?'

'How long will it be before Jennifer will be back with me— with us?'

'Within the fortnight.'

'Why so long now all the paperwork is complete?'

'Because the family who adopted her live a long way from Brisbane. Travel takes time, but we are making arrangements for her imminent return. And now, if you'll excuse me. Good day, Mrs Ransom. Dr Ransom.'

Two weeks felt like forever. Meg cooked, and cleaned, and sewed new summer clothes for Jennifer, but the days dragged in a way she'd never known. If she'd been working in a hospital—

No regrets, she reminded herself when Geoffrey came home from his increasingly busy days and shared snippets of an operation he'd just performed. The intake of first year medical students was happening tomorrow.

And Jennifer was coming home. Of course, both events were on the same day, but Geoffrey had promised he'd get away for an hour to be with her when Jennifer arrived.

Meg stuck her head around the door of the lounge room and marvelled at the decorations. It looked like Christmas and a child's birthday party all rolled into one.

'What do you think? Enough or too much?' Gerry was pinning a garland along the mantelpiece, while an upbeat Jimmy Dorsey record played on the Victrola. Her hips swayed along to the beat. She stepped back to survey her handiwork.

Meg joined her, slipping an arm around her waist.

'Everything is wonderful—or nearly so.'

'You need your daughter to make it perfect.'

Meg thought of her daughter's sweet face the last time she'd been home. Last year felt so long ago. 'I hope Jennifer hasn't forgotten me.'

'No chance, Meg.'

'But she's probably been calling some other woman 'mum' for the past few weeks. And she's only three. And—' The choking sensation hit again, as it did each time she thought of what they had lost. Time they could never recoup.

'Don't expect the worst. She loved you before she was taken, and she'll love you when she comes home again, even if she takes a few days to settle in. If she's a little hesitant, it won't last.' Tipping her head to the side, Gerry eyed off the garland then stepped in close and fiddled with it, hanging it in the same spot.

There was nothing wrong with how it was hung. Likely Gerry guessed Meg was feeling tearful. While Gerry's back was turned, Meg wiped her eyes and took a calming deep breath. 'You're right. Is there anything else to go under the Christmas tree?' The poinsettia was still doing well in its pot. Beneath its red leaves, a small pile of presents waited for Jennifer to open.

'I got carried away and put my gift there this morning. I hope I've got her size right.'

Again, that feeling she'd lost precious time with Jennifer rose like nausea within her. And yet, she couldn't regret the time she'd worked in *Currajong*, or flying medical evacuations and repatriation flights. Did that make her a bad mother, or an overly committed nurse? She shook her head, mainly to stop her own thoughts. 'Do you think she'll have grown very much?'

'In two months? I can't imagine it.' Gerry twined her fingers together and peered at Meg. 'I swapped shifts so I can be here when you get home with Jennifer. I hope that's okay?'

Meg smiled. 'I wouldn't have it any other way. Having her family around her is the most important thing.'

Gerry blew out an audible breath. 'I'm so happy to hear that.

Oh, look at the time. I've got to go or I'll be late for my shift tonight. Hooroo.'

Chapter 29

Her heart was in her throat as they sat on a pair of hard chairs outside the Assistant Director's office. Mr Horsham was running late, the clerk apologised, but he wouldn't be long.

The second hand on the wall clock directly across from Meg's chair clunked from one second to the next, and the minute hand was geriatric, so slowly did it move on from minute to minute.

Geoffrey sat beside her, his hat resting on one knee.

Ten past the hour.

'Do you think there's a problem?' Meg asked. The time seemed not to have moved since she'd last looked.

'This is a busy office, Margaret.' He reached over and, covering her gloved hand with his, gave it a reassuring squeeze.

Meg didn't want reassurance. She wanted Jennifer. Now – here in her arms.

'It won't be long.'

Like a magician's 'Abracadabra', Geoffrey's words produced an immediate effect. The door beside her opened and a man she presumed was Mr Horsham invited them into his office.

'Welcome, Dr and Mrs Ransom. Thank you for your patience. Please be seated.'

'Is Jennifer here?' Meg looked around; her patience was stretched to its limit. Maybe beyond it. She felt like she'd snap if she had to wait one more minute.

'Nearly, Mrs Ransom. I need you to sign these papers, and then your daughter will be brought in. Dr Ransom – sign here and then your wife signs below your name.'

Geoffrey perused the page then signed it and passed it to her.

Meg's signature was a scrawl. She didn't read what the document said before she pushed it across the desk. Mr Horsham examined the document, before adding his name and neatly writing the date below. Meg's muscles quivered with tension. Not even

Geoffrey's hand on her arm stilled her.

'Good. This all seems to be in order.' Mr Horsham crossed the room and opened the door. Meg watched as he stepped outside and made a 'come forward' gesture to someone out of her sight. 'Bring the child in now.'

Meg set her handbag on the floor and stood; her gaze fixed on the doorway. As Jennifer was brought in, her little hand holding that of a woman, Meg sank to one knee and held her arms wide. 'Hello, darling.'

Jennifer shoved her thumb in her mouth and stood.

Meg's heart clenched. Had Jennifer already forgotten her? What if her daughter ended up traumatised by all the changes she'd experienced? Meg kept her smile in place and her voice gentle. 'Mummy's come to take you home.'

Her little girl's blue eyes stared and her thumb slipped out of her mouth. 'Mummy?'

'Yes, darling. It's Mummy.' Her chest was so tight with wanting, it hurt.

Then . . . Jennifer launched herself across the space between them and flung her little arms around Meg's neck.

She clung to her child, raining kisses on her fair hair and silently promising, *I'll never let you go.*

At some point, Geoffrey's hand settled on her shoulder, and without any words needed, Meg stood. Jennifer was wrapped koala-tight to her chest.

He picked up her handbag from the floor and said, 'Let's take our girl home.'

They'd discussed when to tell Jennifer that Geoffrey was her new daddy and agreed it would be best to let her settle in first. Determining when that would be, was up to Meg. But as they rode in the taxi past familiar shops that gave way to familiar houses, and finally, the park where Vera, and Meg too when she'd been home on leave, had taken Jennifer, she wondered if telling her daughter as soon as she was home might be more reassuring. Learning she had a father as soon as she was back in familiar surroundings might be easier than wondering who the strange man with her mother was.

Glancing at Geoffrey, she realised he was angled towards them, his gaze on them unwavering. Had he been watching them throughout the ride?

He smiled, that wonderful slow smile that reached his eyes and felt as though it belonged to her alone. The smile that now included her daughter.

'She looks so much like you, Margaret. My two beautiful girls.'

Jennifer sucked her thumb and watched this man she didn't yet know.

Their eyes met across Jennifer's head. 'You'll be a wonderful father to her.' With the tip of a finger, Meg brushed her daughter's fringe to the side. Perhaps one day, they'd have a child of their own. Maybe a boy for Geoffrey. Watching him making these first tentative connections with Jennifer, Meg thought he wouldn't mind what sex their child was.

The taxi turned around at the river end of the road and pulled up in front of their home. Geoffrey paid the fare then came around to open her door. A hand beneath her elbow helped her step out of the taxi with her armful of child. She couldn't bear to set Jennifer down, not yet. She carried her up the front steps and into the relative coolness of the wide hallway. 'We're home, my darling.'

Gerry stuck her head around the door of the lounge room, and cupped Jennifer's cheek. 'Hello, precious girl.' Glancing at Meg, she stepped back and held the door wide. 'We're in here.'

We? As she stepped through the doorway, Meg wondered who Gerry had invited to join them and felt mildly annoyed. She didn't want to share her daughter with anyone just yet.

Two faces were turned towards her, their smiles slipping as their gazes landed on her.

Her knees went wobbly, and her stomach clenched at the sight of them. Had Gerry invited them? She knew how Meg felt; what she feared.

Today of all days, how could she have allowed them to

ambush her like this?

'Mum, Dad, what are you doing here?'

Chapter 30

'Margaret?' Her mother rose from the sofa and took a step towards Meg. 'Why are you carrying that child?'

Dad caught Mum's hand, stopping her, holding her back, then he too rose. 'Do you have something to tell us?' Was it hurt or anger that lay beneath his words? The quaver in his voice could have been either.

A tide of guilt began building in Meg. Maybe Geoffrey had been right. She *should* have told them about Jennifer. Should have given them the benefit of the doubt. At least then, they would have known they had a granddaughter, even if they chose not to acknowledge her. But she'd not given them a choice.

'I'm sorry.'

Mum twined her fingers, pressing them so tightly together her knuckles turned white. 'We caught the bus all the way from Sydney to see you. The war's been over for months and you haven't come home to us.' It was definitely pain in her mother's expression. The pain of rejection by her only daughter. She darted glances between Meg and Jennifer, having perhaps guessed the child in her arms might be her grandchild.

'I'm sorry,' she said again.

An awkward silence hung over the five adults before Gerry said, 'I'll make a cup of tea and leave you to talk.' She edged past Geoffrey and disappeared down the hallway.

Meg only became aware of Geoffrey's hand on her shoulder, of him standing beside her, when her parents' gazes dropped to where it lay. They'd be wondering what that familiar touch meant, as much as why she hadn't told them about him.

Into the tense silence between them, a gap that might as well have been the distance between earth and moon, he thrust his hand forward. 'I'm Geoffrey Ransom, Margaret's husband.'

Dad looked at Geoffrey's hand then glared at him. 'Husband,

eh? You didn't think to ask my permission before marrying my daughter?'

Meg gasped. 'Is that your only concern – that my husband didn't ask your permission to marry me?'

Geoffrey's hand dropped. 'It's okay, Margaret. Under normal circumstances, I would have asked your father for your hand.'

'It's a father's right and responsibility to choose a life partner for his daughter. Bill Hartnett is still expecting to walk you down the aisle when we bring you home, though that's not going to happen now. Remember home, Margaret? Where your family has been waiting for you all these years while you've been off doing your nursing.'

'I've never forgotten, not once while I was serving. Every time I talked to a patient about where he was from, I thought of all of you.'

Mum's eyes glistened with unshed tears. 'Then why didn't you come home as soon as the war was over?'

'Because it wasn't over just because the Japanese surrendered. It wasn't over until we'd brought home all the men and women who had been prisoners of war. I was working on the last flights to bring them home.'

'Flights? You said you were nursing.' Dad's gaze narrowed on her.

'Their families needed them just as much as you wanted me to come home.'

Mum shook her head. 'But – flying, Margaret? What were you doing on a plane?'

Geoffrey squeezed her shoulder. 'You should be proud of your daughter. She was the first Flying Angel when medical evacuations began last year. She and an orderly cared for our wounded on flights back to Australia. They kept flying through to December last year until every serving man and woman had been repatriated.'

Her mother did look the tiniest bit impressed, but Dad's face had turned red. 'So, you're telling us that you finished last December and now, in February – three months later, you still haven't bothered to return home to your family, and your church, where you belong.'

Something snapped in Meg. 'I belong here, with my husband and my child.'

'Our granddaughter!' Her mother tried to take another step towards Meg, but her father gripped her mother's arm.

'You got married and had a child, and said not a word to us of either event?'

'Actually, I had a child *then* got married. Her name is Jennifer, and she's the reason I didn't return to Sydney.'

Her father's face had turned puce, and Meg had a vision of him collapsing from a heart attack. Dear God, she would never have chosen to tell her parents about Jennifer like this. She could be angry later, but right at this moment, she was worried. 'Dad, are you feeling okay?'

'Mr Dorset, allow me to—' Geoffrey reached for her father, with a clear intention of trying to get him to sit.

Her father wrenched his arm out of Geoffrey's. 'Get your hands off me.'

'I'm a doctor. You need to take it easy and—'

'How dare you not marry my daughter when you made her pregnant? And you, Margaret—' The glare he turned on her burned with anger. Incandescent and righteous, and exactly what she had feared all along. 'We brought you up to be better than that. Giving yourself to a man without God's blessing and love on your union makes you no more than a whore. You're no daughter of mine. And if that child is yours, she's a bastard forever. *You've* condemned her by *your* actions.'

His words lashed Meg like a whip, carving his anger into her heart. Breaking her heart.

Jennifer whimpered and turned her face into Meg's shoulder. And just like that, Meg's guilt and sorrow fell from her. She patted Jennifer's back and rocked her gently. 'It's terrible that you feel like that, Father, but this is my daughter. She's your granddaughter, no matter if you turn from her.'

Geoffrey's arm settled on her shoulder again, and he stood close beside her. She felt his support wrapping around both of them and was grateful. 'Jennifer is my daughter too. I love her like my own child, as much as I love your daughter. They will want for nothing with me, and I'll protect them. It would be nice to have your blessing on our marriage, but if not, that's fine.'

'You'll get no blessing from me. From this day forward, I have no daughter.' He picked up his hat and pushed between them and was gone.

Meg's mother's face crumpled. Tears fell as she touched Jennifer's head. Meg's daughter turned and peeped at her grandmother.

'My granddaughter.' Then she exhaled, the gush of air shaky and final. 'Send me a photo of her care of your oldest brother's address. I'll try to bring your father around.'

Meg nodded and gave her mother a brief hug before she hurried out to join her husband.

Geoffrey drew Meg down onto the sofa so recently vacated by her parents. 'Now I've met your father, I understand your reluctance to tell your family. Mine is different. I can't imagine them responding like that to the news of a wedding and a grandchild, regardless of the order they happened in.'

'My father's response is exactly what I expected, which is why I hadn't told them about Jennifer. I was so focused on his anger I didn't think about how my silence would affect Mum.'

'Mummy?' Jennifer lifted her head from Meg's shoulder and stared with solemn eyes. 'Who's that lady?'

'She's mummy's mummy, your grandma. She loves you almost as much as I do.'

'Who's that?' Jennifer turned her gaze to Geoffrey.

He smiled at Jennifer but spoke to Meg. 'It's your choice when you tell her.'

No more secrets. I don't want Jennifer to ever doubt I'm telling her the truth.

'This is your daddy, and we are never going to go away

again. We'll live together always.'

Jennifer watched him while Meg's heart thudded in her chest. Her daughter had suffered so many changes in her short life. What would she make of this one?

'Howdedoo, Daddy.' She held out her small hand as she'd seen adults do. As perhaps Vera had taught her.

Solemnly, Geoffrey shook her hand, holding it for a moment as he smiled at her. 'Howdedoo, Jennifer.' When he let her go, Meg stood.

'Let's get your suitcase unpacked and have a cool drink, shall we?' Meg kissed her cheek then set Jennifer on the floor but held onto her hand.

'Park, Mummy?'

'After we've had a drink, okay.'

Jennifer nodded. 'Daddy push me on the swing?'

A muscle ticked in Geoffrey's cheek, but he nodded. 'I'll push you on the swing. Whenever I'm home and you want to play, I'll push you on the swing, sweetheart.'

Chapter 31

Late July 1946

The westerly winds are early, Meg thought as she clutched the sides of her coat together with one hand and held tightly to Jennifer's hand with the other. They'd played in the park and fed breadcrumbs to the birds, and swung on the swings until Meg's head spun from watching her daughter's back and forth motion. Now Jennifer needed food and a nap and Meg—she craved some adult conversation.

Closing the front gate behind them she hurried Jennifer up the front steps. She'd left a pot of vegetable soup simmering on the stove that would do for a quick lunch. Once Jennifer had gone down for her nap, Meg picked up the medical journal Geoffrey had brought home and sat at the kitchen table. It was the warmest seat in the house, and she lost herself in reading; so much so that it was only the scrape of chair legs on lino when Gerry sat across from her that lifted her eyes from the page.

'Have you been involved with any epidurals for women in labour?'

Gerry's eyebrows rose and she folded her hands on the table. 'And good afternoon to you, Meg. How was your day? Mine was fine, thank you. Would I like a cup of tea? Why—'

'Sorry, I was immersed in this article about— *Would* you like a cup of tea?'

'Yes please.'

Meg pushed her chair back and lifted the kettle. There was enough water for a small pot, so she moved the kettle onto the hottest part of the stove then opened the wood stove and slipped another small log onto the fire. Dusting off her hands, she dropped back onto her chair. 'I've been reading this article about changes in management of childbirth. Epidurals, inducing labour when a baby's gone well past its due date – and the idea of scans to detect problems early in a pregnancy . . . It all sounds brilliant!'

'They are, although we're seeing resistance from some of the older doctors who want to control every aspect of a woman's labour because it's more convenient for them. But when women come in for their ante-natal check-ups, we're making sure they know all the options now available to them.'

'How they deliver their baby should be their choice.'

'Of course it should, within reason. We had a high-risk delivery yesterday. Fortunately, the mother had had a scan and we knew what to expect.'

Having delivered Jennifer at home with the assistance of Vera and the midwife, Meg was certain how any future babies of hers and Geoffrey would enter the world. If they had any. Seven months into their marriage and she hadn't been blessed with another pregnancy.

The kettle hissed and steamed. Meg made a pot of tea and set it beside two mugs on the table. 'Cake? I had a go at making a sponge cake this morning. It doesn't look that good, but it tastes okay.' She brought the cake platter across from the bench and offered it to Gerry. 'It sank in the middle, so I filled it with preserved cherries.'

Gerry hesitated a moment too long, and Meg sighed.

'I know, but no matter how often I try, I can't master some dishes.'

'I'd love to try your cake, Meg. And don't take this the wrong way, but you aren't really a natural homemaker. You mean well, but other things become more interesting. Like that article you're reading. Put you into an operating theatre and you're like the lead violinist working with the conductor – or in that scenario, the surgeon.' She grinned and cut two slices of cake.

Meg handed her two plates. 'You're right. But Jennifer needs me. I left her with Vera for the first three years of her life, and while I know that was the right thing to do, and Vera was wonderful with her, I can't hand her off to someone else just because I want to go back to nursing. I'm a mother, and my daughter is my top priority.'

'You're a wonderful mother, but Jennifer doesn't need you every minute of every day. Meg, there's a great Lady Gowrie Child Centre near the hospital. You could enrol Jennifer there and work parttime while she was in school.'

'School! She's three years old.'

'Heading for four. The kindergarten has an excellent educational programme, and before you ask, no, I haven't been checking it out. Some of the mums who come into the clinic were talking about it the other day. Lots of other children to play with, outdoor activities and learning . . . And they have to have a rest, even if they don't sleep during it.' Gerry reached across and set her hand on Meg's arm. 'Just think about it for now.'

Since Gerry had mentioned the kindergarten, the idea of returning to a surgical position was impossible to push out of her head. It was seductive and opened possibilities for Meg to be with Jennifer some of the time, and for her daughter to socialise with other children in a safe environment while she worked.

If I can get work at the Herston hospital.

Discreet enquiries using her maiden name elicited an interview. Several mornings later, when Gerry had a day off and offered to take Jennifer shopping for new shoes, Meg declined to go with them.

'I have a few errands to run, and they'll take half the time without Little Miss Munchkin. Thanks, Gerry.' She walked with them to the tram and waved to Jennifer when the bell dinged then watched as the tram juddered away. Then she walked to the bus stop and waited until the bus to Herston arrived.

All the way there, she ran through the positives and negatives of returning to work. One of the biggest negatives was her married status. Now the war was over, women were being encouraged to return to home and hearth and leave the work to the men. Except that men weren't nurses, so maybe she had a chance. And it seemed that the kindergarten kept places for children of mothers working at the hospital. She'd been reassured about that when she rang to make a time to visit the childcare centre.

'Our philosophy includes making it possible for women with children to return to the workplace should they so wish.'

But she hadn't told Geoffrey. It wasn't that she intended to keep it a secret from him, but she wanted to win a position based on merit and not on who her husband was.

'Margaret Dorset?' A nurse with a clipboard stood in front of her.

'That's me.' Meg stood, smoothed down her skirt, and followed the nurse into an office.

'Matron will be with you shortly.' The nurse slipped out on rubber-soled shoes that squeaked only a little on the linoleum floor, closing the door behind her.

Meg took her resumé from her handbag and flattened the folds as best she could. The door opened and she half-turned on the seat. Seeing a woman wearing a matron's cap, she rose and shook the hand extended to her.

'How do you do? Sister Dorset, isn't it?'

'That's correct.' They each took a seat and Meg handed her resumé to Matron Lewis. Her qualifications and service record all carried her maiden name. If she won a position here, she'd tell them then and hope that would be sufficient to explain why she hadn't given her married name. 'I'm keen to work on surgical wards again.' She waited while the matron examined her work history.

'You were in both Darwin and Townsville when they were bombed, and Sister-in-charge of *Currajong*. We have staff who worked there during the war. Do you know Sister Platt?'

Meg hadn't expected to be asked about *Currajong*. 'I do. We worked together for a couple of years on and off. She loves working on the maternity ward whereas I love surgery.'

'Your service record is exemplary, and I see you worked under Dr Ransom for several months. He's Head of Surgery here now. Perhaps I should give him a call and see if he's free to join us. I believe he would appreciate working with you again.' She picked up the phone and requested 'Dr Ransom's office please.'

Feeling guilty and embarrassed, Meg contemplated the awkward position she'd put Geoffrey in, and how he might react when he saw her here.

Why hadn't she thought of this possibility?

Stiffening her spine, she looked straight ahead as a brief knock was followed by the door opening behind her.

Matron smiled and stood. 'Dr Ransom, I have a sister with whom you worked during the war. You mentioned wanting another experienced surgical nurse and she's looking for a surgical position. I thought you might like to speak to her today.'

Meg stood and slowly turned. Her gaze met Geoffrey's and for a moment, it was as though he were seeing her for the first time.

Then he held out a hand. 'Margaret, how unexpected to see you here.'

'Dr Ransom, I should have let you know I was coming in for an interview. I'm sorry I didn't.'

Geoffrey looked at the matron. 'Thank you for calling me, Matron. If you don't mind, I'll take the sister up to my office to complete the interview, and perhaps we can catch up about old times.'

'Certainly, Doctor.' Matron Lewis smiled as she handed over Meg's resumé. 'I expect you'll already know much about Sister Dorset's work.'

'I expect I shall. Thank you. After you, *Sister Dorset.*' He opened the door for her then took her arm as they walked along the corridor.

'Geoffrey, I'm truly sorry I didn't mention I was doing this but—'

'Leave it until we're in my office, Margaret.' He looked straight ahead. Once inside his office, he closed the door and leaned against it. 'What's changed?'

'You mean about—'

'I mean, you were absolutely certain you wanted to stay at home with Jennifer after we got her back, and I supported your decision, and now, six months on, you're applying for a surgical position in my hospital without telling me you planned to do so. I ask again, what's changed?' Geoffrey never raised his voice. He was the calmest man she knew, but he was annoyed. Maybe angry, but she couldn't tell if it because she wanted to work, or because she hadn't told him first.

'I love my daughter, but I miss working in surgery. I miss working with you and working through difficult operations together. Today was mostly about seeing what might be available . . . If there might be an opening—'

'You could have just asked me, Margaret.'

She nodded and rolled her lips together. 'I didn't want to get a job because you're my husband. I want a position here on my merits, but I never expected the matron to call you in. I thought we could talk about it tonight – if I was offered a place. I'm sorry.'

Geoffrey sighed and pushed away from the door. 'You caught me by surprise today, but I never thought you'd stay at home with Jennifer forever. You could be working on my ward again. On your own merits, not because you're my wife. You're a fine nurse, Margaret. One of the best I've worked with, but you know that already. The only question I see is, what do we do about Jennifer?'

'There is a kindergarten near the hospital which gives priority to working mothers. Gerry's patients told her about it, and she mentioned it last week.'

Hurt flashed through his gaze and he frowned. 'Were you talking to Gerry about going back to work before you told me? I thought we had a good marriage; that we could talk about any problems and solve them together?'

The idea clearly pained him, and she mentally kicked herself for phrasing it poorly. 'No, I said nothing to Gerry. She mentioned the kindergarten in the context of an article I was reading in your medical journal. About advances in childbirth practice and her clients.'

Meg perched on a chair and pulled off her gloves. 'Geoffrey, my dear, I want you to know I'm happy in our marriage. You are the best of all husbands, and I'm incredibly grateful to be married to you. But last week, after reading that journal, I realised how terribly I was missing working in an operating theatre. And as much as I love Jennifer, I miss the exchange of ideas and adult conversation, and the solving of medical problems.'

His gaze shuttered before he picked up a file sitting neatly in the middle of his blotter and opened it. 'In that case, it's time for you to return to work. If you can get Jennifer into the childcare centre, you can start immediately. Matron was right; I do need another experienced theatre nurse.'

Meg reeled as if a physical barrier had been thrown up between them. Something wasn't right, and she had no idea what had changed. 'Are you sure you don't mind?'

'I said I don't.' He barely glanced at her. Had he truly accepted her explanation?

'Then there is one other thing that we should probably consider.'

'Only one?' He closed the file around one finger and met her gaze at last. His contained a wealth of pain.

What did I say? Is it because I want to work instead of stay at home?

But since this was a day for discussions, she ploughed on. 'Yes, one I believe is relevant to this discussion. I thought by now I might be pregnant. It's early days, of course, and I could fall pregnant tomorrow, but I understand why employers are less keen to employ married women.'

He held up one hand and she fell silent. 'This is—hard to tell you, but now is as good a time as any. I wondered why our relations haven't been fruitful, since we've been intimate often enough. We know you're fertile; Jennifer is proof of that. But I considered the *problem* might lie with me so . . . I had a test. It seems I have low sperm motility, which means you may never fall pregnant. I'm sorry, Margaret.'

'Oh, Geoffrey, you have nothing to be sorry for. That must have been a blow to hear, but – surely it doesn't mean that it's impossible for us to have a child? Low doesn't mean no chance.'

'You're correct. There is still a chance. I'll pick up some condoms if that will reassure you. Why don't we set a time frame for you to work before we try for a baby? Say, two years?'

He was so practical about everything, even about this possibility that they might not make a child together. Perhaps he'd only just got the test results and that was why he was behaving oddly?

Feeling doubly grateful for his gentle fathering of her daughter, she reached out a hand and touched his arm. 'Thank you, Geoffrey. That's generous of you. I— Thank you.'

'Let me know when you've heard from the kindergarten and I'll let Matron know you'll be joining us. There is one condition.'

Even with Geoffrey's odd mood, Meg's heart felt light at the prospect of nursing again. 'Anything.'

'You will join my staff as Sister Ransom, and everyone will know that you are my wife.'

Meg nodded. 'I'll be very happy with that.'

'You're my wife, and the best surgical nurse I've worked with. Now if you'll excuse me, I have patients to attend.'

Chapter 32

'I talked to the principal of the kindergarten after I left the hospital. She's happy to enrol Jennifer for three days a week, starting next Monday.' A curious mixture of anticipation and dread coursed through Meg as she set Geoffrey's dinner in front of him then took her seat across from him.

'I'll let Matron know in the morning that you'll be joining us. You can work in a supernumerary role until the next roster comes out.' He picked up his cutlery and cut into a potato.

That's it? No discussion tonight? No . . .

'How was your day?'

He didn't look up. 'The same as usual. Busy.' He focused on his food, chewing with a fierce concentration so unlike his usual self when they were together.

There was nothing usual about today for Meg. Something was definitely off with Geoffrey.

'I'm excited about going back to work, but I feel guilty about putting Jennifer into kindy. I must say though, I was impressed by the programme they offer.'

'Matron knows the principal. She holds her in high regard.'

They ate in silence. Geoffrey set his cutlery neatly on his plate and wiped his mouth on his serviette. He pushed his chair back.

Words blurted from Meg's mouth. 'Do you think I'll have missed out on much in the time since I left the RAAF?'

'Since we were married?'

'Er, yes. The two events followed hard on one another.'

Geoffrey took his time, realigning his perfectly aligned knife and fork before he answered. 'There will be a few things new to you. Why don't you look through the last six- or seven-months' worth of my medical journals? That should help direct your attention to areas you need to pick up on.'

He'd pushed his plate away. He'd eaten barely half of his

meal. 'I'm going to bed. I'll probably be gone early in the morning. I have a full day of surgery scheduled. Good night, Margaret.' He paused beside her chair. A moment later, his footsteps receded behind her back.

He didn't kiss me goodnight.

There was a distance between them that Meg had never expected. Each night he left her to sit alone, or with Gerry when she was home. His excuse was reviewing case notes or catching up on reading about some new surgical technique, and if it wasn't either of those, he was simply tired, and going to bed early. Days past and they hadn't made love once. He hadn't even touched her hand, but she'd felt his gaze on her when he thought she wasn't looking.

It can't go on like this. We can't.

When dinner was finished and Gerry had left to go to a movie with a group of nursing friends, Meg stopped him in the hallway with a hand on his arm. 'I know it's late, but can we talk about us?'

'I was going to do some work.' He sighed but let her take his hand and lead him to the veranda. They sat in the swing seat, rocking gently in the dark.

Where did she start? A week ago, everything had been simple. They'd talked about anything and everything and enjoyed each other's company. They'd been *happy,* for goodness' sake, so what had changed? She'd gone over and over their conversation in his office that day at the hospital, but nothing she'd said seemed big enough to have caused the gulf between them.

'You asked me what had changed when I applied to the hospital.'

'And you said you missed working. I told you that first time we had dinner at the Queen's Hotel in Townsville that I'd never stop you working, and I haven't.'

'That's true. You're an amazing man, Geoffrey, and I'm—'

'*Don't* say it.'

'I was only going to say that I'm grateful for your support.'

Despite the night surrounding them, she saw his head bow. She'd just told him she was grateful, as she had that other day. The day when he closed her out. When everything changed.

'Would you—prefer me not to go back to work, or just not with you? Is that the problem?'

'I'll be *grateful* for your experience on my team.'

There it was again. *Grateful.*

'It seems to me you're not happy about the arrangement, and I don't want you to be unhappy.'

'I'm not—unhappy about you working. It's simple, Margaret. If you want to go back to nursing, take the job the hospital is offering. I've no problem with you working. I never have.' He cracked a half smile and so did she, because that's what they always did. Half smiles and skirting around personal topics.

Was that it? They could talk about medicine and politics and any number of broad topics, but they never really talked about feelings.

Not until that *day.*

They sat side by side as Meg gathered her thoughts. She was grateful they were on Vera's swinging seat. Back when she was pregnant and later, after Jennifer's birth, she and Vera had sat and talked through life and disposed of most problems while swinging gently, a soft breeze off the river clearing their minds. She needed that clarity tonight.

'Right from the start after you proposed to me, you were fine with me nursing. But since we've been married, something has changed.' At last, a thought occurred to her, one so big and terrifying, she could hardly breathe. 'Do you think I'm past nursing? Have I been out of it too long?'

Geoffrey reached for her hand. He wasn't a demonstrative man and the action surprised her. His hand was warm and smooth, and grounded her before fear overcame her. His touch, infrequent as it had been, had always done that.

'First up, you're not past doing anything. Maybe you'll be a little slower at first, although I doubt it, but I'll start you on smaller procedures. You'll soon be back in the swing of things. As to the rest of it . . .' He enfolded her hand in both of his. There was real pleasure in his touch, and hope in the small physical connection.

The longer he held her hand, the more she believed she would find a way to break through the barrier he'd thrown up. She liked the feeling that his strength flowed through their clasped hands and into her. Odd to think of her husband in such terms, but the image felt right.

Their eyes met in the lambent light from the street, his, intense. She waited while he gathered words before dispensing them like precious gems—only the best and as few as did the job. 'Do you remember much of the time after Jennifer was gone?'

Meg shook her head. 'It's a blur, but what's that got to do with—'

'What do you remember?'

Meg frowned. 'We got married. Gerry was a witness, and Roger. I was sad. But what has that to do with us now?'

'That's why, Margaret. *You* changed. You were barely functioning with ordinary day-to-day tasks. Your child had disappeared into the adoption system, and when you got her back, you barely let her out of your sight. And that's understandable, but how would you have handled the pressure of working in a hospital when you were worrying about her?'

It slammed into Meg then. The knowledge Geoffrey had protected her from. 'I was grieving for Jennifer as though she'd died.'

He nodded. 'After you got her back, you watched her like a hawk. It took such a long time before you stopped doing even simple things automatically and started to relax. Started living. A long time till you came back.'

Back? The word jumped out at her and snagged her conscience.

'Came back as in I was finally wholly present? Was I so very distracted?'

'Yes, but it was understandable after what you'd been through.'

'I'm so sorry, Geoffrey. I know you cared about helping me get my daughter back, but why ever did you marry me?'

He was quiet for a long time. At last, he took a deep breath, the sort of breath one took before doing something scary. Something that could change everything without knowing if it would be for the better.

'I loved you, Margaret. I knew you weren't in love with me, but I thought I could give you what you needed and maybe one day, you'd see me. Fall in love with me. I wanted to give you everything, but for a time, I feared I couldn't give you the one thing you most wanted – your daughter.'

'Oh, Geoffrey.' Emotion rose like a wave building out at sea and rushing towards the shore. 'I *do* love you.'

He raised the hand he held and kissed it. 'I've waited a long time to hear you say so.'

'Have I never told you? I'm sorry. I don't know when I started loving you. I'm not even sure I recognised it for a long time.'

'But you're sure now?'

She nodded and reached up to cup his cheek. 'Gerry suspected I was falling for you back in the *Currajong* days. Perhaps she was right, and I was afraid to acknowledge the truth.'

She'd been blessed to know the love of two wonderful men, but why had it taken her so long to truly see what Geoffrey had given her? How dark her life must have been that she hadn't understood what he'd done for her. 'I am truly sorry I never spoke those words.'

'It doesn't matter.'

Meg's throat clogged with years of emotion and grief she hadn't acknowledged. But Geoffrey had. Geoffrey—her rock and her strength. He'd saved the shell of a woman she imagined she'd been and slowly, painstakingly, helped her build a new life.

'I love you.' Slipping off the seat she sat on his lap, wound her arms around his neck and kissed him. Intentionally. Deliberately.

With love.

He wrapped both arms round her, enfolding her in his love, a love she'd only now recognised. He'd saved her, loved her, and now . . .

'I love you, Geoffrey Ransom. You are my life.'

Epilogue

Perth, 1952

'Push, Meg.' Geoffrey held her hand tightly as she pushed and pushed then breathed.

Dimly she was aware he'd slipped into calling her 'Meg'. She liked the sound of it on his lips. When the next contraction subsided, her gaze landed on the clock. Two in the morning. Which meant she'd been in labour for nine hours. Through the window, a silver wash of moonlight picked out the creamy white of the grevillea spikes, and she focused on them.

Another contraction gripped her. Sweat ran into her eyes before she scrunched them shut.

'The baby's head is crowning. Not long now, Meg.' Narelle, Meg's midwife who operated out of Geoffrey's new hospital in Perth, gave her an encouraging smile. 'You're nearly there. Next one, I want you to give the biggest push yet, okay?'

Meg nodded, breathed in and—

'Now! Push hard.'

Meg pushed, screamed, and then – a lusty cry brought her eyes open.

'Congratulations. You have a gorgeous little girl.' Narelle lifted the baby to show Meg. Geoffrey cut the umbilical cord. As soon as her baby was clean and wrapped warmly against the cool early morning air, the midwife set their daughter in Meg's arms. 'I'll give you some time together while we wait for the placenta to birth.'

Geoffrey put his arm around her shoulders as she held the baby and looked into her eyes. Blue, of course, although they were just as likely to be hazel if she took after her father.

'Well done, my darling.' He kissed her cheek and stroked the baby's. 'Any thoughts on what you'd like to call her?'

Elated but tired, Meg leaned her head against his shoulder. 'I liked all of your suggestions. Here, hold her while I get more comfortable, will you.'

Geoffrey took his daughter – the baby they'd almost given up on having – and cradled her tenderly. 'She's beautiful, Meg. Like her mother and her big sister.'

Meg lay back on the pillows and watched Geoffrey with their child. He'd been a wonderful father to Jennifer, who adored him, and once again, Meg gave thanks that he'd persevered all those years ago, waiting for her to realise she loved him. 'What does she look like? Is she an Amy, a Susan, or a Marie?'

Geoffrey's expression was tender and full of love. 'There were times when I didn't think we'd have a child together, and that was okay, because we have Jennifer. But I'm very happy this little one's here.' He gazed at their daughter and touched her tiny nose with a gentle finger. 'How about Grace?'

Meg leaned over and took hold of one tiny hand. The baby held onto her finger and lay quiet in her father's arms.

'Grace. That's perfect.'

The End

Thank you for reading Meg's story. If you enjoyed it, please consider leaving a review on Goodreads and/or the retailer from whom you purchased this book, your library, Bookbub, and share the pleasure of reading books you enjoy with others.

Grace's story is coming!

Under the Same Stars   (pre-order available)

It's mid-July 1969 in Perth, Australia. Man has landed on the moon, and Grace Ransom is reaching for the stars. Like her mother, she pushes boundaries, wanting to do more than marry and have babies like her friends.

The chance to work at Jandakot Airport brings her into the world of Robyn Miller, the Flying Nurse, and mechanic, Mike Maguire, who teaches her to ride his Triumph and believes she can be whatever she wants to be. As Grace studies medicine and waits for her boyfriend to return from Vietnam, she challenges the male-dominated establishment as she seeks a path to change her world.

(Read the first chapter below)

***

Acknowledgements:

Many thanks to Dr Peter Burrows for checking my medical details and researching historical usage. Any errors are mine.

For Meg's impressions of Townsville, my thanks to Diane Hillyard, whose recollections of an earlier time colour these scenes.

And as always, many thanks to my wonderful friend and editor, Annie Seaton, and to bestselling author, Darry Fraser for happily reading this story prior to publication and providing a wonderful cover quote.

Read Chapter 1 of Grace's story now.

Chapter 1
21 July 1969, Perth Australia

'It's one small step for man, one giant leap for Mankind.'

Neil Armstrong's voice, tinny, distorted, and so unbelievably far away, sent a thrill through Gracie. Beyond the windows of the school assembly hall, a south-westerly wind rattled the panes of glass. Beyond the coastline, the Indian Ocean rolled in long blue swells that had travelled halfway around the world towards the beaches of Perth.

But the astronaut's voice had travelled much further. Three hundred and eighty-four thousand, four hundred kilometres and almost seventy-six hours in a tiny tin-can spaceship. It was enthralling, exciting and Gracie rather thought she'd like to see the little blue spot that was Earth from the lunar surface one day. Were there Australian astronauts? The only ones mentioned had been Americans . . . And all were men.

The teachers were as focused as the students on the two black and white televisions set up at the front of the assembly hall. Risking a whisper, Gracie leaned towards her best friend, Nora. 'Why are all the astronauts men?'

Nora, her short blonde hair immaculate even after walking to the new assembly hall through the wind, spared a glance for Gracie and shrugged. 'That's just how it is. Men get to go on adventures.' She turned back to the screen and the televised images from the Moon. Neil Armstrong moved in slow motion bounds across the lunar surface.

'It isn't fair. Why should men get to have all the fun? I'm not going to settle for watching adventures happen to others.'

There was a sharp-nailed tap on her shoulder. 'Girls, stop talking. You're watching history in the making.'

'Yes, Miss.' Gracie clamped her mouth shut and turned her attention back to the small screen.

Mr Paxton, Gracie's science teacher and a veteran of World War Two, completed the diagram of the Apollo 11 trajectory then limped with a sailor-like roll from the blackboard and leaned against his desk. 'So, ladies, courtesy of the Australian tracking station at Parkes in New South Wales, you've watched the moon landing. Any questions about the landing itself or shall we move onto the physics of how it all happens?'

Gracie's hand shot up. Yesterday's broadcast had thrown up plenty of questions and one in particular bugged her. 'Mr Paxton, why aren't there any female astronauts?'

Mr Paxton's greying eyebrows rose like a pair of fuzzy caterpillars. 'The most amazing feat of engineering and application of science in the history of mankind and all you, Miss Westall, want to know is why there are no women on the Moon?'

'Yes, sir. In this day and age it seems strange that—'

'It's not strange at all. Grace, the lunar landing is not a plot by men to keep women out of space. Do you remember reading about the Russian cosmonaut, Valentina Tereshkova? She was just twenty-six when she became the first and youngest woman to have flown in space with a solo mission on the Vostok 6 in 1963.'

'Yes, sir.'

'She spent three days orbiting the earth, the first woman to go into space.'

'But she hasn't been to the Moon.'

'Small steps, Grace. Perhaps you'll train as a pilot and become the first Australian woman astronaut. You've got the brains for it. Now, moving on, do you have any questions about the physics of yesterday's momentous achievement . . . *science* questions, *not* social commentary.' He pinned Gracie with a look that told her he'd let her go so far and no further.

Wisely, she held her tongue.

***

'. . . and so, girls . . .' Miss Grant, the headmistress of Perth's prestigious St Margaret's School for Girls, cast a stern eye across the upturned faces of this year's senior class. As she turned her head to make eye contact with girls on the far side of the group, her elegant chignon came into view. Like everything else about the headmistress, it was smooth with not a hair out of place, and her dark grey dress with three-quarter length sleeves was the precise length it should be.

A model of social correctness, thought Gracie.

She gripped Nora's hand and whispered, 'I'm going to apply, Nora.'

Nora leaned closer, her lips barely moving as she replied. 'Bet that will go over like a lead balloon with your dad.'

Miss Grant clasped her hands and held them still at waist height, the very image of decorum, of everything a woman should be. 'I have decided to open the floor to your suggestions for the end of year speaker. Who would you like to speak at the graduation ceremony for the class of 1969?'

A hand shot up somewhere near the front and a voice asked—tentative, hopeful, finishing on a quavering squeak. 'Can we get the Beatles, Miss?'

Miss Grant's nostrils flared and her mouth pinched, prune-like. She pinned the questioner with her cold blue gaze. 'Sandra McKitchie, stand up. Are you really as silly as that question paints you?'

Sandra stood, her cheeks a fiery red and eyes downcast. She was likely to graduate bottom of their class, but Gracie felt a twinge of sympathy for her classmate. Airhead she might be, but she didn't deserve public humiliation because she was infatuated with the British band. Maybe if Sandra's father wasn't one of the wealthiest men in Perth, if he hadn't flown her to Adelaide to see the group, she wouldn't now be getting into trouble for her love of their music.

'No, Miss, sorry, Miss.' Sandra sank onto the bench, head bowed low.

And that posture will score her another scolding unless . . .

Gracie's hand rose straight and tall as the poplars along the school driveway. 'Miss Grant?'

'Grace, I depend on you for a more sensible suggestion.'

Grace stood, a quiver of excitement at her daring tingling in her fingers, down her spine. The eyes of her classmates turned to her, hoping for a suggestion that excited them. 'Yes, Miss.'

Anyone would be better than that minister at last year's graduation. Even Miss Grant's eyes had held a glazed look as she'd waited for him to end his rambling speech about the need to hold fast to social norms.

'What about Sister Robin Miller? You've encouraged us to aspire to the highest ideals of service. In 1967, Sister Miller began flying her own plane on multiple flights and administered the polio vaccine to remote communities in Western Australia. Over the last two years she's flown about 69,000 kilometres to groups scattered over an area of half a million square miles, and dispensed 37,000 doses of Oral Sabin polio vaccine and . . .'

The headmistress' hand rose, as implacable and incapable of being ignored as a stop sign. 'An interesting suggestion, thank you, Grace. I believe we were thinking more along the lines of one of our fine politicians, but I'll keep your suggestion in mind.'

Hands clenched in her lap, Gracie sat stiff-backed, her aside to Nora an angry mutter. 'She's not going to consider it at all. We'll be stuck with some old windbag who condescends to come and talk *at* us and thinks we should be grateful. Times are changing, Nora, but this school is stuck in the Dark Ages.'

'At least you tried, Gracie.'

A heavy hand descended on Gracie's shoulder. 'Listen, don't chatter, girls.'

'Yes, Miss.' Gracie pressed her lips together and stared past the heads of the students seated in front of her. Two telling offs in under a week. She prayed the teachers didn't share that in her school report. But the world-wide excitement of the Moon landing had fired her imagination. Appearing attentive, she'd turned her head to the headmistress, and glanced with quick, sideways looks around the hall.

Nothing has changed. Nothing ever changes.

But the story of Sugarbird Lady spun in her head like a beacon of hope.

If Sister Miller can fly her own plane thousands of miles, if Valentina Tereshkova can orbit the earth, why not Gracie Westall?

***

Social media links

Facebook   **Twitter**   **Website**   **Pinterest**
Bookbub

Head on over to my webpage and find out more about my rural series and other stories:

Website

About the Author
Born and raised in Toowoomba, Susanne is an Australian author of contemporary and rural romances set in Australia and exotic locations. She adores travel with her husband, both at home and overseas.

Her heroes have to be pretty special to live up to her real life hero. He saved her life then married her.

She is published with Harlequin Mira/Escape, and has written several self-published rural series. A popular guest speaker, she has been invited to speak in libraries, book clubs, and to community groups.

MORE BOOKS BY SUSANNE BELLAMY

<u>Rural fiction</u>

Hearts of the Outback (6 book series)

<u>Individual titles – Hearts of the Outback</u>
Just One Kiss
Heartbreak Homestead
Long Way Home
Winds of Change
Wild About Harry
The Cattleman's Promise

<u>Home to Lark Creek</u>
A Promise of Home
Hard Road Home
Turn Left for Home
Home from the Hill

<u>Bindarra Creek Romance</u>
Second Chance Love
Pearls and Green Beer (novella)
In the Heat of the Night
Forgotten Secrets (August 2022)

<u>Through Escape Publishing</u>
Starting Over (Also appears in print bind up: Heart of the Town - four book anthology)
Engaging the Enemy
Her Christmas Kisses (Also appears in print: Christmas Among the Gum Trees)
A Spy for Lady Clementine

Contemporary romance:
White Ginger

Romantic suspense:
The Emerald Lei (originally published as Winning the Heiress' Heart)
High Stakes
Singapore Trap

Novellas:
A Taste of Christmas (in A Season to Remember)
One Night in Tuscany

Regency:

A Spy for Lady Clementine
Spying for the Earl (until mid-2022, included in *Sweet Christmas Secrets* anthology)

Coming 15 November 2022 – **Sweet Secrets of Swain Cove**